CLOUD

~ OF ~

DESTRUCTION

CLOUD OF DESTRUCTION

Mists of Redemption ~ Book 3

M. L. REID

Podium

Cover design by Mario Teodosio

ISBN: 978-1-0394-3660-2

Published in 2024 by Podium Publishing
www.podiumaudio.com

Podium

CLOUD

OF

DESTRUCTION

CHAPTER 1

I'd experienced some very unusual things in the eighteen months since I'd become a Hunter. Scary things. Some of my most memorable ones were: having a monster race toy with me to the death—and somehow surviving. Getting a System that leveled me up like a video game—and not being able to tell anyone about it. Learning that Earth was dying—and no one believing me. And befriending the most powerful person in the entire world—who is not even from Earth.

However, one of the most unusual things I'd ever seen was Bethany Wilks standing in front of the E Hostel. Never mind the fact our friendship was odd to begin with. I mean, I literally spent months thinking she was sending hitmen after me. Somehow that was cleared up, and we became friends. It still blew my mind.

But I never in my life thought I'd see Bethany standing in front of the building where the weakest of the weak lived. My residence. The blonde bombshell and her bodyguards stood out like a sore thumb on the dirty street. Well, it had been dirty before the recent earthquakes. Now it just looked horrible, with the crumbling walls and fallen lampposts added to the litter. Bethany came from the other side of Eden, where they actually had lawns and separate houses—or mansions—and everything was maintained to perfection.

I'd been fighting monsters in the Gate all morning, so I was covered in sweat and muck, from the bottom of my black leather boots to the tips of my pale brown hair and every inch of black leather armor in between. Even my triangular miniskirt and my black hip-satchel Items Bag wasn't spared. But that's what I get for fighting in a bog.

I didn't think I'd be ambushed before I got home to clean up, though. I blinked at her, totally surprised. "What are you doing here?"

This was the first time anyone had ever come to the hostel for me. The reason was simple—I didn't want them to. Even though all my important people knew my life hadn't been easy in the past, I didn't want them to actually see it. I didn't know Bethany knew where I lived, but I got how she figured it out. Her dad was third in command in the Hunter's Council, and as long as she asked him, Bethany had access to nearly every Hunter file. As a spoiled princess, he'd never told her no.

There was something off about seeing the glamorous Bethany Wilks standing outside the dingy E Hostel. Her blonde hair fell down her back in thick loose curls, and her lacey white dress, pink jacket, multicolored silk scarf, and knee-high brown boots stuck out like a sparkling diamond in a bucket of muddy pebbles.

Tenants walked in and out of the front door, craning their heads to get a better look at the celebrity gracing our small neck of the woods. Every time the door opened, it revealed the crowd hiding on the other side, watching Bethany with open curiosity. Most of the windows on the front of the building were also full of watchers.

Seriously, didn't they have more things to do other than stand there and stare?

At least Bethany didn't seem to mind. As the face and spokeswoman of the Hunters, she was probably used to it.

She didn't answer my question. Instead, she asked one of her own. "Is it always so loud around here?" She glanced toward the back of the hostel, where the sounds of construction wailed painfully.

I walked over to her. Bethany had two visible bodyguards and seven invisible ones around her at all times. Before, the two visible ones never glanced in my direction; I wasn't strong enough to be a threat, so they ignored my existence entirely. But now, the looks they sent me were *unfriendly*, to put it kindly. I swallowed a sigh, thinking of the last time I interacted with Bethany's father. I guess Mr. Wilks didn't approve of me anymore.

Despite the subtle glares, the bodyguards didn't prevent me from getting close to her. "The workout building burnt down a couple months ago," I explained in the simplest way possible. Never mind I was the reason it burnt down, with me inside when it happened. "It took a month for the paperwork to go through, and now they're building the new one. It should have been done in a month, but the quake yesterday damaged the new structure. Who knows when it will be ready now?"

Bethany scowled and rubbed her diamond-studded ear. "It's so loud. How do you sleep?"

I smiled and shrugged. "The city rules make them stop working at 9:00 p.m. And I'm usually gone before they start in the morning." I used to be the weakest Hunter in history and learned the hard way that finding a safe party to trail in the Gate was crucial to surviving the brutal Hunter lifestyle. Now that I was stronger, I didn't need to use another team as a shield anymore, but it was a habit to get up early and finish my daily tasks as soon as possible now. "Since I don't spend that much time at the hostel, it's not that big of a deal."

The person who had to deal with it the most was poor Henry, who was here all day long. The sound was driving him nuts. Every time I talked to him, he looked so haggard from the constant noise. But the sweet old man was still excited over the new gym, so he didn't complain too much.

"Hm." She obviously still thought it was a pain. "I've only been here for fifteen minutes, and I already think it's dumb."

I sighed, caught in between amusement and exasperation. "You didn't have to come here, you know. You could have called me, and I would have met you somewhere else."

She grinned and tossed her hair over her shoulder. "I know. But I wanted to surprise you. I mean, you surprised me, so it's only fair."

Mateo—my fellow burning gym victim—walked out of the hostel doors and froze, jaw unhinged at the sight of Bethany. Then he looked at me, and his shocked expression shifted to confusion. I could see the wheels turning in his mind, as if he was debating on what to do. He moved to come closer.

The instant he shifted in our direction, every bodyguards' eyes zeroed in on him. Even the invisible ones—not that Mateo was strong enough to feel them. Mateo went rigid under their menacing stares before he hurried back into the hostel in a rather disgraceful-looking retreat.

Bethany didn't even notice the whole thing.

I glanced at her, trying to figure out what she meant. This woman was the worst at talking in circles. "What surprise?"

"I totally didn't know you were going to the party tonight." She laughed in delight. "I'm excited you're finally coming to a party with me. I mean, it's not really coming with me. I actually can't hang out with you, since I'll be on the job and in charge of entertaining the guests, but you know." She shrugged.

No, I didn't know. "What party? What are you talking about?" A sense of dread sank in my stomach.

She looked at me like I was crazy. "The reception party in a couple hours? The one set up to greet the Hunters from the Quebec and West Coast Gate. I was floored when I saw your name on the expedition list."

I gaped at her, finally remembering a vague sentence Kesstel tossed to me last night. "I thought it was just a small meeting to get to know other Hunters. Kesstel said I didn't have to go if I didn't want to."

There were so many things at stake right now, both on a personal and global level, I didn't have time to go to a party. Excluding the fact the world was dying, it was only two days ago that I found out my System was in danger. How it was and where it was located, I didn't know. All I knew was I needed to find the right portal somewhere in the world—and hope I was strong enough to rescue it. All my strength came from the System. Without it, everything I had now would disappear, along with my family's livelihood.

Bethany snorted and planted a hand on her hip. "Ah, no. It's a big deal. Eden is the headquarters of the Hunter's Association, so they're going to roll out the red carpet to make sure all the other Hunters know we aren't some backwater town. Everyone is required to go."

My stomach sank like a bag of rocks. I could already guess what Bethany was going to do next.

She slipped her arm around my shoulder, ignoring the grime, and gripped it to prevent me from escaping. "So, I'm here to make sure you look absolutely amazing. You're going to be stunning by the time I'm done with you." Her baby blue eyes were practically sparkling with determined excitement. "Those other Hunters are going to know that no matter what your rank is, you are worth your weight in gold, and you have backing."

I patted her arm. "That's really nice of you, but—"

"Nope. It's already a done deal. Let's go. The stylist is already waiting, and we don't have a lot of time. Stylishly late doesn't work for the hostess." Bethany marched me down the street, her bodyguards trailing behind. "My car's just ahead."

"Stylist?" I gaped at her. "Where are we going?"

"My house." Bethany beamed. "I already have your outfit ready for you. You remember the amazing outfit I picked out for you a couple days ago? I thought it would fit perfectly for this occasion. Chic, sexy, but not slutty."

A very black car slowly rolled down the street toward us, avoiding the cracks in the road that hadn't been patched up yet. I doubted such an expensive vehicle had ever graced the streets of E District.

My mouth dropped open. God, I'd only ridden in a car a couple times my whole life. And never one like *that*. It was practically gleaming with money. "Hang on, Bethany. This is a bad idea. I don't think your dad likes me that much."

She actually laughed. "Yeah, Daddy's had a stick up his butt for the last couple days. What did you say to him? I can't count how many times he's started a 'I need to be careful of the charity projects I pick up' talk." She snorted rather unladylike and rolled her eyes. "He just doesn't get it. Anyway, as long as I start to cry, he caves in." Sometimes, her honesty was simply amazing. "Besides, he's not home right now. And even if he was, he wouldn't say anything to you with me there."

A bodyguard opened the door to the car and bent his waist to bow her in.

"Oh, this is going to be fun!" Bethany squealed as she shoved me inside.

Every day in the Gate was a battle to survive. It was a brutal, merciless ordeal that would never end. But compared to the last two hours, I would gladly choose the Gate. I'd been scrubbed, primped, and slathered with so many bottles of stuff, I didn't even feel like myself anymore. The stylist said she was going with a natural-beauty look, but she still covered every inch of my face in layers and layers of makeup. Admittedly, I looked good. I'd never been so beautiful in my life.

My hair was in perfect beachy curls which softened the image my sporty-glam clothes gave. And I smelled like perfume. It wasn't the little-kid, fruity stuff I played with Aliya with; it was feminine and sexy and way over my budget. It smelled fantastic, but it drove me nuts because it muffled my sense of smell.

Bethany's car pulled up to the side of the most prominent club in A District. I looked out the window at the marble, tinted glass, and steel building. Lights were placed in strategic locations to cause the white stone to almost glow in the dying light. Pale blue energy crystals were embedded in the steel, making the building pop all the more.

I swallowed hard, nervously running my hand over the two inches of bare skin on my left thigh. Since my right one was covered in leather,

I couldn't get used to the feeling of air on only my left. I couldn't help tugging on the short black-and-iridescent-blue jacket, as if one more tug would make it cover my stomach.

"I really don't have to go," I said, trying to take the shameful route of retreat.

Bethany reached out and fidgeted with my bangs for a second. "Nope. You're coming. You look amazing, don't worry. I can't hang with you the whole time, but if you run into trouble, you can come get me immediately. Okay?" Her thick blonde hair was half pulled up, creating a beautiful knot on her crown, while the rest of her curls fell down to her butt. Her opalescent wraparound dress hugged her features. Somehow, it made us look like a match, her high-class glam paired with the sporty glam I wore.

"Let's go. We're a little early, but there's things I have to set up." Bethany opened the door and took the hand of the bodyguard standing outside.

Instead of the usual black armor the men normally wore, they were all in black pants, shirts, and leather jackets. Cool and sophisticated looking. For the first time, I noticed that all of her bodyguards were attractive men, something I'd bet was in the job description. They weren't clones of each other, but each had undeniable appeal.

After Bethany exited the car, the bodyguard reached out for me. I waved away his hand and got out by myself, then Bethany grabbed my arm and dragged me up the short steps into the building. The foyer was done in the same aesthetics as outside; nothing out of the ordinary, I guessed.

The lead bodyguard opened the doors in the back of the foyer, and Bethany pulled me in. It was like walking into a whole new world—one I would never be ready for.

The front door opened to a mezzanine which wrapped around the dance floor and bar below. The whole club was dark—the ceiling, walls, and flooring were all solid black or a black-and-navy swirled design. Two large rectangular pillars, which looked like a giant had taken the ends and twisted them, rose from the ground all the way up to the extra-tall ceiling.

Brightly glowing blue crystals gleamed along the sides of the pillars, all the way up, and lined the mezzanine and the dance floors. Round tables adorned with shining crystals in glass vases dotted the mezzanine. Large chandeliers dripping hundreds of rows of crystals dangled from the ceiling, creating tiny rainbows everywhere. In the back of the massive main floor was a sophisticated bar in front of a feature wall made out of diamond-shaped brushed metal and hidden white lighting.

I stopped just inside the threshold and felt my mind explode. "I definitely don't belong here."

Bethany laughed and dragged me in. "Now you do. At least for the night. In a couple years, we'll come back and celebrate your official drinking birthday here. Until then, have a Coke." She motioned to a circular table on the right side. "I gotta go talk to the manager. Anything you order is on me. Literally. It's my club, and friends eat free." She laughed at my shocked face and waltzed off, her bodyguards trailing behind her.

Feeling like an ant in a giant's house, I walked over to the far side of the mezzanine and sat down at a table. The lighting was low, but that didn't matter much to a Hunter; I could still see every detail perfectly. Honestly, I would have been more comfortable if I couldn't see. There wasn't anyone I could people-watch either, since the party didn't start for another twenty minutes—if people were on time.

With nothing else to do, I opened my Guide and started to go over fighting forms and moves. Mentally, I envisioned each move, practicing it over and over, just like I did in real life.

My concentration snapped when someone walked in my direction. I looked up and stiffened.

Mr. Wilks, dressed in a suave pinstriped suit, walked over to me, several bodyguards in black suits following behind. His graying blond hair was combed back away from his high forehead, making him look a little too dashing for a man with an adult daughter. Then again, he was an A-rank mage. He'd probably only physically aged five years in the last two decades. "Good evening," he said, sitting down across from me without asking.

"Good evening." I nodded my head, suddenly not sure what to do with my hands. In the end, I folded them in my lap and sat with my back straight. Was this when he told me to stay away from his daughter, like I was a stupid punk?

He leaned back and crossed his legs, a king in his realm. Then again, if Bethany owned this place, then Mr. Wilks's name was on it too. "I have to say, Miss Devhro, I don't know exactly what to do with you." He narrowed his eyes. "Should I make you disappear or not?"

Jynn Devhro

Rank B

Level 50

EXP to Next Level 6525

HP 2842/2842

Stat Points 0

MP 1253/1253

Strength 90 (+20)

Agility 83

Magic 80

Perception 83

Constitution 83 (+20)

Intelligence 76

Skills

Throw

Critical Hit

Quick Hit

Mirror

High Jump

Abilities

Mist (Improved) (50 ft)

Feather Step

Regen (Limited)

Stealth (Limited)

Poison Fog

Mist Blade

CHAPTER 2

My eyes narrowed. Oh, we were about to have a verbal battle. It happened a lot faster than I thought it would. God, I hated those—debate had never been my strong suit. "I'm not sure what you mean, Mr. Wilks."

Mr. Wilks motioned to a bodyguard standing just behind him without saying a word. The man simply nodded and walked away.

Music suddenly blared from the surround-sound speakers. I nearly jumped out of my seat, surprised at the sudden heavy beat and rapid tempo. It was catchy and heady, encouraging anyone listening to dance, but I wasn't used to music that loud. I glanced down at the floor below and saw Bethany standing in front of the DJ booth, talking to a man behind a bunch of spinning equipment.

I turned back to Mr. Wilks.

He had a finger resting on his lip, watching me with flat blue eyes. His coloring was very similar to Bethany's, but he lacked her whimsical flare. "My little princess has talked a lot about you in the last few months." The music was loud, but I was still able to hear his smooth voice through the booming beat. That being said, someone standing ten feet away would be hard-pressed to hear our conversation. As for someone like Bethany, who was on the lower level, it would be impossible. I couldn't help but think the music was intentional and had nothing to do with her.

"In fact," Mr. Wilks went on, "I'd say that nearly forty percent of what she talks about has your name involved with it. She seems to think you're made out of gold, a true friend. As a member of the Hunter's Association Council, I naturally can't look down on E Hunters. I thought it would be a good thing for Bethany. Give her a better sense of what the world is like outside of her protective bubble. As the face of the Hunters, it was even a good thing for her to be seen with a low-leveled Hunter. Gives an image of compassion." He paused. "Regrettably, I found out that you have some atypical beliefs. And, if I'm not mistaken, you might be the one who causes the Hunter's chat forum to explode negatively every month?"

Hmm. I was starting to think it was unfortunate that this guy was Bethany's dad. In theory, I shouldn't hate him; Bethany thought the world of him. But I had to say, he was more cold-blooded than I was expecting. "I'm not a danger to anyone." Well, as long as they weren't trying to hurt me or my family.

"Not intentionally," he amended.

The guard walked up from behind Mr. Wilks, holding a tray with two cups on it. The first was a short cocktail glass filled with red liquid, several ice balls, and an ornamental orange slice. The second was obviously a Coke with crushed ice and a straw inside a decorative clear glass. The guard set the cocktail in front of Mr. Wilks and the Coke in front of me, then retreated a couple steps back with the tray.

Mr. Wilks motioned to the Coke. "Have a drink." With that, he took a small sip of his cocktail. "The biggest problem is," he said, continuing our conversation. "Bethany is a public figure. If she's caught in the grips of any unsavory activities, the consequences would be astronomical."

I sipped my Coke. I wasn't really in the mood to drink anything, but it would be rude to reject it. Even though this guy was obviously rejecting me, he was still my friend's dad. "I am not, in any way, affiliated with the cult, if that's what you're worried about. I thought it had been stamped out a couple months ago." I mean, I was the one who turned over most of the evidence they used to get rid of it.

Mr. Wilks bobbed his head to the side in mild acknowledgement. "Yes, for the most part. The leaders are all cleared up, and most of the people addicted to the drug are on the mend or they've already killed themselves over the drug withdrawals."

Wow, he said that sentence so blandly. It was clear he didn't have an ounce of compassion for the people suffering. Then again, that was how the harsh Hunter society was. The cult members had chosen to go and partake of the drug. The only one at fault was them, so why pity them?

"But the ideas that those madmen spread around still linger in the back of people's minds," Mr. Wilks continued. "It's causing quite a lot of tension in the people. It would be unfortunate if those ideas spread even more. And my daughter would be the perfect candidate because of her media connections."

I took another drink. "Huh. You mean the bizarre idea that Hunters are going to abandon humans and Earth to hide in a utopia in the Gate? That bogus idea?"

His eyes narrowed. "So you have heard it."

I nodded, not impressed. "Heard it. What about it? It's wrong. It couldn't be more wrong if they tried. Then again, they were more interested in turning a profit than actually helping people or steering them in the right direction. It's unfortunate that so many believed that flashy light show."

Mr. Wilks hummed under his breath and took another sip. "You know a lot." His tone let me know I'd just dropped another notch in his opinion.

I shrugged. "I hear stuff." Hell, I'd watched the light show and then personally beat the leaders down with my own swords. It was my fault they were arrested.

But no one knew that, and I planned to keep it that way. I wasn't looking for glory; I was looking for help to save the world. And I found only disappointment. Much like with this interaction with Mr. Wilks.

"Bethany especially likes to talk," I said casually. I had zero guilt pushing the source of my knowledge onto someone else if it kept me out of the spotlight. And since he knew she liked to talk, it was easy to shrug off most of the fault onto her. She had, after all, told me about what was happening in the investigation and trials.

I glanced down at her. She was now standing by the bar, talking to the handful of bartenders there. The bright blue lights reflected off her dress, nearly making her glow. She caught my look and paused to throw me an exaggerated wink. I smiled back before focusing on the man across from me once more.

"Yes," Mr. Wilks spoke slowly. "I have to say, it's surprising how connected you are, considering you aren't even in a guild. Normally it would be impossible for someone like you to be affiliated with Mr. Noblé, never mind my daughter."

My eyes narrowed, understanding what he was insinuating. "I'm not a leech. They are the ones who came to me." No matter how hard I tried to run away. And I was grateful they didn't let me escape, no matter how chaotic they made my life.

But the average person would never believe that. Hunters lived in a rigid strength caste system. Basically, the strong stepped on the weak. It was common for the weaker Hunters to latch onto stronger Hunters, trying to get glory by riding someone else's coattails.

Leeches, that's what they were called.

According to the papers and the name title that Hunters could see floating over my head, I was an E-ranked Hunter, the bottom of the totem pole. It didn't matter that I was currently B ranked and getting stronger. I knew they couldn't see it, so I didn't blame people for treating me as an E. I was used to it.

But that didn't mean I was okay being called a leech. Everything I owned, I'd bought with my own blood and sweat. I couldn't count all the times I'd stopped Bethany from buying me things. I didn't reject Kesstel's endless snacks and treats, but I drew the line with cell phones and magic items. The outfit I wore right now was the first thing I'd ever actually accepted from Bethany—mostly because there wasn't time to buy one myself. She was a shopaholic with too much money, and I was a convenient target. But that didn't mean I would take advantage of her.

I paused. "You know, Bethany is very generous to those she cares about. I personally think it's a good thing, since it makes her more relatable." I frowned and tapped on the rim of my glass. "However, she has a serious problem where she thinks people only want to be with her because they want something from her. I can't fix that alone. Maybe you should help her with that."

"Yet, you sit there dressed in my money, enjoying her generosity and the backing of an S Hunter." Mr. Wilks took another drink.

I knew I shouldn't let him rile me up, but he'd managed to piss me off in less than twenty words. I glared and flung my right hand in the air. The Guide screen popped up, and I flicked my hand over it. In seconds, I set up the transfer of the cost of my clothes and flipped the screen around for him to accept. It was a ridiculous amount of money for four articles of clothing, especially since I was tight after giving the down payment for my family's new condo in Garden City, but my pride was worth more than this.

"By all means, I'll happily compensate you for it. I'm not lacking in money. And this is money that I earned myself. No *backers* or whatever the hell you call them." My voice was low and hard. "Even though it's not like anything I've worn before, I quite liked this outfit. Because Bethany picked it out and it made her happy. Now I find it rather distasteful. Unfortunately, I don't have anything else appropriate to change into or else I'd leave it with you right now."

He cocked his head to the side, not looking offended at all. "And why would it matter what you wore?" He casually threw out the question like it wasn't a test.

I sneered at him. "I might be a lowly E, but I know full well who I associate with. Even I have to play the part as long as I'm seen together with Kesstel or Bethany. I might not necessarily know exactly how to act, but I know I have to look good so they don't look bad."

He nodded as if I'd given the right answer. "As you should. It's good that you understand that." He waved the transfer screen away, and it came back to me. "If I can't afford this little bit of charity, I have no right to raise my little princess."

My mouth twitched. After a second, I canceled the money transfer screen, but I didn't feel any better. "You know, not everything is about money."

People started to slowly stream into the club. Every Hunter was high leveled and dressed in very expensive clothes that were a mashup of modern and fantasy styles. They paused at the front doors for a moment before they dispersed, some going down to the lower floor and some choosing seats at the tables on the mezzanine. Waiters in black slacks and white button-down shirts began to mingle into the crowd, taking orders and bringing drinks on trays.

Mr. Wilks sipped his drink again. "I feel like this is another subject you and I won't see eye to eye on. You see, everything is about money for me. As long as I have enough money, my little princess can be happy." He rested his elbow on the table and leaned toward me. "If everything isn't about money, why would an E go out of her way to enamor an S Hunter so much that he can't even go on a simple trip without her?"

"We both know it's not a simple trip," I said flatly.

We were going to close a random portal that had popped up in the Las Vegas ruins. How was that simple? This portal could be the gateway to the parasitic planet preying on Earth. In other words, a way to save Earth.

Not that Mr. Wilks believed me about the parasite. In fact, I think that's why he hated me—he thought I was a crazed liar.

Then again, it was also just as likely that the Las Vegas Portal led to the world fragment where my System was. I wouldn't know until I saw it with my own eyes. Even if the portal was neither of those things, it still needed to be closed. For humanity's sake and to buy me and Kesstel a little more time before Earth collapsed.

I glared at Mr. Wilks. "And I can still pull up the transfer request, since it seems to burn you so badly."

He shook his head. "Not at all. What bothers me most is that the little girl my daughter is so attached to is going to a place where no E has business being. Now I'm struggling to find the right bodyguards for you and fit them into the limited number of Hunters allotted to go, just to make sure you don't die."

I shook my head. "No, thank you. I don't need or want bodyguards. I'll be just fine without them." My fighting style, as a Warrior of Mist, was unique. It didn't originate from Earth, and the System wanted me to keep it a secret. If I had bodyguards, I wouldn't be able to fight to my fullest, which meant I wouldn't level up and get stronger. That was a major no-go for me.

He waved his hand dismissively. "That's not an option. You're going to a place that will kill you in seconds. No matter how strong the spell you have on him is, Mr. Noblé won't have time to protect you every minute of the day. The backlash of his fighting aura alone could kill you, so you can't be kept together. This isn't a vacation. He has a job to do."

"I don't need bodyguards," I stressed. "Honestly, would *you* trust the people of someone who just said they wanted you to disappear?"

"*Disappear* can mean a few different things, Miss Devhro. I'm aware of your family situation. I could very easily relocate you and your family in a snap of my fingers. I don't believe you're a bad person, but even good people can cause negative effects." He sipped his drink.

The corner of my lip curled up as my eyes narrowed. Technically, what he proposed wouldn't be a terrible thing for my family. We'd already talked about maybe moving Mom to another city, even though at this point, unfortunately, it wouldn't extend her life.

Only, the fact that I wouldn't have a choice in moving made the idea unbearable. I'd worked so hard to finally be able to control my own life and not be pushed around by other's decisions. I refused to let another person I didn't respect tell me what to do.

"Either way, Kesstel would follow me." It wasn't even a guess. If he was willing to tear through the voids of space to get back to me, he would easily follow me across the country. "Then Eden would lose their strongest Hunter. Isn't his strength something you love to brag about? I might not know a lot about politics, but I understand that much. He used to be under your thumb. How much more are you going to let him get away from you?"

It was easy to tell that Mr. Wilks was a calculating man. This one conversation alone gave me a very deep impression about his desire to control everyone and everything. Bethany was happy in the easy life he'd set up for her, but there must be other people who weren't. There was no way in hell I was going to wear his leash. Any favor I had to repay was just another tether he could use. I always rejected Bethany's offers out of pride and because I wanted her to see herself as more than an ATM. Now, I was even more concerned about accepting her gifts.

He lifted a brow. "You sound so confident."

I took a drink and turned the straw in the cup. "I am."

Mr. Wilks set his cocktail glass down with a decisive *clunk*. "Then do us all a favor and don't go on the expedition. I've spent half my life making sure my little princess doesn't cry. Don't complicate it now. Nor do I want to see Mr. Noblé lose his mind again, especially over something that's completely preventable."

Kesstel's familiar presence entered the room. I turned my head to look toward the door and his backlit figure. Our gazes met from across the distance, and immediately, he started to close the distance between us with a lazy prowl.

I focused on Mr. Wilks again. "I'm sorry, but that's not an option. I'm going. As Kesstel's *emotional support person*"—I never thought I'd actually like that title, but right now it wasn't that bad—"I'm especially obligated to go. I'm not going to die. With or without Kesstel, I'll be just fine."

By now, Kesstel had crossed half the mezzanine along the room. Several people tried to stop him for a conversation, but he brushed them off. Mr. Wilks's bodyguards turned as Kesstel got closer, their bodies stiffening for a second, but they didn't try to stop him.

Not like they could, anyway.

I stood up and pressed out a smile I didn't feel. "I appreciate the intentions. And I do understand where you're coming from, even though I believe it's wrong on nearly all accounts. Don't even bother trying to fit the bodyguards in, please. They'll be useless because I'll lose them as soon as we get there, and they will never find me. I can guarantee that." I nodded toward my half-empty glass. "Thanks for the drink."

CHAPTER 3

Kesstel stopped just inside the circle of bodyguards that surrounded me and Mr. Wilks. He wore simple but expensive designer gray jeans and a black jacket over a white-and-blue shirt. His white-blond hair was pushed back off his forehead, the tips falling around his ears. He didn't care at all about the women who were openly staring at him, some near, some far.

He waited for me to get to his side before he nodded a greeting to Mr. Wilks, but he didn't bother to open his mouth. He glanced at me to make sure I was okay, then turned and walked away.

I followed him.

When we were a comfortable distance away, Kesstel looked at me. "Your fur is all ruffled."

My brows wrinkled as I gaped up at him. "What am I, a cat?"

He smirked. "Might as well be. Cats are easier to tame, though."

I whacked his arm with the back of my fingers, even though it hurt me more than him. I ignored the obvious shocked stares from the surrounding people as I shook my stinging digits and scowled at him. "Between the two of us, you're ten times more cat-like." Okay, more tiger-like, but I didn't want him to take it as a compliment. "Besides, who's taming who?" I challenged.

His lips pursed. "I think we're both changing each other," he amended.

I paused and had to agree. We both had changed a lot since he came into my life.

"What did Mr. Wilks say to make you breathe fire like that?" Kesstel led me around to the other side of the U-shaped mezzanine and leaned against a wall next to an empty table. He crossed his arms over his chest and looked with hooded eyes at the Councilman across the room.

I sat down at the table and followed Kesstel's gaze. A small group of important people were collecting around the man, their movements polite and controlled. The bigwigs of two cities meeting each other, if I had to guess. The question was, at the end of the night, would they be on equal terms, or would one city take the upper hand? Hunters were biologically human, but they couldn't resist fighting for the top-dog position.

But that wasn't my fight. I was happy to stand way, way off to the side and let the politicians duke it out. Then I'd do whatever I wanted.

"He doesn't like me," I said. "He's kinda hard to read because he's so cutthroat. He loves Bethany to pieces, but everyone else is just a tool in his fingers."

"Sounds about right." Kesstel's lips thinned. "He always hated that I never bowed to him, and he took great joy in trying to lord over my life."

A wry smile twisted on my face. "Yeah, that doesn't surprise me." I paused. "He doesn't want me to be friends with his daughter, and he doesn't want me to go with you to Las Vegas." I glanced up and grinned. "What do you think? Should I stay home and be a meek little mouse?"

Kesstel breathed a laugh. "I take it Miss Wilks helped you dress up?" He looked at my outfit. "It has her fingerprints stamped all over it."

I lifted a brow. "What? Do I look that bad?"

He smiled at me. "No, not at all. You're always pretty, and right now, you look very beautiful. But I do admit, it throws me off to see you all dressed up. It's just not quite like the Jynn I know." He paused, an almost helpless expression flashing across his face. "But I do find myself torn between letting you shine and covering you in my jacket to hide you from prying eyes." He pointedly looked at my exposed stomach.

I was grateful for the dark atmosphere because it hid the heat in my cheeks. Then again, Kesstel could probably see just fine right now, anyway.

I cocked my head to the side and tried to brush off his comment. "You also look very beautiful right now. I almost didn't recognize you."

He reached out and gently pushed my forehead with his finger. "Mind your manners."

I laughed. "What, I can't call you beautiful?"

He scoffed and slipped his fingers through my fringe. "I'm a man. I prefer handsome."

"A bred-to-be-handsome man."

He rolled his eyes at me in a very unlordlike manner. "Behave." He lifted his hand and flagged down a waiter passing by.

"Yes, sir," I muttered.

Kesstel talked with the waiter for a second then looked at me. "Do you want something to drink?"

I shook my head, since I was still fine from the Coke, and looked at the small crowd amassing below. Only one hundred Hunters were on the mission list, but there were easily over three hundred on the floor, not counting the people on the mezzanine. There was a clear division of the crowd into three distinct styles.

Across the room from me was a large group of people standing close to one another, most of them wearing the same shade of dark green somewhere on their body, be it their dress or a bandanna around their head. Their style of clothing leaned more heavily on the fantasy side. Very few of them were talking to someone not wearing a matching color.

Right under me was a larger group of Hunters in mostly sky blue. Their clothing was more in line with the usual style I saw among the rich people in Eden, with a flare of club glamour. These people were obviously more outgoing. Their expressions were less guarded, and they were openly talking to the Eden Hunters.

The largest group was obviously Eden Hunters. It wasn't just because their styles were a dead giveaway. It was the fact that there was no color coordination among them. The Eden Hunters took up most of the dance room as they spread out to mix with the rest of the crowd.

It was at that moment that Bethany stepped onto a box placed in front of the bar. The box was just tall enough to lift her above the crowd, so everyone on the dance floor could see her. Most of the people on the floor weren't even dancing; they were simply talking and milling around sipping drinks. The last heavy beat of the song ended, leaving the low sound of talking in its wake. A single light beam from above landed on Bethany, making her hair glow like gold and her opalescent dress shimmer. Diamonds sparkled on her wrists and shoes.

Instantly, the noise stopped, and every eye zeroed in on her.

I stood up, walked over to the glass railing, and leaned against the steel bar that topped the glass. Kesstel came over and stood next to me, his wrists resting casually over the rail. From here, I had a perfect view of nearly the whole floor and the mezzanine, except for right against the wall right under me.

Bethany smiled like a goddess and lifted a mic to her mouth. "Welcome, friends and visitors. My name is Bethany Wilks, the hostess of the night." She paused when the crowd erupted into cheering, Eden Hunters easily the loudest of the bunch. She waited until the noise died down before going on.

"Tonight is the eve of a historical occasion. It's been over fifteen years since the Hunters of all the North American Gates have pooled their strengths together like this. I just wanted to recognize each Gate individually and thank them for their willingness to help our nation at this desperate time."

Another cheer rose up and filled the room.

She grinned. "From the northeast, the Quebec Hunters, led by Logan and Mila Fortin. Welcome." She motioned with her hand to the dark-green group of men and women standing stage left.

Everyone cheered, the loudest noises coming from the crowd around the cool-and-collected group. They were obviously the fans brought by the Quebec party. A man with a strong jaw and straight nose stood in the front, his huge arms crossed, looking imposing. His clothes were dark: a dark-green shirt and black leather pants. At his side was a handsome woman, her chin high in the air, looking like she'd just as soon stab you as smile at you. Dark-green sequins shimmered on her dress as she planted a hand on her hip and leaned to the right. Everything about them screamed power couple. The rest of the group stood behind them, a clear wall between them and the rest of the crowd.

Bethany motioned her hand to stage right. "From the West Coast, the Redding Hunters, led by Ben Saito and Miranda Johnson. Glad to have you here."

The group in pale blue lifted their hands as the people cheered. In the front stood a man with black hair and sharp eyes. He wasn't the tallest, compared to the Eden Hunters, but what he lacked in height, he made up for in presence. With his laid-back smile and a flamboyant pale-blue shirt over stylishly ripped jeans, it was impossible to overlook him. At his side stood a tall, thin woman with short curly brunette hair. Her long black dress with splashes of blue glitter accentuated her delicate features and large eyes. Just like Ben Saito, her magical presence was obvious.

"Last but not least." Bethany pulled everyone's attention back to her. "I want to point out my own people. The Eden Hunters, led by Jack Davis and Laurel Harris." She opened her hand out to the figures in front of her, Blood Sword and Eden's S-ranked healer.

The Eden people cheered the loudest yet, their voices ringing off the black rafters overhead. Blood Sword lifted his hand and waved, his open shirt, red vest, and black pants not losing to anyone else in the room. The pretty healer beamed and waved a hand, the stone blinking on her wrist matching the belt that looped her waist over her maroon pants and multicolored shirtdress.

"Now that all the introductions have been made, it's time to get down to business," Bethany said, pouting slightly for effect. "Sad, but true. As amazing as it is to finally get so many heavy hitters in one room, there is a very urgent reason why." She waved her hand, and the spotlight over her disappeared. The rest of the white lights in the club dimmed, leaving only the glowing blue lines around the mezzanine.

A huge white screen started to roll down from the ceiling, covering the vast accent wall behind the bar. When it was all the way down, an image of the US map was projected on the white screen. I was taken aback for a second. I grew up seeing that map, memorizing the cities and sad history associated with it. Only, this was my first time seeing the new shape of America without the Florida peninsula. All that was left was a jagged rounded edge, as if the peninsula had never been there to begin with.

Gasps and mutters rose in the crowd. Shocked people actually pointed at the map and talked animatedly to their companions.

I glanced around and frowned.

Oh, right. The government had withheld this information. How much longer would it be before the public found out?

Bethany called their attention back to her. "Most of this should not be new information," she said from her location in front of the bar. Her whole body was backlit against the image, leaving just a shadow and a tiny glimmer of her clothes around the sides. "But just to make sure everyone is on the same page, I'm going to go over it all again." She turned and pointed at the map.

"Yesterday, a portal opened up in the Las Vegas ruins. It caused a large earthquake that shook up Eden and Redding a fair bit, and even Quebec felt the tremors," Bethany spoke. "As a result, a part of America sank into the ocean. No one was lost that we know of, since it was already an abandoned area, but it proves how dangerous this event is. If we leave the Las Vegas Portal alone, is it going to trigger another earthquake? Or will other portals open near it?"

She paused. "As you just heard, it is not a Gate. Yet. It is just a portal, but it has unloaded a very large amount of monsters into the area. In fact, the day the Las Vegas Portal opened, all the monsters in the Eden, Redding, and Quebec Gates vanished. Based on the monsters that have been spotted in the last twenty-four hours, we speculate that nearly fifty percent of the missing monsters of various ranks were somehow transferred to the Las Vegas Portal."

CHAPTER 4

———

M y eyes widened as a murmur rippled through the crowd. That was a lot of monsters. If they were all lower leveled, it wouldn't be that much a problem. If they were upper leveled, it would be a handful. Then again, that was why they'd employed ten S ranks, eighty-eight As, and two B-ranked Hunters.

Well, a B and an E, because that was still recorded as my official rank. For a little bit longer.

Although the fifty-grand payout for this trip sure shortened that time-line by a lot. I'd have enough for a down payment as soon as I got back, so I wouldn't need to keep my E status anymore. The S and A Hunters were getting paid more because of their rank, but I wasn't going to complain. I was just grateful for the boost. Then again, I'd only get paid if I came back alive. The Association wasn't going to pay the families of the dead bodies.

Bethany motioned to the map behind her. "The mission, which you have already accepted, is to go into Las Vegas, eradicate the monsters there, and find the portal. The Gates are over two hundred meters tall; you can't miss them no matter where you are standing for miles away. This portal is completely different. We know it's there, but we can't find its loca-tion. For all we know, it's inside a building or basement, or even attached to one of the fissures that opened up from the earthquake. With the high concentration of monsters, we aren't able to pinpoint the exact location. It's up to you to find it. Once the portal is found, a plan will be developed to close it. The sooner, the better."

Two-thirds of the crowd muttered in surprise. The hundred people who were part of the mission didn't show a reaction—they obviously already knew. But the Hunters who were there for the party didn't expect it.

Bethany glanced up in my direction. Her eyes locked on mine for a split second, and the smile on her face became more natural. Then her gaze flicked over to Kesstel. All the welcoming in her face vanished in an instant.

When I first met Bethany, she was infatuated with Kesstel. Since we became friends, she started to view him as a competitor for my attention, and any fiery feeling she had for him turned frigid.

Bethany looked back at the crowd and spoke, taking control of the noise. "Yes, close the portal. A method of closing it has been made known to the Hunter's Association Council. Inside each portal, there is a supreme monster, the Boss. Once that being is killed, the portal will disappear. How strong that being is, we don't know yet, but we believe we have the manpower to make it happen."

She lifted her hand. "Because this method will not work on a Gate, we want to get rid of it before it becomes one. America, as a whole, doesn't have the manpower to tackle another Gate at this point, and after two decades of neglect, turning that area into a livable place for people—taking the cost of clean water, housing, and food—is simply not affordable either. If left unchecked, the people who would suffer the most—outside of the North Mexican No-Man's-Land—are the locations under the Redding's and Eden's Gates protection. Which is why it's best to take it down. The sooner the better. And we are grateful for the Quebec Hunters who have come to help." She smiled and nodded at them.

I tapped my chin, watching the people dressed in dark green. Bethany made them sound so gracious, but I'd bet fifty bucks they weren't here strictly by choice. I bet they were ordered to bring a group of people, a set number of S and A Hunters.

Ironically, the single B and E Hunters were from Eden.

The crowd cheered the Quebec Hunters, who took it like champs.

A movement to my side stole my attention, and I looked over. The waiter was coming back with a silver tray balanced on his hand. He stopped at the table just behind me and set a tall drink down before placing a white plate filled with appetizer-like snacks.

Kesstel walked over to the waiter and touched the pay screen the waiter pulled up.

"So," Bethany sighed. "That was a lot of information on what has happened. Let's talk about what will happen." The US map behind her zoomed in until it showed a satellite image with bright yellow state lines drawn in where Utah, Nevada, and Arizona touched. Several blue dots were lit up and labeled. Bethany motioned to the map. "Because of the monsters in Las Vegas, it is not safe to land a plane in the area. The closest city with a large enough airport is St. George, Utah." A blue dot lit up brighter than the rest in the northwest region of the map. "The city has been vacant for years, but the strip is still in good enough condition. A team entered St. George this morning to clean it up enough to land commercial planes. They have already sent notice that everything is ready to go."

I leaned against the rail and stared at the map. All of this was new information to me. Honestly, I'd probably joined the mission a little too fast, since I didn't even wait for the facts first, but I was eager to find those two portals—both the one to the System's home world and the passage to the parasitic planet.

A frown wrinkled my brow. There was quite a distance between St. George and Las Vegas . . .

An orange line snaked across the map, connecting the two cities along the winding interstate through a canyon. There wasn't a spec of green on the satellite picture, just all varying shades of brown and red desert. Even the tiny line labeled the Virgin River, which twisted with the interstate for most of the path before it broke off to make a couple lakes to the southeast of Las Vegas, was more brown green than any other color. Considering the beauty I saw in the Gate every day, this map wasn't that encouraging. Then again, I wasn't going there to sightsee, even if it was my first time leaving Garden City.

"After landing in St. George, the expedition team will take the waiting vehicles to Las Vegas," Bethany said. "It will take roughly two hours of driving before you enter the Las Vegas metropolitan area from the northwest corner. From there, the expedition team will break into three groups."

The map zoomed in on Las Vegas. Two decades ago, this city was known for the lights and glam of the rich. Casinos and clubs fought for attention, enticing people all over the world to visit this diamond in the desert. Now, it was nothing but ruins. The torn buildings were barely a different shade from the surrounding desert. If it wasn't for the yellow lines that highlighted the city, I might have overlooked it, taken for a small mountain in the satellite view. Two more yellow lines divided the map into three parts.

"Each team will be in charge of searching Las Vegas and the surrounding sister cities in their designated areas to find the portal and kill all the monsters." Bethany paused and tilted her head to the side, showing a charming smile that was completely different from her usual pampered imperial princess air. "And remember. This is a joint operation. There is no competition, no prize for actually finding the portal. The real winner is humanity, and the reward is knowing you kept it safe."

And the money you will get when you get home. That could be in a couple days, or even a couple weeks, depending on how long this operation took. I pursed my lips, thinking about it.

"Camps and meeting locations will be set up according to your team leaders. They will also be in charge of setting up the game plan after the portal is found," Bethany explained. She took a deep breath and gave a bright smile. "Now that all the formal stuff is done, it's time to play, yeah? But just to remind you —the planes leave at 8:00 a.m. tomorrow. Play hard, but don't be late!"

I cheered with everyone else, the sound echoing off the walls and rafters. It hadn't even fully died before the loud, beat-heavy music came back on. Hunters eagerly turned to their companions and talked animatedly, adding a low murmur to the song.

Kesstel appeared at my elbow and held out a napkin with . . . two somethings on it. "My mother used to get so distracted when she got ready for parties that she'd forget to eat. I thought you might have suffered from the same plight."

He wasn't that far off the mark. Food had not been in the picture when Bethany's people tortured me into shape. I slowly took the napkin and peered down at the grilled circular pieces of bread with a smear of cheese and tiny roasted tomatoes. It looked like something straight out of a cooking show. I was so used to him handing me easily packaged snacks, it was weird looking at such fancy food. "What is this?"

"Confit tomato and ricotta crostini," Kesstel replied, taking a drink.

My brows lifted. "Gazoontite," I muttered.

He frowned at me. "Is that a word?"

I blinked back at him. "Isn't it? Doesn't it mean *bless you*? Or German for *health* or something like that?"

His brow wrinkled as he shook his head. "I don't believe that's a word. I don't recognize it."

I laughed and bumped his elbow with mine. "You aren't even from Earth. How would you know?" Because I didn't want to waste the snack, I took a bite. The roasted tomatoes burst in my mouth in a pop of bright acidic flavor, which was smoothed over by the herby ricotta, and anchored together with the mellow taste of sourdough. My brows rose as I instantly fell in love with it.

Kesstel hummed under his breath, the sound barely audible over the loud music. He opened his mouth but paused and glanced over his shoulder instead.

I also felt the presence of someone closing in on us. Curious, I leaned around Kesstel.

A man walked toward us in a flamboyant strut. His flaming red shirt was half unbuttoned, revealing a fair amount of his muscular chest, and tight black pants with silver studs hung low on his waist. His wild brown hair was brushed to the right in a roguish way, the tips falling into his handsome, tanned face. His brown eyes were locked on Kesstel, a friendly smile on his face.

He stopped on the other side of Kesstel, his S-ranked aura as thick as his musky cologne. "Hey, there you are, Kesstel. I was starting to think you didn't actually come." The man's eyes lowered and zeroed in on me. "Hm, this must be the little E girl everyone is talking about. Cute."

I swallowed my food hard, trying to think about how to respond to that. Did he come for Kesstel, or to get a look at me? Which S Hunter was he? Without seeing the emblem on his armor, I didn't have a clue.

Kesstel, without even glancing at me, palmed the top of my head and turned me to face the lower floor. "Tyson," Kesstel said in greeting, tone neutral, neither welcoming nor rejecting. "Why aren't your clothes on properly?"

What was he doing? Was Kesstel trying to prevent me from looking at Tyson?

I used my finger to push up on Kesstel's wrist, lifting his hand off the top of my head. He could have easily resisted, however, he allowed me to move his arm at will. Instead, he dropped his palm on the rail next to me, still blocking me from view.

Tyson snorted with laughter, not the least bit offended. "Come on, man. Don't be like that." He stepped around Kesstel and held out a hand to me. "I'm Tyson Walker, also known as the Warlock."

Color me surprised. Weren't warlocks supposed to be old guys who spent all their time studying magic? With pointed hats and a thick book of spells? There was nothing studious or researchy about this man. I knew there was an S god lightning mage named Warlock; I just didn't think he looked like this.

I reached out with my free hand and shook his. "Jynn. Nice to meet you."

His fingers barely closed around mine, like he thought I was going to break at any second. "The rumors are true. You are the girl who's coming along. Interesting." He let go and tapped a knuckle on Kesstel's shoulder. "I don't know how you talked President Anderson into letting her come; I can't get shit out of that man. Tell me how you did it. I wanna bring my lover to Vegas, too. I mean, it's nothing like it was in its heyday, but it's Vegas, baby. A little danger is exciting, am I right?"

Instantly, I choked on the bite I'd just put in my mouth. I gasped and sputtered as food started down the wrong tube. After struggling a second, I swallowed and blinked away the instinctive tears in my eyes. All thoughts of eating were completely wiped out of my shocked mind.

Was he saying what I thought he was?

Kesstel turned his head and glared at Tyson. "Those rumors are groundless. Have a mind of what you say around her so you don't dirty her ears." His angry aura flickered out in warning.

Tyson held up his hands in surrender. "Hey, I'm just commenting on what I'm seeing with my eyes. After the stunt you pulled the other day at the Gate, there's quite a few rumors running around about this girl. Everyone is dying to find out more about the girl you're so damn protective of. I mean, if she's not a lover, what is she?"

It's true; Kesstel and I had a bit of an ambiguous relationship. I didn't even know exactly when it'd turned in that direction, but it was fun and comfortable. There was no question that I found him attractive, and he was very important to me, right up there with my family. But a lover? I wasn't ready for any relationship close to that stage.

The amazing taste I should have had after the crostini was sand in my mouth. I set the rest of the snack on the table and stepped back. "I'm, ah, going to . . . " But I couldn't come up with a good excuse. Instead, I flashed an awkward smile and walked away.

Behind me, I could hear Kesstel hiss, "Are you an idiot?"

I glanced over my shoulder to see Tyson reach out to hook his arm around Kesstel's shoulder, as if the action was second nature. He paused just before he actually touched Kesstel and dropped his arm. "Hey, I didn't mean to scare her away." He hummed and tapped his brow, as if thinking hard. "But seriously, how do you not lose control and kill her in bed? Such restrained sex sounds so . . . boring."

Kesstel whacked him in the back of his head and sent the man stumbling.

My whole body went up in flames. I turned and hurried away. It didn't matter where, as long as I couldn't hear Tyson anymore.

CHAPTER 5

I didn't know that sitting and doing nothing for four hours could be so exhausting. The plane ride was exciting at first, feeling the inertia of the takeoff and seeing the city I grew up in get smaller and smaller. But then there was nothing to do. It was the first time I'd ever been in a plane; I didn't know I should bring my own entertainment.

After a little bit, I leaned over Kesstel's shoulder to see what he was reading. It was US history, specifically about what had been going on in the last twenty years around the Las Vegas region. How, after the fight with monsters destroyed the pipes between Lake Mead and the water treatment plants, the people were forced to abandon the area. Not only that, but the transportation of food had stopped since monsters attacked anything that moved. What few trucks could make it there definitely didn't have enough supplies for a population of two and a half million. Very few people made it out of that desert terrain.

Kesstel continued to read the detailed report the whole time, but I lost interest after an hour and looked blankly out the window.

The landing was more hectic than the takeoff, with a very fast stop. Apparently, the runway wasn't long enough for a plane this size to land. After we exited the plane, the party of one hundred were sorted into two old dark-blue buses labeled Greyhound on the side, Kesstel and I still sitting next to each other. Since Eden was the largest Hunter city, forty percent of the Hunters were from Eden, and the rest of the members were split evenly between the two other participating cities. I recognized a couple of the other people sitting behind me—unfortunately, in some of the cases. But I ignored them and looked out the window when the bus rumbled to a start.

I didn't think there would be anything to look at in the desert, and for the most part, there wasn't. But I did notice the dry landscape had a bit of . . . charm? Or was it beauty? I couldn't help but stare at the amazing patterns on the tan and red rocks as we drove through a narrow gorge, the road bending and twisting with a man-made cliff face on one side and the Virgin River on the other. There were even some geological features that were so cool looking that I bumped Kesstel to get him out of his report and pointed them out.

What made everyone pause was when we all drove past a cave at the bottom of the gorge. There were monsters in there, but the buses didn't stop to take care of them. Our priority was closing the Las Vegas Portal. Then we could take care of the monsters outside of the area.

The gorge opened up to a bland, pale brown desert. We drove past abandoned houses, settlements, and cars, the same thing over and over again. In the end, my eyes drooped, and I couldn't resist leaning my head on Kesstel's warm shoulder. The bus smelled old and dusty, as if it hadn't been used in a very long time, and the seats were stiff and a little coarse on my bare arms. It had probably been abandoned in St. George until a couple days ago, and it was fixed up just for this trip. But Kesstel smelled good, like spicy, earthy soap. It made it easier to relax in the unfamiliar environment, around all the people I would have kept my guard up around otherwise.

I must have fallen asleep, because the next thing I knew, Kesstel nudged my forehead with his chin.

"Hey," he said softly in my ear. "We're almost there."

I blinked awake and sat up. Luckily, I couldn't feel any crusties on my cheek, so in theory, I didn't drool in my sleep, right?

I glanced at Kesstel's shoulder just to make sure. After a brief burst of relief that there wasn't a wet spot, I looked out the window ahead of us. Kesstel stuffed a snack in my hand, and I absentmindedly ate it, the cheesy crackers becoming an afterthought as I took in the scene before me.

In its heyday, Las Vegas was known as the "Entertainment Capital of the World" and the "Neon Capital of the World," along with other nicknames. I'd seen pictures of the bright lights glowing in the desert at night, the glam and flare of the casinos and the amazing shows that left people in awe. Even the parts that weren't attached to the Strip still had a Vegas flare.

None of that applied to the city that was coming into view. There was nothing but desert for miles until the flat land turned into pointy mountains in the distance. What little vegetation there was, growing between the cracks of the interstate, was rough and bare, easily smashed under the bus tires. Sand drifts were piled up along rusted cars abandoned on the roadsides. Most of them showed traces of old monster attacks, and some even had parts of aged, chewed up skeletons hanging out of the smashed windows and missing doors. I guess it was a little messed up, seeing those sights and not being bothered in the slightest. But no matter what I felt, they weren't going to come back to life.

A pileup of broken cars blocked off a bridge on the interstate, forcing the buses to stop. I leaned against my window and watched as a mage in dark-green robes stepped out of the front bus. She waved her hand, and the rusted cars were tossed into the air, dropping debris, ruined luggage, bits of dry skeletons, and clothes as they went. The cars fell over the side of the bridge and landed in a loud, messed-up pile on the road below. As soon as the way was clear, she climbed back onto the bus, and we moved forward.

"I thought there would be more monsters," a man muttered from somewhere behind me. "Isn't that why we're here?" He'd barely finished talking when everyone on the bus stiffened.

I looked up to the metal ceiling as the presence of a lot of monsters closed in from above.

The bus driver slammed on the brakes, and the bus lurched to a stop, the tires skidding on the uneven, broken road and leaving the smell of hot rubber in the air. The lead bus braked just as fast.

The vehicles had barely stopped moving when something—several somethings—smashed on top of the buses. The steel over my head concaved toward me, but I didn't bother looking up. My eyes were locked on the scene outside my window.

The monsters were a disgusting combination of a bat and a mosquito, with bodies as large as a medium-size dog. Their limbs ended in lobster-like pincers, and their ugly faces were elongated to long, swordlike points. Leather wings beat at the air as they dive-bombed the buses, stabbing at the tops with their noses. According to my System, they were called stirges, most of them ranging between levels forty and fifty.

Hundreds of them swarmed the air, spilling out of a huge, battered white-and-gray rectangular building off the side of the road. The stirges took turns attacking the buses, leaving dents on the metal and cracks on the reinforced windows.

Suddenly, a sharp point stabbed through the ceiling right above me.

Kesstel reached out and grabbed the nose, stopping the proboscis a foot from my head. His mouth slanted in an angry line.

At the tip of the monster's mouth, I could see a hole opening and closing and dripping clear liquid. I jumped out of my seat and flattened against my window so that the liquid didn't touch me. Wherever a drop landed, smoke drifted up as the material of my seat melted away.

The monster banged on the ceiling and shrieked, but no matter how it moved, it couldn't get its mouth out of Kesstel's grip.

With a jerk of his wrist, Kesstel snapped the long point in half with a loud *crack*. More clear liquid and black monster blood rained down on my seat.

The monster screeched and jerked back out of the hole, leaving a foot of its proboscis in Kesstel's hand. It didn't have time to clear the opening before I lunged up and thrust my crystal-steel blade into the hole Kesstel had made in its face. The monster died, spilling more liquids down, completely ruining my seat.

While that happened, the rest of the people on the bus weren't idle. Hunters evacuated the vehicles in a flash and started to attack the monsters. We were outnumbered, but every Hunter attack cut down a stirge. The monsters dropped to the ground one after another, their black blood tainting the red dirt.

Kesstel stayed on the bus and pushed the jagged piece of metal back into place where the monster had jabbed through the ceiling. Meanwhile, I went to the doorway and watched the Hunters. It was impressive to see the synchronized moves of teammates working together, their moves limpid with years of practiced coordination. Other Hunters were obviously working together for the first time, trying to kill monsters without injuring the person next to them. The longer they fought, the more fluid their movements became, matching the Hunters around them. Magic flashed and metal glinted as black blood and monster bodies rained down.

I jumped out of the bus and joined the fray, using this moment as practice for my Throw and Critical Hit abilities. I was fast enough—and the other people were distracted enough—that I doubted anyone saw anything strange. As it was, when the monsters finally stopped spilling out of the battered white-and-gray building, no one asked me why the monsters I killed disappeared.

Breathing heavily, I stood and put my kindjal away.

A Hunter next to me with a long cut on his shoulder turned to his teammate and smacked him upside the head.

The teammate yelped and stumbled a couple feet forward. "What was that for?" he whined while he rubbed the back of his head.

"Couldn't keep your mouth shut, could you?" the injured Hunter complained. "Just had to jinx it all before anyone even got their armor on!" He turned his head and scowled down at his injury. "It's not like healers have endless MP."

It took me a second to realize that the teammate was the guy in the back of my bus who'd complained about the lack of monsters.

The injured Hunter wasn't wrong either. There were very few Hunters with armor on right now. Most of us were all in comfortable clothes—sweats and loose-fitting wear—for the long ride. Some of the Hunters were even barefoot on the blackened red sand.

The pig teammate whined and scowled at the injured Hunter. "I didn't know this was going to happen. You can't blame me."

"Hell no. You jinx everything," he insisted. "It's only your insanely dumb strength that gets you out of it. Just keep your trap shut, and everything will be fine." He humphed in irritation, but his hand was gentler when he patted his teammate on the back. The two men walked toward the group of healers moving through the party.

"Alright," a loud voice shouted over the crowd's talking. "Since we've stopped, we might as well talk now."

I recognized Blood Sword's voice and shifted until I could see him through the crowd. A second later, Kesstel appeared by my shoulder.

I glanced at him. "Nice of you to finally show up."

He nodded his head to the side dismissively. "They didn't need my help. I wasn't the only S who sat out this fight." He nodded across the way to the other bus, at a woman stepping down from it.

I blinked, recognizing Miranda Johnson from the Redding Gate. Her shorts showed off her long legs, and her loose shirt only emphasized her thin, model-like frame. As if she could feel my gaze, she looked toward me. Her soft brown eyes met mine for a second before she looked away with disinterest. Her gaze landed on Kesstel. She paused, her eyes narrowing for a second, then she stepped all the way down and walked over to stand by Ben Saito.

The six Ss in charge stood together, with Blood Sword in the middle.

He lifted his hand, and a holographic map of Las Vegas appeared over everyone's head. "Alright then," Blood Sword said. "As you all know, Las Vegas and the surrounding terrain have been divided into three areas. Each team will take a third, and each team will be divided, according to your team leads, into groups of ten. If there is a problem with your group, take it up with your team lead. Drama is for the TV—leave it there. There's going to be enough things in that city trying to kill us; we shouldn't have to worry about watching our backs from our own people, too." He looked around at all the Hunters.

I couldn't help but glance over to the right. Two regretfully handsome, square-faced men stood just ten feet away, surrounded by a small group of Hunters. The moment I looked over, Blake, Mark, Penny, and President Price all looked in my direction.

CHAPTER 6

I'd seen the list; I already knew that Blake and his posse were coming to Las Vegas. I mean, Blake was the only person besides me who wasn't an A Hunter or higher, so it was pretty easy to pick him out when I looked at the list. I could understand why Price, Mark, and Penny were on the mission. They were all As, so it made sense, and I knew from experience that Penny was good value, though her ability to notice me when I was using Stealth was a little concerning. Mark and President Price—they must be good, too, since the Stone Mace continued to rise on the guild list. As for why Blake was here, I could only assume he'd cried to his cousin. I'd never actually seen Blake in action. It was always his higher-leveled party that followed his beck and call.

Since I had no say on who could and could not come on the expedition, I had been trying to ignore the fact that this particular group existed. They sat in the back of the bus; I sat in the front. With so many people between us, they were nothing but a figment of my imagination.

I sighed and shifted a little, putting Kesstel between me and them so I didn't have to look at Blake anymore. Blood Sword wanted everyone to be friends, but when had that shithead Blake ever left me alone?

Blood Sword kept talking. "The team leads have talked, and it has been decided that as the largest group, the Eden party will take the middle section of Las Vegas." He motioned to the area that followed the interstate through the city, which also included most of the old and new Strips on the southern half of the interstate. "According to the detectors, more monsters are concentrated there, so a larger party should be given that job. We don't know the ranks, and just because there are more monsters, it doesn't mean that the portal is in this section. Monsters spread and claim domains, as you all know." The map disappeared, and Blood Sword looked around, meeting everyone's eyes. "It's our job to claim it back."

Ben Saito stepped forward and spoke in a deep voice. "There are still a couple miles before we get to the drop-off point. Once there, teams will go to their designated areas. The drop-off point is going to be the rendez-vous location, at the I15 and 573 junction. Tomorrow, that rendezvous point is going to be I15 and 574 junction. Please be sure to have your section cleared off by then. Even though that is the rendezvous point, teams have decided that for the most part, we will be camping separately." He glanced at the leads around him. "I think that's everything I need to share with you. Details will be taken care of by your team leads." He clapped his hands. "Let's break."

Since time was an issue, the Hunters didn't go back to their kills to salvage the sellables. A second team would be following after us in a couple days, when that area was safe, to take care of the carcasses. The money from that would go toward funding the expedition and paying the Hunters in it.

However, that didn't make a lick of difference to my drop item orbs. The glowing white balls hovered on the ground like little ghosts, completely unaffected by the Hunters walking through them as everyone headed back to the buses.

I shifted around the group, bending awkwardly so I could reach down. To the people watching me, it looked like I was picking through the red rocks on the ground, finding ones that weren't bloody. In actuality, I was touching the drop orbs as I picked half-heartedly through the rocks. Soon enough there was just me, the patiently waiting Kesstel, and one other person.

I looked over at Jonovan, who was standing very naturally next to Kesstel, watching me with a soft smile. Glancing at Kesstel, I noticed his body wasn't rigid at all. Were they friends? I focused on the healer. "Afternoon, Healer Jonovan. I haven't had the chance to talk to you yet."

Although he was one of the few people I knew here, we hadn't been able to talk yet. Jonovan sat with the S-ranked healer, Laurel, and President Price had been hovering over all the Ss this whole time. And where Price was, Blake was, too, like a turd tail on a fish. Kesstel was the only exception, and that was because Kesstel wouldn't let Price get near him. As soon as he got too close, Kesstel would release a very focused aura assault on him. The last one made Price's leg give out, and Mark's quick reflexes were the only reason the president didn't eat dirt.

The whole event caused most people to steer clear of Kesstel. The other Ss who knew him took it in stride—Kesstel'd never been a cuddly bunny—but it drew a lot of confused looks from everyone else. Never mind the already strange looks people gave him because of me.

All this meant I hadn't been able to greet Jonovan with more than a passing smile since we'd started the trip.

Jonovan glanced at my hip satchel as I slipped another rock into the bag, his face curious. "Afternoon, Miss Jynn. I noticed you haven't been helped by a healer yet."

I glanced at the cut on my arm. I was so used to getting injured and waiting for it to be healed with Regen, I'd gotten used to ignoring the pain. "It's okay."

He smiled gently and walked up. "But it would be better if I took it away."

When I opened my mouth to object, Kesstel spoke up. "Just let him. It's one less thing to worry about."

I pinched my mouth together but stuck out my arm.

Jonovan's fingers started to glow faintly with gold magic as he reached out. His fingers ghosted over my skin, and the warm magic seeped into my cut. In seconds, it was gone.

"You've gotten so much stronger," he said quietly. Kesstel could hear him, but it was doubtful that the Hunters in the buses could, even with their amazing hearing. "That's a good thing. I hated always seeing you so beat up." Jonovan's soft brown eyes locked with mine. "But we are still going to a very dangerous place. Be sure to stay by Kesstel and your guards, do you understand?"

I blinked at him. "My guards? What does that mean?"

The golden light disappeared from Jonovan's fingers, and he drew back. "I thought you knew? Two Hunters on your team are to act as your guards first and Hunters second when Kesstel isn't around. Since they haven't already, I assume they'll introduce themselves later." Jonovan glanced at Kesstel. "Though they might wait until Kesstel steps away first."

I groaned and thumped my fist on my thigh. *Damn it!*

Kesstel didn't look the least bit guilty. "If they have a job to do, they should do it. Regardless of who is around."

"Kesstel, this is a team endeavor," Jonovan reminded him. "Please play nice." It was debatable who was actually older between Kesstel and Jonovan, but since Kesstel only looked like he was in his early twenties and Jonovan looked about fifteen years older, it didn't seem out of place for Jonovan to admonish him.

Kesstel simply gave a lordly I-don't-give-a-damn smile back. But he still didn't get angry. "I'm aware of the situation, Jonovan."

Jonovan gave a short laugh and shook his head. "Well, shall we go? The buses are waiting." He nodded toward the vehicles, where dozens of eyes were staring at us.

Kesstel glanced at me.

I reached out and picked up one more rock, brushing against the last drop orb as I did. "Yep, all done."

"What exactly are you doing?" Jonovan asked as we headed back to the bus.

"Collecting rocks for my sister," I lied right to his face. "She has a thing for rocks, and I thought it would be cool to get some from Vegas. It's not like it's easy to come here, you know. It's just hard finding ones that aren't covered in blood or other stuff, you know?"

Sorry, Aliya, I thought. Hopefully, Jonovan forgot this before they met later. If he asked her about rocks, that might be very embarrassing.

Jonovan hummed in interest. "You're a dedicated sister."

A true smile softened my face. "She's my reason for living."

Kesstel turned his head and looked at me. It was impossible to guess what he was thinking behind his blank mask. I'd gotten used to figuring out his emotions at least, but not this time.

Since Jonovan was seated in the back, he got on the bus first. I went next and Kesstel followed. It wasn't until I saw my seat that I stopped.

Oh, right. My seat got ruined. Where was I going to sit? There wasn't an open spot in the entire bus.

Kesstel grabbed my shoulder and pushed me into his chair. "Sit here." Then he reached up and rested his hand on the rail which ran along the luggage compartment. Was he really planning on standing the rest of the trip?

I wasn't the only person staring at him. After all, he was the only one standing in the whole bus.

"Um, Kesstel?" I asked.

He cut me off. "It's fine." He glanced at the bus driver. "Let's go."

The bus driver jumped like a frightened cat, but he started the engine and quickly caught up to the first bus. Meanwhile, Kesstel leaned casually on his hip, completely unaffected by the moving vehicle. He lifted his hand, and his Guide popped up. His fingers danced over the blue screen before he paused.

A Partner Message (PM) popped up in front of me. I blinked at the teal Guide screen then glanced at Kesstel. There was only one person who could give me a PM.

He stared down at me, expecting.

Lips pursed, I opened my first ever PM.

Kesstel: [**What were you actually doing out there? It wasn't just picking rocks.**]

I bit my lips. How much was I allowed to tell him?

I slowly pressed Reply. I wasn't used to this function on the Guide, and I didn't quite know what to say, so my typing was a lot slower than Kesstel's. [**When I kill a monster, I can collect the sellable parts without having to do the work of taking them apart. That's what I was doing. But it only applies to the monsters I kill myself.**]

Kesstel focused on the screen, obviously reading my message. His brows lifted. [**I see.**] He paused and tapped out another message. [**If this portal isn't the one we need, I was planning on leaving from here. Since we now have visas, we can go anywhere we want.**]

I bit my lips. [**Leave without going back to Eden?**]

[**Yes.**] He looked down, taking in my expression. [**Is there a problem with that?**]

[**I . . .**] I stopped typing and paused, staring at the blinking line, waiting for the rest of my response.

Technically, no. There wasn't a problem. At the same time, there was. I had a lot of responsibility right now—even more than I did half a year ago. I couldn't just up and leave. How would my family cope? Financially, they'd be okay. The condo was almost ready for them to move into, and I could transfer the money I got from this expedition to them. That would hold them over until I came back. In theory.

Only, my family meant more than a financial obligation. They meant everything to me. I could still see the worried expressions on their faces when I told them I was going away for a couple weeks—if this expedition only took that long. Technically, we were contracted to finish the job, no matter how long it took. I couldn't imagine what they would think if they found out I wasn't coming home for an unknown period of time.

Yet, this was the end goal. Me and Kesstel came on this expedition to fast-track getting our passports so we could leave Eden. I just wasn't expecting to leave so fast without talking to my family about it. And there was no phone service in this area, so I couldn't even call them.

The sooner we found the portal to the parasitic planet, the better. Still, now that I found myself at this point, I was unnerved. My tiny world was suddenly growing so quickly, I felt whiplashed.

Before I could finish putting my thoughts together, Kesstel sent another PM.

[**Think about it.**]

I pressed my lips together and nodded.

CHAPTER 7

The Eden group was divided into four teams of ten. Blood Sword—who was the overall manager of the Eden Hunters—and Healer Laurel were in charge of their own teams. Tyson Walker was in charge of team three, which included President Price and his people, and even though Kesstel had the highest rank on team four, he refused to be the leader.

Team four's leader was a fire mage named Charlie Moon. Even though she was a mage, she wore as much black leather armor as I did. A deep red cape cascaded down her back and bunched around her neck so that if she tilted her head down enough, half of her face could be hidden. Her black hair was cut short and spiked up.

She stood in front of our team, eyes narrowed with determination. "Okay." Her voice was crisp and clear. "You all know what we have to do, right? We have one day to clear out our section. The sooner it's done, the sooner we can call it a day. I, for one, hate working at night, so let's get this over with as soon as possible, shall we?"

Her eyes landed on me. Her lips dipped down slightly. That fraction of a second in which her expression changed told me she was frustrated I was here. Obviously, she wanted to get the job done, but she probably felt obligated to babysit me. Her eyes flicked over to the two Hunters standing behind me whose names I'd already forgotten, then rested on Kesstel at my side.

Charlie hesitated for a second, uncertainty flickering on her face. She probably wasn't too thrilled to have a lone-wolf S Hunter in her group either.

She motioned behind us. "Let's go."

I turned around with the rest of my team. Across a parking lot was a battered two-story apartment building. The colors were bland and faded, big gaps spread across the tiled roof, and sand had collected in pools around the structure. It was just the first building, the beginning of a deserted city. Endless more spread out behind, as faded and battered as the apartments in front of us.

And we were going to check every single one of them.

"We aren't going to use a set formation today," Charlie said. "Grab a buddy and stick together. If we spread out, we can cover more ground faster. Keep a watch on your surroundings. It's mostly weak monsters on the outside of the city, but we never know when that's going to change. If you get in over your head, fall back and regroup with the rest of us. Don't be a hero; they die too fast." She pointed to the single healer, a man in navy blue robes. "Phil's with me. We'll stay in the middle of our area, clearing things out there. If you need healing, find us or send a distress flare."

People in the group glanced at each other and left in pairs, spreading out in all directions. I turned to Kesstel to ask what he wanted to do. I didn't actually plan on working with him—I simply wasn't strong enough yet. No matter how careful he was, it was possible he could accidentally hurt me in a battle. I didn't want him to hold back just for me. I figured he'd do what he wanted—which probably involved going to the inner city with the stronger monsters—and I would wander around, looking for the portal. Maybe we would search together, maybe not. Hell, he was strong enough he might already know where it was.

I looked at him and whispered, "Can you feel the portal right now?"

His lips thinned. "There's interference." He didn't elaborate, probably because of the people right in front of us. "It would be easier to just destroy the city."

"That's not even funny," I muttered, thinking. If Kesstel couldn't feel it, did that mean the parasitic planet was purposefully hiding it from him? If it was hidden like that, did that mean it was important? Could it be the one that would lead us to the parasitic planet?

A System notice flashed in front of my eyes. [**Daily Task: Kill five Dust Mephits.**]

I blinked at the task, completely distracted. There was more talking and movement around me as people wandered off, but it was all background noise. It'd been three days since the System gave me a daily task—ever since it told me to find it. Since then, it had been strangely quiet. Now, it was talking to me again.

Kesstel put his hand on my back, instantly drawing me out of my thoughts. He waited for me to look up. "What is it?" He glanced at my screen even though he couldn't read the words.

I put it away. "It's nothing."

What was a dust mephit? There was no telling how many of these things there were. If there were only ten in the area, I couldn't afford to let anyone else kill them, which meant it would be best if I didn't have any partners at all. And it wasn't exactly abandoning the mission either, I reasoned with myself. I would still kill monsters, and I'd be looking for the portal at the same time. I'd just be doing it with a very specific goal in mind.

I heard my name called. I looked at Charlie.

Two Hunters in black armor stood at her side. She motioned to the tall, thin man with dyed red hair just visible under his helmet. "This is Alex Mann." Then she motioned to a sturdy woman with a broad nose and brown eyes. Her puff of curly black hair was tied at the back of her head, exploding out of the bottom of her helmet. "This Mona Keliki. They are your partners during this expedition, Miss Devhro."

My lips twitched. I'd been around Bethany enough to recognize the style of their armor at a glance. These two were obviously Wilks employees, aka, my babysitters. Annoyance tightened in my throat. "I thought he was my partner." I glanced at Kesstel. "Since I'm, you know, his emotional support person."

Kesstel folded his arms over his chest. "I was under that impression too."

Charlie shifted nervously, intimidated by his frigid stare. The two Hunters at her side looked away, obviously just as uncomfortable.

"With your capabilities, Noble, I thought it would be best for you to work alone. That way, you can freely move as much as you need," Charlie said.

No, they were Mr. Wilks's orders. He wouldn't have put bodyguards on the team otherwise, and poor Charlie was going to take the fall. Still, they weren't wrong. Kesstel worked best alone. And if weaker monsters fled in his presence, I'd never finish my daily task. Right now would be the worst time to get a probation penalty.

I nudged Kesstel with my elbow to distract him from scaring people. "We're here on a mission so that everyone can be safer. You have the ability, and I'll only hold you back. We'll split up here and meet back up tonight."

His eyes narrowed. A wisp of oppressive aura danced around our feet. "You are under no obligation to listen to anyone's orders."

The faces of the people across from us went white. Alex even took an unsteady step back, while Charlie and Mona stood their ground on trembling knees.

I smiled, appeasing him. "No, it's fine. This is my choice." I didn't plan on being babysat, anyway. I also didn't want him to cause a scene.

His aura pulled back, and he slowly nodded. "Very well. I'll keep an eye on you. If you need anything, send a PM."

Given how far Kesstel's search ability was, he would probably know exactly where I was no matter where I went during this mission. He might not know my exact situation, but he'd know my location. I nodded.

His fingers softly slid through the hair at the end of my ponytail. "See you soon."

I grinned and waved. "Yep."

He took a second to flick a dissatisfied glance at Alex and Mona, making both of them lose what color they had gotten back in their faces, before he turned. He disappeared, leaving behind a small puff of dust where he had been standing.

Charlie let out a breath. "I didn't know he was *that* temperamental."

I snorted. "You have no idea." Admittedly, I only saw him act like that when it involved me. A soft smile touched my mouth, just thinking about it.

"We should head out," Mona prompted. As soon as Kesstel was gone, the polite look on her face faded a bit.

I glanced at her and nodded slowly. I could already hear fighting in the distance. Dust drifted in the air from between several buildings a block to the south. Alex and Mona walked in the other direction, away from that fight. Charlie joined the healer, and they disappeared around the building.

I followed Mona and Alex, wondering what to do now. As we walked around the apartment building, I paused and looked toward it. It obviously hadn't been a great place to live before the Gates appeared, just good enough to fill out the basic needs. In other words, it was a type of building I was very familiar with. Doors and windows were either left or smashed open, leaving gaping black holes in the sand-covered building. It appeared empty. I couldn't hear or see movement inside, but there was something . . .

I frowned and walked toward the apartment.

"Miss Devhro?" Alex asked.

I glanced at him. "Don't you think that building is odd?" I motioned to it.

He glanced at it then shook his head. "There's nothing in there."

I shook my head. "I think we should check it out."

What little politeness was left in Mona's expression was quickly fading. "No one else stopped at the building, Miss Devhro. There's obviously nothing in it."

It was true. The other Hunters—including Kesstel—went right past this place, and I couldn't really feel anything inside. Still, there was something about it that just seemed . . . wrong.

"I'm going to check it out," I said and kept walking.

"Miss Devhro, we need to hurry and do our part," Mona reminded, her polite voice strained.

I glanced at her, completely seeing through to the look she was trying to hide. Annoyance. It looked like she wasn't as willing to babysit me as I thought. "Yes, and our part is searching *every* building. Just because you can't feel the portal doesn't mean it's not there. That's why we need to visually check everything, remember?"

"You don't need to worry about searching," Alex jumped into the conversation. "Just leave the messy stuff to us." He gave a forced, lopsided smile.

They thought I was useless. I wasn't surprised. I was titled an E, and the only reason I was here was because Kesstel had made it that way. Judging from the way people looked at me last night at the party and today, it was obvious what they thought of me. I was a pet that Kesstel was appeasing.

I sighed, annoyed, even though I understood why. They could think whatever they wanted. I had a job to do, and as long as they were here, that wasn't going to happen. Frustrated, I marched up to the ground floor door labeled 101 and kicked it open harder than I meant to. To be exact, it was more eroded than I thought. The aged doorframe splintered, and the whole thing fell back. It landed on the ground and sent up a dusty cloud.

Coughing, I went inside. Barely two steps in, Alex appeared and grabbed my arm to pull me back behind him. I jerked my arm out of his hold and stepped around his form.

Inside should have been a small apartment—one bedroom, small kitchenette, roughly seven hundred square feet—but not anymore. A monster had ripped through the walls between at least three apartments, and there was a giant hole in the ceiling connecting to the apartments above too. The light from the broken windows illuminated the inside enough to see sandy leftovers from the last owner's hoarding thrown everywhere, with several partial skeletons in the middle of it all. The cabinets were torn off the walls in the kitchenette, and nearly every piece of furniture was shredded. I bet the rest of the apartments looked the same.

"There's nothing here," Alex said. He gave me an accusing glance.

As soon as he turned his head, the wall moved just behind him. No, something camouflaged on the off-white wall moved. More than one something.

I swung my arm up, grabbed Alex's head, and bent over, taking the surprised man with me as whatever it was opened its mouth and spit a gush of liquid, which shot right through where Alex's head used to be. It sailed over our bodies and landed on the ground where Mona had been standing a second ago. The concrete turned green where the liquid touched.

"Camouflage?" Mona hissed. She grabbed my arm and threw me out of the apartment. "Stay there!" she ordered as a pair of knives appeared in her hands. "We'll be back after we deal with this."

Alex spun back as he stood up, his arm swinging out. A sword materialized in his hand and smashed where the barely visible things were. Black blood splattered on the wall, which cracked then crumbled all together, filling the air with a brown cloud of dust and particles. From the pile of rubble, several huge spiders easily over a foot across crawled out. By the way the far wall continued to ripple, there were at least a dozen camouflaged spiders in this apartment alone.

I stood outside the door, just like they told me to, and watched. Hopefully Alex had something smaller than a sword, because that area was too tight for a long weapon. The building was already so run down, if he took out too many more walls, the whole building might come down on them.

Mona slipped around Alex and dove into the room, knives slashing. She was like a madwoman, flashing her blades every which way, dropping the level twenty-three spiders to the ground one after another. The biggest problem for her was, as soon as one spider was killed, another one took its place, spitting yet another jet of liquid that she had to dodge. There had to be a nest or something somewhere in the hole between the apartments.

I pursed my lips and rocked back on my heels. Well, they were going to be busy for a while with that, and I had a checklist to cross off. Alone. I didn't have a time limit for finding the portal other than soon, but the daily task had to be done today. I seriously couldn't afford to be stripped of my stats tomorrow. Not here.

I activated Stealth and walked away. If two A-ranked Hunters couldn't handle a bunch of level twenty-three monsters by themselves, they didn't deserve to be bodyguards.

As soon as I got around the building, I took in the abandoned structures and listened to the sounds of fighting. Then I picked a spot where I couldn't hear anything and ran in that direction.

CHAPTER 8

According to the Guide, a dust mephit was like a large dirt imp found in the Redding Gate. They liked to hide and jump out at their victims, blinding them with a small dust devil then hacking them to pieces with their sharp claws. Pleasant.

I released my mist and stretched it out to its full range, fifty feet in all directions around me. The thin water vapor rushed out, hit the run-down buildings, and pooled over street curbs. It rose in the dry, hot air and formed a bubble around me, swallowing any short building within my radius. I'd seen this happen so many times in Gate Vale, it was a novel experience to see it on Earth.

Unfortunately, I was already aware of how the dry climate wanted to evaporate my mist. If it weren't for my strong will, this cloud would have already blown away. It was going to take effort—and a lot of water—on my part to keep my ability at max capacity. Even so, if I was going to search for anything, this was the best way.

Instantly, I found some small larvae-like monsters hiding behind a building to my right. I turned and made quick work of them, then started to run. It took me an hour to realize that when Charlie said the lower-ranked monsters were on the outside of the city, she meant between levels twenty and thirty-five. They were easy enough to handle, but I couldn't just cake-walk over them while I kept a look out for dust mephits and the portal.

After a couple hours of fighting and avoiding the rest of my team, I stopped and leaned against a building to take a breather. The higher my level, the more resistant my body was to the elements. I knew it was hot and dry, but I didn't feel the heat as much as a normal human would. Even so, after a while, I had to hide in the shade for a minute to cool off.

I pulled a water bottle out of my Items Bag and chugged the whole thing down.

"I should have brought more of these," I muttered. I had learned a lot during my first trip. This was a lot different from a quick day trip to Alous Wasteland. I had enough supplies for today, but I was going to have to fill up for tomorrow. The water mages could help with that. They might not want to share with an E, but they'd never say no to Kesstel.

My stomach roared to life, letting me know I'd already burned off the calories from my afternoon snack and that it was almost time to call it a day. There was probably only an hour left before the sun set, and I still hadn't found my task monsters. I didn't think the Las Vegas Portal would release an army of monsters after dark like Gate Vale—I was sure the Association would have given us a heads-up if it did—but I couldn't say I really wanted to fight monsters in the dark. I guess with my mist, it wasn't that big of a deal, but it put a whole new spin on childhood terrors for me.

While I caught my breath, I opened my stats. **EXP to Next Level: 34.** Gah, so agonizingly close to the next level. I just needed a little bump to get there.

A breeze gently brushed by me, carrying the smell of hot, dry dirt. The dust particles danced in the air, little wisps of pale brown the same color as the surrounding sand. Without warning, the breeze whipped around and aimed right at me. I jumped to the side a split second before the particles rammed into the wall I was leaning on. Cracks spread like a huge web across the wall, and dry stucco crumbled down like blue snowflakes. The air turned to the side and rushed around, scooping up more dust and picking up speed until a twenty-foot funnel formed.

"Here we go," I whispered, Mirroring my kindjal.

I pushed out my mist, searching for the monster I couldn't feel. I could see the movement of four things, but I couldn't exactly tell what they were. They didn't seem to have physical bodies per se. The only features I could make out were that they had bodies and wings, but even that fact kept shifting in my 3D vision.

One of the monsters flew toward the dust devil. Through the sand flying in the air, I saw something which looked like a cross between a gargoyle and a pig, with a big, squished nose, huge pointed ears, and a potbelly body supported by batty wings. It was dark brown, but it wasn't solid. It was like it was made out of sand that shifted around, forming and deforming a body with each flap of its wings.

The level forty-eight dust mephit flew toward the funnel.

I coupled Critical Hit and Throw together and flung my right kindjal at the monster. As soon as the blade left my hand, I shot forward after it with my left sword at the ready. Dust whipped at my face, making it hard to see, but my senses were locked onto the monster.

The dust mephit jerked to the side just as the kindjal hit it. Although my attack landed, it was on its side instead of the middle of the chest, where I'd aimed. The dust mephit let out a crackly sort of sound, like dry leaves being stepped on, and its unstable body exploded into a cloud of dust. The kindjal kept going right through it, as if it never hit anything at all. The sand that belonged to the monster's body swirled and merged back.

With a strong beat of its wings, the dust mephit moved toward the dust devil. My right kindjal appeared back in my hand just as I lunged at the monster, swinging both swords down. I missed by an inch as the dust mephit merged with the funnel.

As soon as it joined, the tiny dusty tornado spun faster. Nearly blind, I staggered back and jumped away to crouch against a nearby building. It gave enough of a buffer from the dust devil for me to take a breath without inhaling dirt. Wind dragged at my mist, trying to pull it out of my control.

I tsked and canceled it. I'd rather fight with my mist for the stat boost, but right now, it wouldn't help enough to make up for its loss. I took out a handkerchief from my Items Bag and wrapped it around my nose and mouth. Luckily, I'd listened to Aunt Mina's worrying when she went on and on about freak sandstorms—which Las Vegas didn't normally get— and bought some goggles. I'd felt like an idiot at the time and only brought them to make her feel better, but now I was grateful.

I hated the feeling of the things covering my face—it was like my senses were cut in half. But at least I'd be able to see and breathe.

I felt movement to my right and dodged to the side just as another gust hit the wall I was hiding against. That gust of wind wrapped around and started a new dust devil. Just to the side of that, I spotted another dust mephit flying toward the new funnel.

Like hell was I going to let it merge and create a bigger tornado.

I flung my kindjal at it again. This time, I didn't aim for the monster; I aimed right in front of it. The dust mephit sensed the weapon and jerked back, and the kindjal shot right past it without touching the monster in the slightest—but it stopped it long enough for me to get there.

My kindjal sliced right through the monster's wing, cleaving it in half. It let out a crackling sound as it beat its uneven wings furiously. With each beat, particles of sand wafted off the broken ends and disappeared into the wind. Did this monster not even have flesh and black blood? Just sand?

The dust mephit lashed out with its long, spindly arms. The claws at the end of its three digits solidified from sand particles to sharp rocks as it aimed for my face.

My right kindjal appeared back in my hand just then. I blocked with my left and countered with my right, aiming for the other wing. If I could drop it to the ground, it would be a useless lump. The monster shifted out of the way again, but the injury on its wing significantly slowed it down. I quickly followed with another attack while it was still recovering its balance. My kindjal slashed across its chest, displacing its body's sand. The sand moved back into place, but at least the monster's HP dropped.

A burst of sandy air shot out of the dust devil ten feet away.

I dropped to the ground and stabbed my kindjal into the ground for an anchor. The main attack missed me, but its still powerful undercurrent hit me. The gritty air blast peppered my forehead numb with sand and tore at my hair, nearly pulling it from the ponytail. A normal human would have been skinned. Still, I gripped my handle and braced against the attack. As soon as the blast was over, the dust mephit fell on me, slashing and tearing me with its suddenly solid claws.

I gritted my teeth against the pain and twisted around until I could kick it right in its ugly face. The monster crackled and fell back. Jumping up, I attacked the injured dust mephit as it flew toward the dust devil, stabbing right through its body with my right kindjal.

The monster's body lost its solidity, and I fell right through it. The sand rippled around me, blocking my vision for a second. In the back of my mind, I screamed, *Oh my god, I'm inside a monster!* As soon as I was through, I planted my foot and swung around as if I wasn't freaked out. Both my kindjals went up, slashing at its head. It had just barely solidified when my blades went through its neck and across its eyes.

My kindjal hit a solid object in its left eye. A second later, I felt the crack of an energy crystal. The dust mephit disappeared in a shimmer of light that was a lot prettier than the monster. Two drop item orbs fell to the ground.

[+325 EXP]

[You have Leveled Up!]

[Daily Task: Kill five Dust Mephits. (1/5)]

I didn't have time to respond before another shot of sand-filled air exploded out of the side of the dust devil. It hit me dead-on. I groaned, unwilling to open my mouth, as I was thrown off my feet. Hitting the hard, cracked cement, I was pushed along by the wind attack until I hit the side of a building.

The attack ended, and I scrambled to my feet, gasping and dizzy. I slid around the side of the building, looking for a place to catch my breath. On the north side, the first and larger dust devil still raged, slowly getting closer to me. On the south side, the smaller but still just as painful funnel closed in on me.

I shifted into a more comfortable position so that my arm didn't put so much weight on the bruises forming on my back and sides, and my foot bumped against something I hadn't seen in the small blind spot my goggles gave me. Instinctively, I looked down.

On the ground was a huge, crude-looking sword. The blade wasn't perfectly straight, and the material that was wrapped and tied around the handle was tattered. But I recognized that style of sword.

One just like it had sliced me to death bit by painful bit while monsters laughed with glee.

Jynn Devhro

Rank B	**Level** 51
	EXP to Next Level 7489

HP 1074/2997	**Stat Points** 3
MP 702/1301	

Strength 91 (+20)	**Agility** 84
Magic 81	**Perception** 84
Constitution 84 (+20)	**Intelligence** 77

Skills	**Abilities**
Throw	Mist (Improved) (50 ft)
Critical Hit	Feather Step
Quick Hit	Regen (Limited)
Mirror	Stealth (Limited)
High Jump	Poison Fog
	Mist Blade

CHAPTER 9

My eyes widened and my heart stopped. Even though I didn't want to see them, the horrible memories crashed through my mind like a wrecking ball. The pain of losing layer after layer of skin and muscle. The smell of my own blood dripping from my body. The desperation to live. The oppressive knowledge that I wasn't going to. The derisive laughter of the orcs. Fear for me. Fear for my family. Fear of the unbeatable terror that treated me like a toy.

The memory threatened to overtake my being. My breath came short and fast as I leaned back, away from the sword. My trembling hands fell useless to my sides, and the left kindjal winked out of existence.

A blast of sand brushed past my face, tugging at the hankie. I blinked, pushing the memory back down into the dark hole in my mind, somewhere I'd never let it escape from again. Slowly, the dim room lit with green fire faded away until the sandy, deserted city came back.

I took a breath, finally getting enough air in my lungs.

No, I wasn't going to fall apart. I wasn't a weakling anymore. I would not be a victim anymore.

The chaotic waves in my mind settled down to a perfect clarity. It was like there was no more flying sand distracting me, no more grit getting into my ears, no sting of tiny particles on my skin. The double threats of the dust devils lessened. As soon as I defeated one twister and the monster inside, there would only be one dust devil left. I could do that.

My hands tightened around my right kindjal. Lunging around the southern corner, I sprinted to the smaller funnel. I closed in on the dust devil in seconds, and just before I got there, I activated Mist and Mist Blade at the same time. A small, tightly controlled ball of mist formed at the edge of my crystal-steel blade. As I swung across my chest, the mist lengthened out around the blade, turning my seventeen-inch blade into a ten-foot-long sword. The translucent blade slashed through the funnel, leaving a gaping hole, and I thrust my hand out and forced a mist ball into the opening, preventing the twister from closing up again.

My toes tapped on the ground, and I leapt through the hole seconds before my mist ball was shredded. Unlike the spinning outer wall, the air was calm enough in the eye of the dust devil that I could finally breathe a decent amount of air.

There wasn't enough room for the Mist Blade—at least three feet of the blade were inside the twister wall. The dust tore at my mist, but I forced it to stay in place.

I could feel a monster presence above me in the spinning wall, shifting and changing, sometimes with the rotation of the wind and other times against it. Suddenly, it broke out of the sand and dived toward me. Stepping to the side, I swung, the long blade light as a feather as it whipped around in a silvery blur. The dust mephit crackled in alarm and beat its wings furiously backward. My blade missed by centimeters, and the monster was swallowed in the dust devil, its body dissolving then merging with the spinning sand.

A second later, it shot out of the funnel from behind me. I evaded and swung my Mist Blade. The quick monster dodged to the side, but I still managed to cut off the corner of its pointed ear, and it dove back into the sand to hide.

I Mirrored my sword again and ended up with a normal kindjal and a long blade. From there, I waited for the monster to materialize and attack again. Meanwhile, the funnel wasn't stationary. It was slowly and steadily moving across the cracked cement, forcing me to constantly move to stay in the middle of it while me and the monster played a deadly peekaboo game. Sometimes, I hit the dust mephit; other times, I was the one who took damage.

The dust mephit popped out of the sand right above my head. I whipped my Mist Blade up. This time, instead of slashing at the monster, I morphed the fog around it. My blade became a block which latched onto the monster's wing. I gritted my teeth and used all my will to force the block of mist to the ground.

The dust mephit crackled as it landed with a *psh* of sand hitting the ground. Its legs and body dissolved into a pile of sand, leaving only its head and mist-encased right wing and arm intact. My kindjal flashed, stabbing down where the energy crystal was in its eye. The monster exploded into tiny white lights, and two drop orbs appeared.

[+325 EXP]

[Daily Task: Kill five Dust Mephits. (2/5)]

"Three to go," I said softly, my voice muffled by the hankie. I touched the drop item orbs, absorbing them into my Items Bag.

The dust devil dissipated around me . . . revealing the first, larger one advancing at a steady pace. Maybe I should have been glad that these weren't as fast as natural dust devils, but damn, were they slow. If only the dust mephit's attacks were too.

Right on cue, a rush of dust and wind shot at me like a lance.

I threw my kindjal to the side, right at the window of the building. It shattered, and I quickly dove in after my sword. A sandy gust followed me in. Flattening against the wall, the attack skimmed right past. I paused, finally realizing I'd been fighting around a bank this whole time. The furniture was in disarray, with desks and chairs overturned, and dead plants lay on the ground. There was dried blood on the teller's windows.

I sprinted to the other side of the large room and broke another window. Jumping out of it, I then leapt up to the roof and ran to the very tiptop. The dust devil spun right next to the building, slowly inching along as if meandering. Did the monster lose my location?

I took a deep breath and jumped up to where the wind was weakest. My High Jump took me right over the rim of the funnel, and I fell down the middle.

Two dust mephits hovered inside, one at full health and the other a bit depleted—obviously the first one I'd hit when I started this battle. I aimed for the injured one and activated Mist Blade one more time. Both monsters looked up just as I slashed down with all my might on the injured dust mephit. It didn't even have time to move before I cut it in half, from the crown of the head to its toes. The monster dissolved, leaving two drop orbs, and the energy crystal clattered to the ground ten feet below.

[+325 EXP]

[Daily Task: Kill five Dust Mephits. (3/5)]

The other monster crackled in agitation and merged with the swirling sand wall. I landed on the ground and turned, sensing for the hiding monster. With a jerk of my wrist, I destroyed the energy crystal at my feet.

With a threatening crackle, the level fifty-three dust mephit attacked me. As it burst out of the funnel, it sent out a blast of sand. I dodged, clearing its vicious claws, but the sand attack hit me right on the side, hard enough to cause the soles of my boots to skid across the gritty cement. Pain seared through me, but I held my stance. Foot by foot, I was pushed closer to the side of the funnel. From the vicious speed of the sand, I bet they would feel like little bullets if I was caught inside.

I sank my Mist Blade into the cement and stopped the sliding motion. Now that I wasn't moving with the air, the energy of the sand pelting me increased painfully, but it was better than being inside the wall.

The dust mephit came at me again. While one of my hands was preoccupied with anchoring me to the ground, my other blocked and parried the monster's attack with my kindjal. We slowly hacked at each other and continued to drop HP.

Only, I didn't have time to take this slowly. The sun was starting to lower, and the building cast long shadows on the ground. I still had one more dust mephit to look for, and my HP was already in the yellow.

The monster popped out of the wall above my head. Bracing my hand on the blade anchored to the ground, I used that to kick and spin at the same time. My ankle caught its wing, and I hooked my foot around the back of its head. With the momentum, I smashed the monster to the ground. A second later, I stabbed it through the head, and it disappeared along with the dust devil.

[+365 EXP]

[Daily Task: Kill five Dust Mephits. (4/5)]

Breathing heavily and aching all over, I leaned down to pick up the drop orbs, then I hurried over to where I'd killed the first dust mephit and picked up those drop orbs too. For the first time, I had enough time to read the names of the drop items; a floating eye and a vial of mephit sand. My System didn't react to these items, meaning they didn't have anything to do with the cure for Dreamers.

I sighed in disappointment before chugging a water bottle and eating a granola bar. It wasn't a meal, but it was enough to hold me over till I got to a safe place.

When I was ready, I trekked back to where the bank was, now several blocks away.

From around the corner of the building ahead, I saw a wisp of sand dance in the air. That was the exact same thing the other dust mephits did before they attacked me. Instantly, I flattened myself against the building and turned on Stealth. Now that I'd fought the monsters multiple times, I could think of several different ways to approach this. Honestly, the easiest way I could think of was if I surprise attacked it first.

I sent my senses out, just a quick flicker so I didn't spook it. I wasn't surprised that I couldn't completely sense a monster, but what I could see was a large cluster of sand that moved in a very specific way. It was just five feet away, coming in my direction.

I leapt out from my hiding spot, facing the monster.

The sand stalled and condensed, forming a startled dust mephit. Before it could do anything, I encased it in a large ball of poisoned mist and solidified the edges. The monster's wings beat against the solid sides, crumbling on the edges until sand collected on the bottom of the mist ball. Its claws slashed against the sides, but every time a little cut was formed, I fixed it.

Slowly, I shrunk the ball, forcing the monster into a tighter and tighter spot. I could tell by the way its HP started to slowly go down that it was poisoned. The dust mephit waved its arms wildly, obviously trying to create sandy wind magic, but it was completely cut off from the outside world. Even the sand of its body was sluggish, clumped together inside the moist ball rather than morphing and changing as it usually did.

I didn't wait too long before I took out my kindjal. It was a higher level than me, so it was only a matter of time before it broke out of the mist barrier. I activated Mist Blade, ignoring my flashing red MP, and killed the monster.

[+355 EXP]

[Daily Task (Kill five Dust Mephits) Completed. +200 EXP]

Breathing hard, I pulled the goggles and hankie off my face then rested my hands on my knees and bent over. I was so tired. I couldn't tell what hurt more, my head from the excessive use of MP or my body from the battle.

I straightened and looked at the red streaks in the sky. I hoped the camp wasn't too far away; I'd totally lost track of where I was. But first, there was something else I had to do.

I turned and finally went back to where the red orc sword was. It was still there, lying on the dirty ground. Unlike everything around it, it only had a very light layer of sand on it, as if it were new to the environment.

Reaching down, my hand paused an inch from the handle. Painful memories threatened to flood my mind again, but I forced them back before they overtook me. The thought of touching this sword nauseated my already empty stomach. Still, I forced my fingers to lower and grasp the rough handle. The last time I'd touched a sword like this, I could barely lift it, a fact that the red orcs found hilarious. Now, not only could I lift it, but it was easy to swing even with how unbalanced the blade was.

Now that my mind was clear, I could see the bit of black blood caked with sand that clung to the dark, crooked blade. That had to be fresh—well, fresher than two decades ago.

Did that mean the Las Vegas Portal was the one I was looking for? The portal the System was in?

CHAPTER 10

I opened up my System and clicked on Kesstel's name to send a PM. **[Where are you? Do you know where the campsite is?]** As soon as I hit send, I looked up and noticed a group of people coming my way.

A moment later, President Price, Blake, and their posse—plus another guy who I didn't know—appeared at the end of the street. I hadn't even realized I'd gotten so close to the other team's area. Several abandoned cars and a bunch of garbage lay between us. Hopefully, they wouldn't notice me.

As soon as the thought crossed my mind, Penny paused and looked over at me, as usual the first one to detect me. Mark noticed and followed her look, which notified the rest of the group. Price instantly walked toward me, the rest following.

I groaned inwardly. Was I fast enough to run away from them? I was still thirty levels lower than Price. It was a big enough difference that I doubted I'd get far. Not to mention, Penny was faster and could actually perceive my Stealth mode. In theory, they shouldn't try anything while we were on a mission, right?

Psh, yeah, right.

A PM from Kesstel popped up. Right as I went to open it, Price spoke up.

"Evening, Miss Devhro. I'm surprised to see you out by yourself." He put on a cordial smile, which nearly cracked his face in half.

My mouth twitched. "Right. I was just on my way back. I'll see you there."

Price's narrowed eyes looked me up and down, taking in my very messy appearance. "It really is too dangerous for a . . . *Hunter* like you to be out in the open alone like this. Since we're all going to the same place, why don't we go together?" he asked, as if he were the most considerate gentleman in the world. Never mind the fact he was looking at me like a piece of meat with a price tag.

Hunter, huh? I bet that wasn't the original word he was thinking of. Still, I didn't mind it so much. Just watching the disgruntled look on Blake's face made it worth it. "Thanks, but no thanks," I replied. "I can get back on my own." As soon as Kesstel told me where to go.

I reached out to finally open the PM Kesstel had sent.

"Hey, didn't you hear my cousin?" Blake demanded.

The man I didn't know lunged over and grabbed my wrist before I could step back. "Some*thing* like you should show more respect to your superiors." As he scolded me, he quickly glanced at Price and Blake, clearly looking for praise.

What the hell? Who was this guy? Didn't all the people on this expedition have good credentials? Why was this guy sucking up to them? Then I noticed the Stone Mace symbol on his sleeve.

Oh, he was one of their people. No wonder he was a brownnoser.

I scowled and jerked my wrist. "Let go."

His hand tightened, making my wrist hurt. Price simply watched, a small light of amusement in his eyes. Apparently, he was done trying to cater toward a tiny E.

My fist tightened, itching for the feel of my kindjal. If this guy didn't let me go in three seconds, I was going to *make* him let go. Seriously, if he didn't know how to use this hand properly, he didn't need it anymore.

Blake stepped forward. "He's right. Backing or not, something like you—"

A blur of movement shot over my shoulder, the air pressure ruffling the loose fringe around my face. A split second later, a large palm gripped the man's face, and an arm wrapped around me, locking me against the warm chest behind. At the same time, the man was thrown at a car beside Blake so hard that the door bent and the whole vehicle slid back several feet. He collapsed to the ground, unconscious.

I blinked, still trying to catch up on everything because it happened so fast. The only reason I didn't struggle against the hold locking me into place was because I recognized the presence of the man behind me.

Kesstel's now free hand touched under my chin and lifted my face so the other four Hunters could get a good look at me. "This young lady is mine," Kesstel announced. His aura seeped out of him, thick with anger.

"Anyone who touches her will die a very, very painful death. I will not give you another warning."

The Hunters dropped to the ground one by one under Kesstel's pressure. Face pale and covered in sweat, President Price looked up with an unwilling expression. Blake, the weakest person, was bent over on his hands and knees, gasping for air.

My eyes were wide from Kesstel's possessive words. My heart stopped then stuttered, pounding painfully hard in my chest. Did he know the full meaning of his words? Was that what he intended? Or was he referring to me as his emotional support person again?

I was still trying to process them when Kesstel scooped me up into his arms and I was surrounded by his freshly showered smell. I looked up, still shocked, as he cradled the back of my head with a large hand and pressed it to his chest. Then he moved. Air blasted around me as Kesstel ran and jumped so fast that I could barely make out the desolate city as it passed.

Seconds later, he came to a stop and set my feet down. "You're a mess," he said softly. "Did you roll in a sand hill?" A towel appeared in his hand. He wet it with a water bottle then started to gently wipe my face clean. Now that I had a good look at him, I realized he was dressed casually. It was obvious he was done for the day.

I propped a hand on his arm and let him clean my face. When I thought it was good enough, I leaned back and looked around. We were on top of a tall building with the whole city spread out before us. The red-and-orange sunset lit up the already reddish-brown color of the crumbling city, making the reds vibrant. The hot colors blended and contrasted with the shadows the buildings cast, as the tall structures cut through the dying sun like knives. It really was quite the sight to see.

But that wasn't what was really on my mind.

"'This young lady is mine,'" I whispered the words that kept looping in my mind before I glanced up into Kesstel's diamond blue eyes. "Yours, huh?"

His mouth twitched, and he tilted his head up to look at the sunset. His hands tightened around the towel.

I could tell he was thinking. Since I wanted to know what it was, I didn't break the silence. Truth be told, my heart was still pounding from his statement. I didn't even fully know how I felt about it, but I knew I didn't hate his possessive words. They made my chest feel like it was full of soda bubbles, shifting and bursting while my heart did flips and little fireworks went off in my mind. It was uncomfortable and wonderful at the same time. I wanted to run away from the feeling, but I didn't want to miss out on what else Kesstel had to say.

In the end, I was so torn, I just stayed still.

"You are mine," Kesstel said slowly. "More than anyone else in this world, you could only be mine." He looked down into my eyes. "You are no longer an Earthling. Because of that, when this world collapses, I can take you away with me. You and I won't have to be alone when we move to the next world. We could have a constant companion; someone we always feel familiar with in a world of strangers."

My eyes widened. That wasn't exactly what I thought he was going to say. "Is that why you're always so nice to me? You want a constant companion?"

His lips thinned. "It was to begin with," he admitted. "And even a little now. I just wanted someone—anyone or anything—like an anchor I could hold on to in the endless battle I was thrust into. Even if I couldn't feel anything for them, it didn't matter. When I realized you were changing and I might be able to take you with me to the next worlds, I figured you could be that someone. That's why I forced my way into your life."

My mouth dropped open, but I couldn't find any words to say. I'd never thought that might be the reason he wanted to be with me.

"But that isn't the case now." He reached out, took my hand, and started to meticulously wipe it clean. "It can't be just anyone now. It has to be you."

It took everything in me to not wiggle away from the ticklish touch. The damp towel was cold on my fingers, but his skin was so warm on mine. It would be so easy to turn my hand over and hold his. "So, *if* Earth actually collapsed—which I'm going to make sure it doesn't—and *if* I agreed to go with you, what would that make us? Friends, friends with benefits, or something more solid? What exactly do you want from me?"

He took my other hand and started to clean it. "Originally, I just wanted to be friends. I wanted a familiar smiling face I could see every day. Now, I admit my feelings have changed. But I'd never degrade you to friends with benefits. My mother would never rest in peace if she knew she raised a scoundrel." The corner of his mouth kicked up, revealing a bit of a smile for the first time since I cornered him into this discussion. "It's an all-or-nothing thing with me."

The towel disappeared, and he cupped my cheek softly so I could only look into his serious eyes. "I want more. I want everything when it comes to you." He paused. "But I'm also not going to force you into anything you don't want. I respect you more than that. So I'll be content as long as you stay by my side, where you can be safe and neither of us have to be alone."

I swallowed hard and lowered my head. There was so much I didn't even know how to feel about. It felt wonderful to know he had romantic feelings for me, but at the same time, it felt forced. Were they his real feelings? Or was it because of my special constitution which soothed the chaotic energy of the crystal in his chest? "How do you know that you don't feel that way just because I'm the only one who makes you feel emotions? And you're not clinging to me because of that?"

The corner of his mouth kicked up. "I also thought about that. But even before I became a Boss, I'd never felt like this for another woman."

Heat colored my cheeks, and my heart was pounding a million beats per minute. *Get a hold of yourself,* I thought. Right now was the worst time to even consider a relationship.

I looked toward the dying sunset. "How do you know you're the only one for me? What if we go to another world and I fall in love with a man over there?"

"I have confidence in my looks," Kesstel drawled flatly. "Not to mention, you're just like me. Someone who stays guarded against everyone else. I haven't seen you open up to anyone else as much as you have to me, either." There was a challenge in his tone.

My fingers tapped on my thigh. "You're . . . not wrong about that."

Kesstel shrugged. "And in the end, if you did take interest in another person, I'd just have to make them disappear." He was so nonchalant about that declaration.

I gasped and whacked him on the shoulder. "That's not something to joke about!"

"Who said I was joking?" He smirked.

I rolled my eyes. "Right. Anything your lordship says is fact." Then I paused, turning serious again. "If this world collapses, I'll go with you. And if this world doesn't, I'll still stay with you." I looked into his eyes. "Honestly, I don't know how to feel. I'm not looking for a relationship right now. But I know that when you were gone, I was lonely. I threw myself into hunting monsters, but even that didn't distract me enough to forget about missing you. I don't want to feel that again. I don't want you to be alone anymore either." Slowly, I reached out. My fingers hesitated a second before I touched his pale cheek just under his eyes which fascinated me so much. Feeling the warm skin under my touch, I became bolder and ran my fingers over his face, touching and feeling this perfectly sculpted face.

He closed his eyes and lowered his head, letting me touch as much as I wanted. His hands reached out and gently rested on my waist.

My heart jumped and I had to swallow a couple times before I was sure I could talk in a calm voice. "I'll go with you anywhere you want . . . but why can't you make Earth your new home?"

He opened his eyes and focused on me. The red light of the sunset darkened the pale blue shade to a true blue.

"You want revenge for your planet, I know. But I don't want to watch you kill yourself," I said softly. "I want to see you live with me. For me. I want to see your face every day and see the faces of my family every day. Maybe it's selfish to want that, but when it comes to the people I care about, I am selfish."

He grabbed my hand and pressed my fingers to his lips.

My eyes widened and blush burned my cheeks. "I don't see why we both can't get what we want. We can work together and save this world. Then you can come back here and live together with me. Earth can be your new home. No more jumping from world to world, no more starting over in a strange place. No more fighting."

"It sounds like a dream." Kesstel's lips brushed against my fingertips. "One I wish I could believe in."

"Then tell me," I started. "What would happen to me after we found the parasitic planet? If you kamikazed, what would happen to me? Would I die on it with you? Or would I pop up on another planet and live the life you're living now, alone on a foreign place with no one by my side? Is that what you want by bringing me with you?"

He paused, and a glint sharpened his eyes. "No. I don't want that."

I shook my head. "I don't want that either."

"However, I can't see a way to save this planet," Kesstel said. "It's already too infected. Even if the parasitic planet dies, this world will still collapse."

CHAPTER 11

———

The fiery sunset dimmed and gave way to the dark night sky, just like the hope in my heart. One by one, the stars came out, spreading across the dark blue void.

Slowly, I stepped back from Kesstel. I was willing to follow him, and I liked him, but that didn't mean I was ready for an intimate relationship. I shifted to his side and looked up at the night sky. There was no light pollution here, unlike in Eden, and my enhanced sight helped differentiate the colors in the sky.

For the first time in my life, the fullness of the solar system was revealed to me. Billions of pale colorful bits of glitter spread across the dark sky, twinkling and winking just like in pictures. The background wasn't just solid black but a mixture of dark blues and even violets. My lips parted as I stared at the view. It was gorgeous.

Still, there was another thought on my mind. "How many of those stars have habitable worlds like this one?" I whispered. "Only eight of those lights are planets from this solar system. The rest are solar systems and galaxies with countless worlds. It makes me wonder how many of those lights are the parasitic planet's next targets. And how many planets have already collapsed but we can't tell because the light hasn't stopped reaching Earth yet?" I paused. "Maybe even your world's light is still visible right now."

Kesstel's hand closed in a fist.

Ah, I didn't mean to make him sad. My finger reached out and touched the back of his hand. He turned his until our fingers hooked together. I wasn't ready to talk about the heavy subjects again, so I reached for a lighter one.

"Have you had dinner yet? I haven't, so why don't we eat?" I turned and looked around for a place to sit. All I saw on the flat roof was dirt and garbage. The skylights were covered with curved semitransparent plastic bubbles, but they were all broken and jagged looking.

Kesstel looked around too. He picked out a large space and waved his hand, then a fifteen-foot camper appeared right there on the roof.

I gaped. "You brought that?"

He frowned at me. "The Association gave it to me with all the other equipment I needed for the stay. Didn't they give you one?"

I snorted and shook my head. "No, they gave me a tent and a sleeping bag. Oh, and a camp chair. At least they gave me a full two weeks' worth of food and snacks."

He hummed under his breath. "Generous as always. They must have assumed we'd share; I noticed mine is larger than the other Hunters'." He walked toward the camper and opened the door. "There's a shower if you want to clean up before eating." He stepped into the dark, and a second later, several ceiling lights flicked on inside.

The thought of being clean sounded heavenly. I admit, that was a problem I hadn't thought of until today. How were we going to stay clean in this waterless desert?

But how had they fit a shower in such a small camper? I followed him in.

To the right of the door was a full-size bed, half hidden behind a folding curtain. To the left, a small counter and stove sat below a cabinet. Across from that was a raised box with a door and white lid over it. Maybe a storage bin? A small eating nook with a table and benches took up the space on the other side of the kitchenette. There wasn't a single inch of unused space in the camper, everything tidy and clean and decorated in tans, blues, and faux wood.

"It's really nice. I'm impressed you could fit this in your Items Bag." I ran my hand over the smooth wooden countertop.

Kesstel went to the storage box. "It came with the industrial Items Bag they gave me." He looked at me over his shoulder. "I take it they didn't give you one of those either?"

I shook my head. "Just a normal one with a bunch of equipment in it."

He humphed under his breath and opened the white lid to the box. I'd thought it was for storage, but I was wrong. Inside was a toilet with a small space next to it, all white plastic. Kesstel took a shower curtain from his Items Bag and hung it on a square rail on the ceiling directly above the toilet area. That was when I noticed the water nozzle on the ceiling.

He demonstrated how to turn the shower on then stepped back. "There's a water purifier, but that doesn't mean there's endless water. Hot or not. We can replenish the water from a water mage, but that won't happen until we meet up with the rest of the team." With that, he slipped by me and left the camper.

I stood in place, feeling awkward. Did I really have to undress in a place where another person—a man—was going to live in too? My fist thumped on my thigh as my mind ran in circles. It just felt wrong being naked somewhere that wasn't my bedroom or bathroom. I couldn't help but glance at all the closed windows and the locked door, as if they were going to blow open any second. Still, this was my life until the Las Vegas Portal closed.

I steeled myself and took the fastest shower of my life. The water hadn't even warmed up all the way before I was done. Still, after the dirty day, I was more concerned about being clean than being warm. *Maybe I shouldn't have brought such flowery shampoo*, I thought as I toweled my hair dry after I was dressed in jeans and a shirt. Embarrassed, I opened the windows to air out the camper then went out.

Kesstel was sitting in one of two camping chairs, staring up at the night sky. He glanced at me when I came to a stop next to him. "You could have taken longer," he commented before he started to stand. "Let's go in and eat."

I shook my head and dropped into the chair next to him. "Why don't we eat out here?" I motioned to the sky.

Apart from the occasional monster cry, it was quiet, and the dark hid the desolate atmosphere of the abandoned city. Right now, it was easy enough to pretend it was just me, him, and the endless night sky.

He nodded and sank back into his chair. "I've already eaten, so you go ahead." He took out a drink and twisted off the cap.

I took out my dinner—a deli sandwich with chips and a Gatorade. My two weeks of meals included fourteen sandwiches with chips and drinks, fourteen cereal packets with milk, and fourteen MRE instant meals. If we weren't done with the mission in two weeks, we'd meet with a supplier outside of the city and refill our needs.

I'd heard MREs weren't that bad tasting, but I wasn't going to try it right now. All I wanted was to enjoy a ham sandwich under a starry sky. Since I could already feel Kesstel's barrier around us, I knew that was perfectly possible.

"I take it you didn't find the portal?" I asked.

He shook his head. "It's not in this location."

I nodded and swallowed my bite. "Did you actually kill monsters, or did you just run around looking?"

He glanced at me, frowning. "Of course I eradicated monsters as I went. I made a deal to get our passports, and I'll hold up my end of the bargain."

I couldn't help but laugh at his admonishing tone. "Right, right."

"What did you run into to get so sandy?" he asked.

We talked about our day as I ate. After I was done, I looked at him. "Can you look at something for me?"

He paused at my serious tone and nodded.

I took the orc's sword out of my Items Bag. "Do you know how to track things?" I handed him the sword. "I need to find where this sword came from. I think it came from the portal we're trying to find."

Kesstel held it and shifted it in his hand. "It's not very well made," he muttered. "The blade is crooked, and the grip on the handle is off. The balance is poor." He held it up, the light of the camper gleaming on one side of the blade while the moonlight lit up the other. Then he shook his head. "I'm not a tracker. You're different, since I know what to look for when I feel for you. Unless I know what the monster feels like, I can't just find them." He handed the weapon back. "It seems like the monsters in the portal have a civilization. That's very unusual."

I didn't want to hold the blade longer than I had to, so I immediately stored it away. "Yes. They do."

He frowned. "You sound so sure."

I bit my lips and nodded. "I've—" My voice was cut off by the System. I paused and closed my mouth.

Kesstel didn't miss that second. His eyes narrowed as a frown marred his face.

"I've fought them before," I finally said. Apparently, that was vague enough that the System allowed me to finish. "Fought and miserably lost."

"I see," he whispered.

"If you see another sword like that or a red orc, let me know."

His brows lifted. "A red orc?" he asked in surprise.

I looked at him. "You know about them?"

He nodded. "Yes. While I was under the control of the parasitic planet, the people of one of the worlds I raided turned into red orcs after they were injected with energy crystals. But that world completely collapsed. It didn't even turn into a remnant world under the parasite's control. It just vanished. That's all I know about them."

"Hm." I tapped on my chin. "Honestly, you know more about them than I do. All I know is that they're big, ugly, and red." *And their swords hurt.* But I didn't say that last part out loud in case it upset Kesstel.

I stood up and stretched. "It's late. We should join up with the rest of the team."

Kesstel stood up and glanced at the camper. "We don't actually have to. We can stay here. The team is a mile to the northwest of us right now."

I looked in that direction. Sure enough, I could spot a few lights in the distance, barely visible between the buildings.

"They have safety in numbers," Kesstel continued. "But we'll be just fine here. We'll meet up with them in the morning."

I paused before nodding. It's not like I really wanted to share a camp with Blake, anyway. I simply suggested we go back for the sake of being a team player. Then again, Kesstel was his own team. "Make sure you tell Charlie what we're doing," I reminded him. "And find out what time we need to meet up." I paused. "You can PM her, right?" I didn't have the option, but Kesstel must have.

He didn't look too interested in checking in with her, but he opened his Guide and tapped on the screen. Meanwhile, I folded up the chairs, walked to the camper, and leaned them against the side. It wasn't until I was standing next to the table inside that I realized the problem. There was only one bed. If we were supposed to share the space, where was I supposed to sleep?

My lips twitched and I moved to leave. Or planned to, but Kesstel was in the doorway.

He looked at me. "What's wrong?"

My fist thumped on my thigh before I noticed it and forced my body to stop the movement. Why was I always so nervous when it came to Kesstel? "I'm going to set up my tent." I'd never set one up before, but the instructions said it was an easy three-minute setup, so I should be okay.

His brows wrinkled in a frown, and he examined my face. He suddenly stepped forward, using his body to force me back into the camper, and shut the door behind him. "I'm not going to let you sleep on the ground while I lounge on a mattress." He pushed on my shoulder.

We were already so close together in such a tight place that there was nowhere to go. He easily overbalanced me and caused me to sit back on the bed behind the folding curtain. I blinked up at him, alarmed.

"You sleep there." He patted my head like he was appeasing a spooked cat, then walked to the back of the camper where the table was. After a minute of adjusting things around the table, he set the tabletop down flat on the gap between the bench seats and laid the bench pads down over it all. In the end, it created a narrow, not quite twin-size bed. "I'll sleep here." He motioned to the new bed.

I stood up. "I should sleep there. I'm smaller than you."

He shook his head. "But that bed has a curtain and you're a young lady. Stop making a fuss and listen to me."

No matter how I argued, he wouldn't budge from his decision. In the end, I collapsed onto the full bed. So many things had happened today that I was exhausted and couldn't keep my eyes open anymore. I was in a foreign abandoned city full of monsters, but with Kesstel reassuringly close on the other side of the curtain, I felt safe enough to fall into a deep sleep.

CHAPTER 12

*L*ivid was a good description of Charlie's face when Kesstel and I showed up at camp the next morning in our armor.

She narrowed her eyes and her cheeks turned red. "We are a *team*," she gritted out. "In order to ensure *everyone's safety*, we need to work *together* as a *team*. That includes following orders. Noble, please do not up and vanish in the middle of a planning meeting. You are just as responsible as I am when it comes to coming up with a plan for the expedition."

I glanced at him in shock. He seriously bailed on that?

Kesstel didn't look bothered at all. He glanced down at me and shrugged. "You didn't respond fast enough."

If I wasn't getting the stink eye from Charlie, I might have slapped my palm on my forehead.

The red flush on Charlie's cheeks spread to her whole face, but she didn't blow her lid. It wouldn't have done her any good, anyway—Kesstel didn't care. She must have realized that because she took a breath and her complexion mellowed out a bit. "Miss Devhro, you were given *bodyguards* for *your safety*. There are a lot of dangerous monsters out there, and it was decided for *your safety* that Alex and Mona were the best Hunters to take care of *your safety*."

I glanced at the two Hunters standing just behind her with cloudy faces. Every time Charlie said "safety," their glowering deepened.

"They spent six hours running around looking for you," Charlie stressed, her face going red again. "We thought you were dead. It wasn't until we met up with Noble after 6:00 p.m. that we found out you were, in fact, alive."

I pursed my lips and glanced down, feeling a little guilty. I didn't think they would waste that much time looking for me. I thought they'd give up after a while and just do the expedition job. It was possible that I'd killed more monsters than they did yesterday.

Charlie took another deep breath, and her angry flush lessened a bit. "And then, neither of you returned for camp last night." Her narrowed eyes flicked between the two of us. "Noble can handle himself, I'm fully aware. And I understand that as long as you two are together, neither of you will be injured. I understand that. But the Association has decided that we will all camp together to make sure that *everyone* is *safe*. This isn't a pleasure trip or a honeymoon. This is real life, where mistakes make dead people. To ensure the *safety* of all of our families back in Eden, we need to follow the rules set down by the Association."

And that's why Charlie was the leader of team four, not Kesstel. She cared about rules, and Kesstel honestly didn't give a damn about what she was saying. In fact, he probably would have already wandered off if I wasn't standing here. He might not be the best teammate for the expedition, but as my partner, he took the punishment with me.

Then again, I was just as bad of a teammate, since I ran off to do my own thing yesterday too. And I was going to do it again. The System didn't give me a daily task today, but I was going to be on the lookout for a red orc. Of course, that meant I was going to travel back to the site where the dust mephits were and look for clues there.

Charlie rubbed her brows and sighed. Apparently, she'd finally gotten it all off her chest because she rolled her shoulders and assumed her normal, cool expression. "Now, we're going to try this again. Noble, you did a wonderful job yesterday. Please do the same today. Miss Devhro, stick to Alex and Mona today. It would save all of us a lot of effort and running around, especially now that we're going deeper into the city. The monsters are going to be getting harder from here on out. Mr. Wilks was very clear on the conditions you're supposed to return to Eden in. We plan to make sure that happens."

My mouth twitched. "I would think Mr. Wilks is far enough away that he shouldn't have much say over what we do." Even if he was right next to me, I still wouldn't care.

Charlie rubbed her face wearily. "I'm going to pretend I didn't hear that." She shook her head and walked away. "How did I get stuck with the hard ones?" she muttered, apparently forgetting that Hunters have good hearing.

I glanced at Kesstel. "You seriously walked out of a planning meeting?"

He shrugged. "They didn't need me there, anyway. And I knew there had to be a reason for you not answering me immediately. It was getting late, and it was time to call it a day. I wasn't wrong either. Those people were getting hostile to you." He paused. "Maybe I should make them—"

"No," I said firmly, cutting him off. My eyes narrowed as anger settled in my chest. Not at him, obviously, but at President Price and his people. Since they weren't going to pretend to be cordial anymore, I didn't have to either. "I don't want you to fight my battles. I can do it."

Kesstel took in my sharp eyes and nodded. "Alright." He reached out and brushed his hands through my hair. "Then I'll see you later. If you delay on PMing me, I'll come find you again," he warned then walked away between the buildings.

As soon as he was gone, Alex and Mona approached me.

"Where did you go?" Alex demanded, his face tight.

I shook my head and motioned to the east. "That way. I thought it was a good place to look for monsters I could handle."

He shook his head. "There aren't any weak enough for you. You need to stay with us. We'll take care of everything."

Mona folded her arms over her chest. "Well, what do you have to say?" she demanded.

I opened my mouth and paused. "I'm sorry I stressed you out yesterday. In the future, if I disappear again, just keep going. I'll catch up later."

Alex gaped at me while Mona blinked in shock.

I smiled at them. "Well, now that we said what we wanted to say, we should go." I pointed to the east. "That way." With that, I turned and started walking. If they wanted to stick with me, they could. But I wasn't going to deviate from my plan.

The two Hunters caught up to me.

"What's over here?" Mona asked, looking at all the desolate shops on both sides of the street.

My eyes narrowed. "A mystery I need to solve."

They gave me odd looks.

"That doesn't make any sense," Mona objected.

I snorted and shook my head. "A lot of my life doesn't. If you think about it, monsters from another dimension and the Hunters who kill them don't make sense. If you told someone twenty-five years ago this is how Earth would be today, they'd lock you up in a padded room." I casually waved my hand. "Try explaining that to me first, then we can talk about my random actions."

Now they looked at me like I actually needed a padded room.

Alex motioned to the west. "We should head in that direction. We're getting too close to the Redding section."

I shook my head. "I'm going to start over there and then see where I end up next." That explanation was not a game plan, but it was all I had to go off of. Maybe one of these two babysitters actually knew how to track. Before I could open my mouth to ask, Alex grabbed my arm.

"Hey, you need to listen to me," he said, an annoyed edge to his words. "Didn't you hear Charlie? This isn't a pleasure trip. I'm not here to sightsee or spend all day looking for you. We have a job to do, so stop screwing around." His hand tightened painfully on my arm. Whether or not he meant it, his aura flickered out. If I was a real E, I would have collapsed.

I frowned at him. I got where he was coming from; I was being a horrible teammate, and I wasn't following the team lead's orders. I knew that. But what I was doing was just as important.

I tried to pull my arm away, but his hand only tightened more.

Mona grabbed his arm. "Hey, be careful. She's not like you and me. You'll hurt her."

Alex let go of me like I was made of fire. He scowled and looked away in frustration.

I refused to rub the bruise forming under my left arm bracer. I wasn't going to show him that weakness. I frowned and glanced in the direction I wanted to go. "I doubt you'd believe me, but I found a lead to the portal yesterday. At least, I'm ninety percent certain it's a lead to the portal. That's why I want to go back and check it out now that it's day again."

Mona looked at me in surprise. "You think the portal is over there? Why didn't you say something to Charlie?"

I shook my head. "It's not over there. But I think clues over there could lead to the portal." How was I going to convince them I needed to look for red orc footprints to lead me to a portal? And that I knew what portal that red orc belonged to? If my random ramblings earlier sounded crazy, that explanation would be downright insane. And it wasn't like I could admit I'd been in the portal the red orcs were in and "survived," either. They wouldn't believe that.

Like I said, a lot of things in my life didn't make sense.

I paused. "Do either of you have any tracking abilities?" That orc sword couldn't have just landed there by accident. A red orc had to have been in that location and dropped it. If we could find where that monster had come from, we'd be able to find the direction the portal was in.

Mona shook her head.

Alex rolled his eyes. "Some."

Good, that was all I needed.

He opened his mouth, still looking bad tempered, but Mona cut him off. "We'll go look over there, like you want," she told me. "But if there's nothing over there, no more making our lives difficult. Understand?" She looked between Alex and me. "That way, we're both compromising, and we can start working instead of standing here in the middle of nowhere."

I nodded. "Deal." What were they going to do when I was right?

We started working our way over, with me sandwiched between the two of them. Since this area had already been cleared, we only ran into a couple spiders like the ones in the apartment duplex yesterday. Like yesterday, they made me sit back and watch all the EXP I could have gotten die in front of my eyes.

It sucked. Bad. God, I really missed Emma and her team. At least they attempted to treat me like an equal.

"These things are everywhere," Mona huffed and stood up when the last one was dead. "It's not like they're hard; they're just constant."

"Hm, I didn't notice any of them yesterday," I said, thinking. "Do you think there's a big nest somewhere and they're traveling from there?"

"I wouldn't know how monsters think," Alex barked darkly.

Yeah, the shithead still hated me. Unfortunately for him, I could handle that. In fact, it was people who were nice to me without reason that I had more problems with. Alex didn't have to like me; he just couldn't obstruct me. The moment he did, I was out of here. I didn't mind letting them see what I was doing until then. And if they stayed long enough to be converted over to my cause, that would be ideal. Sadly, I wasn't expecting it.

"They want to spread out and eat humans," I answered Alex's comment, looking at the dozens of giant spider carcasses on the ground. "That's all they can think about." That's what the energy crystals mindlessly drove them to do. Fill up the world with energy crystals and destroy the current intelligent species.

So, how were the red orcs able to function as a society and have a language? The nixies had a bit of social structure, like a pack of wolves, but they were still driven to maim and kill by the energy crystals, and they had no definite language, just screeching and whatnot. They were both monsters controlled by the parasitic planet.

So why were the red orcs different?

CHAPTER 13

———

This is it." I motioned to the bank where I'd found the sword yesterday. My battle with the dust mephits certainly took a toll on the building. While the rest of the surrounding structures had piles of sand scattered around them, the bank was nearly buried in a mountain on the north side. It was missing more tiles on the roof, and the gaping holes in the windows were ominous looking.

Alex's gaze was locked on the bank. "Do you think the money is still in the vault?"

My brows pinched together as I stared at him. What the hell was he thinking about?

Mona turned her head and gave him a hard look.

He noticed our gazes and flinched back like he was caught with his hand in the cookie jar. "What? I was just wondering. I mean, everyone who had money in there would be dead by now. Shit, this bank isn't even in business anymore. So . . . that's just free money in there. Right?"

Technically, what he said was true. It also wouldn't surprise me if other Hunters were taking detours to do the same thing. After all, money was also a kind of strength, and Hunters were obsessed with power. Even I was guilty of that desire. But the money in that building wasn't mine, and I wasn't going to take the time to peek in the vault.

I rolled my eyes. "And you said I was distracting you from the mission? Look, if you want to take a stroll tonight and check it out, be my guest. But wait until working hours are done." With a huff, I walked to the side of the building where I'd found the sword.

Mona looked around as she followed me. She stopped and leaned down to stare at the markings on the ground. "There was a battle here, right?"

I glanced over to see her examining the indent my body had made on the sandy ground when a wind attack had smacked me against the building. "Yep. There were five dust mephits."

Alex let out a low whistle. "I've heard of those. Apparently, they're a pain to fight." He stopped and motioned to a rusty red mark on the wall where I'd hit. "Human blood." He looked at me. "Did you see the fight?"

I frowned at the blood splash. Hm, I hadn't even noticed I'd bled. I was too distracted with other things at the time—like a sand attack trying to crush me. It took me a second to blink out of my thoughts before I answered him. "It was the Josu Ghost." Man, I never thought I'd use that name for myself willingly.

Alex's thin face screwed up in confusion. "What?"

Mona turned to me. "The Josu Ghost? He's on this mission? How do you know it was him?"

I opened my mouth to correct the gender, but paused. Never mind. It didn't matter if anyone knew what gender the Ghost was. "I've heard the stories about how the Josu Ghost walks around in a cloud. That's what I saw: a cloud moving around the street. Then the dust mephits came out and they fought." I shrugged. "The dust mephits died, and the Josu Ghost left before I could catch up." At least the first part of that story was true. Go me.

"Did you see his face?" Alex pressed, geeking out like a fanboy. "What team is he in?"

I shook my head, nonplussed by his two-facedness. "I don't know. Anyway," I said before they could ask me more about the Ghost. "This is what I wanted to look at." I led them to the spot where the blade had been. I paused for a second before taking out the orc sword. "I found this here. It belongs to a red orc." Carefully, I put it back in the exact same position. "I believe this sword is connected to the portal we're trying to find." If nothing else, it was a portal I was desperate to find.

Mona's mouth dropped open. "This is a red orc's sword?" She leaned down and peered at it. "How do you know?" She felt the crudely made blade. "It's huge."

I pursed my lips. "I've seen a red orc holding one before. I recognized it as soon as I saw it."

Alex made a sound of disbelief. "An E saw a red orc and lived? You must have been in a really strong team. Whose was it?"

"You mean, who did I leech on?" I gritted out the words. "Believe me, I was not with them by choice." My eyes narrowed as I stared at him.

"But that's not why we're here. Can you track the monster that owned this sword or not?"

Alex frowned. He took a breath and started to speak like a civil person again. "Just because you know what monster owned the sword—if that's true at all—it doesn't mean that monster can lead us to the Las Vegas Portal."

Mona nodded. "It's true. Monsters were pulled from all the North American Gates and dumped here. The red orc could have just popped up here." She paused. "It's just as likely that the red orc is already dead. Why else would it lose its sword?"

I gritted my teeth, frustrated with their logical reasoning. "I know that. I completely understand. But I *need* to find the portal, and this is the only clue we have." It was the only clue I'd ever gotten to finding the System's world. I couldn't stop now.

Alex sighed and shook his head. "This is a wild-goose chase."

"Even so," I pressed. "Can you track it or not?"

He frowned and knelt down next to the sword. His fingers touched the blade lightly. "How did they make this? By banging on it with a rock?" he muttered. "Never mind." Closing his eyes, his brows tightened like he was concentrating. He lifted his head and turned this way and that with his eyes still closed.

My heart pounded heavily as I watched him. I'd never seen any tracking skills before, since I normally didn't work in a team. There were several ways to do it, I knew. The first was reading the physical marks on the ground. That was a learned skill anyone could acquire if they found someone to teach them, and as old as humanity. The second was tracking the magic signature of the target. A Hunter either had to get a Skill Stone or suddenly develop this hard-to-come-by skill. Apparently, Alex's skill fell into the second category.

A long while later, Alex sighed and shook his head. "I can't find anything." He opened his eyes and motioned to the marks all over the ground. "Whatever happened here—you said the Josu Ghost was in a battle, right?—messed up the magical signature. I can't even catch a trace of the owner of this sword. For all I can tell, it might've just randomly appeared here."

My heart sank to the ground. So I was the reason why it couldn't be tracked right now? I bounced my fist rhythmically on my thigh as I thought. "What if we get out of this spot? Walk around and see if we can find the trail outside of the fight zone?"

He frowned. "I don't have that ability. My tracking skills aren't the greatest."

My fist tightened in frustration. It was like helplessly watching liquid gold slip through my fingers. "We could—"

"We should give the sword to Charlie," Mona said, cutting me off. "She can give it to Jack or Laurel, and they can find someone with a stronger tracking skill. I think I remember Tyson's team had a very strong tracker."

It took me a second to remember that Blood Sword's name was Jack. Laurel was the S-ranked healer in charge of team two.

"If this sword can do what you think it can—lead us to the portal we're trying to find—it should be brought to the attention of the leaders." Mona reached out to pick it up.

I jumped forward and scooped it up before she could. It was fine if they touched it, but any more than that agitated me. I gripped the sword possessively and frowned at her. "I'll hang onto it until we show them." Before she could say anything, I put the sword back in my Items Bag.

I didn't want to show it to anyone else. God knew how hard it was for me to show these two. I was so used to protecting myself by keeping everything close to my chest, it felt wrong to reveal my secrets to anyone other than Kesstel. It was a bad mentality and certainly not helpful in some situations, but it was second nature now. If more people were helping me track this sword to the portal, I'd find it faster. But this blade was tied to such an emotionally traumatic situation, I just wanted to keep it all to myself.

I looked down at my empty hand. I could still feel the weight of the blade on my fingers. Would Blake or his people recognize the weapon if they saw it? After all, some of their teammates were killed by blades like it.

Mona's mouth twitched, and she looked like she was going to say something harsh. Then she huffed a breath. "Either way, we had a deal. We came here just like you asked. We didn't find anything, so now you're going to hold up your end of the deal. You're going to let us concentrate on the mission without any trouble. Correct?"

I nodded slowly. As long as we kept moving around, I'd have another chance to search for more traces of red orcs.

Mona stood up. "Good, let's go."

Since I promised, all I could do was follow behind as my "bodyguards" led the way. The city seemed like an endless maze of broken buildings, dirty streets, and bits of humanity fading away in the harsh sun.

As soon as we got out of the cleared area, monsters popped up one after another. I wasn't allowed to fight since I was *too weak*, so Alex had me keep track of the map to prevent us from going in circles or wandering into another team's area.

For the sixth time in two hours, Mona pushed me behind her. She glared toward the other side of the cul-de-sac we were in, knives gripped tight in her hands. Townhomes lined the street, all two stories tall and the same color as the sand on the ground. Movement shifted between the farthest buildings. At first it was hard to see because of the monsters' excellent camouflage, but the same colors that hid the eight-legged creatures so well also gave them away when they moved to a new spot.

"Get behind the car!" Mona ordered me, pointing to a rusted black SUV parked in the drive of the closest townhome. She didn't even make sure I followed her instructions before she brandished her two knives and sprinted at the giant spiders.

"These things are everywhere," Alex complained as he took out his own sword. "Is it just me or are they getting bigger?" He didn't wait for an answer before he joined Mona.

Why did he ask if he didn't care for an answer? I rolled my eyes as if I hadn't done the exact same thing before.

As it was, he was right. Every time we encountered a group of spiders, they got bigger and stronger. This group of twenty, the fourth group we'd found today, were level thirty and almost two feet across. When they weren't camouflaged, they were a pale brown color with tufts of hair along their eight disgusting legs. Fortunately—or unfortunately—I only had to see their bodies for five seconds before they blended in with the background. After they moved, it was another five seconds before their exoskeleton could adjust and camouflage again.

The weird thing was, most of the creatures we were fighting today were spiders. The information we were given said that half the monsters in the North American Gates appeared here. So where were they all? I doubted the Hunters had killed that many in the last twenty-four hours. I couldn't help but remember the Josu Rainforest, how I'd witnessed monsters eat each other. It also happened in Gate Vale every night—monsters preying on weaker monsters. Was that happening here too? That's the only thing which made sense.

I stepped behind the SUV and leaned on the hood with my chin in my palm as I watched the fight. Yeah, I was so done with this pretending-to-be-a-weak-E thing. The last couple hours had been really hard. Normally, my rank wasn't an issue because no one was there to stop me from doing what I wanted. Now I was being choked, yet again, by the strings of my rank.

Not because I didn't have the strength to fight against everyone's prejudice, but because I was still holding on to those strings for convenience.

I huffed a breath and pushed off the car. What the hell? It didn't matter what Mona and Alex said, I wasn't going to miss out on all that EXP anymore. As for destroying energy crystals and making the monsters vanish . . . Well, I'd think about that in a minute.

My kindjal appeared in my hand and—

A cold chill rushed down my spine to my toes then back up to my skull. The hair rose on the back of my neck. I whipped around, brandishing my kindjal at whatever was behind me.

All I could see was a cracked sidewalk and driveway between the buildings, completely empty. Dead shrubbery and messy rocks filled the lawn, and several dead palm trees rested against the tan townhomes. The only noise I could hear were the sounds of fighting coming from the far side of the cul-de-sac. But in the small dark gap between the two tall buildings, there was . . . something.

Goose bumps spread across my skin. Whatever it was, it was staring at me. I could feel the hostile gaze like a smothering pillow, even though I couldn't see it.

My eyes narrowed. Poison Fog billowed from me, washing over the dead lawn and into the gap between the townhomes.

In the shadows, a large humanoid figure at least seven feet tall moved. It turned and ran, my mist wafting around it as it moved. Sunlight flashed over it as it turned the corner and disappeared behind the townhome.

I gasped. That shape! That red skin!

A red orc.

CHAPTER 14

The red orc ran out of the range of my fog and disappeared from my view.

Instantly, I activated Feather Step and sprinted after it through the gap between the tan townhomes. Behind me, I could hear Mona yelling, "Where are you going?!"

"How did she get so . . . " Alex's voice died out behind me.

They could scream all they wanted; I refused to lose the red orc. I didn't know when I'd find another one. I slid around the corner to the back of the building and looked east, in the direction the monster was headed. One street over, a huge red humanoid with long, very dark red dreadlocks and wearing a brown loincloth jumped over the fence of a construction area.

Damn, it was fast.

I canceled the fog and activated Stealth then sprinted in that direction, Feather Stepping across fences, buildings, and cars—anything that was in my way. I was fast, but the red orc stayed two blocks ahead of me despite its large build. I thought it would find a place to hide and I could ambush it there, but it just kept running southeast, mile after mile. Was it going to the portal? My blood pumped faster in excitement, boosting my speed.

A huge worm, at least three feet in diameter, popped out of the cement in front of the red orc, startling it. It didn't have eyes or a nose, only a wide mouth full of sharp teeth and a wiggly tongue. The level forty worm lunged at the red orc, who sidestepped the attack and swung the massive sword it was holding at the other monster. The worm screeched and writhed as the sword cleaved halfway through its body, then it wiggled away and sank back into its hole. It was all over in seconds.

The red orc didn't pursue it, simply turned and ran again, rushing down the long street.

So that I didn't run into the same problem, I Feather Stepped along the sidewalk a good twenty feet from where the monster's hole was. I didn't expect that as soon as my toe touched the ground, another giant worm would erupt out of the cement in front of me like a gray geyser, peppering me with chunks of cement and gray dust. I gasped and lifted my foot as I put on the brakes, the heel of my boot sinking a couple inches into the monster's soft body to stop my forward momentum. I used that inertia to bend and twist to the right just as the worm snapped at my feet with its toothy mouth. It must react to vibrations on the ground, since it couldn't see and my Stealth was still on.

The monster missed, but it was close enough that the bottom of its head brushed against my shoulder, leaving a thick string of rotten-smelling mucus.

My kindjal appeared in my hand as I lashed out. The blade hit the worm and kept going, leaving a thick cut across most of its body. Unlike the red orc's jagged attack, my cut was sharp and clean, leaving a gaping hole which revealed the red flesh underneath.

The monster screamed and sank back into its hole.

Breathing heavily, I turned and looked down the street where the red orc had gone.

It had stopped three blocks away and was staring at me. Or more like, staring between the hole in the sidewalk and the glob of worm mucus floating in the air on my invisible shoulder. The orc's red eyes narrowed and its mouth pulled back, revealing its pointed teeth. I couldn't hear it from here, but I knew it was growling.

It turned around and sprinted east at full speed.

"Shit," I muttered. Did it just change directions because it finally noticed it was being tailed? Whether or not that was the case, what else could I do? Of course I followed it.

A mile later, the red orc ducked into the broken front doors of a large home improvement store.

I landed in front of the building and looked at the tan-and-blue exterior. When it came to the damage on the outside, compared to other ransacked stores, this one looked like it'd escaped most of it. Mostly, it just showed wear and tear from neglect in a desert environment. Then again, this was a hardware store, not a food chain. Building up your shelter was important, but not if you only had three days before you dehydrated to death.

I took a second to wipe the mucus off my shoulder. I couldn't do much about the smell, but at least there wasn't floating goo on me anymore. Hopefully, the red orc didn't have that sensitive of a nose.

My eyes narrowed as I frowned at the gaping entrance. It wouldn't surprise me if the red orc was waiting just inside, ready to kill me as soon as I stepped through the doors. I could barge my way in, sword flashing. Or . . .

I glanced at the exit door thirty feet away, thinking. I waved my hand, and Poison Fog poured into the entrance. Last time the red orc encountered the fog, it ran away like it knew it was harmful. Maybe this way I could prevent it from fleeing before I could capture it.

I anchored the Poison Fog there and sprinted over to the exit door. Unlike the front doors, they weren't ripped off their hinges, just slightly pushed apart. The red orc wouldn't fit in without bumping the doors, but there was enough room that I could slide in.

Silently, I crept along the dusty cash registers and paused, listening. Without electricity, the huge store was dark inside. Sparse skylights let in a dull yellowed light, but it wasn't much. Fortunately, my enhanced senses were just fine with this light. The air was thick with the smell of dust, a slight smell of decay, and animal musk. An inch of dry grime covered the blue registers and the brittle, curled pages of the magazines on the racks in the queue. The candy boxes and broken soda coolers were, not surprisingly, empty.

Something rattled and fell to the ground, as if it had been bumped. Carefully, I stood up and peered over the register toward the entrance.

The red orc crouched behind an empty merchandise wall, facing where the Poison Fog pooled. It clenched its huge sword in its hand and shifted restlessly, obviously waiting to ambush whatever came through the open doors.

I glared at the monster. The first red orcs I'd ever met had been invisible. Completely. No one—not even A-ranked Penny in Blake's team—had heard, seen, or felt them as the group of monsters got closer. Not until they started chopping off Hunter heads. I didn't have the System then, so I didn't know what their levels were, but they were strong enough to take down a group of A-ranked Hunters like it was child's play.

This red orc in front of me was different. It was level fifty-eight. Judging by how it crouched, waiting to ambush me when I came through the front door, it would have already turned invisible if it could; so it didn't have Stealth, meaning this red orc was not an elite. And it was alone. Was it a scout? Were the orcs checking out the city before they made a move?

I had so many questions for this monster, but half of them would have to go unanswered. Questions like, *Where is your portal?* were ten times more important, which meant I couldn't kill the red orc, at least until I got an answer to that most important question. A tall order, considering its level was so much higher than mine. I was going to have to give it my all just to be on par with it. Going all out while trying not to actually kill something wasn't the easiest.

Only, now that I was in the position of getting ready to fight a red orc, memories of the last time I fought one plagued my mind. My hands started to tremble as nausea rolled in my stomach.

I swallowed and gripped my kindjal hard enough to make my hands shake for a whole other reason. Focusing on the dull pain in my fingers, I let it force back the memories I refused to see again and took a deep breath before Mirroring my weapon. After obsessively leveling up for the last half year, this was my first step on the path to revenge. I wasn't going to trip now.

I stood up and threw my kindjal at the red orc's chest, where an energy crystal shone faintly. Like a rocket, the crystal-steel blade shot at the monster, who jolted and turned at the last second. Instead of hitting the energy crystal where it was by its heart, my sword sank into the red orc's left shoulder blade. It howled and reached back, trying to pull the short sword out, but every time its beefy fingers touched the slender sword, it howled in pain, and its skin blackened like a burn.

After a moment, the blade disappeared, leaving a bleeding hole in its wake, and reappeared in my hand. My brows pinched together as I stared at the black scorch mark around the orc's wound. I'd never seen the kindjal do that to a monster before.

My shock only lasted a split second before I lunged forward, Feather Stepping over merchandise racks, and closed in on the red orc like a bullet. Unfortunately, the dust was so thick, it left small poofs in the air as soon as I touched it, giving away my location.

The red orc lifted its sword just as my kindjal came down at its head. A loud *clang* rang out as my crystal-steel blades hit the red orc's crude metal. For a second, I was suspended in the air as my attack came to an abrupt halt, all my weight on the red orc, then it swung its arm and flung me toward the wall.

I twisted and landed with my feet on the wall, legs bent to absorb the impact. The wall vibrated and groaned, raining down more dry grime on me. Seriously, what was the use of Stealth in this place?

As soon as I landed, I jumped to the side. A half second later, a large box smashed into the spot where I had been, exploding, and the ceramic pieces of a sink clattered to the ground. Landing on top of the short merchandise stand, I dodged box after box as the red orc threw an entire pallet of kitchen sinks at me.

Annoyed, I waved my hand. The Poison Fog filling the entrance enlarged and moved, washing over the red orc. The seven-foot-tall monster froze then let out a short, high-pitched sound.

Wait, I knew it was wary of my power, but was it actually . . . *scared* of the mist?

The red orc rushed straight at me, crashing straight through the display racks and scattering merchandise everywhere like a freight train. Its roar echoed loudly off the steel rafters overhead as it swung its huge blade down at me.

I flicked my own kindjal out. The red orc's strength was a lot higher than mine—hell, its arms were as thick as my waist—but I had enough strength to deflect its assault and guide it to the side. The attack smashed into the stand I was on, which completely collapsed into a pile of wood rubble, bent metal wires, and merchandise casualties.

I lunged at the red orc's exposed back and attacked. Yet again, the monster was fast enough to shift out of the way, so I missed its vitals, but its skin hissed and burned black to match the wound on its other shoulder.

Twisting, it backhanded me, its shovel-like hand catching my hip and shaving off a chunk of HP in one hit. I groaned painfully as I was thrown away, landing halfway down the lighting aisle, where I rolled to my feet and immediately started dodging more thrown merchandise. Since Stealth was useless—I was so covered in dust, it gave away my every move—I canceled it and waved my hands. Fifty feet of Poison Fog spread out around me, filling the store all the way up to the ceiling.

The building opened up to me like a 3D map in my head. I could see every piece of merchandise and every mouse carcass along the sides of the building, but most importantly, I could see the red orc perfectly.

The red orc howled and ran for the door, slamming right into the barrier I had placed over the exit and bouncing back. My brows wrinkled at the effort it took to keep the barrier in place.

The monster could have attacked it. The orc was strong enough; it could break the barrier with little effort. But it turned and ran toward the large glow of light to its right—the entrance to the garden area on the side of the store.

I didn't know if it was the prolonged exposure or if my attacks had weakened it enough, but the red orc was finally inflicted with Poison and Bleed. Its HP began to steadily drop, which was a good and bad thing. I didn't want the monster to die before I had a chance to get answers out of it, but it would be easier to subdue if it was weaker.

The monster broke through the glass doors between the main store and the garden area. I was just a step behind.

The space was fenced in with thick steel thirty feet high. On the right were rows of tall metal shelves full of bricks, wood, and other wares. On the left were rows of short tables full of hundreds of dead plants.

As soon as we were outside the range of the fog, the orc turned on its heel and attacked me. I dodged and counterattacked as I shaved off its HP a little at a time, trying to avoid the red orc's heavy attacks. I was mostly successful, but my body and HP took a heavy beating regardless. Our fight continued until the garden area was destroyed in our wake.

"Yah!" I screamed, kicking the monster in the chin.

It yelled, momentarily stunned, as its sword slipped from its hand and fell into a pile of dry soil. The red orc fell back heavily into a pile of scattered gray bricks. Black blood seeped from dozens of cuts on its mostly exposed body, turning the clay-red skin a dark maroon color and dripping from its tan loincloth. A large chunk of its dreadlocks had been torn off, making its hair very lopsided. Then again, with or without hair, it was still ugly as shit.

I didn't wait another second before I created a mist barrier around the monster, locking it into place. It shrieked and tried to twist free, but it was too weak to break the barrier now.

Breathing heavily, I leaned on my knees to get a little strength back. With the back of my hand, I wiped at the sweat and blood on my forehead threatening to leak into my eyes. As messy as the monster looked, I wasn't much better. I was littered with aching bruises and cuts. None of my injuries were as deep as the red orc's, but my HP was still in the yellow.

I spat out a quick breath then stood up tall. I pointed my kindjal at the red orc's nose, finally level with mine.

"Talk," I commanded. "I know you can."

CHAPTER 15

The red orc's upper lip pulled back and flashed its yellowed teeth as it growled at me.

I glared back. "Where is your portal?"

It didn't respond.

Maybe it didn't know what a portal was. We could communicate, but that didn't mean it knew our terms. It was something I'd noticed from being around Kesstel.

"Where did you come from?" I asked. "Where is the hole you came out of to come to this world?" I flicked my wrist and left a cut on the red orc's cheek.

Its skin sizzled and blackened, dripping black blood. It flinched, but it was the kindjal, not the actual injury, which hurt the red orc. Still, the monster didn't talk, just growled at me.

My eyes narrowed. A year ago—hell, even six months ago—I might have been stuck, unwilling to use force to get what I wanted, with no reason to be that determined or know how to be that vicious. Unfortunately for this monster, that wasn't the case today. And honestly, its own species had been a large contributor for that change.

I Mirrored my kindjal and lifted a sword up. The harsh sun's rays hit the blade, and the crystal threading through the bright steel caught the light, seeming to glow as the metal flashed bright. It was truly a beautiful sight, completely unique from any other weapon I'd ever seen.

"You fear this," I stated. "It burns and hurts with just a simple touch, doesn't it?" To make my point, I lightly brushed the flat of the blade over the red orc's forehead. It whimpered as I left a burning black mark. It was shocking that such an ugly consequence could come from such a beautiful item. Then again, in a Hunter's world, the more beautiful a thing was, the more it wanted to kill you.

I leaned closer to the red orc, forcing its red eyes to look into mine. "If a simple touch hurts that much, how would it feel if I inserted it in you and left it there?" I ghosted the tip of the kindjal along the monster's right wrist—its dominant hand. "I could slide it in and go all the way up"—I trailed the tip of the blade up to its elbow—"and leave it there. Just under the skin. I'm sure that would feel . . . good." My nose wrinkled with disgust, but a cruel smile curled my lips.

God, I never knew I could have thoughts like this, but I hated this monster. No, I loathed it. I wanted it dead. I wanted all of them dead. I hadn't realized that until right this second. I tried to be a good person for my sister, and because of that, I put up with a lot of shit I really didn't have to. But with this monster—with all the red orcs—there was no line I wouldn't cross. I wanted them to die horribly, just like I did in front of them.

It made me as much of a monster as they were. I knew that.

And I accepted it.

The red orc shuddered, the black pupils of its red eyes shrinking in fear.

"We can talk like civilized people," I spoke, soft and slow. "Or we can talk with my sword in you. It's your pick. I honestly don't care; I'll get answers out of you, regardless." I dipped my kindjal, angling it to align with its wrist.

The red orc gasped and yelled something in a rough, guttural voice. A teal screen appeared in front of me as the System translated the language for me. [**C-Cloud witch!**]

Cloud witch? That was a new title to add to my ever-growing list. It was still freaky to see the universal translator in the System work on a red orc. It felt wrong to see a monster talk, but at least it was finally talking. I couldn't let it stop now. "I'm glad you finally agreed to cooperate," I said, shifting back a half step. "Now, tell me, where do I get into your world?"

It shook its square head. [**No. No more cloud witches!**]

My eyes narrowed. "Are there others like me?"

Kesstel and the System said there weren't any other Warriors of Mist. Were they wrong? For Kesstel, it wouldn't be that much of a stretch, but for the System to be wrong—the very thing that made me a Warrior of Mist—it didn't seem possible. But a part of me wanted it to be true.

The red orc kept shaking its head. [**No more! No more!**] It just kept repeating that short sentence over and over again.

I scowled. What the hell—it didn't need to actually answer that question. As soon as I found the portal, I could get the answer myself.

With that in mind, I went back to my original question. "Where is the opening to your world?" I demanded over its rough voice. It just kept saying the same thing over and over again. I didn't even think it heard me. Annoyed, I motioned to its wrist, ready to dig the kindjal in.

It clamped its mouth shut. It stopped talking, but it still didn't give me the answer I wanted.

I glanced at its HP bar over its head. The red orc only had ten percent of its HP left, and the red line was still dropping because of its status effects. Unfortunately, I didn't have a way to make it stop. My Regen only applied to me, although I wouldn't have cast it on the red orc anyway. It was too much of a pain in the butt when it was healthy.

Still, I couldn't let it die just yet.

"Tell me," I said, pressing the kindjal against the red orc's wrist.

It growled and moaned in pain, but still shook its head.

I glanced at the HP. Would it even survive if I did what I threatened? I doubted it.

I tsked and dug the tip of the blade in enough to make the red orc howl in pain while being careful of its veins. Blood dripped off its thick wrist, but it couldn't move away.

"Where is the entrance to your world?" I demanded, watching its HP slip lower and lower.

I'd said the same thing in so many different ways, it had to know what I was talking about. At this point, I knew it wasn't going to tell me. And that was a problem. Even if I found another red orc, I couldn't guarantee it would be one I could subdue. I already knew how strong they were.

I stepped back, removing my blade from its arm. What should I do? It wouldn't tell me where the portal was, and it was a lot more dead than alive. How would an injured monster react? The energy crystals in them drove monsters to mindlessly attack the current intelligent species no matter how injured they were. But the red orcs weren't completely taken over by the parasitic planet—they had a language and civilization. So, did that mean they had a fight-or-flight reaction too?

If I released the red orc, would it attack me? Or would it run away to heal itself? Did red orcs have a Hunter-like society, complete with healers? Or a way to heal itself in its own world?

I shifted my body to the side, away from the red orc, and pulled my left glove off to tap my clean finger on my chin as if I was thinking. My mist slowly pulled back into my body and thinned around the orc, as if I was accidentally letting it happen. All the while, I was completely focused on the monster.

If it showed any attack reaction, it would be best to just reap the EXP from it. Given the monster's level, it would be more than enough to get me to the next one. But if it ran off—which I was hoping it would so I could follow it home—then I'd just have to make sure it didn't notice me this time.

The last of the mist disappeared around us, leaving nothing but hot, dry air.

Soundlessly, the red orc shifted while keeping its eyes on me, as if testing the lack of restrictions. Its gaze flickered to the side where its huge sword was half buried under a pile of dry soil from when it fell earlier. Then it peeked toward the metal gate of the garden area that had been knocked out of its frame long ago. Then it looked toward the gate again. And again.

So it was going to run. Good. I suppressed a smile and continued to pretend I didn't notice it moving.

Suddenly, all the muscles in my body tensed in alarm.

A flash of strong power shot past me, missing my body by inches. It was so close I felt the whiplash of the magic vibrate through my body, and my arm bruised purple without even actually being touched by the attack. I turned my head just in time to see as a water arrow pierced the red orc's chest.

A large hole exploded in its chest, clear through, and half the bricks behind it crumbled into dust. The force of the explosion pushed the red orc to the side. Its messy corpse splatted to the ground, the gruesome sound echoing through the silent steel cage, followed with the tinkling sound of the red orc's golf ball-size energy crystal skittering across the ground.

My eyes were wide as I watched it all happen, my mouth parted in dismay. *No! No! I needed that red orc!* Rage flared in my heart. My hands tightened around my kindjals until my fingers hurt even more than my arm.

Slowly, I turned in the direction the water arrow had come from. That attack had come from a Hunter—a Hunter who was blatantly flaunting their strength, exerting much more power than necessary to kill a wounded monster. There weren't any water mages on my team, plus I was pretty sure I was way out of my team's allotted area.

So who the hell stole my kill?

A large hole gaped through the roof of the steel fence surrounding the garden area. Standing beside that hole was a mage in a silvery blue robe, the light material catching the sunlight and shimmering softly as it fluttered around her long legs. A whimsical silver circlet tamed the bangs of her shoulder-length brown curls and dropped a gleaming blue gem between her graceful eyebrows. She looked like an elf, holding an elegant silver staff topped with a large shining magic crystal in her hand.

Miranda Johnson from the Redding Gate smiled gently. "Oh my. I came just in time. You almost died." She didn't sound like that was a bad thing. She jumped down from the second floor, her robe fluttering gracefully around her as she practically floated down. She walked over to me, her feet barely touching the ground, like a beacon of hope in this messy, ruined world. It wasn't until she was closer that I noticed her graceful pointed ear cuffs, which helped her enchanting elvish appearance even more.

I stared at her. *Calm down*, I ordered myself. *She doesn't know what she did. Calm down. Don't slash her face; you're not strong enough to handle the consequences yet.*

I plastered on a smile I didn't feel. "Yes, ah, thank you, Mrs. Johnson."

Okay, she looked around twenty, but she'd also been an S Hunter for over ten years. I didn't know her real age—I wasn't an S stalker like other people—but she had to be at least thirty. She was beautiful, powerful, and loaded. She could be married.

She froze midstep, and the soft curl on her pink lips went stagnant for a split second. Then she smiled brighter, flooding the world with her gentle light. "Miss. It's *Miss*. Please, just call me Tári."

Tári. Hang on, I knew that word. One of my high school friends totally geeked out over an old movie with elves, halflings, and a really big eye. It meant *queen* in some made-up elvish language from that movie. I'd forgotten that an S mage had adopted that name for herself.

It was a fight to keep the frown from my face. So basically, I was supposed to call her a queen every time I spoke to her? Even though I knew her real name? Ah, it was better to just never reference her nickname.

The other dozen Hunters on her team jumped down, displacing the dust that had finally settled. They walked behind her, not bothering to repress their auras at all.

Miranda stopped next to me and touched her cheek in an *oh, dear* manner. "You must have been separated from your party, you poor thing."

She glanced at the Hunters behind her. "We should take her safely back to her team."

I couldn't help but glance at the red orc corpse, still burning inside. I pressed the anger down and kept my painful smile in place. "That's okay. I'm sure you're busy."

She reached out and rested a slender hand on my bruised arm. The bruise that she gave me. She smiled, her face kind, but her brown eyes were commanding. "It's no trouble. After all, we Hunters need to watch out for each other."

I shifted a little, just enough to make her stop pressing on my painful arm. "I'm grateful, but—"

She cut me off before I could finish my sentence. "Of course, it's no trouble." She turned to her group and tapped her fingers together in front of her, her moves graceful. "Well, it looks like Eden lost a Hunter. As good neighbors, we should return her." With that, she floated to the open exit.

I gaped after her, then rolled my eyes mentally.

The rest of the team followed behind her, except for a short man in bright red armor. He walked in my direction before jerking his chin to the side. "Let's go."

"You know, I'm really fine," I said. "You don't need to stop whatever you're doing for this." Maybe he'd at least listen to me.

He scowled. "You're wasting my time. Get walking." He moved purposefully after his team. None of them even bothered looking for the energy crystal.

What the hell? They weren't going to let me off? What kind of logic was this? Their attitude was normal—oppress the weaker Hunters. But what was up with insisting on "helping" someone, regardless of what that person wanted? That was totally not normal. Most Hunters couldn't care less about helping another person.

Annoyance boiled in me as I scowled at their backs, gripping my kindjals. Since I couldn't do anything to the Hunters, I flicked my right wrist and threw my weapon to the side. It shot straight and stabbed right into the red orc's energy crystal gleaming in the shadows to my right. It shattered and disappeared, along with the monster's carcass and its sword.

Unfortunately, I didn't get any EXP from it.

When the short Hunter glanced back at me, I finally followed him.

CHAPTER 16

It was a smooth walk toward the middle of the city. My . . . *escorts* were very quick at clearing out every obstacle, and they enjoyed pleasant conversations between them.

And treated me like I was a balloon on a string that they wouldn't let fly away.

Miranda lifted her silvery staff into the air. With a flourish, she waved it and twisted her body like she was performing a dance move. Water condensed around her like liquid lace until it created three beautiful water arrows. When her move ended, she stabbed the bottom of her staff into the cracked concrete and struck an impressive pose. The arrows shot out, water rippling around their blue tips and sparkling like diamonds in the dying red sun. The action was smooth and breathtaking to watch, even if the whole theatrical act was completely unnecessary.

Three monkey monsters with scorpion tails died instantly. Miranda turned and smiled at me. "We're almost there. No reason to worry."

I nodded slowly. What was her deal with acting like the most generous hostess in the world? She was both condescending and trying to win brownie points at the same time. The whole thing just stank of the color brown.

She gently beamed at me and walked forward.

Her team shot daggers at me with their eyes. In the thirty minutes I'd been with them, I'd been degraded from a stray mongrel they had to return to a lucky piece of shit that didn't show the right amount of gratitude in their eyes. As if I wanted their company, anyway. Even though it was bumpy, my day had been a hundred times better before they showed up and screwed over my lead—and my EXP.

I inwardly rolled my eyes and followed them. Seriously, why was she so insistent on bringing me back to my camp? The city teams weren't even supposed to camp together.

Since I didn't want to spend too much time trying to figure them out, I concentrated on thinking about what I should do about my red orc—or lack of red orc—problem. After all, I'd done exactly what I said I wouldn't do and ditched my babysitters again just to run after a dead end. Now I was in trouble again, and I didn't have anything to worm my way out of it. At this point, nothing but the location of the portal would get me off the hook.

A teal PM box popped up in front of me. [**What's taking so long?**] I could practically hear Kesstel's voice as I read the message.

The short man next to me glared in my direction. Was I not supposed to message people while I watched them fight? What else was I going to do?

I ignored him and tapped a response. If I didn't, Kesstel might come charging over again. [**I'm coming. Apparently, I'm almost there.**]

A second later, Kesstel messaged back. [**You've been walking back and forth on our perimeter for the last ten minutes.**]

I stiffened with surprise. *We'd what? Seriously? Why?*

Because I didn't want to get on my *escorts'* radar, I hadn't pushed out my senses to try to locate Kesstel. What if anyone in their group was sensitive to other people's probing? As an S, Miranda should at least be able to sense me. Who knew who else could? It'd kept me blind as I followed them.

[**The camp is four blocks north and one block west from your location.**] Kesstel added.

[**Got it.**] I glanced at Miranda as she leisurely walked west, her entourage trailing behind. The short man who'd been watching me this whole time sent another nasty glare my way.

I stared back. "I'm going to go this way." I motioned to the north. "Thanks for seeing me this far."

Miranda turned around, the blue gem between her eyebrows gleaming. "Ah, is that the direction? I've been so busy killing monsters I must have gotten mixed up. Silly me. I've always been horrible with directions." She gave a small laugh. "I'm sure you'll forgive me." *Says the woman who interrupts me every time I try to tell her my name.*

I was sure that's exactly what she wanted me to do. Fall over myself to forgive her. I just smiled.

She brushed her brown curls behind her ear, only to have them fall back into perfect place. She floated back to me and rested her hand on my bruised arm. Again. "You don't have to be so nervous around me, you know," she said graciously. "I'm sure we could be good friends." She didn't wait for me to respond before she turned and started toward the camp. "Well, since that's the direction we need to go, we might as well go that way."

Since I knew where I was going, I didn't stick to their leisurely pace. I was tired, covered in blood and filth, and sure as hell didn't want to spend an extra minute with these people. Miranda's team was forced to speed up to keep pace with me, sending another wave of death glares in my direction. They could glare all they wanted. If they wanted to stay with me, they had to keep up.

"You must be tired," Miranda commented.

"Famished," I responded flatly without looking at her. "I just want to call it a day."

She hummed under her breath but didn't respond anymore.

I nearly sighed aloud with relief when the camp came into view. Nearly thirty campers were spread out in a double ring on a large old baseball field. An arched backstop fence rose up on one side of the camper circle, with rusted bleachers on the side. The grass was all gone, leaving only packed dirt and a few desert plants. But the chain-link fence around the field gave a small sense of false security, a clear visual of the surrounding area, and enough space for everyone on the field.

I paused and tossed a glance over my shoulder. "Thanks for the walk." I didn't bother to see their reactions before I hopped over the fence, making sure it didn't look too easy, and speed walked toward the ring of RVs.

Kesstel was leaning against the largest RV, obviously his, on the outside of the ring. His arms were folded over his chest, and he was wearing casual clothes. Well, as casual as a duke would let himself wear; his gray pants and maroon shirt were still designer grade. As soon as I landed inside the field, he tipped his chin up and opened his eyes. Our eyes locked together as he waited for me to come to him.

I'd like to say I finally relaxed now that Kesstel was within sight, but I couldn't. The reason was simple—Miranda and her entourage were a half step behind me.

Seriously? Just go back to your own camp!

Halfway across the field, a dozen Hunters came out of the circle holding weapons. It didn't take a lot of thought to realize they were the guards reacting to the strong aura of Miranda's team. They paused in disbelief at the sight of me and the group following me.

Then Jonovan stepped around the guards and hurried over, his open green mage robe wafting behind him. Even on a mission, he was still dressed in business casual underneath. "Jynn, why . . . what . . . " He stopped in front of me, his usual relaxed demeanor completely destroyed as he gaped at me. "Whose blood is all this?" he demanded, reaching out his hand.

My lips pursed together, but I didn't dodge his healing touch. "At the moment, I couldn't tell you. Some of it is mine. The other half . . . well, your guess is as good as mine."

"I found her just as a red orc was going to kill her," Miranda cut in and smiled kindly. "The poor thing was scared to death."

In a flash, Jonovan calmed down and faced the Redding Hunters. "Thank you for bringing her back to us."

Blood Sword and the S-ranked healer, Laurel Harris, came up and greeted the Redding Hunters.

Jonovan pulled me away from the group. "What have you gotten yourself into this time, Jynn?" He looked at my bruised arm, obviously aware of it under my dark-gray under armor suit. "This wasn't caused by a monster, was it?" He flicked a glance toward the group of Hunters.

Since anyone could hear my answer, I just pressed my lips into a bland smile.

His lips twitched, but he sighed and poured more of his gentle healing magic into me. "Jynn, what is this I hear about you running away from your escorts?"

I tilted my head to the side so I couldn't see his disappointed expression. I could count the number of people who could influence me with two hands. Although last on the list, Jonovan was still there. After all, he was a large part of the reason I had survived my first year of being a Hunter. He'd done so much for me, and I'd returned that kindness with hiding and lies. It sucked.

Kesstel was still in his relaxed position leaning against his RV, watching the show. When our eyes met, his lips curled up slightly, like he thought it was funny that Jonovan was lecturing me and I was taking it.

I scowled at him.

Jonovan, oblivious of the interactions between me and Kesstel, obviously thought I was making a face at him. "I understand that you're stronger now, but—"

"Miss Devhro!" Charlie appeared beside us. Her eyes narrowed as she examined me. "Oh my god, look at you! This! This is what I'm talking about! Why do you keep running out on your own? Are you trying to get me punished? What would have happened if the Redding Hunters hadn't found you in time?" She shoved a hand through her short hair in exasperation.

Three steps behind her, Alex and Mona were glaring at me. To be fair, I did tell them to proceed with the expedition if I disappeared. They didn't miss out too much, did they?

Still, I bit my lips and looked away. Guilt tried to lower my head, but I refused to bow to anyone. "I was chasing a red orc," I admitted.

Mona and Alex gave me an odd look, as if they couldn't decide whether or not to believe me.

"A red orc? You saw a red orc and decided to run after it?" Charlie demanded as if she couldn't believe her ears. "Do you have a death wish? Red orcs weren't even on the list of monsters in the area. Are you sure it was a red orc? It could have been a goblin."

I shook my head. "It was a red orc. The Redding Hunters can vouch for me. They saw it too." And stole the kill right from under my nose.

Charlie pursed her lips and drew in a deep breath. After a second, she pushed the air out. I must be a lost cause because she looked at Jonovan. "How is she?"

Jonovan, who had watched our whole interaction with interest, finally spoke up. "She's just fine now. Healthy as a Hunter." The golden light in his fingers faded, and he stepped back.

I smiled at him. "Thank you, Mr. Jonovan."

"Of course, Miss Jynn," he responded with a complicated smile and reached out to pat my head. Before I could decide if I was going to let him, he paused and drew back his hand. "Maybe later." He stared pointedly at my messy hair.

I rolled my eyes. "You're a healer. You've touched a lot worse than red orc blood before."

He bobbed his head. "True. But that was saving a life."

Nice to know I was reduced to grosser than the dead. I guess everyone needed something to strive for.

Charlie hummed under her breath, drawing our attention again. She glanced at Jonovan. "Thank you for your assistance, Healer Jonovan. It's always a pleasure to work with you." Now that she wasn't dealing with a wayward underling, Charlie was the model of a polite leader. "If you'll excuse us, we have something to talk about." She turned her livid eyes in my direction. Ah, she'd been holding back, hadn't she?

Kesstel appeared at my side. "Anything else that needs to be said can wait until Jynn's cleaned up." His blue eyes went right over my head and bore into Charlie's.

Charlie opened her mouth, obviously not okay with his suggestion, but it was clear that his gaze unnerved her. She pursed her lips and looked away. With a stiff nod, she turned and dragged Alex and Mona away with her.

Kesstel rested his hand on my shoulder, not caring how clean I was, then nodded to Jonovan. "Thanks." With that, he guided me away toward his RV.

I waved bye to Jonovan and fell into step with Kesstel. I glanced up at him. "Did you enjoy the show?"

He jerked a shoulder up in a semishrug. "Somewhat. Mostly, I was wondering how long you were going to take it. You didn't have to, you know. If you don't want to listen, walk away."

Yeah, he'd say that. "That would be rude," I said. "Jonovan was only concerned. And what Charlie was saying was correct, even if she was losing her temper with me. It wasn't being mean just to be mean. There's a difference. I am trying to get along with people, you know. Even if our interests conflict."

He shook his head. "It's just adding obligations on you that you don't need. The more strings you have around your neck, the harder it is to do what you need to."

I looked down at my messy boots and the small puffs of dirt that kicked up every time I stepped. There was truth in his words, but I still couldn't bring myself to adopt that principle just yet. The difference was, I wasn't ready to give up on humanity—even if he never cared about them to begin with.

Kesstel's finger tapped under my chin and lifted my head. "Don't bow your head to anyone. Not even me."

What he was saying was serious, and I took it seriously, but it also seemed to crack the ice. Just like that, all the guilt washed away. If he didn't want me to belittle myself to others, I wouldn't. I huffed a laugh. "If your lordship says so."

The corner of his lips hooked up as his eyes softened in a gorgeous smile. "His lordship does."

My cheeks colored, but I didn't let myself look away.

CHAPTER 17

Just before we walked around the corner of Kesstel's RV, someone called out, "Noble!"

Kesstel and I turned to see Blood Sword waving in our direction. The group of Eden and Redding Hunters were slowly walking toward the circle of campers. Blood Sword locked eyes with Kesstel then jerked his chin toward the Redding Hunters, obviously wanting Kesstel to join them.

Kesstel's lips formed a hard slant. He glanced from me to the Hunters then back. He sighed. "Obligations and getting along with people, right?"

I smiled at him. "Yep."

Okay, I didn't really want him to get along with the Redding Hunters, but it would be better for humanity if this Boss could form some sort of attachment to Earth. If he could start seeing this place as his new home, he'd have a reason to fight for it.

Kesstel nodded toward his camper. "The shower is already set up for you. Take as much time as you need. I'll see you when you get out."

He turned and headed toward the group of Hunters forming in the middle of the camper circle. Tables and chairs were set out, with people milling around and interacting. They were all rich, and they dressed like it. All they needed was music, a bonfire, and alcohol, and this could be a bona fide party instead of a Hunting expedition.

And in the middle of it all was the Tári, looking right at home under the flattery of the Eden Hunters. Even Blake and President Price were smarming up to the elf-like woman. When Kesstel joined the group, she smiled at him with gentle eyes.

My eyes narrowed, and I couldn't keep the frown from pulling at my lips. Unable to watch anymore, I hurried into the RV and locked the door behind me. After I was clean, I took a minute to scowl at my clothes. Yesterday, it didn't matter what I threw on. Jeans and a cheap shirt were just fine around Kesstel because I knew he didn't care what I wore, and I was used to his upscale look. Now that I was with a bunch of people who judged based on a person's appearance, I found myself wishing I owned something better. In the end, I picked my nicest shirt and a pair of black leggings. They looked nice, and the outfit was flexible, in case monsters suddenly came.

I reached for the handle and paused. It would be easier if I just hid inside the camper for the rest of the night. No one would have the guts to interrogate me here, not even Charlie or my babysitters. And I wouldn't have to see the Redding Hunters again.

Ironically, it was the image of those people which motivated me to open the door. I wasn't going to hide in here because of them.

All the introductions had ended by the time I came out. Hunters were mixing with each other, casually talking. On the surface, it was all fun and games, the air thick with happy voices and laughter, but underneath, they were feeling each other out, checking to see who was stronger than who. It was like a shiver of sharks circling and bumping each other, never taking the first bite to start a feeding frenzy but each still asserting their dominance as a predator.

Apparently, I wasn't the only one who thought they needed drinks, because someone had passed out beer while I was gone, and some snack trays were spread out on the tables in the middle of the circle.

Kesstel and the other S-ranked Hunters were standing together on the outside of the mingling group. There were too many people between me and him to know what they were talking about, but Miranda said something, and everyone laughed. Well, everyone but Kesstel. He nodded his head slightly and sipped his bottle.

When it came to people I was comfortable enough to hang with, right now, it was narrowed down to two people—Kesstel, standing with the other Ss, and Jonovan, talking with several other Hunters, including the Redding healer. I knew exactly where I wanted to be. Even if that position was way out of my league, I belonged at Kesstel's side. Just like I promised.

As I walked around the mingling Hunters, I heard snippets of their conversations.

"Damn, so you're saying that most of the areas in the Redding's Gate Vale are dry? We have some dry places, but most of Eden's Gate Vale is forested."

"I'm already up to fifty-six kills since the start of the expedition. Me and my buddy have a bet to see who's going to get more kills."

"Wow, Tári really made all these snacks herself? God, traveling with her must be a dream."

I silently snorted at the last one and kept moving on toward my target location.

Charlie walked up to Blood Sword and Healer Laurel and whispered something in Blood Sword's ear. His face settled into a serious frown, then he bumped Laurel and nodded to the side. The three of them walked away, leaving Miranda and Kesstel together.

Miranda looked into Kesstel's face, a smile softening her elvish features. I had to admit, they looked good standing together. Her elegance was a perfect pair to his sophisticated arrogance.

It wasn't the first time I thought he looked good with another woman, but unlike with Bethany, seeing them stand so close together left a sour taste in my mouth.

A dry breeze wafted between the campers, causing some people to bow over their food to protect it from the dust. Miranda brushed a casual hand through her hair, effortlessly putting her curls back into place while subtly showing off the beautiful, whimsical gem-studded design on her skin around the Guide pearl in her temple. She looked up at Kesstel and softly laughed. "Oh my. Your hair got ruffled," she lied right in his face and reached out.

Kesstel's eyes narrowed in displeasure, and he tilted his head slightly away from her incoming hand. I didn't know if Miranda's skin was too thick or if she didn't notice he was rejecting her action. Either way, she kept reaching for his hair.

It felt like a bomb went off in my mind. I'd never thought I was a possessive person, but the sense of distaste in me exploded into full-on rage at her intimate actions. *Don't touch him!*

In the blink of an eye, I was standing right in front of them, my hand up beside Kesstel's head like a shield. Miranda's fingers hit the back of my hand. She paused, as if startled that I was suddenly there. She sharply turned to me and drew back her hand, a dark emotion flashing in her eyes.

I didn't even look at her. I kept my gaze locked on Kesstel's face and generously smiled, even though I was still boiling inside. "Here. Let me fix that for you." My fingers brushed through his soft hair like I was soothing an upset cat.

The apathetic glint in his blue eyes softened as a hint of a smile touched his face, as if he'd already seen through her actions to mine. But he still leaned his head into my hand, letting me play all I wanted. He relaxed and rested his hand on my waist.

His actions soothed the anger boiling in my chest.

Miranda's eyes flared in a flash of anger before she hid the emotion behind an exaggeratedly kind smile. "Oh, I almost didn't recognize you, little girl. You clean up well." Her flattery was like a knife, but I was getting used to it.

Kesstel's finger twitched on my waist, and his eyes sharpened.

Miranda didn't seem to notice the pressure building around him. She turned to me and said, "I set out a bunch of snacks to share on the table. Why don't you fill your stomach? They're free for everyone." Her words were kind, but there was an obvious message behind her smooth tone: Go away, you poor little bum.

It felt good to finally get in her way, even if it was just a fraction of the damage she inflicted on me.

Before I could come up with some words to rub her raw, Kesstel straightened. "There's no need. She's fine." He pulled me closer to his side. The brown bottle in his hand disappeared, replaced with a familiar pink pastry box.

He handed it to me.

A thrill of excitement went through me as I took the box. The smell of sugar, chocolate, and nuts pushed away the dry decay that had been assaulting my nose the last two days. "Kesstel, why didn't you give this to me last night?" I asked, cradling the box.

He flashed a brief smile. "I can't give you all the treats at the same time. They need to be spread out so they can last the whole trip."

Miranda's smile spasmed as she tried to keep it in place.

I completely ignored her and opened the lid, revealing a chocolate puffed pastry, a ricotta sfogliatelle, and several other pastries. The snacks that Miranda brought looked good, but nothing like this. Happily, I handed Kesstel the ricotta sfogliatelle, careful not to break the hundreds of paper-thin layers, and took the chocolate one for myself. The box disappeared in my Items Bag for later splurging. I grinned at him. "Thank you."

He nodded in response and ate his Italian pastry.

Miranda looked completely at a loss for words. How long had it been since she was so thoroughly neglected? Too bad for her, both me and

Kesstel were used to handling a dramatic princess. "I have to say, those pastries did look wonderful," she said, trying to break the ice. "Where are they from?"

I swallowed my bite. "There's a pastry shop in Eden that Kesstel and I go to a lot." Was I showing off too much? Probably. I thought I'd feel more awkward than this, but I had to admit, it felt good declaring my position at Kesstel's side. Especially after she was so blatantly flirting with him.

Kesstel and I turned our heads when Blood Sword walked up to us. Miranda glanced at him and revamped her efforts to appear like a queenly elf, but she didn't even get a glance.

Blood Sword's gaze was locked on me. "Evening, Miss Devhro. Your team lead told me you found a clue to the Las Vegas Portal?" His rough voice was a low rumble, obviously not wanting other people to hear.

Miranda, who was standing close to us, stiffened and gave me a sharp look.

I ignored her. When Mona had brought up the idea of telling others about the red orc sword, I knew it was the right thing to do. But now that I was in this position, my first instinct was to hide it so they couldn't take the sword from me.

In the end, I nodded slowly. "Yes. I believe so."

Blood Sword's face tightened. "Is that so? Come with me." He used his head to motion over his shoulder. In the gap between the campers where he was indicating, I could see Laurel, Charlie, Alex, and Mona watching.

"Oh," Miranda spoke up, not bothering to lower her voice. Just like that, she regained her queenly persona and turned it up to an eleven. "If there's something that involves the portal, doesn't everyone have the right to know about it?" She softly touched her cheek with a delicate hand. "After all, this is a joint operation, isn't it? If it's a clue to finding the portal, we all should hear about it."

The closest Hunters turned at her first sentence and quieted, open curiosity and shock on their faces. This caught other people's attention. Like dominoes, one by one, all the Hunters quieted and turned in our direction.

Miranda smiled gently and tapped her fingertips in front of her, forming a triangle with her hands. She glanced between Blood Sword's stiff face and Kesstel's apathetic stare before settling on my annoyed expression. "Please, Miss Devhro. Show us this clue." Hidden in her soft tone was a challenge.

CHAPTER 18

—

Don't cut her face. Don't cut her face. Don't cut her pointy-ass face, I chanted fervently in my head like a prayer, over and over. No matter how much I repeated it, my fingers itched for my kindjal. Just a quick swipe, right up the sharp curve of her high cheekbones. Jonovan was good enough that he could make it look like it never happened, and he wasn't even the strongest healer around me. It would be like it never happened, but I'd still have the satisfaction of making this woman bleed. I forcibly froze my body to keep from doing something stupid.

But god, I really wanted to do it.

Over fifty Hunters locked their eyes on me, like lions ready to pounce at any moment. Curiosity, derision, and mockery played on their faces, but that didn't change the fact that each of them were absolutely focused on me. And the possible clue I had to the portal.

It was uncomfortable, being stared at like this, but the most unbearable thing was having to show my red orc sword to another person. Okay, mostly to Miranda. Shallow, I know, but I didn't want to share anything with her. Not Kesstel. Not my monster sword. They were mine.

My whole life, I'd scrabbled for scraps. With few exceptions, I'd never had the chance to get possessive over something. After all, all the best things I ever got were given to Aliya—which I'd never regretted.

I could keep Kesstel to myself because he naturally rejected everyone else. Unfortunately, the same couldn't be said about the red orc sword. I didn't want to show it off, but at the same time, I loathed the idea of cowering under Miranda's provocation.

I held my hands out, and the huge, heavy sword appeared. My fingers couldn't even fully wrap about the handle as I gripped it and lifted the blade—which was much taller than me—so everyone could see it.

Everyone's expression changed, and whispers broke out.

"That's a red orc sword?"

"It's huge."

"What is that made out of? It's so crude."

"Is that the real thing or a toy she found to play with?"

On the side of the crowd, I glimpsed Blake and his people. Penny's eyes widened, and she turned to whisper to the shocked Mark. Blake's face darkened and he scowled, glaring at me like he wanted to kill me. President Price glanced from his cousin to me before his expression set to stone. The fifth person in the group, the guy I didn't know, looked completely lost.

"This is the red orc sword," I said, my voice ringing out and quieting the noise. "I found it several miles to the east of here. I know a little about the portal it came from; I thought it might be the portal we're trying to find, but I wanted to make sure before I told people, in case I was wrong." Okay, that last part was BS, but I figured I should add something so people didn't blame me for purposefully withholding information. Which I totally had.

"Are you sure that's a red orc sword? I just killed one, and there was nothing like that in its hand," Miranda asked loudly enough for everyone to hear. To be fair, from her angle earlier, she wouldn't have been able to see the sword. It had been ten feet to the right of the red orc and half buried in a pile of dry soil.

But she wasn't done talking yet. "It's crude looking, yes, but how do we know it wasn't just . . . put together?"

What she meant was, did I make the sword so I could fool people and become important?

I scowled at her.

Kesstel shifted at my side. His aura wisped around his feet before he pulled it back. "I can attest that it's not from Earth. But if there's an armorer in the group, step forward and examine the metal."

The Hunters looked at each other. None of them wanted to get closer, obviously spooked by the aura Kesstel barely kept under control—which was most likely on purpose. Even Miranda stiffened, her gentle smile becoming stressed.

Blood Sword glanced at Kesstel a couple times before approaching me. Impressive, really, considering he was the only person in the whole group who had personally felt what it was like when Kesstel lost control.

He glanced at the crowd. "Violet, get over here."

A short woman with blonde hair hurried through the crowd to the front.

Blood Sword motioned for me to hand the weapon over. As soon as it settled into his hands, he paused and glanced at me. "It's heavy." There was an obvious question in his gaze. After all, a normal human or E wouldn't have been able to handle it as easily as I just had. But Blood Sword didn't comment on that; instead, he held out the weapon for Violet to examine.

She pushed her shoulder-length hair behind her ears and leaned over the blade. "It doesn't look man-made. So sloppy." She pointed to the uneven handle. A brass circular loupe appeared in her hand while a flashlight appeared in the other. She clicked the flashlight on and held the lens over her right eye as the bright light flashed off the blade in the darkness. It wasn't until I noticed the difference that I remembered how late it was.

"I want a second opinion," Miranda announced. "Elijah!"

A tall man from Redding stepped closer to Violet and leaned over to examine the blade. Violet wrinkled her nose at him and Miranda but didn't comment.

Blood Sword's face stayed impassive. He focused on me again. "You know for sure that this is a red orc sword?"

I nodded. "I've seen them use it." I paused, then casually tossed out the words, "Blake Hans and his crew were there too." I peeked at them.

Blake looked like he was choking on a bitter lemon. His usually handsome features were pinched together as his face slowly turned purple. Penny was staring at her toes as she kicked at the dirt, and Mark looked away, frowning.

Blood Sword turned to them. "Is that true?" he called out.

President Price stepped forward, his square face in a business smile. "A half a year ago, there was a Portal Burst that my cousin and his party were involved in. It was reported to the Hunter's Association in a timely manner, but before the Association could act, the portal disappeared." Everything—from his facial expression to his words—was perfectly polite while overbearing enough to discourage contradictions. He was both admitting it had happened and stating Blake was protected under him.

Then Price leveled his gaze on me. "However, I don't remember this young woman being mentioned at the time. My guild doesn't employ E Hunters; we deal with too many dangerous situations to put them in harm's way like that. I can't see why she would have been involved with the Portal Burst."

I smirked and lifted my head. "I was there because Mr. Hans tried to turn me into entertainment, and we all got caught by the red orcs. Isn't that how it happened, Mr. Hans?" I stared right into Blake's eyes.

We were in a large group of highly regarded Hunters. If I threw shit at the fan now, the mess would be considerable. I doubted, outside of Jonovan, there were too many completely clean hands in this group. Even if they didn't go out of their way to kill someone, most Hunters wouldn't risk their own necks for a weaker person. After all, the saying, "What happens in the Gate, stays in the Gate," was true for a reason. Anything could happen in there, as long as you didn't get caught. If you did something illegal and didn't clean up the evidence, it was your fault, and you deserved to be arrested.

Right now, it was a "he said, she said" situation. Emma would back me, but we'd be against all of Blake's gang. With Kesstel behind me, the Hunter's Association wouldn't just brush it to the side anymore. In other words, Blake could really be in trouble now.

Only, that wasn't necessarily the trouble I wanted him to feel. I wanted him to feel the powerlessness of not being able to control your own fate.

"Now, now." Miranda stepped up, putting herself in the middle of everything. "I'm sure there's a fascinating story behind all this, but I believe the main issue is whether or not this sword belonged to a red orc. And if it has anything to do with the portal that we're all trying to find."

Her people nodded and voiced their agreement.

Kesstel rested his hand on my shoulder. His glacier blue eyes were zeroed in on Blake. He knew someone had been bothering me lately, although he didn't know the extent of the hitmen I'd shaken off my trail, since I'd never told him what was going on. Kesstel wasn't a stupid man, and it was easy enough to connect the dots.

I nudged his side with my elbow until he looked at me. The corner of my mouth kicked up in an almost smile. "It's okay," I mouthed. I'd been holding it in for months now. What was a little longer?

He frowned, obviously not liking my decision. He leaned down and whispered in my ear, "If you want revenge, you just need to say the word. Why don't you take advantage of my status more? What's the use of having it if you don't use it?"

I huffed a laugh. "I think I take advantage of you enough. And if I lean on you too much, I'll get fat and lazy."

He disagreed with a low hum. "Not possible."

Blood Sword read my expression before he turned back to Violet. "So, what's it made out of?"

The whole time this had been going on, she'd been humming under her breath and muttering to herself—much to the other guy's displeasure. She obviously didn't care. Violet put away her loupe and flashlight. "I don't know, sir," she gushed out, a trace of excitement in her voice. "I don't even think this metal exists on Earth. It's amazing! I can't wait to research more about it." She ran a finger down the side of the blade. "It doesn't have any energy crystals in it, but it's still hella sharp. There's monster blood on it, meaning it's obviously damaging monsters without the crystals, unlike our own weapons. That's amazing! I mean, we've never seen anything this advanced—I mean, produced metal?!—on a monster before."

Elijah, the Redding Hunter, tsked under his tongue when Violet's light disappeared, shrouding the metal in darkness. He looked at Miranda. "Everything she said is correct, Tári. This metal is not from Earth. It's impossible to say which monster it belongs to, but for sure, the metal came from a portal."

Miranda opened her mouth, but Blood Sword beat her to the punch.

"Can it be tracked?" he asked. "The monsters can't be tracked; we've already tried. But is this sword different?" He glanced at me.

I shook my head. "I don't have that ability. I tried earlier"—I glanced at Alex standing in the back of the group—"but it didn't work." Not that I blamed him, obstinate as he was.

Put on the spot, Alex spoke out. "I only have a little skill in tracking. Only enough to claim that I have the skill, nothing more. A stronger person would definitely have a better chance at tracking it back to the portal." For the first time, there was a bit of regret in his voice.

Finding the portal wasn't a race, but that didn't mean people didn't covet the glory of finding it. It was something much better to boast about than being a babysitter who kept losing his ward.

Blood Sword nodded. "Alright. Everyone with a tracking ability or skill, come here." He looked at Miranda. "We are working together in a joint operation. I believe both of us should have equal chances to track this sword, isn't that right?"

Miranda beamed at him. "Yes." She motioned to a couple people on her team.

Blood Sword walked to an empty table next to the snacks and set the weapon down before stepping back. Eight people took turns approaching it and holding their hands over it. Their colorless auras, completely different from the flare of magic, fluctuated and flickered out repeatedly, like a hand reaching out to grasp an invisible rope. In the end, every one of them shook their heads and said they couldn't track it.

President Price muttered something to Penny then nudged her forward with his elbow.

She strolled up with her hands in her pockets and stared down at the sword. Her lips twitched a little before she hovered her hand an inch above the blade. Her aura flickered around briefly before it stopped. She stepped back and shook her head. "I can't track it."

Miranda hummed under her breath. "Well, since we can't figure it out right now, it should be kept in safe hands." She walked up to it and reached for the sword.

My chest seized up and an alarm went off in my mind. "Hey—"

Before the syllable could fully exit my mouth, Kesstel disappeared from my side, reappearing on the other side of the table with the red orc sword in his hands. "If that's the case, I'll take care of it."

Miranda blinked at where the sword had been on the table, just inches under her fingers, then looked up at Kesstel in surprise. She flinched back from his chilly blue eyes before she collected herself and put on a gentle smile. "Are you sure? I'm worried it would be a lot of hassle, Kesstel." There was an affectionate ring in her tone when she said his name. As if they'd always been intimate. "I'll gladly take on that responsibility so you can focus your all on your task." It was like she was taking one for the team for the greater good.

My eyes narrowed as my hands clenched into fists.

If Miranda was looking for an emotional response, she was facing the wrong direction. "No," Kesstel replied flatly, a slightly sarcastic tone hiding in his voice. "I'll take care of this. As a team leader, you need to have all of your attention on directing your team. It would be unfortunate if one of them died because you were distracted and neglected them."

Her eyes widened from his backhanded threat.

He didn't even give her enough time to come up with a comeback. The sword disappeared, obviously put in his Items Bag, then he gave a brief nod to Blood Sword before heading back to me.

The crowd parted for him. Even though Kesstel's aura was under control, so he wasn't oppressing anyone, the Hunters were still alarmed. He'd moved at a speed that none of them could contend with. In fact, I got the impression some of them weren't even aware he'd moved until he had the sword in his hand.

Kesstel settled back at my side. "Should we go have dinner now? It's getting late."

I nodded. "I wanna eat under the stars again." I couldn't resist glancing toward the Redding Hunters. It was late enough in the day it was obvious they were going to camp with us tonight. Just the thought killed my appetite. "It's so crowded here."

I was being willful and petty, but at the moment, I couldn't help it. I didn't want to be here, and I couldn't find a reason I should force myself to. With Kesstel's barrier, we were perfectly safe, even though we were alone. And both of us could relax and say whatever we wanted.

Kesstel seemed to understand what I meant instantly. "Sounds like a good plan." He waved his hand, and his camper disappeared into his Items Bag. He turned and looked at Charlie over everyone's head. "We'll be back in the morning. Good night."

The poor team lead didn't even have time to sputter in protest before Kesstel picked me up and we were gone.

Jynn Devhro

Rank	B	**Level**	51
		EXP to Next Level	5261

HP	1074/2997	**Stat Points**	3
MP	702/1301		

Strength	91 (+20)	**Agility**	85
Magic	82	**Perception**	85
Constitution	84 (+20)	**Intelligence**	77

Skills	**Abilities**
Throw	Mist (Improved) (50 ft)
Critical Hit	Feather Step
Quick Hit	Regen (Limited)
Mirror	Stealth (Limited)
High Jump	Poison Fog
	Mist Blade

CHAPTER 19

[Come find me.]

My eyes snapped open. Instantly, I was alert and awake without the faintest bit of morning grogginess. The teal System message hovered in front of my face. It hadn't made a sound when it appeared, but it still woke me up like I had been shocked.

The original message disappeared, replaced with a new one. [Hurry.]

I sat up and quietly changed from my PJs into my dark-gray under armor suit. I didn't know what was going on, but if the System was acting like this, something had happened. Or was going to happen. It was better to be prepared.

Silently, I opened the tan curtain and peeked out.

Kesstel was sleeping on the fold-down table bed, his large frame squished into the small space. His face was angled away from me, giving me a good look at his messy hair in the pale predawn light streaking through the open air vent over the stove. His blue blanket was bunched around the waistband of his PJ pants, revealing his bare back gently rising and falling.

I froze, unable to take my eyes off him. The longer I stared, the hotter my face got. Just when I was about to go up in flames, I bit my lips and looked away.

Quietly, I opened the front door and fled into the chilly, dry air, managing to silently shut the door. I breathed out a sigh and hurried across the top of the school building we were camping on to the edge of Kesstel's barrier. Once I was far enough away to make sure I wouldn't wake him up as I moved, I put on my armor.

Just as I was done tying my hair up in a ponytail, I caught the sound of voices coming closer. I paused, recognizing them. I hurried through

Kesstel's barrier, feeling the now-familiar shiver going up my spine, and crouched down at the edge of the roof.

Below, four very familiar Hunters in full armor were jogging down the dim street right in front of the school.

"Look, Blake," Mark said, a half a step behind the other man. "I know what the pres said, but do you really think this is a good idea? Last time we went into that portal, we got our asses handed to us."

Instantly, my attention was piqued.

Blake scoffed at him. "Don't be a dumbass. We made it out just fine." He kept going with his head high.

"Has anyone else wondered where all the monsters are?" Penny, jogging ahead of all three men, commented. Her words were completely ignored by them.

Mark snorted. "A third of our party dying doesn't count as fine, Blake." He hopped over a pitch-black crevice which broke the sidewalk in two. As he did, he passed in front of me so I could only see his back now.

The nameless fourth man nearly jumped out of his skin in reaction to Mark's words. He stumbled a bit as he landed when he jumped over the crevice. "We—we aren't actually going in though, right? We're just supposed to find it? That's what President Price said."

Blake didn't answer either man. Instead, his head angled toward Penny. "You're going in the right direction, right?"

She bobbed her head without looking back. "Yeah, boss. It's that way." She pointed southwest.

"How much farther?" he demanded as he ran right over the top of a rusty suburban.

She shook her head. "I can't tell. I just know the matching energy to the sword is this way." I could barely hear what she said, she was getting so far away. She jumped up to the top of a street post as light as a bird and peered down the road. "It could be miles, boss."

Mark said something, but distance jumbled the words together.

My eyes narrowed. So Penny had lied last night when she said she couldn't track the sword. President Price must have stayed behind now to cover their asses, I bet. Just to find the portal first. Then again, I was sure it was President Price who had instigated the whole thing. Just how far would that man go for glory?

Well, since they were going to be nice enough to show me the way to the portal, I might as well take them up on the offer. I stood up, the muscles in my legs bunching, ready to jump down.

Someone appeared behind me. My kindjal was in my hand as I twisted to attack.

Kesstel grabbed my right wrist and crossed my arm over my stomach, hugging my body into his in the process. His other hand covered my eyes.

I froze, shocked. "What are you doing?"

"It's not polite to sneak off," he said low in my ear. "I might get frustrated if that becomes a habit."

I wiggled around, completely aware of his bare chest behind me, but he didn't let me go. Finally, I grabbed his hand with my free one and pulled it off my face. As soon as I could see, I stopped struggling. He, in turn, rested his hand on my shoulder. Even though I was restricted, he wasn't hurting me, and I was actually quite comfortable.

"There are things I have to do." I glared up at him.

He hummed and rested his chin on the top of my head. "I see. So we finally get to go to the portal? I was starting to get bored." I didn't have to see him to know he was staring in the direction of Blake and his team as they got farther away.

I paused, not sure how to proceed. I already knew the System didn't like him. How would it react if I brought him along? When it came to fighting the red orcs in the portal, he'd make things a million times easier, but that was only if the System didn't freak out because of him.

System, can I bring him? I asked in my mind. Grabbing his hand on my shoulder, I turned it over before carefully setting the kindjal in his hand. The instant it touched his skin, the sword disappeared back into the Items Bag.

I frowned, knowing it was the System's answer. It didn't want him near it. I turned my head, watching as a group of dog-like creatures attacked Blake and his team. They must be far enough away that Kesstel's presence didn't scare off the monsters.

"This portal is special," I started slowly. "And I need to go by myself."

"I see," he said again. "I take it this portal has something to do with the Warriors of Mist?"

I nodded.

His free hand crossed over and rested on my shoulder again, caging me in all the more. "I don't like the idea of you going into a portal without me. There are too many things that can go wrong. The reason I can move from portal to portal without problems is because I have an energy crystal. You don't have one. In fact, I've never seen you even touch one. Who knows what will happen if you go inside."

I looked up at him and smiled. "I've been in that particular portal before. I have an idea what's going to happen." Okay, I had no idea what was going to happen. My only experience had become a mental scar which still hadn't completely healed. And probably never would. But for Kesstel's peace of mind, I didn't mind stretching the truth.

He hummed again, obviously not reassured. "There's also the time difference, and if the portal closes while you're in it . . . hell, Earth might not even exist anymore by the time you come back."

A jolt of alarm went down my back. I watched Blake and his team finish off the last of the monsters, leaving a pile of carcasses behind them. For a second, I hesitated. Everything that Kesstel said was true, but it didn't change the fact I had to go.

I gripped his hand on my shoulder. "I gotta go. I'll see you tonight." I smiled at him, lifted onto my toes, and brushed my lips across his cheek.

He froze and looked down at me, his wide eyes a deep, deep blue.

I froze, just as shocked. I hadn't even thought about it before I kissed him. It felt like a natural impulse. I just . . . did it. It wasn't even the first time I'd kissed a boy, but it felt so much more important because it was Kesstel.

A humiliatingly hot blush seared my whole face red. Horrified, I looked down, wishing my hair was loose so it could hide my burning ears.

"I . . . I gotta go." Unable to take it anymore, I activated Stealth. He still knew where I was, but at least he couldn't see me anymore. Right?

. . . Right?

"Okay. See you tonight." Kesstel took a second to squeeze me before he opened his arms and let me go.

I bolted and jumped right off the side of the school like my tail was on fire. Landing on top of a light post, I activated Feather Step and sprinted after Blake's team. After a couple blocks, I was able to banish thoughts of Kesstel to the back of my mind so I could focus on trailing the other Hunters.

Kesstel and I had set up camp a mile away from the others, and Blake's aggressive pace was taking us farther and farther away from them. All too soon, the sun arched into the sky, chasing away the slight desert night chill and replacing it with dry heat. I followed them south, around buildings, down streets, and through a dozen battles.

I wasn't just idle while they were fighting, either. I was pitted against my own fair share of monsters along the way, staying two blocks away and maintaining Stealth the whole time so they wouldn't notice. I thought

Penny had caught me once or twice, but in the end, they didn't discover me, which was exactly what I wanted to happen.

Mark hacked a huge flying bug monster with thin wings and baseball-size eyes in half. "I think we're in Redding territory now." He flicked the black blood off his great sword and looked at the leaning streetlight.

Blake grunted, still winded from the battle. "What does it matter? As long as we find the portal, it could be in China for all I care." A water bottle appeared in his hand. He tipped his head back and guzzled it down.

Two blocks away but still within line of sight of them, I bent down and picked up the drop orbs of the bug monsters I had just killed. Breathing heavily, I leaned against the remains of a dark tan brick wall which used to surround a trailer park and chugged my own water down. We'd run six miles already, fighting monsters the whole way, and it was barely noon. Didn't they need to eat too? I hadn't had breakfast, and my empty stomach was cramping up.

The fourth guy in their group took off his helmet and wiped his brow before looking up at a sign to their right. "Las Vegas RV Resort? That's a thing? How can an RV place be a resort?" He looked across the large stretch of broken pavement and random dead trees. Several trashed RVs dotted the parking pad. One was even flipped on its side, the windows and door broken. "Doesn't look like a resort."

Mark snorted. "Well, what did you expect? None of this looks like what it used to. Besides, they could call it whatever they wanted. If they wanted to call it a resort, they could call it a resort."

Penny tossed her long dark hair over her shoulder and motioned down the street. "There's a pool. Well, it used to be a pool."

Mark laughed. "See? There you have it. There's a pool. It's a resort."

Blake walked over and thumped Mark on the shoulder. "Knock it off." He grabbed Penny's arm and dragged the young woman closer. He loomed over her, using his height to intimidate her because he couldn't use his rank. "We've been running for miles in ninety-degree weather. And all you keep saying is 'this way, this way.' How much longer until we're there?"

"Calm down, Blake." Mark reached out to pull Blake off her. "You know it's not like GPS."

Penny didn't even flinch. She just pointed at a tall building on the other side of the RV resort. "There. The trail ends there."

CHAPTER 20

The casino spread out across the whole block, consisting of a huge building with several towers, the tallest of which was topped with a steel-and-glass A-frame roof and two attached parking structures. Half of the side parking structure was a pile of rubble, the chunks of pale cement forming a small mountain. The front of the casino had been originally decorated like buildings from an old western town. Decades of neglect, coupled with the withered and dirt-covered garden area, added an even more authentic touch to this ghost town of a city. The pillars holding up the awning that covered the valet parking at the front door had collapsed at an odd angle, smashing several cars under it. It was hard to tell if this had happened recently or if it was old damage.

Penny, along with the rest of her team, stopped beside the downed awning. "Have you noticed that some of the buildings are damaged and others are just fine?" She tapped the rubble with her wakizashi. "It makes you wonder how much the earthquake that hit Eden affected this place. If this was the epicenter of the earthquake, shouldn't every building in Las Vegas have fallen down, based on the damage that Garden City sustained?"

No one answered her question. After all, there wasn't a logical answer.

Mark glanced up at the tall, cream-colored hotel town topped with steel and glass. "How structurally sound do you think this building is? It's not like it's small. If it falls down on us, we won't be able to dig ourselves out."

The fourth man snorted. "I'm more worried about the monsters that could be inside. If that sword is a red orc sword, this place must be crawling with them."

They were quiet for a minute.

Blake reached out and whacked the fourth man on the back of the head. I guess he was tired enough that he didn't even try to put on a charismatic leader facade anymore. "Stop bitching and get going. This building is huge, and we don't know how big the portal is. It's going to take hours just to search through the whole place." He pointed at the entrance of the casino, which had been reduced to a small black gap under the crumbled valet roof. "Check it out."

From my hiding spot behind a dead tree, I watched the man jump as if the request freaked him out, but he gripped his sword and crept closer to the gaping black hole. He slipped inside.

After a minute, a Guide screen popped up in front of Blake. He closed it down and motioned to the remaining Hunters. "Let's go." They climbed into the hole and disappeared.

I waited a minute, listening for any sounds of distress. I didn't know if I was too far away or at an odd angle, but I couldn't hear any signs of trouble. Penny said the portal was in here, even if she couldn't find its exact location. At this point, she was the best tip I had, even if I hadn't seen any red orcs to confirm it.

I hurried over to the pile of steel and rubble and slipped through the hole.

It was like a tomb inside. The air was thick and dry, so heavy with decay it was hard to breathe. Blackness stretched out on either side of me, like voids swallowing up everything. Pale light beamed from the hole behind me, and a large dim light from an open area ahead gave enough illumination to reflect off the metal of the rows and rows of gambling machines filling the middle of the space ahead of me. Two walkways along the side of the machines directed toward the bright, open area ahead.

Blake and his team crept along the gambling machines. For the first time, I saw a weapon in Blake's hand, a red and silver longsword.

It was uncomfortable with my vision so limited, so I spread out a thin layer of mist around me. Just enough to build a map of everything within a thirty-foot radius. Hopefully, it was light enough that Penny didn't notice it through the oppressive odor of the casino. Since I was going to shamelessly use these Hunters as a guide to get to the portal, it wouldn't do any good to have them find me before we found it.

Whether or not it was a good thing, I didn't find any monsters. Odd, since the portal was so close. I was expecting to find an army of monsters that would attack as soon as we entered the casino, or at least a squadron of red orcs. Neither of those things happened.

I hurried and caught up to Blake's team, trailing thirty feet behind. If I could, I would have preferred to tail them from above, but this was a building, not a forest. Jumping from branch to branch was completely different from swinging from light fixture to fixture.

The darkness faded away, revealing a huge conservatory. As soon as I caught sight of it, I stopped and gaped along with Blake's team.

It must have been pretty decades ago, but not now. Paved pathways wound through dead gardens and over a dried-up indoor stream. In the middle of the conservatory were the ruins of a tropical-themed open bar, and on the far side was a fake mountain which might have been a water feature, judging from the discoloration on it. Rows of windows surrounded the conservatory, all faced like tall row houses, up to the steel-and-glass A-frame ceiling. It should have been bright inside, with the midday sun directly above.

But it wasn't. The reason why was horrifyingly obvious.

Thick spiderwebs filled the open air of the conservatory, stretching from all four walls. They started at the fourth floor and went all the way up to the broken glass ceiling. Hundreds of platter-size spiders crawled along the webs, flashing different colors as if they couldn't decide on a camouflage tone to settle on. Every single one of them was between levels thirty-five and forty-five. The higher the level, the bigger they were, between two to three feet. They were the same spiders I'd encountered since day one. I finally knew where they all came from.

In the middle of the humongous nest was a massive spider, larger than a 4x4 truck. Its hairy brown abdomen was at least six feet long and was covered in pale brown stripes. The arm-length spinnerets pinched and brushed together, thick white web stretching and gumming between the appendages. Eight thick legs spread out wide, the second pair longer than all the others, giving the spider monsters an uneven, scarier appearance. The thorax was just as long and hairy as the abdomen. Under a dozen large black eyes were two thick pincers tipped with curved, sword-length fangs. Above it was a name written in red letters: [Uttu Lv82].

I wasn't arachnophobic, but the sight of that giant spider twisted my stomach and sent freezing shivers all over my body.

Fast as a flash, Penny grabbed onto Mark's arm with a clawed hand. She didn't look away from the huge monster, but her whole body was shivering, and she was white as a ghost.

Mark glanced at her and shifted a little closer.

The uttu stretched out a leg and tapped against a large webbed bundle next to it. The bunch shivered, and suddenly, a dozen platter-size spiders became visible as their colors changed. It wasn't until the smaller spiders scurried away that I could see through the webbing enough to identify what was wrapped up—a red orc. It was obviously dead and already half eaten by the smaller spiders. From the distorted look frozen on its face, it wasn't a good death. A dozen other bundles with different monsters inside dotted the nest, each one feeding any number of smaller spiders.

The uttu shifted its body. Behind it was a huge white ball. An egg sac.

Oh my god. There had to be hundreds more spiders in that sac! I swallowed back the nausea that burned at the back of my throat.

The fourth man beside Blake was shaking so badly his armor was rattling. He mouthed a word over and over but, thankfully, didn't say whatever it was out loud. Even Blake was wide-eyed with a sick expression on his face. The only one who hadn't lost his cool was Mark, who let Penny grip his arm as much as she needed while she tried to get her expression under control.

Blake turned his body and silently motioned for his team to retreat.

I stayed crouched behind the slot machine, torn on what to do. Penny had said the portal I needed was in this building, but damn, I really didn't want to deal with a giant spider that was thirty levels higher than I was. And that wasn't counting the army of baby spiders behind it.

If I was quiet, I might be able to sneak around the building. Hopefully, the spiders were all concentrated in the conservatory. If I ran into the smaller ones and killed them without alerting the uttu, it could work, and hopefully, there wasn't another uttu somewhere. I didn't even know that monsters could reproduce, but the evidence was right in front of me.

The other Hunters crept toward the hole at the entrance of the casino. Blake had high aspirations, but even he had to admit they couldn't take on a legion of spiders alone. They'd done what they wanted to do—they'd found the location of the portal. Now it was time to get all the other Hunters here to help clear out the place.

I was conflicted. I wanted to do this alone. I needed the EXP, plus the System was still adamant that I didn't reveal anything to anyone. Only, I couldn't take out the uttu alone, and finding the System was more important than EXP. That only left me with one option—call for backup. Kesstel liked to ask questions and he was smart, but maybe I could still hide what was going on after the uttu was dead.

I opened a Partner Message to him and paused. I felt a little guilty knowing I was preparing to use him then lose him, but too much was at stake. Besides, he'd told me it was okay to take advantage of him, right? Letting him help wasn't a weakness. I could still stand on my own feet. Right?

I pursed my lips and started tapping on the screen. [**I think I—**]

A man let out a startled, pained scream. The sound echoed from the other side of the rows of gambling machines. In the silence of the dark room, his scream bounced around, seemingly getting louder and louder. It felt like it lasted forever, even though it was just a split second. After that came the sounds of armor rattling, and something heavy hit a slot machine hard enough to send the whole structure screeching sharply across the stone floor.

The sounds finally died, leaving a stifling stillness behind. The hair on my body stood up, and I stopped breathing. All of my focus was on listening.

Click, click, click, sounded from the conservatory.

I twisted around and stared up at the huge brown monster. High in its nest, the uttu's many eyes were pointed in our direction. Its fangs tapped together—*click, click, click*—and it jerked its legs around, bending and straightening them out. It was staying in position by the egg sac, but it was obviously agitated.

Dozens of smaller spiders dropped out of the nest, blending into the dead gardens and walkways. The ground seemed to ripple as they scurried in my direction.

In the darkness behind me, there was another tussle with more sounds.

"Get it off me!" the fourth man moaned.

He stumbled back into the edge of my mist, and I was finally able to see what was going on. See the spider that clung to his back, trying to stab through his armor with its fangs. There were more sounds of fighting from the other side of my mist.

Suddenly, the small opening at the front of the casino dimmed.

"They—they blocked it off," Penny whispered in shock. "How do we get out?"

Boom! rumbled from the conservatory behind me.

My gut twisted together painfully.

The tropical-themed bar in the middle of the garden collapsed under the weight of the giant uttu spider landing on it. The monster didn't seem to mind the cloud of dust that exploded as it crawled over the pile of broken rubble. The smaller spiders scurried out of the way each time one of its eight legs stepped down, their camouflage colors clashing with their surroundings and giving away their location. The uttu tapped its fangs together—*click, click, click*—as it crawled in our direction. My direction.

A huge spider was closing in from the front, and the exit behind had been cut off by enough small spiders to give a B and three A-ranked Hunters trouble. Without hesitation, I turned and silently sprinted into the pitch-black void to the right of the conservatory.

CHAPTER 21

—

My sight was restricted to just five feet in front of my toes, but luckily, my mist more than made up for the limitation. Webs spread across the rows of gambling machines, random tables, and pillars, creating a maze. I bent and twisted like a gymnast, maxing out all the moves that the System had added into my Guide to study, just to make it through quickly without touching the webs. Behind me, I could hear the scurrying of many legs, the hard exoskeletons brushing and tapping against each other.

Farther behind me came screaming—mostly a man screaming. It echoed so much that I couldn't make out his words.

But I didn't have time for that.

I twisted over a stretch of web, my horizontal body spinning through the slender gap with only inches between me and the white filament on either side. Three spiders dropped from the ceiling, their uneven legs spread wide, clicking their pinky-size fangs together.

My kindjal appeared in my hands midtwist and my arms came into action. By the time I landed, one spider was dead, another half dead, and the last wasn't far behind. Several quick moves later, I collected their EXP and drop orbs and ran on before their bodies even finished dissolving into little lights which lit up the dark for a split second.

More and more of the spiders came at me. I didn't know where I was going; even with a mental 3D map, between hurrying through the web maze and killing spiders that rained down, I didn't have time to find a way out. Vaguely, I heard the System notify me that I leveled up, but even that information was secondary. I was too busy dealing with the spiders.

I twisted and slashed at the monsters closest to me while creating numerous blocks of mist and smashing them down on the others. Guts and broken exoskeletons piled around the slot machines, but the spiders never seemed to end.

I was currently winning, but that didn't mean I got away scot-free. Countless holes and injuries dotted my body where a spider had gotten through my defense long enough to attack. Most of them were stabs from the needle-hooks on the tips of their legs, but I could also feel several venomous bites on my legs and arms. Luckily, the venom didn't seem to be a neurotoxin, but where I was bit felt like it was on fire.

I flicked my wrist, snapping my arm straight, and cast Mist Blade. The water vapor solidified in a ten-foot blade around my kindjal. My face twisted in a scowl as I swung the weightless weapon while I used my left kindjal for defense and attack. Since Stealth didn't work on these monsters—I had a feeling it had to do with the webs wafting around when I moved—I canceled it so I didn't waste more MP than I needed to.

Loud crashes and yelling echoed behind me, from Blake's team fighting the uttu and other spiders. They were obviously having a hard time, but that wasn't my business. It's not like I was faring much better.

Slowly, the sounds of their fighting got farther and farther away.

The Mist Blade slashed through the webbing, clearing a way through and killing several monsters at the same time. Finally, I had enough of a break to pay attention to the layout of the 3D map in my mind. To my right was a restaurant with overturned tables and chairs. Not far away to my left was an open room with rows of tables and chairs.

And just past that was a pair of closed double doors. The exit?

I sprinted forward, slashing the Mist Blade in front of me as I went.

Spiders ran after me, their feet scuttling across the crusty carpet. Landing in front of the door, I pushed the bar handle. The door wiggled then hit something on the other side. That was when I noticed that the door was made out of glass but there wasn't a lumen of light coming through it. Something huge was completely blocking the way.

I kicked at the door. The glass shattered, and my foot hit the rubble behind hard enough to jar my bones. It didn't budge. Was this concrete? From the partially collapsed parking garage?

"Damn," I hissed and turned around, swinging my blades as I went and killing more spiders.

The System dinged, alerting me that I'd just gained another level, but I could hardly celebrate. All I could think about was how many had I killed to level up already? Had it been a short time? I couldn't tell.

Leveling was great, but I was in over my head. My HP was dropping steadily, and the fiery burn around the bite wounds was slowly growing. I needed to get out of here. After I healed up, I could come back here with Kesstel. If he could take out a dragon, he could squash a bunch of spiders.

I could fight my way back to the front entrance and cut it open with my Mist Blade, but then, I'd have to run past the conservatory. I didn't know how many spiders I'd killed so far, but it wasn't hundreds. There had to be a lot more monsters in the nest. Also, I didn't know where the uttu was. I could hear the fighting going on somewhere in the building, but I couldn't pinpoint it. If I ran that way, I could accidentally get mixed up in a worse situation than what I was in now. There was another exit around a corner from where I was, but I could already tell there was no light coming from it. It was probably barricaded just like the door behind me.

Instead, I focused on a staircase, one of the two which I had run past a short distance back. I couldn't see what was on top—hell it could be worse than this—but I had to take the risk. I couldn't stay cornered forever.

Fighting my way to the stairs, I jumped up in one leap. Not surprisingly, there were more webs. However, there seemed to be fewer spiders. But that fact was quickly changing as more crawled up from the staircase. Creating a solid piece of mist, I slammed it on top of the stairs like a lid, then took care of the few that had made it out of the hole first. Spiders below stabbed at the solid fog blocking their way, but since they weren't stronger than me, it stayed in place.

I looked around, completely flabbergasted. Seriously, there wasn't a single window in sight on the corridor I was in or in the several empty conference rooms attached to it. The only light source came from ahead of me, where the second floor opened up to overlook the conservatory.

Do they just not believe in windows in Las Vegas? I wanted to yell out. *What was so wrong with a window in a building? Every building needed an escape route in case of a fire, or a horde of huge spiders attacked.* But the only windows I'd seen in this building were the ones that lined the conservatory walls—probably "viewing specials" to the hotel room's visitors.

There really was only one way to go now. Frustrated and a little desperate, I ran toward the light. I was starting to regret following Blake into this building. I should have scoped it out more first. But there was no time to regret now. More spiders were pouring in, blanketing the ceiling and scurrying across the floor.

On and on, I swung my blades and smashed monsters, all the while trying to get to the conservatory, gaining yet another level at an alarming rate. Maybe at this point, if Blake's team was still alive and keeping the uttu distracted, I could climb up the windowed walls. If I couldn't make it to the glass ceiling—which I doubted I could—I could at least break through a window in the conservatory and leave through the other side of the hotel. I knew from looking at the hotel tower that it was covered in unblocked windows; I just didn't know where the rooms started and the prison-like casino ended.

Muted light poured through the open doors to a balcony overlooking the dead garden. Above, the spider nest stretched out, seemingly thicker than ever. It wasn't flickering with as many smaller spiders anymore, but there were still a lot on it. It was going to be a rough escape, but I was running out of options.

With a calculated swing, the four spiders between me and the curved, dirty white-marble-and-dark-wood balcony died, leaving me a clear path. I lunged through the opening, blinking hard as my eyes adjusted to the sudden light change. Elevator shafts rose over the balcony, going all the way up, with rows of hotel room windows on either side. It was an easy jump up to the next floor, less than twenty feet. And there was ten feet before the webbing started. Good.

Now that I was actually in the conservatory, I realized all I needed were three or four High Jumps to get to the glass top. If I could avoid the webs and spiders, I could be out of here in less than a minute. The question was, did I want to deal with spiders and webs in the dark or in the light?

My knees bent, ready to jump.

The wall on the other side of the elevator shafts exploded. From the first hotel floor, Blake's team came flying out and landed on the balcony ten feet from me. They were obviously battered, covered in wounds and thick white film, but still alive—although I didn't know how much longer for the fourth man. Red blood leaked from puncture wounds on the back of his throat, and his face had a grayish hue. Still, by the way he gripped his sword, he wasn't ready to lie down and die.

The other Hunters spotted me and gasped.

"Y-You!" Blake hissed, pointing his sword at me.

My attention was split when the horde of spiders chasing me started to spill out onto the balcony. Thrusting my hand out, a huge block of solid mist fell over the entrance, smashing the handful of monsters in the light and blocking the others from coming in.

"I thought she was an E," Mark said, confused.

Out of the gaping hole the Hunters had just come from, thick, long brown spider legs crept out. The uttu's head appeared, then the rest of its humongous body. It spread across the wall like a nightmare from hell, looking at us with its many black eyes, *click, click, clicking* its fangs together. There were clear signs of damage to it, but it still had more than half its HP, and it didn't seem tired.

I spun around and located a gap in the webs on the wall left of the elevators, opposite of the uttu. As soon as I saw it, I jumped in that direction—anything to put distance between me and the huge spider. Swinging my Mist Blade, I cut the hole bigger so I didn't touch the web as I sailed through, and a small mist block appeared on the wall, a perfect place for me to land.

My boots had barely touched it when Blake and his team landed on the wall right next to me, using the hole I'd just cut.

I scowled at them—well, *him*—but I didn't have time for more than that. The Hunters weren't the only thing leaping after me. My stomach twisted in fear when the uttu sprang off the wall in our direction, uneven legs outstretched.

Truly desperate now, I jumped up to the next level, the other Hunters right behind me. Forget going through the building to the outer walls now. I just wanted to get out of here. The closest exit was up, above the nest. I had my mist blocks to help me jump, but the other Hunters didn't. They clung to the walls like the monsters we were fighting, trailing after me.

The uttu landed on the wall, making the whole side shake. Windows cracked and shattered, raining shards down as the giant spider sped after us with its eight legs. But the very thing slowing us down—the webs—was also preventing the uttu from catching us. It also had to crawl through the holes in the webs.

Speed was my thing right now, my whole body focused on getting to the glass ceiling. However, the smaller spiders weren't willing to let us go easily. Fighting them slowed me down, eating up every advantage I had over the uttu. Unfettered, I could reach the top in three or four jumps. Because of the webs and killing the spiders on them, I was forced to make one small jump at a time, the uttu hot on my heels.

Blake's constant cursing hummed in my ear. He hadn't stopped swearing this whole time, as if it would help him go any faster. He had tried several times to get above me, but the other Hunters quickly found out that their weapons couldn't cut the sticky webbing—Mark was actually forced

to abandon one of his swords. They reluctantly let me go first, much to
Blake's disgust. He must hate that he was below an E, below the person
he'd been trying to kill for months, and wasn't afraid to spew his poison-
ous words at me even as he used me to save his life.

Mark and Penny stayed even with Blake, killing most of the spiders
and saving Blake's ass more than once. The fourth man was several steps
behind, every desperate move just inches away from the uttu's front legs.
If his face had been gray before, it was flat-out ghastly now.

Another three-foot spider died at the tip of my Mist Blade. The two
halves of its carcass hit the uttu on the back, leaving a trail of black blood
on the giant brown abdomen before the halves fell and caught on the thick
white web. The uttu, only ten feet below me, didn't pause as it climbed
after me and the other Hunters.

I looked up to the steel-framed glass top. So close; twenty more feet.
Just one more jump. Unfortunately, a dozen thick strands of the white
web crisscrossed in front of me. From the corner of my vision, my MP
bar flashed red. I had been using MP like running water all day, and now
I was starting to run dry. I gritted my feet and put more effort into my
Mist Blade.

Jumping up I swung hard, hacking the strands away from the side of
the wall. Dozens of carcasses and Mark's swords weighed down the fila-
ments. Cutting the web enabled the uttu to go faster as well, but if I could
take away the threat of the smaller spiders, I could move faster too.

With one last swing, I cut the last strands of the spider's nest, detaching
it from the wall. The weight of the nest shifted to the other side, pulling
the few strands attached to this wall taut. Slowly at first, then faster and
faster, the remaining strands were stretched thinner and thinner. With an
audible *snap*, the strands broke, and this side of the nest collapsed. The
huge egg sac in the middle swung to the side with the movement, acting
like a wrecking ball. More strands snapped from other places on the nest,
and the egg sac smashed into the wall and completely flattened on one
side. Small spiders rained down to the ground, dislodged from the violent
web.

The uttu paused. There were no emotions on its ugly face, but it
seemed shocked by the sudden chaos.

A war hammer appeared in Mark's hand, and he threw it up as hard as
he could. The weapon hit the window overhead, and the whole square of
slanted glass exploded. Me and the other Hunters took advantage of the
chaos to jump through the hole.

I couldn't be more excited to breathe in the dry, hot Las Vegas air. Wind and sand whipped around me and tugged at the thin veil of mist that I kept around my feet. Small glass particles stuck in my hair and pricked at my scalp, but none of that mattered. I sprinted to the edge of the building, ready to jump down to freedom.

A small black spot caught my eye, and I turned my head in that direction. Far, far down below, half hidden between two dead palm trees and next to the dried-up swimming pool was a small black arch. As soon as I saw it, a rush of emotion surged inside me. I knew what that was.

The portal to the System.

CHAPTER 22

I didn't have time to fully process the shock of finding the portal before two things happened at the same time. Both sent my internal alarms screaming.

The uttu broke out through the glass-and-steel roof, sending debris everywhere.

Simultaneously, a big, thick hand reached for me from behind. I stepped to the side, but I wasn't fast enough. The strong hand snagged onto my shoulder guard and jerked me backward. I barely had a chance to look at Blake's determined face before he flung me across the ceiling, right at the uttu.

"Son of a bitch!" I yelled. Damned if I was going to be spider food so they could get away. I twisted in the air and stabbed my kindjal down. It pierced into the rough ceiling, and I came to a sharp stop—right under the uttu.

The spider's ugly mouth bit down at me, fast as a blur. I rolled to the side, and the giant spider's sword-length fangs stabbed into the ceiling, piercing right through. I swung my kindjal at them. If I could disarm it, the fight would be much easier. The crystal-steel blade hit the fang's smooth black surface, and a four-inch crack splintered out over the fang before my kindjal bounced off. While the monster withered and thrashed in obvious pain, I rolled to a crouch under its belly.

Out of the corner of my eyes, I saw the legs of the smaller spiders reaching out of the hole just ten feet away from me. I absolutely refused to deal with those and the uttu at the same time, so I quickly slammed a mist barrier over the hole, cutting them off, then turned my immediate attention back to surviving the uttu.

Every time I tried to escape my spidery prison, a huge, thick leg would stab down and cut off my escape route with the sharp claws at the tips of its legs. Our moves were frantic, me jerking out around under it while it tried to stomp and stab me to death with its feet, fangs, or the spinnerets on its butt.

I tried to use the long Mist Blade, but for the first time, I found something it couldn't cut through. The long blade was so long that it kept catching on the spider's legs—which more often than not, put me at a disadvantage. In the end, I canceled the blade and used my short swords. But no matter how much I slashed and cut, the uttu's exoskeleton was harder than anything I'd ever dealt with. My best attacks were like paper cuts, chipping its HP away one point at a time, and leaving tiny scratches here and there. Every time I tried to hit the same place twice, the uttu always shifted away to prevent it.

I was getting just as beat up. I was able to avoid the worst attacks, but the uttu was doing a helluva job adding to the injuries I'd already sustained throughout the day.

The uttu didn't have a nose. I didn't know how it breathed, but I was getting desperate. Casting Poison Fog, I pooled it thick around me, covering the whole monster. The dry wind ripped at the condensed cloud, but I didn't let it float away. A normal person wouldn't be able to see an inch in front of their noses, but the uttu's vision didn't seem affected. Probably because of the millions of hairs all over its body.

At first, nothing changed as we continued our awkward shuffling, but then, suddenly, the uttu stiffened.

I took the chance to stab straight up into the underside of its abdomen, right where I'd hit it before. *Crack!* My kindjal broke through the thick exoskeleton and sank into the huge cavity all the way to the hilt. Black blood and innards gushed out, covering my hand and arm.

The uttu arched up high away from me, pulling the kindjal right out of my slick hand, its four uneven front legs flailing around in the thick Poison Fog. I dove away and rolled to my feet, coming up short right next to Penny and Mark, who stood in front of Blake with their weapons out. The fourth injured man stood off to the side, breathing heavily with sweat covering his gray face.

Penny barely glanced at me; her whole attention was on the uttu, wakizashi at the ready.

"You don't know how to die, do you?" Mark muttered, another modest but sharp-looking war axe in one hand and a bastard sword in the other.

I sneered but didn't answer.

"It's injured," Penny said, watching the spider legs play peekaboo in the Poison Fog. "Where? I can't see. Did that cloud come from you?"

I glanced at her. Was she seriously asking for help? As in, almost-teaming-up help? I gritted my teeth. If Blake or Mark had asked, I for sure wouldn't say anything. But I didn't actually have a bone to pick with Penny. She was part of their team, but she'd never actually done anything to me.

Technically, I could just jump off the building and leave the uttu and Blake's team behind. Only, they didn't know that. As far as they were concerned, I was stuck on top of the building with them. Blake obviously wanted to kill me—the dumbass did just throw me under the spider—but I wasn't opposed to teaming up with Penny for a minute. Even if I didn't get EXP from teaming up with them, I did want the energy crystal from the uttu, since its energy could still be absorbed by the System. And if the System was in trouble, it needed all the help it could get.

" . . . I stabbed through its abdomen underneath," I replied softly as I looked at the uttu's title bar, the HP bar under its name—and the status effects it was inflicted with. "And . . . it's poisoned with Bleed and partial Paralysis."

"Bullshit," Blake hissed. "Even we couldn't crack its skin."

"Exoskeleton," Penny corrected flatly under her breath.

"I made several cracks on its legs and underbelly. And the right fang," I continued like they never spoke at all. "If you can hit one of those spots, you might be able to deal real damage." Whether or not they believed me, that was their problem.

The uttu rushed out of the Poison Fog, its movements now slightly slower than before. I didn't keep the fog on it. I wouldn't be hurt, but if I was going to temporarily team up, I shouldn't poison them. Well, at least one of them. The other two deserved it for sure, and I couldn't decide on the third.

Mark and Penny rushed forward and met the uttu head-on. Blake stayed back, throwing out random orders, but his strategies weren't that great; the two Hunters mostly ignored him. They worked together somewhat, but they still lacked the smooth teamwork I appreciated with Emma's team. The fourth man hung beside Blake, holding his sword and shivering.

Since Mark and Penny were distracting the monster in front, I went high, creating a mist platform above it and jumping up.

Apparently, the monster had some animosity toward me because it abandoned Penny and Mark to lift on its hind legs, reaching out for me with its long front legs. I tsked and jumped off my block, up at another one out of its thirty-foot reach.

In a flash, Penny lunged forward and stabbed into the hole I'd left in the uttu's underbelly, shaving off a huge chunk of HP. The uttu jerked and withered, and dropped down right on top of the young woman, trapping her under it. She yelled out as she was suddenly crushed under its weight.

Mark swore and jumped forward, attacking the uttu's multiple eyes with his weapons like a madman. "Move, damn you!" he yelled.

One of its eyes popped. The uttu jerked and rose on its feet, revealing the motionless girl underneath.

From up here, out of the fray, I could finally locate the exact place the energy crystal was on the giant spider: in the middle of its abdomen, closer to the top than the bottom. Too deep for my kindjals to reach, but I should be able to get through it with the Mist Blade. However, at this point, if I used the Mist Blade, I'd skewer Penny, too.

I leaned over and kicked off the mist block, putting as much speed as I could behind me. I shot like a bullet at the distracted uttu. My second kindjal disappeared, and I gripped my right one with both hands, stabbing down with all my might right where the faint light was gleaming. With a loud crack, a foot-long crevice opened up, and my kindjal plunged right into its back.

The uttu arched back in pain and surprise. Mark took advantage of that time to grab Penny and run back to where Blake was. The uttu's movement was so violent, I was thrown completely off it. I flipped wildly through the air and barely managed to catch myself on a mist block. Breathing heavily, I stared down below. The hole was right where I needed it to be; now, I just needed a chance to attack one more time.

"What are you doing?" Blake yelled at Mark, his face pale. "Just leave her. She's dead anyway." He reached out to pull Penny out of Mark's arms.

Mark shifted so Blake couldn't touch her, juggling the young woman and his sword at the same time. "She's still breathing."

"Your job is to protect *me*," Blake snarled. "Not her."

Mark scoffed. "You don't need to remind me." He set her on the ceiling a little ways away from the two men, then pointed at them with his sword and threatened, "If you want me to keep doing my job, don't touch her. Let's see you get out of here without me." He was battered and covered in red and black blood, but he still came across as imposing.

Blake and the other guy stiffened, as if Mark had read their minds.

The uttu came rushing forward, enraged by its injuries.

A large shield with a huge spike in the middle appeared on Mark's left arm before he ran forward and met the monster head-on. Hunter and monster clashed and started to exchange heavy blows.

From above, I threw my kindjal at the uttu, trying to distract it enough for Mark to land a good hit. Once it was distracted, I could attack the hole above the energy crystal again. Unfortunately, there was a clear difference between the fight before and now. Mark just wasn't enough without Penny, especially with how tired he already was.

Finally, the giant monster swept its leg out and smacked right into Mark's shield. The spike on its front bent in half as the rest of the metal contorted around his arm from the force of the hit, and Mark was thrown back. He smashed into the ceiling and skidded across the dirty surface, his limp body hitting the short rim around the building with enough force still to vault him over the edge.

Shocked, I thrust out my hand and collected the faint fog I had spread over the entire ceiling under him. He landed on a large mist platform several feet below the line of the ceiling. I could see him from this angle, but anyone else would think he was gone.

I paused, hand still out and conflicted. I hated the guy. Hated his indifference to my life. But I couldn't say that was a new concept for Hunters—it was how everyone was. I also hated how he was so entangled with Blake. I was sure that everything Blake had done to me, Mark also had a hand in it.

Only, I couldn't deny I was impressed with how Mark was determined to save Penny. It made him seem like he could be a normal person. It was that tiny thought which had made me stretch out my hand impulsively. And now that I had him in my grasp, I was torn on whether I should drop him or leave him there.

Before I could sort my thoughts out, the uttu charged at Blake and the fourth guy. Both men yelled and stumbled back, lifting their swords, but neither of them looked like they had confidence in fighting.

Suddenly, Blake reached out and grabbed the other guy.

"What are you doing?" he yelled, weakly struggling. Unfortunately for him, he was so injured, he couldn't throw off Blake's hand. "Stop!"

Blake didn't even answer. He just threw the screaming man right at the uttu in true Blake fashion.

The monster's huge fangs stabbed into his chest, nearly breaking the man in half. His screaming cut off, and his dead body went limp.

The uttu paused and focused on the meal in its fangs while Blake backed away, looking for a way down.

Finally!

I cast Mist Blade and kicked off my mist block. Silently, I shot down. Gripping my blade with two hands, I stabbed down into the hole I'd made earlier. The ten-foot blade sank into the black cavity, down, down. The uttu didn't even have time to react before I felt the slight resistance of the energy crystal. The crystal broke, and the uttu exploded into tiny lights. The Hunter's body thudded to the ground in a heap of flesh and blood.

I dropped through the lights and landed in a crouch, my Mist Blade stabbing a hole through the ceiling. As expected, I didn't get any EXP, but there were two drop item orbs at my feet. I picked them up and stood, looking at Blake.

He stared at me with wide eyes full of shock and hate. "What the hell . . . was that?"

I sneered at him. "I wonder."

Blake glared. Never mind the fact that his team was either dead or unconscious; he obviously didn't care. Now that the uttu was gone, it was like he'd been shot with courage. He pointed his sword at me. "A little insect like you should have died a long time ago. This time, I'm going to make sure you stay dead. There's no one here to stop me this time."

I looked at him, taking in all his injuries and comparing them to mine. He was ten levels above me, but without a doubt, I had a lot more training and technique compared to him.

And I was sick and tired of his bullshit.

I settled into a fighting stance. "You're right. There's no one here now. Come get me," I taunted.

CHAPTER 23

"Hah!" Blake gripped his sword with both hands and swung down, performing an advanced move, but he lacked the control a Hunter should have learned in basic training.

I blocked his sword. My arm shook under the force of his attack, but I held firm and didn't budge an inch.

Blake's eyes widened in shock. After watching me fight against the uttu while he cowered in fear, did he seriously still think I was a weak little E? With a snarl, he continued to attack me.

He might be stronger than me, but I had him in speed. We exchanged several blows, then he performed the same move on me—a downward two-handed strike. I blocked again, and before he could pull back, I locked his arms in a mist block.

He flailed madly against the seemingly invisible force and cursed at me. If he exerted his Hunter aura, he could break it, since he was higher level than me. But he either was too panicked to figure that out or he was just that pampered. When was the last time this man had to do anything for himself? Every time I'd seen him, he was with a huge pack of Hunters who did everything he told them. Did he get spoiled so much growing up that he didn't even learn the basics?

While he was throwing a fit, I slid behind him. With a simple flick of my wrist, I cut through both his Achilles tendons.

Blake screamed and dropped to his knees. His arms were still suspended above his head, and blood gushed from his ankles. "I'm going to kill you!" he raged and proceeded to hurl insult after insult at me.

I stared down at him, feeling conflicted. *This should have been harder,* I thought. This human was a monster who had nearly hounded me to death more than once. He was the cause of all my trauma. In my mind, we should have had a big fight where I finally got to defeat him in a blaze of glory, showing him who was the better Hunter. Beat him into the dust like the insect he kept calling me. Instead, it was over in minutes.

I was disappointed, seeing how easily I was able to subdue him. But I didn't pity him. In fact, there was only one thing I wanted when I looked at this pathetic person.

Resolution.

He finally exerted his aura and broke the blocks holding him captive. Immediately, he overbalanced and fell forward.

I didn't hesitate to slam the flat of my blade down on his arms. He screamed in pain, but I didn't stop until I heard his bones break. One bone for every time he'd thrown me to my death.

"What the hell are you doing?" he gasped, tears and snot covering his pain-contorted face.

"I think we got off on the wrong foot," I said, not bothering to answer him in the slightest. Unlike his broken whine, my voice was calm. The kindjals disappeared as I stood over him. "From the very beginning, you were a shit-headed bastard, and I hated you for it. I still do." Calmly, I grabbed the rim on the collar of his expensive armor and started to drag him toward the hole where big spiders were pressing against the barrier, still trying to come out.

He yelled and tried to resist me, but his limbs were too broken to do anything but leave a trail of blood as I pulled him across the dirty ceiling.

"You know, I'm not a religious person," I continued in a conversational tone over his loud cursing. Maybe I should have been more upset than I was. In fact, I didn't really feel like I was doing anything bad as I walked closer and closer to the hole of spiders. "I barely know anything about Western religions, never mind the Asian variety. So I can't really tell you what karma actually means. From what I understand, it basically means, 'what goes around, comes around.' Or something like that."

I stopped right next to the hole and watched as half a dozen spiders stabbed and poked at the mist barrier with their fangs and legs. They couldn't get through—I was too strong for them—but it was still a freaky thing to watch. Behind them, hundreds of spiders swarmed the half-collapsed nest, their bodies flickering between red and brown, as if agitated. Were they going to try to rebuild the nest?

Blake thrashed and screamed louder than ever, but he couldn't get away from my hold. He pounded his head back against my arm, which hurt, but not enough to make me let go.

I lifted my hand over the opening, and the barrier shrank until it was the same size as the hole. Then I thrust it down. Like a cork popping out of a bottle, the barrier shot down, and the spiders around it fell to the ground, leaving a gaping hole.

"No," Blake begged. "Don't!"

I wanted him to feel that. The fear, the helplessness, the pain. And finally, the crushing disappointment of giving up and accepting your death.

"The only thing I know for sure about karma," I said, continuing my earlier train of thought, "is that karma's a bitch."

I tossed him in.

Blake screamed as he fell, his wide eyes staring at me in disbelief the whole way. He landed on the thick white webbing of the spider nest, which cushioned his fall and grabbed onto his body like glue. Instantly, spiders swarmed over his body. He screamed again and again as the monsters bit him over and over, chipping away at his HP two or three points at a time. His broken limbs stuck to the webbing, completely unable to fight against the monsters that took him apart bit by bit. His cries slowly faded until they stopped.

I stood there and watched the whole time. I needed to see it. I needed closure. And I needed to see how much of a monster I was.

I never thought I'd ever plot the murder of another person. This wasn't a mistake which happened in the heat of battle—this was so much more. And I understood that I would do it all over again if I had to. As long as that man was alive, he'd try to kill me. I didn't even know why. Was there an actual reason? I just knew the only way I'd have peace was when he was dead. And now he was.

I wasn't excited or relieved. It was just what it was. A fact of life, just like breathing. And it was a fact that Las Vegas was just like Gate Vale. No one would question how Blake died—or even care—as long as there weren't any obvious clues which pointed his death toward someone. Or I should say, there were only a couple people who would ask. But if Kesstel backed me up, even President Price would have to let it go. In theory.

As for Kesstel backing me—well, I was pretty sure the only thing he'd be disappointed in was not doing the deed himself.

I turned back to the mess behind me. The uttu was gone, but the dead man and most of his blood was still there. I grabbed his arm, dragged him over to the hole, and threw him down to the spiders still swarming over Blake's body, which couldn't be more excited to have another bag of bones to suck dry.

After that, I placed another barrier over the hole to contain the few spiders climbing back up. The ones I'd knocked off earlier were dead on the ground far below, their legs curled around their bodies or broken off completely, but there were enough spiders in there to replace them easily.

With that settled, I turned back to the still unconscious Penny. That must have been some hit for her to be out this long after. Mark, too. That guy was still limply floating a few feet off the top of the roof. A symptom like this would merit a rush to the ER, even for a Hunter, but that wasn't an option right now.

I walked over and looked down at Penny. She was older than me, but her slightly gothic style, long brown pigtails, and thick eyeliner gave her a more teenish vibe. I could leave her here, but for the same reason I'd decided to join her in battle, I didn't hate her enough to let her die when I finally let the spiders out of the hole. After all, the barrier was going to disappear as soon as I went into the portal.

I scowled and huffed a breath. "So dumb," I muttered. "Seriously, mentally insane."

I grabbed her and hoisted her over my shoulder. With that, I jumped off the side of the hundred-foot-tall hotel. I had to admit, it was a little freaky taking the first step, but I'd gotten used to heights—even if this was the highest I'd ever been. It wasn't a problem to carry Penny down, just a matter of hopping from one block to the next all the way down to the half-crumbled parking garage. I couldn't sense any monsters, so they must not have respawned from when we cleared out the area recently.

I set Penny down on top of the structure, then looked back up at the figure floating next to the top. God, I wished he'd wake up right then and there. What face would that dirtbag make if he opened his eyes and stared straight down at the ground from up there? It would be priceless.

But he didn't wake up. Not even when I leapt all the way back up there and hauled his heavy ass over my shoulder and jumped back down. Penny was easy enough; I mean, she was a five-and-a-half-foot girl in light armor. This guy was over six feet, built like a bull, and in full heavy armor. Even with my enhanced strength, the jumps down sucked. I had to settle for one little hop at a time instead of long drops. I was panting heavily by the time I dumped him in a heap next to the young woman.

"You need to go on a diet," I grumbled, kicking him just hard enough to turn him on his back without leaving any real damage—payback for

Mason from a couple months ago. "Alright, that's all the sympathy I have for you," I told the unconscious people. "If you die now, that's on your head."

An emergency flare stone appeared in my hand, and I activated it. A bright light flashed up into the air and formed the huge symbol of the Hunter's Association a hundred feet overhead. I looked up at the huge *H* with the weapons behind it. In the dull sandy ruins, the bright primary colors were very obvious.

"And that's as good as it gets," I muttered. "Good luck." Without another glance, I jumped down from the broken parking garage and ran to the back of the hotel casino.

A short, rusted gate surrounded the pool area. Dead palm trees scattered around the area, some still standing, but most were on the ground. A few were tipped into the dried-up pool, the tops half buried in the piles of sandy dirt collecting inside, and others lay with piles of broken lounge chairs under them.

But what interested me most were two palm trees leaning against each other. And the black void between them.

It was just like in Glenn Holt: a small portal stretched between two trees. Back then, the original portal was barely big enough for Mark to walk in without ducking. The seven-foot red orcs had needed to duck low just to climb in. This portal was taller, but not by much, maybe eight or nine feet tall, and looked like a black triangle stretched between the palm trees. A cool, rippling black triangle. It looked 3D, but it was flat as paper.

I slowly walked up to it and stopped. I thought there'd be a red orc or five guarding the entrance, but I couldn't sense one. Or any other monster, for that matter.

Did the spiders keep them away? Having neighbors like that would be a big turn off. Could the spiders enter the portal? Or were they simply preventing the red orcs from unleashing an army?

My HP and MP were very low, and going into a portal was very, very dangerous. But I didn't want the rest of the Hunters to find the portal yet. Not when I had such a personal attachment to it. I almost felt like it was mine. Stupid, I knew. But I couldn't shake the feeling.

[**Come find me.**] The System urged. [**Find me. Now.**]

I glanced up at my red HP and MP numbers. Logic said I should wait an hour and heal myself, but the System needed me now.

I stepped into the portal.

Jynn Devhro

Rank B

Level 54

EXP to Next Level 8304

HP 674/3496

MP 225/1513

Stat Points 0

Strength 97 (+20)

Agility 90

Magic 85

Perception 89

Constitution 90 (+20)

Intelligence 80

Skills

Throw

Critical Hit

Quick Hit

Mirror

High Jump

Abilities

Mist (Improved) (100 ft)

Feather Step

Regen (Limited)

Stealth (Limited)

Poison Fog

Mist Blade

CHAPTER 24

I stepped out of the black hole–like portal onto a tall, grass-topped hill under a cloudy sky. A city stretched out below, as foreign as the alien world I was in. A shock of worry jolted down my back. Was I in the wrong place? Did I find the wrong portal?

Then I recognized the artistic Roman-style architecture of the crumbling buildings, with their smooth white walls and cream-colored tile ceilings; the random broken sculptures that should have decorated small squares throughout the city but now were just piles of rubble.

The last time I saw this city, I was in the thick of it, being chased by red orcs and scared out of my mind. The chaos of the situation had blurred the details of my memories, even though the last moments were as solid as a movie.

Even with faulty memories, one thing was very obvious—the city was in a lot better condition back then. In just the half year since I was here, the place had gone from trashed to ruins.

To the right of the city, a large lake of mist rose a hundred feet into the air and spread all the way to the mountains in the distance. Stone pillars pierced through the thick cloud.

I couldn't tell if they were natural or not. From the outside, they seemed to be random, but who's to say there wasn't another city inside that mist?

Movement drew my attention back to the city. Several red orcs were walking quickly through the yellow-sanded streets in the distance. Ducking down, I used the height of the hill as cover and watched as they hurried to the center of the city where the massive palace with a triangular roof and rows of pillars stood. I knew that building well. Knew the huge green fires on the outside and inside of the building. Knew the sounds of monstrous laughter from the red orcs inside. Knew the huge red orc king that sat on the throne.

After all, it was the building I'd nearly died in. Or did die in.

Honestly, I wasn't too sure.

Was the System down there? If so, I was in trouble. I was only level fifty-four; I couldn't possibly take on a city of red orcs. Even with Stealth, how long would it take for me to search that whole place alone? The red orcs obviously knew about the Mist ability, given the way the one I'd found yesterday responded. If I used it to search, I would get swarmed by red orcs. I already knew from experience that the one Miranda had killed was not the strongest one here. It was sheer dumb luck that I'd encountered one I could actually handle then—and that he was scared enough of my ability that he kept making mistakes.

"Find me," a female voice whispered to my right.

My eyes widened with surprise—I hadn't sensed anyone getting close!—and I turned toward the sound. I was alone on the grassy hill.

But the voice didn't stop. "Come find me."

I knew that voice. I'd only heard it once before, and it'd only said six words, "*Then I will make you stronger,*" but that voice was ingrained into my mind like a tattoo. Somehow, I knew it more intimately than my own mother's laugh and Aliya's silly teasing. It was a sound I'd craved deep in my soul to hear again.

Instinctively, I knew where the voice came from. I turned and ran across a large yellowing field toward the thick mist cloud. I encountered several monsters on the way, but I was able to take care of the smaller ones without losing too much HP or dodge around the large ones which looked like hell cows on steroids. I also found that as soon as I created mist, every monster in the area, no matter what their level was, would turn tail and run.

They were deathly scared of the mist. Just like that red orc in Las Vegas.

I stopped outside the mist cloud and looked up. I didn't grow up around lakes or oceans, and the only time I encountered fog that wasn't my own was in Gate Vale. More specifically, Fogmire. But even that musky place, with its terrible visibility, wasn't this tall. This oppressive. For the first time in a long, long time, I couldn't see what was inside the mist. I was so used to being in control of the water vapor around me, it felt wrong that I couldn't bend it to my will.

I reached out and touched it. It slid through my fingers like liquid velvet, soft and cool.

But it didn't respond to my will.

There was something almost... alive about the mist. But not quite. Like it had a purpose, but not a will. Instinctively, I could sense that, although it seemed to reject every other living thing in this world, it would let me in. But it didn't consider me its master.

Curious, I let out some of my mist and watched. My mist touched the cloud and stopped abruptly. They were both particles of water, both the same thing, but they didn't blend together. It was like two oils in a cup with different density, and it was blatantly obvious that my mist was the lightweight of the two. I didn't even know there could be a difference. I mean, mist was just a type of physical state of water. It wasn't until now that I found out it could be so much more.

I stopped playing around and stepped into the thick cloud. Even though I didn't own the mist, it didn't drench me. It sifted over me and curled into swirls behind my feet as I walked. There was a freshness in the air, like the smell of a cool summer rain with a faint hint of flowers, even though I couldn't see any.

My visibility and perception were reduced to ten feet. It was uncomfortable, since I had gotten used to my enhanced stats, but somehow, I knew I was safe here. There were no monsters; nothing that was going to attack me.

Only, I wasn't alone in this mist. The System was in here ... whatever that meant.

Just when I started to get worried about walking in circles, the dying grass turned into a pebble path, the first marker I'd seen this whole time. I used the heel of my boot to make a mark to help in case I did walk in circles, then started down the way.

After a couple minutes, two gray shadows appeared on either side of the path. I frowned and slowed to approach them cautiously. It wasn't until I was closer that I realized they were the columns of a decorative stone arch which straddled the pebble path. The details etched in cloudy gray and white marble were beautiful and whimsical, but the most shocking thing was that the freestanding arch was one massive, solid piece of stone. There were no lines to indicate that multiple blocks had been used to make it.

On the other side of the arch, the pebble trail stopped and became soft white marble. In the pale light which penetrated the mist, I could see little flecks of crystal in the flooring. It was undoubtedly the most expensive floor I'd ever seen. It felt almost blasphemous to step on it with my dirty boots. Unfortunately, I was getting too low on supplies to entertain that notion enough to actually clean my soles.

Silently, I kept going.

The arch faded behind me, and another structure appeared, made out of the same material as the first arch. A thought dawned on me, and I turned in a circle, analyzing the structure around me. That was when I realized I was standing in the entrance hall to a Roman-like palace. Decorative arches connected the columns somewhere high above me where I couldn't see.

This palace wasn't like the one in the city. The city palace might have been pretty before the world collapsed, but right now, it gave off a confined and oppressive air. The palace I was in now was airy, with no apparent walls or ceiling. Everything was clean, a mix of cool grays and white marble without a single seam in sight, as if the whole place was one giant piece of stone.

The entrance hall opened up to a garden courtyard. I could tell by the shape of the planter boxes that it should have been a gorgeous garden, but the boxes were mostly dirt with a handful of beautiful, colorful exotic flowers inside.

As soon as I stepped in the courtyard, the mist lifted, revealing the whole large area surrounded by the pillared hallways.

In the middle of the garden stood a beautiful young woman with very long, silvery hair. Half of her hair was piled on top of her head in a sophisticated bun while the rest fluttered in loose curls to her knees. *Fluttered* was the right term, because her hair kept drifting around as if there was a breeze. Her long white dress was always on the move, too. The modest bodice hugged her slender form, and a thick, intricate silver band wrapped around her waist. The white, multilayered skirt flared out from there.

I couldn't pinpoint how old she was. She could pass for a fourteen-year-old as well as a twenty-year-old. But there was something timeless in her steady silver eyes. It was different from Kesstel's gaze, which looked like he'd seen more hardships than I ever will. No, this young woman's eyes had seen *everything*.

A warm smile curled her pink lips. "Hello, Jynn. I've been waiting a long time to meet you." I knew that voice. It was the one which had called me here.

I blinked at her. I'd lived long enough to know I should be wary of a strange person who knew my name, but a stronger part of me wanted to trust her. It wasn't a cheap trick like the nixies in Prine Lake. The desire—and her—were real. "Who are you?"

She didn't seem bothered by my guarded words. She walked—no, *glided* toward me. I thought Miranda looked ethereal when she moved. It wasn't until I saw this young woman move that I realized what a knockoff Miranda was.

"I will answer all of your questions, but first, there's something I need from you." Even though her hair was silver, her brows and thick lashes were black. Her childish cheeks had a faint pink tint, all making her gorgeous instead of washed-out. She reached up with her slender hand. "I know you aren't much for physical affection, but I hope you'll permit me." She wrapped her arms around my neck and hugged me tight. She didn't seem bothered by the fact I was covered in blood.

I stiffened in surprise. Not because of her sudden physical closeness but because I didn't reject it. I never thought I'd accept a stranger's touch like this. Only, she didn't feel like a stranger. In the end, I was so lost—should I hug back or not?—that I didn't move.

"Did you really call me here for a hug?" It was like with Kesstel. Was there a sign over my head which said free hugs to nonhumans?

"No, silly child." But she didn't let go either. A musical chuckle fluttered out of her lips, soft and sad. "So warm. I remember hugs, but I'd forgotten how warm they are. It's been so, so long since I've touched another person." She stepped back and tilted her head, smiling at me. "Thank you."

I thought she'd be smeared with the grime all over me, but her person was still perfectly clean. In fact . . . I glanced down at my body. I was perfectly clean now.

I wasn't just clean—my HP and MP were full.

"Now that that's out of the way for now, shall we get back to your first question?" the young woman asked. She lifted her hands and spread them out, displaying the garden.

"Welcome to Vapria," she said. "You know me as System. My actual name is Goddess. I am the soul of this planet."

CHAPTER 25

———

G oddess?" I asked. "Not *the* goddess?"

Maybe I shouldn't have been as shocked as I was. I'd already figured out that someone powerful had created the System and attached it to me. I just didn't think it would be a goddess. Still, the truth in her words was like a hammer to the head. I knew—like, I *knew* down to my very cells—that every word she spoke was true.

She shook her head, sending her long hair dancing again. "No. There is no pantheon here. Just me. I alone created this world. Its mornings and evenings. Its plants and people. Life and death. Once upon a time, it was all under my control."

"Until you were absorbed by the parasite," I finished.

She nodded. A touch of ruthlessness creased the smooth skin between her brows. Her eyes flashed bright silver before she controlled her expression. "Yes. Before that giant parasite appeared, we were happy. Now, there's just me."

I tapped my fist on my thigh, thinking. "I didn't know that gods and stuff actually existed. I thought that was just made-up stuff to make people feel better."

"Every planet with life on it has a soul who created it," Goddess said. "Even Earth. Some of those souls choose to have a separate body like me. And some are like the parasitic planet, where the planet is their body."

"And Earth?" I asked.

She pursed her lips. "I can't say for sure. I didn't even know the planet existed until the parasite attached to it. What little I know about it is from the time I was attached to you while you were on Earth. Since my body is stuck in this portal, I wasn't able to actually communicate with Earth; just impressions here and there. Whether or not it had a second body, right now, it's too weak to hold a separate form. Actually, when the Las Vegas Portal opened up, the sudden flood of parasitic magic forced Earth's soul into sleep. With its current state of health, it might be thousands of years before Earth's soul wakes again."

My eyes widened. "When the Las Vegas Portal opened? You mean, this isn't the Las Vegas Portal?"

She shook her head. "No. When the parasite opened that portal, I used the unstable connection between the two planets to force open one to here. It was the only way I could open a path to you. We were lucky enough to get it on the same continent as you."

So there was a second portal which had to be taken care of. I shelved that information for later and focused on the immediate situation. "What happens when the soul of a planet sleeps?"

"Well, the soul of the planet keeps life going," she said simply. "Just like how when a human stops working and goes to sleep, their productivity stops, the soul of a planet is the same. If there's nothing to keep life going, it dies off."

"Dies off," I whispered in shock. My knees weakened, and I had to lock them to stay upright. "Earth is, like, really dying?"

She nodded. "Some things are preprogrammed, such as the weather, gravity, tides, and such. But even those will slow to a stop. Of course, that's if the planet isn't being assaulted. Putting the planet to sleep is the first step of the last phase before the parasite eats a planet."

I pressed my palm to my forehead, taking it all in. I knew from Kesstel that the planet was dying, but he was so vague on the details that it hadn't seemed to be an impending threat until now. "Is that what happened to you?" I looked up at her. "You're still in your human form."

She reached out and casually touched my arm. "My case was different. I'm much younger than Earth. I didn't take the time to play with dinosaurs and experiment with the weather. I didn't like being alone, so I created a suitable environment and my people as soon as I could. And my people were still considered young when I was attacked, barely five thousand years old. I was naive and didn't even know another planet could attack me, so I didn't have much of a defense against it. The parasite didn't have to wait till I was unconscious before it tore my world apart."

She didn't like to be alone, yet I could tell just by her needy hug that she'd been alone for a long, long time. She obviously hadn't gotten over her need to touch, judging from the way she stayed by me. But I didn't find her touch revolting, so I just let her.

"And the red orcs?" I asked, motioning to the side walls in the direction of the city. "Is that what happened to your people?" Kesstel talked about the Blood Mists, but maybe not all of them had turned into ghosts.

Just like when she mentioned the parasitic planet, fury flashed over her face. "Those disgusting monsters appeared here after I was absorbed and my people were taken away. Those monsters defiled the last remains I have of my beloved children, but I was too powerless to destroy them. And yet, because they live near me, they are blessed by my aura and able to keep some semblance of a civilization—regardless of how unwilling I am." She gripped my arm and stared into my eyes. "I will not allow them any longer."

I tilted my head to the side. "What do you want from me?" I finally asked the question that'd been haunting me for so long.

"Revenge." Goddess said it so simply, as if it was easy to do. "That parasite took everything from me. I can't get my people back, but I want to make that vile creature feel the pain of being ripped apart, just like I felt."

My eyes widened. I already knew I was a tool for the System; I just didn't think the System and I were working toward the same goal so closely.

Kesstel and I were planning on finding the way to the parasitic planet, but we'd never developed a plan on what to do when we got there. Kesstel wanted to go all kamikaze, but I didn't want him to die. I didn't plan on dying either, even though I didn't actually oppose the idea. If that's what it took to keep my family safe, that was the price I'd pay. But if I had my choice, I'd choose to live together with Kesstel and my family, happy and free.

Goddess lifted her hand. I felt my kindjal disappear from my Items Bag, and the short sword appeared in her hands, floating inches above her skin. Slowly, the crystal in the blade started to glow like a faint star.

Goddess smiled affectionately as she stared down at the sword. "Her Will. The name of this sword is lost a little in translation from my language to yours. Its true name is *Her Holiness's Guidance.*" She said the actual name in a language I didn't know, but instinctively, I understood her words.

I gasped. "I understood that."

She laughed at me. "Of course you did. You are my person now. From the time you accepted the System, you ceased being an Earthling and became mine. My last beloved child."

Her words blew me away yet again, but they also made sense. I wasn't human anymore; I was a Warrior of Mist. They belonged to this world. I just didn't think I was going to get my own goddess along with it. It explained why I was instinctively drawn to her.

She moved her hand to the side. The blade lifted into the air and shifted until it hovered vertically above her palm, the tip inches from her fair skin. "When my people were made, I didn't understand that I needed to create order. I was saddened when I found out my children were fighting and killing each other for my attention. Couldn't they see that I loved all of them the same?" she asked sadly. "I created this sword and gave it to the most appropriate person. He then used it to unite my people, and together, we created a peaceful kingdom which lasted until the collapse of my world."

She paused. "I created a sword as a show of power, but it was never intended for bloodshed." She looked at me, a sad smile on her face. "But now we are drenched in it. This sword will be the symbol of my revenge, my will to destroy the parasitic planet which shattered my happy home. I'm sorry I forced this burden on you. And yet, a part of me is not."

I shook my head. "I'm just grateful you gave me the power to protect my family."

Her hair rippled in big waves as she nodded. "Yes." A nostalgic air touched her perfect features. "You are so much like my last king. When a prince, he hated being in the spotlight, but he took his duties seriously and fulfilled them to his best ability. He was willing to pay any price to protect his family. Since he lost his parents as a child, I raised him. His family were my people. He was very dear to me. I'd never had a favorite before, but he was mine." She stopped with a sad smile.

I frowned, thinking. "Is that why you picked me?" I paused. "I mean, I wasn't the only Hunter who came through the portal. There were much stronger people there, even if they aren't the best. Emma is a great person, though. Much kinder than me."

Goddess laughed and softly touched my cheek. "I'm afraid I have to disappoint you."

"Huh?"

She shook her head and rubbed her thumb over my skin before she drew back. "I didn't pick you for your admirable personality, or because I saw the glimmer of greatness in your soul." She paused. "I chose you because you were the *only* person in my world who was weak enough for me to influence. I'm just glad you *are* a good person, so then I didn't have to use too much effort to control you."

I gaped at her. "What?"

She stepped back. "Before you came, I was nearly dead. I'd even lost my separate appearance. I was nothing but a stretch of land on the verge of accepting I was going to die. Then a random portal opened up and a group of Earthlings were brought into my world. Since you didn't have energy crystals in you, I could influence and use you like tools. But after I gathered all the remaining power I had left, I found I was too weak to bestow it on anyone. It wasn't until you, Jynn, were dying that I was able to overpower your body enough to change it."

She rested her hand on my arm. "It was the last desperate move I could make. If you hadn't accepted me, then the effort of that action alone would have killed me. But you did, and I was able to expel you from my world and back onto Earth safely. Then your man found you on the ground inside the Gate Vale and brought you to the hospital. It took me several days to set up the System, and that's why it took you so long to wake up."

My hand thumped on my thigh, digesting what she just said. "My man?" Who was that? "Wait, do you mean Kesstel?"

She nodded. "Although you didn't know each other at the time. Knowing him now, I'm surprised at his show of mercy. After all, he didn't know what you were. Or have feelings yet."

I blushed so hard, my face hurt. "He's not, really, my man. I mean . . . " I only kissed him on the cheek once. And I was starting to turn possessive of him. And I was totally fine with him being possessive over me. All after I'd decided I wasn't ready for a relationship.

God, I was good at living a double standard. This just got complicated.

I huffed a breath and changed the subject. It was nearly impossible to lie to myself when Goddess was staring at me with her steady silver eyes. "Why the System? Why couldn't I just get stronger all in one go?"

She laughed, clearly enjoying my obvious evasion, but she let it slide. "I didn't have the power to make you strong 'all in one go.' I was just as powerless; a flame on a candle ready to be snuffed out. But every time you destroyed an energy crystal, I could refine that energy and use it to power both of us." She smiled as brightly as the sun. "After so much effort, I think we have enough." She lifted her right hand. A bright ball of light like a mini star appeared floating in her palm.

I squinted from the light; only, it didn't actually hurt my eyes. The gentle power washed over me, like her warm hug from earlier. As soon as the light touched the flowers in the garden beside me, they grew and bloomed at a visible rate. More flowers broke out of the soil and bloomed. The still mist suddenly started to ripple and curl, moving lovingly around us.

Goddess lifted the light. "This is the remaining portion of all the energy you have collected." She paused. "This is me. My soul. The heart of Vapria."

Her silvery gaze bore into mine, a marble-size star floating above her right palm and the kindjal hovering vertically over her left. "I will be the virus who will poison the parasite."

CHAPTER 26

I will be the virus who will poison the parasite.

Her words crashed into my mind like a wrecking ball. For a second, the pressure of trying to save my family was lighter. I finally felt like I could breathe. The truth in her divine voice was mesmerizing, as if it really could happen. Then that moment was over, and I had to pay attention to details.

"How?" I asked softly.

"When you're ready, I'll merge with Her Will," Goddess explained. "Then you will carry me to the parasitic planet. Every planet has a heart." She motioned with her right hand, the soul star staying perfectly in place over her palm, to the garden around her. "This palace is my heart. The beginning of me, where my soul resided while my world was being created. Earth's is the Garden of Eden, which has always stayed hidden from humans. The parasitic planet has one, too. If you stab Her Will into the altar there, I can inject myself into the parasite and fight it from the inside. That way we can bypass any defense it has set up."

I stared at the glowing kindjal floating above her left palm. It sounded possible, but there were a couple issues. "I don't even know how to find the portal to the parasite. Do you?"

She shook her head. "It hasn't opened up yet. So there's no reason for you to take a trip to Siberia." A smile touched her mouth, as if she'd thought of a funny joke.

My mouth twitched. "We had to check," I muttered.

"And that's the right idea." She sounded like she was soothing a sulking child, but I didn't actually hate her tone. Maybe it was because she was the Goddess of the Warriors of Mist, but I doubted I'd ever hate anything she did. It felt like it was programmed into me, and I didn't mind because I instinctively knew she wanted the best for me, even if I had to learn the hard way.

"Like a fly who spews acid onto its food then extends a straw-like mouth to suck up the decomposed remains, the parasite is much the same. It won't open a direct portal to Earth until it is ready to absorb the planet," Goddess explained. "I'll be able to feel it when that happens. If we move fast enough, we can intercept it before it damages Earth beyond repair."

My eyes widened, and I took a step forward. "You . . . care what happens to Earth?" It was almost too good to be true. After all, I'd talked circles and circles around Kesstel trying to get him to care.

She laughed. "Well, it's the birthplace of my only child. If we succeed, it will be the land where my children will live until I can make another world for them. Which will take a long time." She paused. "If things go as planned, I'll have leverage over Earth to convince it to host my people for a time. After all, if not for me and my person, Earth won't exist in the future." She laughed again and shook her head. "I can't believe I'm talking about the future. I've lived in the past for so long."

I smiled and nodded.

It was still a little weird to hear a woman younger than me keep calling me her child. Hell, it was weird to hear anyone other than my mom call me that. But at the same time, it slipped off Goddess's tongue so naturally that it didn't make me uncomfortable. It was actually very reassuring how much she cared about my well-being.

When I first got the System, I had to work for what I got. It would give impossible requests, and I'd fulfill them. It almost didn't feel like the System and Goddess were the same person. Maybe it was because in the beginning, we didn't know each other; we were both simply using the other person to get what we wanted. I wanted to be strong enough to protect my family and give them a better future, and I was willing to pay any price. Goddess wanted revenge and didn't care what "tool" she had to use.

"I know what you mean. The future was always so bleak before I met you. Every day, I woke up thinking I might just die that day. I wanted to live; I just couldn't see how. But . . . " I looked around at the palace features barely visible in the hazy mist. "What about Vapria? Are you going to try to rebuild it?"

Her own gaze swept around the sparse garden courtyard and elegant palace. She looked so sad, like she was going to cry, but her eyes stayed dry. "No. My beloved Vapria is dead, and has been for a long, long time.

I'll never be able to repair it. When we leave to go back to Earth, it will collapse and cease to exist." Her voice trembled.

I bit my lips. My experience with this world was short and, honestly, not pleasant. It was more like trauma, even with meeting Goddess. But I could understand how hard it was for her to say that. She was going to be just like Kesstel—someone who lost everything. "I'm sorry."

Goddess drew in a breath and composed her expression, her silvery hair fluttering around her. "I am too. But finally, there's hope for the future. For both of us."

She stepped back until she stood in the middle of the garden. The kindjal and her soul light lifted into the air, rising until they were floating ten feet above our heads. The crystal in the blade of the kindjal started to glow brighter until it was as bright as the soul light.

"You have a choice now," Goddess spoke. Her flowing white dress—so different from my mostly black armor—danced in the air more than ever, revealing peeks of the silver sandals on Goddess's pale feet. "When you get Her Will back, you will have access to the other seventy percent of the energy you have collected—until the time when I need it to attack the parasite."

I paused. "That's a lot of energy." If I'd gotten to level fifty-four with only thirty percent of the energy I'd collected, what level would I be with all of it?

"I originally chose to slowly give you the energy, not only because I needed some but because there was a chance your body couldn't accept it and you would have exploded." It was amazing how she could say such heavy things with such a matter-of-fact voice. She looked me in the eye. "Now, I think your body is strong enough to handle the weight of it. You can choose to continue to slowly absorb the energy level by level, like you have so far, or you can accept it all at once. I won't lie, the first choice would be easier, albeit very time consuming; I'm not even sure how long it would take. The latter choice will be painful, and there's a fifty percent chance you won't be able to handle it, physically or mentally. If so, you and I will both die. Then no one can stop the parasite."

"But Earth doesn't have a lot of time left, huh?" I asked. I didn't even need to see her nod before I decided. There was no telling if I had enough time to slowly absorb it. I could risk not being able to handle absorbing the energy or risk Earth collapsing before I was strong enough to protect it. I didn't have time to play it safe anymore. "I'll take it all at once."

A proud smile spread across her face. "I knew you'd say that." She lifted her hands into the air. Bright white magic covered her fingers and then arced up until it touched the sword and the floating ball of light.

A tremendous magical pressure spread out, whipping her long silvery hair and white dress around. The thick mist started to swirl around us like a tornado, the obscure features of the palace going in and out of focus as the water vapor pooled and sifted around it. I flinched as it hit, and I bent my knees to brace against it. My ponytail lashed at my face, but I couldn't take my eyes off what was happening.

Goddess's eyes began to glow with the same bright magic. Slowly, she brought her hands together. As she did, her soul light and the glowing kindjal grew closer. The closer they got, the more pressure flooded the area. The ground began to shake, and all the petals on the flowers were ripped off their stems. The bright colors joined the cloudy tornado, flashing pops of colors in the off-white walls.

Instinctively I held out my hand for my kindjal to anchor myself to the ground, but it was useless. With nothing else, I bent down a little lower so I didn't catch as much pressure.

Goddess touched her hands together, and the kindjal and soul light merged. A bright pulse of magic exploded out, nearly blinding me.

I covered my eyes and bent over, but I could still see the afterimage behind my closed lids. After a second, I became aware of the stillness around me and peaked my eyes open.

The cloud funnel had stopped. Instead, the mist stood unusually still, like it was a form of art instead of water particles in the ever-moving air. Light beams stabbed into the mist, forming shapes on the wall when they bounced off random marble features hiding on the other side.

In the middle of the garden, Goddess levitated three feet off the ground. She looked like a picture from an art book, with her dress and hair dancing around her. Above her raised hands was the still glowing kindjal, but it was different. The blade was no longer half steel, half crystal—it was all crystal. The inside of the blade shifted and moved, as if there was a real cloud inside, and the handle was bright steel with the same whimsical cloud-like pattern I'd seen on the palace columns.

It was hands down the most beautiful weapon I'd ever seen.

The glow started to fade from the kindjal until it was just a faint light, barely more than a trick of the light. Slowly, Goddess's body began to fade, as if she were turning into mist herself. She lowered her hand and brought the sword down to float horizontally, level with her chest.

Then she drifted over to me as if she didn't care that her body was fading away.

She smiled gently. "The parasitic planet has made many Bosses. But you are mine. The Boss I have made for our end goal."

My eyes widened. "I'm . . . a Boss? I thought you would be the Boss of this world? Or the red orc king?"

She shook her head. "A planet's soul can't be a Boss. The orc king is the Boss the parasite put here, but you are *my* chosen Boss. As soon as you take Her Will, Vapria and my existence will be tied to you. A portion of my power will still be withheld from you, to be used only when you desperately need it. After all, I'll need that energy to infect the parasitic planet. As for the rest of the energy you will receive . . . bear with it."

She held out the kindjal.

I stared at the glowing sword, so familiar and so foreign at the same time. I felt like I was standing at the edge of a tall building, knowing there was a net down there, somewhere, but I was going to have to freefall first. Freefall while I was in pain.

Still, what else was I going to do? Walk away now that we were at this point because I was scared of the pain? Since when was that ever an option?

I reached out and gripped the smooth handle. It still fit like it was made for my hand. The pattern-weld steel was warm against my skin, and for the first time, there seemed to be a . . . current in the sword. Almost like the handle was pulsing while the mist moved and swirled inside the blade. Alive.

This sword, with the soul of Goddess inside, was alive.

I didn't feel the pain I was expecting, just the calming feeling I always felt when I held the kindjal. No, it was more than that. It was the reassuring feeling I had standing in Goddess's presence.

Goddess reached out and wrapped her arms tight around my neck. "Don't be afraid. I'm here with you," she whispered in my neck. "Don't resist and don't give up. Be as strong as I know you can be."

Before I could ask what she meant or even hug her back, she vanished in a ball of light that was absorbed into the kindjal.

Pain—mind-numbing, incapacitating agony—erupted in my body.

CHAPTER 27

It felt like my body was being ripped apart, right down to my very cells. I could almost feel each cell as it was flooded with so much power that it erupted, only to have a new one replace it instantly and repeat the same process all over again.

The agony was so intense my mouth gaped open, but no sound came out. I think I still gripped the kindjal with both hands, but I couldn't quite tell. There was nothing but pain. Continual, piercing torture. I collapsed onto the marble walkway, but even the cold stone on my face didn't bring any relief.

I tried to tell myself it was okay, but I couldn't. My mind was a mess. Had I been too confident? I knew it would hurt, but what I felt was way more intense than just *hurt*. Thoughts of doubt, surprise, and agony flashed in and out of my mind so fast, I couldn't make sense of it. Distress piled up in me.

On and on, the process went. How long had I been lying on the ground? Long enough that the light—the sun?—was fading when I cracked my eyes open.

Slowly, through the anguish, I became aware that some cells weren't being replaced after they exploded. My body was starting to shut down.

No! The one thought broke through my jumbled thoughts. *No, I won't die.*

Only, my body was under the control of the torrent of energy flooding in. No matter what I thought, it wouldn't respond. Wouldn't repair itself.

My mind jumped in panic.

Shh. Goddess' calming voice quieted my chaotic mind. *It's going to be okay. The more you panic, the more your body will resist. It'll rip your body apart.*

I couldn't see her—I couldn't even open my eyes properly. I couldn't tell if she was standing over me or if I was hearing her words in my mind. But her words were enough. Her voice was the first clear thing I understood since this pain started. Mentally, I latched onto it, desperate for something to distract myself with.

Very well, she said, as if responding to my thoughts even though I couldn't form a coherent line. *Let me tell you a story. The story of my beginning and end. Concentrate on my story, not the energy.*

A clear picture appeared in my mind, like a movie. The vision overwhelmed me until I was like a ghost in the middle of a set. Below me, a small planet floated in the void of space. It was beautiful, painted in vibrant greens, browns, and blues. Just like Earth, though the shapes of the continents were different.

I could still feel the pain ripping through my body, but the more I focused on the planet, the less I felt the piercing torture.

This was what my world looked like before it collapsed. My beautiful Vapria, Goddess said in my mind.

Suddenly, I was dropped down to the planet. I could see it happening, but I didn't feel the horrible gut-wrenching motion. I found myself standing in the same courtyard my body was lying in. Only, instead of a half-dead and silent place, it was vibrant and full of color. Exotic plants filled the planter beds, overflowing with flowers as if each plant were vying for attention. The marble of the arched walkway surrounding the garden seemed to glow slightly. Mist hung lightly in the air, soft and carefree. The way it swirled about was almost . . . playful. And in the middle, sitting on the side of a gorgeous water feature in a white flowing dress, was Goddess. Instead of the quiet smiles she gave me, an infectious, happy grin spread across her beautiful face.

"Goddess," a man called out behind me.

I turned—flinching slightly when the sudden move intensified my pain for that second—and saw a tall middle-aged man in a decorated European suit, a long red cape, and a white gold circlet on his brow. A very familiar kindjal and scabbard hung from his belt. He walked toward me, his eyes on Goddess. It was like he couldn't even see me directly in front of him.

I threw my hands out to stop him, but he passed right through my hands and body. My mouth wrinkled uncomfortably. I couldn't say it was pleasant knowing that a ghost had just passed through my body. Or was I the ghost who went through him? Still, I bore the pain of moving and turned to watch the scene.

The king stopped in front of Goddess and dropped to one knee, his gloved hand over his heart "I have returned. I have completed the task you gave me."

She flicked the water off her white fingers and turned her body to face him. "Welcome back, young king. I missed you."

Without willing it, my body drifted to the side of the garden so I could see their profiles instead of looking at the king's back.

The king turned and motioned with his hand. A dozen men and women walked into the garden. Some had their heads up high in pride, while others stared at the ground as if they couldn't believe where they were. Their clothes were a mix of European and Roman styles, some in obviously expensive clothing and jewels, while others wore barely more than rags.

The light mist which lingered in the air drifted around them and clung to their bodies, like metal fiber to a magnet.

"Wonderful," Goddess said happily and stood up. She patted the king's head as if he were a child as she walked by.

He smiled wide and ducked his head to hide his expression, but I still saw the red flush on his ears.

The group of men and women dropped to their knees as Goddess went closer to them. Even the most arrogant one, a woman in a very fine dress, bowed her head in humble adoration. I didn't know what Goddess saw as she stared at the people one by one, but in the end, she stepped back.

"You are all wonderful. Just what I was looking for." She brushed her fluttering hair out of her way so she could glance over her shoulder at the king still on his knees. "You did a marvelous job as always, Valen. But why are you still kneeling there, silly child?"

He smiled helplessly and stood up.

"And you as well. Stand up." Goddess turned back to the people.

One by one, they rose to their feet. When they were all standing, Goddess went on.

"From now on, you will be trained by me to help King Valen keep the peace between my children. Half of you will directly assist King Valen"— she motioned to him—"while the others will go out and fulfill my will."

The group of people murmured in amazement, as if they couldn't believe their ears. Obviously, they had no idea what was going to happen to them before now; they were just following orders. I was starting to notice a trend on how Goddess handled things. She did the same thing to me when I first got the System.

"Whatever your rank or position was before you came here, that doesn't matter anymore," Goddess continued. "From now on, you will be my Warriors of Mist. Upholders of peace and protectors of my children."

My eyes widened as I finally understood that I was watching the start of something great. The start of what I was now.

The set froze as if someone had hit the pause button and turned everything and everyone inside the scene into a wax museum display.

Valen, my first king, was the first Warrior of Mist I created, Goddess's voice spoke in my mind. *But obviously, he couldn't both be a king and personally walk among my children to manage the peace at the same time. So I had him find more of my children who had a natural affinity to mist, those who were good people, to help him. They became my first team of warriors and did great things among my people. More joined the Warriors of Mist until the ranks grew into the thousands, and while there were very powerful warriors over the years, none accomplished such great feats as these few people. They laid the groundwork which resulted in peace till the end of my world's time.*

Thick mist rushed in and covered the scene, masking it behind a gray wall.

The pain intensified, ripping at my body and mind. I groaned and collapsed on the ground. I didn't want to move, but I couldn't resist curling into a fetal position. Even the act of moving on the smooth marble was agonizing.

Laughter—Goddess's laughter—echoed in my ears, breaking the pain enough for me to open my eyes.

The mist had thinned back to a light accent which floated around happily in response to Goddess's laughter. She was seated on the rim of a flowerbed, still in a white dress, the sun reflecting off her floating silvery hair.

A young man, roughly fourteen, with youthful blond hair and the long, lean body of a growing adolescent was kneeling in front of her. His hands rested on Goddess's knees while he laid his head in her lap.

"It's not funny!" he moaned, his voice cracking with emotion.

She raised her hand and laughed behind her fingers yet again. Then she took a breath and grinned at the boy, her silvery eyes narrowing happily. "I know it seems like that to you, but it is so sweet, I can't help it. I love hearing stories about budding first love."

He pouted and turned his head, but his ears couldn't hide the bright red flush behind his short hair. "I'm glad you find this entertaining." He let out a sigh and sat back. "I just . . . don't know what to do." He moaned and grabbed the white golden circlet off his head so he could mess with his hair. "It's just, I know I love her ten times more than he does."

Slowly, I stood up, even though each move was excruciating. But I wanted to be able to see what was happening better. They were so familiar with each other. It was different from when Goddess interacted with King Valen. She treated this young man almost like her own child. Was this boy the last king she'd called her favorite?

Goddess's brows rose high as she smiled helplessly. She took the circlet from his hands and ran her thumb around the rim. The crown, although never dirty at all, gave a more illustrious shine. "Oh, do you?" She smoothed his hair and put the crown back on.

He nodded adamantly. "Of course I do! She's the one for me!"

"And how many times have you talked to this love of your life, young King Terre?"

The young man stalled. "Ah, well. Only a couple times . . . " His voice trailed off. "I'm busy, you know. And she's shy." His cheeks colored.

"Since the two of them are engaged, I would assume this girl and that boy have talked more than a couple times, wouldn't you?" Goddess asked softly, her tone educating. "How can you be sure that you love her more than he does?"

He sputtered again. "Well, it was an arranged engagement from when they were babies. It doesn't mean they actually have feelings for each other," he said as if it was the greatest insult. "She deserves better than that. I'm the king. It wouldn't be hard at all for me to break that engagement." He nodded, obviously approving of his train of thought.

The smile melted off Goddess's face. She tilted her head to the side and stared into the young man's face. "Tell me, Terre. As king, just because you can do it, does that mean you should?"

He paused and looked up into Goddess's face. His confident expression melted with insecurity. "Ah." He swallowed and looked around, his fists resting on his thighs.

"Have I taught you so poorly?" Goddess continued, her heavy words kind.

He frowned. "I-It's just that, I want her to be happy."

Goddess reached out and gently lifted his chin so their eyes met. "Is the decision to break an alliance between two influential families for the greater good, for her happiness, or to appease the unrest *you* feel because your first love is taken?"

He paused, thinking. His expression shifted. He obviously knew he was in the wrong; he just didn't know how to admit his mistake. "I—"

The blue sky flashed a dark red color.

Instantly, I stiffened in alarm. It was just like a Portal Burst or the Gate Vale at night. The same light which stained everything the color of blood.

At the same time, Goddess jumped up to her feet, her pale face strained and shocked. Her wide eyes started to glow silver then she wobbled and bent over, clutching her head. "Wha—!"

King Terre was thrown to the ground by her actions. His circlet clattered to the smooth marble behind him as he sat up in panic. "Goddess?" his voice cracked. "What's wrong?" He scrambled up and touched her arms like he was scared of hurting her. "Goddess?"

I looked around, trying to see what was going on, but I could only see the palace with the still mist. Tension hung in the air, but there was no obvious problem. Yet I knew what was happening.

The sky flashed red again.

Goddess moaned in pain and clutched her head, the long strands of hair tangling in a mess around her fingers.

"Don't hurt yourself!" the young man nearly sobbed, tears pooling in his eyes. He carefully touched her hands, trying to pull her nails away from her skin. "What's wrong? How do I help? Goddess!"

She threw her head back and screamed in agony. The piercing scream seemed to echo from the air, the flowers, the palace pillars, and even the very ground itself.

The ground rumbled hard enough that the young king couldn't hold on to Goddess and fell to his knees. Behind me, on the other side of the mist wall surrounding the memory, came the ripping, thunderous sounds of heavy structures collapsing and thousands of people screaming. Dust filled the air, smothering the sweet flowery scent.

Painfully, I half turned. As I did, the mist wall opened up like a window, revealing what was on the other side: a manicured field with a large city beyond—the same one I'd seen earlier today. But unlike the last time I saw it, there was only comparatively minimal damage to the pretty buildings. People ran around the streets in panic, their screams reaching all the way here.

On the other side of the city, a two-hundred-foot Gate arch rose out of the ground. Then another appeared in the distance. Then another. Then another.

Goddess let out a breathy gasp, drawing my attention just in time to see her collapse to the ground. For the first time, her hair and dress weren't fluttering around her. They were still—lifeless—on her trembling body.

King Terre shifted to her side and helped her sit up. They stared at the Gate arches in equal terror.

"What . . . what are those?" he whispered in a scared voice.

Goddess's eyes were still glowing, panic wrinkling her face. "I don't know."

Monsters spilled out of the Gates, instinctively honing in on the people, and the screaming intensified.

A thick cloud mist rushed in and blanketed the scene.

Goddess's voice echoed in my mind, staving off the pain which threatened to overwhelm me once again. *My sweet King Terre. He never would get to be with his little love. She died fleeing to safety a month later, while her fiancé fell trying to save her. My little king was heartbroken, but he was so busy helping protect my people, he never had the chance to grieve. He never had the chance to become an adult, either.*

CHAPTER 28

The mists receded again.

Black smoke collected under the clouded sky and spread out like a stain, growing larger and larger. All the flowers in the garden courtyard were wilted, their brittle brown stems warped and bent until the heads of the dead flowers touched the dry soil. Broken leaves scattered across the flowerbeds and the dull marble walkways, crunching under the feet of the few hundreds of people crammed into the courtyard and surrounding walkways.

Their clothes were dirty and torn. Everyone held a weapon. Even the very few children were sporting daggers. Unfortunately, those weapons looked just as worn and dull as the people who wielded them.

I stared at them, enduring the sharp pains I felt every time I breathed, recognizing their looks. Their expressions. Grief. Pain. Hopelessness. Despair. Denial. Anger. Fear. It was all there. The look of a people on the verge of extinction.

In the middle of the group sat Goddess, but not the Goddess I knew. The only reason I knew who she was was because I recognized the white dress and color of her hair. She'd aged from a gorgeous young woman to an old crone. Thin skin sagged on her chin and bagged under her tired, grief-stricken eyes. Her arms were like sticks wrapped in skin, and her shoulders dropped with despair. There was nothing vibrant about her; even her hair and dress were motionless. She literally looked like she was ready to die.

King Terre was at her side. He didn't even look much older, still a stretching adolescent youth. He'd lost obvious weight and the youthful, happy gleam in his countenance. A familiar kindjal hung at his hip.

Instead of the crystal blade glowing with power, the blade was mostly steel with only a sliver of crystal in it—just like the kindjal I received when I first gained the System. He looked around at the panicked people, eyes serious, trying to organize them.

"Warriors! Surround and protect the people," he ordered. "We are not dead yet! As long as even a single person is alive, we will keep fighting." He was shaking, and his adolescent voice broke, but he kept trying to put on a strong show.

His voice was drowned out by screams.

"The monsters are coming!"

"They're here!"

"We're going to die!"

People jostled and pushed each other, trying to get to the back of the crowd. They didn't seem to care who they stepped on, be it man, woman, or child. Other people simply dropped their weapons and sat in the dirt.

"What's the use? Everyone else is already dead."

"I just want to join my husband in death."

"Why fight? This is the end."

King Terre drew his kindjal. "Don't give up! We will survive another day!" he yelled for all he was worth over the despairing sounds of his people. "Warriors, at the ready!"

Before anyone could respond, the ground started to shake. Dust fell from the thousands of cracks which marred the marble columns around the garden. A huge shadow of a monster appeared, completely covering the people and the surrounding building.

Everyone started to scream, no matter their age.

Terre's eyes widened and his arm holding the kindjal went slack as he stared up at whatever was making the shadow. The brave face he'd been holding cracked into an expression of terror and disbelief.

I turned and gasped up at the monster.

It was over a hundred feet tall and more than twice as long. It had the torso of a man and a mostly humanish face, both a sickly gray. The bottom half of its body was a steel-colored scorpion with eight huge, armored legs, two powerful pincers, and a huge scorpion tail, tipped with a deadly stinger. The mostly human head was bald, with oversized bug eyes and insect-like pincers coming out of its mouth. Its extralong human fingers were tipped with claws.

I knew it was a vision, but my heart still pounded with terror and shock. I'd seen a lot of horrifying monsters in my life, and this one ranked up at the top five.

The ground shook as the monster stepped closer and closer, shrouding the terrified people deeper and deeper in its shadow. The monster stopped and opened its mouth, the insect limbs twitching. A long, low roar pummeled through the air, the sound rattling into the chest painfully and nearly bursting the eardrums.

The people screamed and covered their ears.

Out of the group of terrified people, a slender white figure slowly rose into the air. Goddess was like a tiny speck compared to the monster; a brittle piece of glass ready to break. Even so, she stared at it with disgust and disdain. "You will not touch my people," she declared. Her voice was like the wind, a breathy gust that was over too soon.

She lifted her hands, palms toward the monster and fingers spread wide. A ball of power grew in her hands, getting large and larger. The light swirled like mist, so bright it was hard to look at.

The monster roared, the sound practically an attack by itself. Its pincers rushed out to snap the small white figure in half. Goddess jumped higher in the air, right over the giant pincers. They clamped shut where she used to be with a boom, all while the ball of power grew bigger still. When it was the same size as her, it exploded into a beam of light which smashed into the monster's chest. It pierced its left pectoral where the heart was and cut to the side. It screamed as its massive left arm was cut off and dropped to the ground in an earthshaking crash. Black blood gushed onto the ground and flowed into the entrance hall of the palace, staining the white marble.

Goddess bent over slightly, breathing hard. More wrinkles grew on her face at a visible rate, and her hair faded from silver to a muted gray, as if the shine was starting to diminish.

The monster roared and swung its remaining hand and both the pincers. Goddess dodged the pincers again, but she couldn't get out of the way of the hand. The monster swatted her at full force. She didn't even make a sound as she shot down into the garden courtyard.

People screamed and scrambled out of the way as Goddess smashed into the marble. The white stone cracked and indented around her, dust exploding into the air.

"Goddess!" King Terre yelled in horror as he rushed to her side.

The people clambered around her, but they were too scared to touch her.

A hundred men and women in armor just like mine turned their backs to the crowd in the courtyard and drew their swords at the monster. They were like ants to a giant, but that didn't stop them from charging.

"For Vapria! For Goddess! For King Terre!" the Warriors of Mist cheered as they ran at the creature. Thick mist surrounded them, and they jumped into the air, trying to get high enough to reach the monster's face. Ten of them died before they even reached the monster's waist.

It was amazing to see the full potential of the Warriors of Mist for the first time. To see how they moved together with the mist, as if it was a part of them, an extra limb they could morph at their will. But it didn't matter. It was a one-sided bloodbath.

Even so, the Warriors didn't give up.

Finally, I had to look away. This was a memory. No matter how much I wanted to charge to help them, I couldn't even freely move. I just couldn't watch their sad end.

Goddess lay in the hole, breathing shallowly through her thin, parted lips. Her eyes cracked open, and she looked weakly around at the crying crowd. "I'm . . . sorry," she whispered. Tears pooled in her eyes and leaked down her withered face. "My beloved children. I'm so sorry. I can't . . . save you."

It was like a heavy blanket settled over the people. The crying stopped and terror faded. Even the sounds of fighting in the background seemed to dim. They knew at that moment it was all over. There was nothing they could do. If even the very soul of their planet had given up, there really was no way out of death.

I swallowed the burning lump in my throat hard, staring at the scene. The absolute despair. For a moment, the pain which had been wracking me continuously faded, and all I could feel was heartbreak for a people I didn't even know. Or maybe it was because I understood the self-loathing and anguish in Goddess's eyes.

Another earthquake shook the ground. Pillars cracked and fell, crushing people under them. This time, no one screamed. It wouldn't change anything.

It had nothing to do with the giant Scorpion Man. The monster was still fighting the last of the Warriors of Mist, who were slowly forcing it back even though they were on the losing end.

The cloudy heavens shattered like a mirror. The pieces of the sky vanished, revealing a blood-red starry sky, just like Gate Vale at night. In the middle of that bleeding firmament was a huge planet made completely out of glowing, bright blue crystal. It didn't have any water or land—after all, it was a parasite of death, not a giver of life. It was actually a beautiful picture, straight out of a fantasy art book, with how the colors contrasted and complemented each other. The fact that so much death was so pretty was disgusting.

I stared up at the parasite, unable to take my eyes off it. I'd heard so much about it and seen the effects it had on my world, but this was the first time it felt as *real* as the situation was. I finally had a visual on the threat that was trying to kill my planet—the monster I was determined to kill myself.

The sheer size of it was oppressive. How was I going to find the weak spot on that planet? How long would I have to run around its surface just to get there? The parasitic planet would feel me moving on it for sure. How long would I be able to survive before it overwhelmed me with monsters?

Goddess gaped up at the sky with the rest of her people. There were still sounds going on—like the thundering steps of the monster as it backed away from the palace, and the scared whimpering of the remaining people, the wounded Warriors who were still alive and in pain—but the noise was muted. The calm before the storm.

Bright lights winked in the red sky, then started to move. The shooting stars fell to the ground, aiming at the palace where the people hid.

I gasped when I finally saw what the falling stars were—energy crystals.

The crystals rained down onto the people, who swung at them with their weapons, trying to hit them away, but the energy crystals zoomed around and buried into their chests anyway. It was chaos; people screaming and swinging wildly, trying to protect themselves and their loved ones.

King Terre stood over Goddess, protecting her with everything he had. But no matter how he tried, he couldn't stop an energy crystal from piercing into his chest.

He gasped and stumbled back, away from Goddess. I waited for one to target her now that Terre no longer protected her, but none came. The energy crystals weren't interested in Goddess—just the people.

"Little king!" Goddess gasped in horror as she struggled to sit up. "My children!"

An earsplitting thunderous sound, like nothing I'd ever heard in my life, rumbled in the air. The very ground broke apart like a glass plate under a hammer.

Huge slabs of earth ripped away from each other and lifted into the air as gravity stopped working altogether. The beautiful marble palace fell, cracked and broken into pieces, the dull white mixing with the deep brown rocks, bits of dead vegetation, and the sandy blocks from the large city which used to exist next to the palace. The rocks and vegetation started to dissolve, turning into particle flecks which funneled up toward the glowing parasitic planet looming overhead. As the ground dissolved, it revealed the black void of space beneath it.

In the middle of it all, the remaining people floated before me. They gasped and cried in a new sense of fear at the endless black depths under their feet. They reached for each other, but unless they were touching before the ground split, the more they reached, the more they were pushed apart, like magnets repelling each other.

With each fleck of her planet that the parasite absorbed, Goddess aged. She was literally withering away before my very eyes. But it didn't stop her desperate struggle.

She'd lost the aura of holiness that her white glow gave. Now, she just looked like a ghost, the black void of space below her and the red tainted light surrounding the parasitic planet above her. Her skin-and-bones arms flailed in the air as she reached for her people, struggling against an unseen force which kept her in place. Tears rained from her eyes as she screamed their names. "Terre! Olivia! Jordan! Lillie!" On and on, she wailed their names until her voice cracked. Even then, she kept screaming.

King Terre pressed a hand to the bleeding hole in his chest and reached back for her. "Goddess!"

Others did too, begging her to save them.

But no matter how she struggled and writhed, she couldn't reach them. She couldn't save them.

My heart broke watching the desperate struggle. I didn't know what hurt more: my body or my heart. I couldn't resist reaching out to the closest person—a bloody Warrior of Mist—to me. I knew it was a mirage; I knew my hand would pass through the pitiful man—and it did—but I wanted to help. Somehow. Only, I couldn't.

Then, the first person started to change.

A child clutched onto his mother's clothes, soaking her stained shirt with blood from the hole in his stomach and sobbing in terror. When her hand slipped off his back, he looked up into her face. "Mom!"

She wasn't even looking at him. Her eyes were out of focus, staring up at the giant crystal planet overhead. Slowly, her mouth dropped open in a silent scream, and her body went rigid.

"Mommy!" the boy cried in a new wave of fear.

The begging and pleading for Goddess to save them died out as one by one, the people stopped moving and stared up at the parasite above them with gaping mouths. Their bodies started to fade away, as if someone were draining the color out of their very cells. And it wasn't just their color; the solidity of their bodies started to diminish as they faded into ghosts. Their bodies began to stretch, warping their features into frightening images.

I looked back at the little boy, the youngest person in the group, my heart bleeding for him. He must have been so scared to see this happen to his mother. But his face was blank, fading away and stretching like the others. He wasn't holding his mother anymore. His arms were limp at his sides, like hers, and they drifted away from each other as if they were strangers.

My hands trembled as I covered my mouth in horror.

The Warriors of Mist were the last ones to change, starting with the weakest and most badly wounded.

Terre, floating in the dissolving world debris just ten feet from Goddess, still reached out to her with his blood-smeared hands. "Goddess!" he yelled. Tears poured from his eyes and drifted in the space around him. He looked around at his people with grieving eyes then back at Goddess, pumping his arms like he was trying to swim through space to her.

"Terre!" she cried, desperately reaching for him—the last one left of her people. "My baby! Terre!" She glanced at the phantoms her people had turned into, anguish and horror in her wide eyes. "Why?" she screamed. "Why!"

"Goddess!" Terre's arms started to stretch, his already slender fingers elongating into stick-like claws. He gasped and screamed in pain. His eyes glazed over, and the expression dimmed from his face. Then he gasped and shook his head, breaking out of the spell.

"No!" Goddess wailed. "No! No! Terre!" She groped at the air, whimpering. "Terre!"

He reached back for her. His mouth opened, but no words came out. He was screaming her name with his lips, his eyes, every fiber of his being, only there was no sound. The color of his skin leached away. Then from his hair. Then his clothes. He was still reaching for her as his body began to stretch.

"Terre!" Goddess screamed. "Terre!"

The expression died from his ghoulish face. His hands fell limp and his face turned away from her, staring up at the parasite. Any speck of the handsome young king was gone. All that was left was the king of the Blood Mists.

"NO! NO!" Goddess clawed at the air, wailing and weeping for her people.

Only they weren't her people anymore.

A huge glass orb, like a mini transparent moon, appeared behind Goddess. She, the particles left of her planet, and the Blood Mists were sucked into it. The particles of earth collected back together and formed a flat stretch of land inside. On one side, a familiar city, the one the red orcs inhabited now, formed. The Blood Mists were sent there. On the other side, Goddess was hurled into the middle of a field. The rubble remains of the white palace landed in a pile on top of her, exploding dust into the air.

I clutched my chest as another wave of heartbreak offset the physical pain still wracking my body.

The glass orb arose with its new contents and floated over to the parasitic planet. It was then I noticed hundreds of other orbs in the airspace around the parasite. The remnants of other planets looked like cat's-eye marbles, their flat lands floating in the middle of round clear orbs. Vapria, Goddess's beloved world, joined their ranks.

Another remnant. Another victim to the parasite.

This is Earth's future, Goddess said slowly in my mind. *If we don't stop the parasite.*

CHAPTER 29

The image disappeared into a puff of clouds, leaving me floating in a black void. There weren't any stars or lights of any kind, but my own body glowed faintly and gave light around me.

The history I'd just witnessed was still thick in my mind. I couldn't make my body stop trembling as emotions ripped through me.

Fear of what I just saw. Fear for the people I didn't even know, for a people who didn't even exist anymore. And fear knowing it was going to happen to Earth. Just the thought of watching my family turn into monsters in front of me nearly shattered my soul.

Grief for the lives so easily swallowed up washed over me. I didn't know if it was because of my connection to Goddess, but I felt all her heartbreak in my chest. It was like a fist was tightening around my heart, making it hard to breathe. I empathized with her desire to protect her people, and her devastation at not being able to.

I felt anger, too; both Goddess's and my own. Anger at the parasite; that it did this over and over again. And that it wanted to do the same to Earth.

I'd die before I let it succeed.

But another part of me was sad. Sad for Goddess. And sad for Kesstel, because he went through the same thing too. Only he didn't just watch his people fall; he physically experienced the change that turned his people—and his only surviving brother—into monsters.

All those emotions and more which I couldn't even name mixed in me and blended with the physical pain still terrorizing my body. Now that I didn't have anything to distract me, the physical pain came back, though it wasn't as intense anymore, no longer threatening to kill me.

Mentally, I started to piece everything together, joining the clues I'd gleaned since I got the System. Goddess's planet was attacked, and her people were turned into Blood Mists. The next planet was Kesstel's, and the Blood Mists were responsible for killing most of his people. He turned into the Boss of his remnant world and, under the parasite's control, wiped out several more planets, including the one whose people turned into the red orcs.

After some time, Kesstel was able to get his mind back and left his portal, which collapsed the remnant of his world, Kathar. He then killed all the Blood Mists, and sometime after that, the red orcs' remnant world dissolved, and they were put into Goddess's world. Then after several worlds, Kesstel ended up on Earth, and the red orcs took me into the remnant world of Vapria, where Goddess gave me the System.

As I put things in order, the blackness began to brighten, and shapes started to form around me. It took me a second to realize I was back in the courtyard in Goddess's palace again. I was in the same position I was before Goddess handed me the kindjal, and the dead garden looked exactly the same as before the visions.

A transparent image of Goddess appeared, the same gorgeous young woman I first talked to. She smiled, her silver hair and dress dancing around her. "Congratulations on not dying," she said simply. "I know it still hurts, but you're through the worst part now. Now there are several things I need to talk to you about. First off, your reward."

I swallowed painfully. "A reward for what?" It hurt moving my mouth to talk, just like it hurt holding the weightless kindjal in my right hand.

"For surviving everything I've asked you to do. I didn't want you to die, but I didn't hold back on treating you like a puppet for everything I wanted. You, after all, were originally just a tool I was using. I think it's only fair you are rewarded for it. And I know how desperately you've been looking for it." She cupped her hands in front of her. An intricate glass bottle appeared, floating over her palms, with a pink liquid inside.

All in all, it looked a lot like an expensive perfume.

"What is this?" I asked as I took the bottle she offered, trying to ignore the stinging needles that assaulted my muscles when I moved. It landed gently in my left hand, and I could feel the chill of the glass through my open finger gloves.

"The antidote for the Dreamer's disease," Goddess replied simply.

My breathing stopped, and my eyes widened with shock. My lips parted as I stared down at the delicate bottle in my hand. "The antidote?" My voice shook.

"Mm-hmm," she hummed as she nodded. "But that's the only dose. It can only heal one person. My world's technology was never as advanced as Earth's, so making the antidote was difficult for me. That bottle is the only one that survived when my world collapsed."

It was like holding my mother's life in my hands. The idea terrified me, especially with how much my hands were trembling. Carefully, I stored it in my Items Bag before I could drop it. Then I paused. There were so many afflicted with the Dreamer's disease. "So only one person can be healed," I muttered. I looked into her eyes. "What's the formula? If I had that, the scientists on Earth could replicate it, right?"

She sighed and moved her hands in a lost manner. "Yes, I believe they could make it. All the ingredients are available on Earth, whether natural or introduced through the Gates. However, I'm limited by your vocabulary." When I stared at her blankly, she explained more. "All of my understanding of your dialect is through you. If you don't know the word, I don't know it. I could tell you the ingredients of the antidote, but more than half of it would be in my dialect. Earth's scientists wouldn't understand it because there's no way for me to translate it, simply because I don't know the words to translate it into—since you don't know the terms. You would understand the term a little, but it's like an eight-year-old reading an advanced chemistry book. You could sound out the word but wouldn't understand what it means." She paused. "Do you understand?"

I nodded dully. "But this will save my mother?" I asked again, resting a hand protectively on my hip satchel. That was all I could ask for. After all, I wasn't really so determined to save Earth for all the people. I wanted to save it for my family, because they lived on it. That included my mom. I would never let them turn into monsters like Goddess's people.

Goddess nodded. "Yes. It will wake her up." She looked me up and down, like she was looking at more than my face. It was like her silver eyes could see into my very soul. "I think you are ready for the next step."

Really? There's more? I was still in such pain. Even so, I nodded. "Okay."

She opened her arms and motioned to the thick mist swirling around us. "Cultivate and absorb this mist. All of it. This mist, which is a part of me, is the last item I can give you. From then on, anything you get will be acquired by your own hands." She paused. "In return, Jynn, purify the remnant of my city of those disgusting monsters." Her eyes started to glow in anger. "Every single red orc tainting the last memento of my people must be erased."

My eyes widened. It was a tall order, just like everything else she'd told me to do. Still, I nodded. "Okay."

She grinned, tilting her head to the side in an almost girlish manner. "Thank you." She drifted over to me for a hug. Her transparent arms wrapped around me, but I couldn't feel her body at all before she converged into a small ball of light and merged with the glowing kindjal. The kindjal disappeared into my Items Bag.

I looked around at the mist filling the palace. It was so thick, I couldn't see the actual structure of the building. I knew the palace was huge from the visions, but I'd been too busy watching what was happening to remember to actually look at it. All I could remember was that it was pretty. Maybe I'd finally have time to admire it when all the mist was gone.

I slowly sat, crossed my aching legs, and naturally relaxed into the right position. As soon as I stopped moving, the pain subsided enough for me to open my mind to cultivate.

Mentally, I reached out and touched the mist floating around me. At first it resisted me, like when I first encountered the wall of mist around the palace. Then it wrapped around my will like a handshake and willingly moved into my body.

At first, it was like a dip. Then a trickle. The mist pooled in my stomach and spread throughout my body, causing all my new cells to zing. It was both cold and hot at the same time, the two extremes fluctuating endlessly.

Cold sweat clung to my skin. Whenever I cultivated in Gate Vale, I could feel my power growing because of the extra mist I was storing inside of me. It wasn't the mist itself which was necessarily empowering me, but the filling up of my magic stores. The more there was in them, the more I could do with it. But this mist was completely different. I could feel the essence of Goddess inside the water particles. The mist itself was enhancing me. It collided with the energy still upgrading my body and clashed like a lightning storm. Jolts of pain added to the hot-and-cold sensations coursing through my muscles.

I gasped and almost collapsed. Luckily, I was already so rigid that I didn't slip out of form, but god, did it hurt.

It wasn't just the mist filling me either. The more I cultivated, the more thoughts that didn't belong to me flooded my mind. It was as if someone was turning the pages of a book in my mind; each time the page was turned, that knowledge downloaded into my mind. As soon as that was done, a new page turned. Information on the Warriors of Mist overloaded my brain, cramming into every available corner. More than fascinating, it was overwhelming.

My face contorted as a stabbing migraine threatened to split my head in half, but still, I didn't stop cultivating the mist. I couldn't stop, even if I wanted to. The mist was now on autopilot, actively funneling into me without any effort on my part—and with the mist, the knowledge that came with it.

It was all so much. Too much. The chaos of the energy and mist colliding in my cells, the endless terms, fight moves, and battle plans for the Warriors of Mist. It was out of my control.

A slight panic sparked inside me. I'd spent an entire year of hell, not being able to control my life. I'd gotten used to finally having a say in what I did and how I did it.

But this—this was completely beyond me. The more I couldn't force the mist and energy to obey my will, the more the small seed of panic grew.

What if I lost my mind like Kesstel? I believed Goddess wasn't trying to hurt or subjugate me, but a human's mind was different from a goddess's. What if she was wrong? What if this was too much for me?

As doubts crept in, the pain in my body and mind intensified.

Panting painfully, I cracked my eyes open. I just needed a little distraction, just enough to settle my mind.

In my narrow field of vision, I could see the mist twisting and funneling into my body. My body which . . . wasn't completely solid anymore.

My eyes flared wide as I stared at my fingers still pressed together in cultivating position. I could see my legs through their outline. Like I was turning into a ghost.

CHAPTER 30

Panic screamed in my mind. In a tiny corner of my awareness, tucked away from the endless information overwhelming my brain, the memory of Goddess's people turning into Blood Mists popped up.

I didn't want to become a ghost. It was stupid of me to want all the power at once. Stupid and greedy. Now, I was paying for it. I should have been patient. I'd spent years being patient; I should have just waited a little longer.

The pain in my body and mind intensified sharply. As I watched, my fingers faded even more, until I could barely see my fingertips.

No! No! No! I wanted to yell, but I was immobilized, completely frozen in place, unable to do anything but accept the mist that was washing away my being.

You're okay, Goddess whispered softly in my ear. I couldn't see her, but her warm voice broke through the hysteria setting in. *As soon as you lose focus, you will lose yourself. What are you fighting for?*

What was I fighting for? In an unoccupied corner of my mind, Aliya's face came into view. She smiled at me, her face bright with excitement as she cradled the red fanged snapper bracelet against her chest. Then Aunt Mina and Uncle Carl as the four of us happily sat together and played games on the dinky, rundown table. Then my mother from my childhood memories as she engulfed me in a loving hug. And finally, Kesstel. Proud, noble Kesstel, so strong and gentle.

As I thought of them, my frenzied emotions began to settle. I squeezed my eyes shut and focused on my important people.

I was fighting for them. Every single day, everything I did was for them. Even Kesstel. I wasn't just desperate to keep my family safe on Earth. I also wanted to give Kesstel a home on Earth, too. With me.

Pain didn't go away, neither did the flood of information, but as long as I focused on my family and Kesstel, I could handle it.

I lost track of time. It felt like a long time, though I never got hungry or fell asleep. All I knew was absorbing the mist and allowing the information to cram into my mind. Finally, I felt the flood start to slow down.

Yet again, my eyes peeked open. The first thing I saw were my fingers, normal and whole, as if they'd never turned transparent to begin with. Then I turned, ready to finally see Goddess's palace. Instead, I received a shock.

It wasn't just the mist that was thinning as I absorbed it—the actual palace was fading away with it. Even now, with mere wisps of mist left, the columns of beautiful marble were barely more than pale shadows which slightly distorted the light. The flowers were nothing more than faint hues of colorful gas, like a rainbow caught in place and fading away.

The last of the mist absorbed into my chest, and the palace completely vanished, like a popped bubble. I was left sitting in the dirt. Behind me was a short mountain, just as bare as the ground I was sitting on.

Finally, *finally*, the pain wracking my body faded away, and the hustle and bustle in my brain quieted down and stopped. I never knew how wonderful it was to have a blank mind. Usually, my mind failed me when I needed it the most, and that sucked. But right now, the quiet was just what I needed.

In relief, I flopped back onto the ground like a marionette with its strings cut. A slight breeze brushed across me, chilling my sweaty body, but it felt great. Anything that wasn't painful felt great.

Most noticeable was how much I could sense—all six of my senses had drastically improved. I could hear the dry blades of grass brushing against each other hundreds of feet away, where the dirt became a field. I could sense the movement of cow monsters in that field, timidly approaching the space where the mist barrier used to be, but skittering away when they got too close. I could smell the scent of the dirt and the grass, the stink of the monsters, the freshness of the immediate air around me which slowly changed as the air circulated, bringing in the outside smells.

I was just as aware of my own body. I could feel the strength hibernating in my limbs, ready to explode out, the steady beating of my heart, and the blood coursing through my veins. Even the ends of my hair, spread out on the dirt under my head, seemed to have a bit of awareness in them.

I had gotten used to the Hunter's enhanced senses, but the sudden sharp intensity was a little disorienting. I felt physically empowered and mentally drained at the same time. All I wanted was just a second to stare up at the cloudy sky and regroup myself.

I didn't get that chance.

A System notice popped up in my vision. [**You have Leveled Up!**] That wasn't the only screen which appeared.

[**Mist upgraded to True Mist.**]

[**Regen (Limited) upgraded to Regen.**]

[**Stealth (Limited) upgraded to Stealth.**]

[**Mist Blade upgraded to Mist Blade (Enhanced).**]

[**Gained Ability: Merge.**]

[**Gained Ability: Warp.**]

[**Gained Ability: Telekinesis.**]

[**Mirror skill upgraded to Mirror (Improved).**]

[**Gained Skill: Float.**]

I gaped at the System screens that just kept coming. Even when they finally stopped, I still stared up, expecting more to come. The abilities didn't surprise me; after all the information that was crammed into my head, I knew what they were and what they did.

No, there was something else which confused me.

"All that pain, and I only gained one level?" I muttered to myself. "I thought I got the rest of the seventy percent of energy that was held back."

Feeling a little cheated, I opened my Stats menu . . . and gasped.

I'd jumped from level fifty-four all the way up to level eighty-seven.

I was an A—a high A, if I was guessing right.

Technically, Goddess' voice whispered in my ear, *you don't need the System anymore. All the energy you collect will go directly into your body now, since I'm with you. But it is convenient for you to have a visual, and the System is already set up.*

"True," I said. "I guess this means we won't be communicating through the System anymore, huh?"

The System is a semi-independent program, Goddess supplied. *I am the System, but there are some things preprogrammed, such as notifying you when you level up. Conversational prompts are mostly me, outside of reminding you not to talk about the System. So, when it comes to talking with each other, it will be done this way.*

I frowned, looking up at the cloudy sky. "So, can I tell Kesstel about what's going on yet?"

My question was met with silence. Just when I figured she wasn't going to say anything, Goddess finally spoke up. *I am conflicted about that monster.*

A jolt went through me, and I sat up quickly. "He's not a monster!"

Yes, technically, he is. Just because he looks human, it doesn't change the fact that there is an energy crystal in him, even if the cleansing effect you get through me enables him to fully break free of the control and act like a normal human. He is a very powerful monster. Powerful enough to hunt down the remnants of my people through several worlds—an act which I haven't forgiven him for. In a way, I'm grateful he was able to put them to rest, but I'm also bitter about it.

There was very little I could argue about her logic. I sighed, completely understanding what she was talking about. After all, I saw with my own eyes how much she loved her people.

"I trust him," I said softly. "He's one of the few people I trust."

I know. I can understand how you feel about him, although I don't think it's a good idea. Not as long as there is an energy crystal in him.

My head tilted to the side as a thought came to me. "Is there a way to take it out of him?"

Kill him. There was no pity in her tone. *His life force is infused with the energy crystal. It's what has kept him alive all these years and given power to his body. If you separate one, the other will collapse.*

A chill went through my body which had nothing to do with the breeze racing over the dirt. "I can't do that." Even if I had the power to, I couldn't. Not when he meant so much to me. As for how much, I wasn't ready to fully examine it. There were too many things I had to deal with before I could consider romance.

Starting with clearing out the red orcs.

I took a breath and rolled to my feet. I felt light and nimble, as if there was a trampoline under my feet. I stopped and did a couple warm-up exercises, getting the feel of my new body.

Then I turned to the east, where the ruins of Vapria's capital city were.

Mist, thick as mud, spread out and flooded down the yellow dirt roads. It washed up against the crumbling buildings and climbed higher until it covered the walls and spilled over into the surrounding streets. On and on, the fog spread, swallowing one building at a time, then five buildings at a time, then ten. As the mist reached the center of the city where the red orc's palace stood, loud roars and monster cries of alarm filled the air.

Unlike the last time I was in this city, when Emma and I were scrambling to flee from murderous monsters, I was completely relaxed as I walked through the streets. Now that I was going slower, I could finally see the exquisite architecture this place used to have. Appreciate the cloud designs on the keystone of Roman-like arches and triangle spaces above the columns. Pause and look at the designs of the ruined fountain plazas, imagining what it used to look like in its heyday. Try to picture how the city was when it was full of happy people walking, talking, laughing, and playing with each other.

The image in my head was drastically different from what my eyes were seeing, with all the broken rubble everywhere. And what my ears were hearing, with the red orc's howling in the wind.

It was important that I dealt with the red orcs, but if this world was going to crumble when I left it, then I should take a second and remember what it looked like first. Especially since I was going to be the last one to see it. And I should give Goddess one last time to reminisce about what was left of her people. The only things I would take with me out of the portal were Goddess, the kindjal, and my armor. Everything else which had to do with Vapria would vanish.

Thank you for being considerate, Goddess whispered. *I'm okay. No matter how similar it looks, this place, this capital, isn't mine.*

Okay, I thought back, and stopped to admire the detailed decoration around a raised garden box. The intricate flower design was all carved into the off-white marble, and it must have taken a lot of effort when it was originally made.

As I stood there, I felt ten beings move through my mist, which filled every inch of the entire city. The ten red orcs closed in on me, two each in the buildings on my left and right, and three on the road ahead and behind me. It was obviously an ambush in the making.

Too bad for them, I could see everything they were trying to do.

I just stood there, waiting for them.

Jynn Devhro

Rank	A	**Level**	87
		EXP to Next Level	32,569

HP	13,354/13,354	**Stat Points**	6
MP	5691/5691		

Strength	145 (+30)	**Agility**	138
Magic	136	**Perception**	137
Constitution	138 (+30)	**Intelligence**	128

Skills	**Abilities**
Throw	True Mist
Critical Hit	Feather Step
Quick Hit	Regen
Mirror (Improved)	Stealth
High Jump	Poison Fog
Float	Mist Blade (Enhanced)
	Merge
	Warp
	Telekinesis

CHAPTER 31

Even though I could see the red orcs "sneaking" up on me, I didn't know their levels. If they were the same level as the red orc I'd encountered in Las Vegas, I could take them all on at once. If they were the same level as the ones that ambushed me and Blake's team before I got the System, I would be in trouble, even with my new levels. It would be best if I took them down one at a time first.

With that in mind, I changed from Mist to Poison Fog.

I waited until the red orcs on the ground reached the outside of the plaza, then I activated Merge. The cells in my body separated and blended together with the mist. It was a funny feeling, as if I was suddenly weightless, like a balloon. I couldn't feel my limbs because I didn't have a body, but I was aware of my body's essence. I was nothing but a ghost in the fog, as much a part of the mist as it was of me.

I flew up to the building on the left. A seven-foot-tall red orc stood at the top, holding a javelin. Its burly body was several times wider than my own, its black hair hung in messy dreads down its bare back, and a brown loincloth was wrapped around its waist. I didn't have a nose at the moment, but I was distinctly aware of the strong odor which arose from its skin, something my heightened senses picked up easily. It smelled like dirty body, blood, and old food. Ugh.

The level eighty-six red orc didn't notice my ghostly presence behind it as it stared down into the plaza where I had been, turning its head this way and that, trying to locate me.

I materialized my body on top of it, kneeling on its shoulders. Before it could make a sound, I grabbed its chin and jerked it up, slicing the kindjal across the red orc's throat, making sure to cut the vocals. The monster was so surprised it didn't even resist. I flipped my wrist around and stabbed into the orc's chest where the energy crystal was. The body exploded into thousands of tiny lights, and the javelin fell to the ground.

[+1625 EXP]

I caught the javelin so it didn't clatter to the ground, but I couldn't hide the lights which lit up the mist where I floated in the air. The red orc on the other side of the building, thirty feet away, let out a startled cry.

I didn't wait for it to make a ruckus. Storing the javelin in my Items Bag, I activated Warp. For a fraction of a second, my body felt like it was being squeezed through a rubber tube. A half a second later, I appeared behind the red orc.

It turned around, swinging a giant war axe down at my head.

Damn, it had fast reflexes for holding a weapon as big as I was tall. Then again, compared to the size of the huge red orc, it wasn't that out of proportion. I blocked the attack with my kindjal, the force behind it causing the tiles under my feet to shatter and my boots to slide back down the slanted roof several feet. My arms shook under the pressure, and I could feel the building under me shift. The attack didn't even land, but it still shaved off some of my HP. Double damn.

Before the red orc could rebalance itself and start another attack, I Merged with the mist.

When the pressure against its axe suddenly disappeared, the monster was thrown off-balance. It staggered forward, right through where my body had been, huge bare feet struggling to steady itself on the uneven roof.

I appeared behind the monster and swung my kindjal. The red orc's head fell. Before it landed on the ground, I destroyed the energy crystal in its chest, and the whole body exploded into shining lights.

[+1650 EXP]

I caught the huge war axe just as my senses let me know an attack was coming. I turned and swung the heavy weapon broadside like a shield toward the incoming threat. A twelve-foot javelin struck the axe just as I moved it in front of my face, the force sending a shock of numbing pain through my hand and knocking the axe right out of my fingers. Both weapons clattered to the roof with bent blades, but that hardly mattered. The eight red orcs running in my direction did.

I lifted my hand and cast Mist. Huge blocks appeared over the red orcs and slammed down right on them, catching two of the monsters by surprise and smashing them under the pressure. They weren't dead, but they were pinned belly down on the ground with several broken limbs. That was good enough for now.

Three red orcs blocked my attacks in time; one with its huge sword and the other two with their bare hands. Their arms shook under the pressure as they knelt like Atlas holding the weight of the world. I quickly morphed the blocks into domes around them. They were stuck in place for now, but since we were on par levelwise, it might not be too long before they broke their cages.

The last three monsters dodged out of the way entirely. I stared down at them, my stomach twisting. I hadn't felt a thing when I killed the last two red orcs, but the level ninety-one S-rank lead standing in the middle of the plaza was entirely different.

Because it'd almost killed me.

Just seeing its nightmarish square red face and titan-like body was enough to send shivers down my spine. Refresh the pain I felt as my skin and muscles were shaved off a layer at a time. Hear the mocking laughter because I was too weak to even lift the child's sword it gave me.

The leader stared up at me with anger . . . and a slight puzzlement. Did it recognize me?

I took a breath and forced my emotions to settle. I was a Warrior of Mist now. S rank or not, that monster was going to know what it felt like to helplessly watch itself die.

I Warped behind the orc and swung at its neck.

It turned and blocked my attack, sending me flying with a swing of its massive sword. I twisted in the air and landed on a mist barrier. A trail of blood leaked down from my side, a surprise backlash of our powers colliding. As soon as I landed, a tall, thin red orc lunged after me. As I twisted out of the way, I lashed out and left a long burning slash down its arm. Unfortunately, I didn't have time to do more before the third red orc, who was built like a mountain and had short hair with a single ratty braid dangling from its right temple, attacked from the other side.

I kicked off the huge monster's face and backflipped onto one of the domes holding the red orcs. It roared in rage and punched the barrier with its beefy fists. I scowled down at it and smashed my hand against the surface, thickening and intensifying the Poison Fog inside. The orc yelped and howled in surprise.

A tingle of alarm went down my spine, and I instantly Merged with the mist. A split second later, the leader's sword sliced through where I had been standing. Solidifying behind it, I went after the leader and the two free red orcs at its side.

Dozens of attacks from both sides were exchanged in minutes. I was higher leveled and empowered with the knowledge I'd inherited by absorbing Goddess's mist, but even I was surprised at the fast pace. As I exchanged blows with the three red orcs, I Merged and Warped to dodge their attacks and attempt sneak attacks on them. Blood spilled on both sides, two buildings collapsed, and one of the red orcs pinned down by a block died from friendly fire. Unfortunately, I didn't get EXP from that, but it was one less monster I had to deal with.

The mountain-size orc swung its huge sword with a roar. I Merged with the mist and let the blade pass right through me, then I dodged to the side and solidified as I drove my kindjal into the exposed black-haired armpit. The red orc's mouth dropped open with pain right before it exploded into little white lights.

One more down, I thought, turning to the two others.

The Poison Fog was thick as mud, but they could still tell where I was. The tall thin red orc was covered in the most cuts, and the name title over its head indicated it was inflicted with Paralysis and Bleed. Good. The ailments were enough to slow the monster down so it was easier to handle. The leader was breathing hard, but it didn't have nearly as many injuries—probably because it didn't have any problems with using its posse as meat shields to block my attacks. It also didn't seem to be that affected by my Poison Fog. It slowed its movements down a little, but didn't have any afflictions.

They ran at me, closing the distance in seconds. By the time they got to me, I'd already jumped twenty feet into the air and cast my newly enhanced Mirror, even though I already had a kindjal in both hands. The crystal blades started to glow, then two more kindjals appeared in the air around me. The ability Telekinesis automatically activated, causing the two swords to float in the air at my sides. It was a heavy MP hit—the two combined abilities cost eighty points—but it was worth it.

I Merged with the mist and disappeared before the lead red orc could skewer me with a javelin. The two kindjals in my hands disappeared with me, but the two floating kindjals stayed in place, waiting for directions. I knew the theory of how to use them, but I'd never actually executed the actions. I preferred to practice abilities before I applied them in battle, but right now seemed as good a time as any.

The two floating kindjals shot like bullets in opposite directions—right at a trapped red orc on either side of the ruined plaza. The kindjals stabbed right through the barriers and pierced the red orcs' energy crystals. Two monsters exploded.

[+1650 EXP]

[+1600 EXP]

The leader and the thin red orc beside him looked both ways, growling in concern.

Good. I took the chance to Warp behind the disoriented thin orc. I dipped and slashed the back of its knees, causing it to howl and collapse. The lead red orc reacted instantly and attacked, and I was forced to jump out of the way before I could finish off the thin monster. I skidded to a stop ten feet away.

My two floating kindjals shot at the leader. The S monster growled loudly and engaged with the kindjals, trying to destroy them, but no matter how hard it chopped at the blades and flung them away, the kindjals kept diving back like angry eagles. Without a physical body to restrict their movements, I could wield them in ways I never thought possible until now. The lead red orc, although powerful, had trouble keeping up.

My eyes narrowed as the mental strain of controlling them started to throb at my temples. But I didn't keep my full attention on that fight long; there were other monsters I needed to kill. Relying on the 3D moving picture in my mind, I used that to continue attacking the leader with a portion of my attention. The floating kindjals slowed down a little, but they were still active enough to pose a threat.

Meanwhile, I went after the thin red orc. It pushed up, trying to stand on its knees to face me, but as soon as too much weight was on its bleeding knees, it collapsed to the ground. It swung its giant weapon as I closed in, but I jumped back just in time and flung the kindjal in my right hand. It shot out and stabbed the red orc right in the chest all the way up to the hilt. The monster exploded into little lights.

The sudden bright light distracted the leader for just two seconds. That was all I needed.

One of the floating kindjals shot right under the monster's arm and stabbed into its side. While the leader paused in pain, the second kindjal dove in. Unfortunately, both attacks missed the energy crystal in its chest by inches.

Damn.

The red orc stabbed its sword into the ground to prop itself up, then grabbed the kindjals and pulled them out of its body with a roar. As if it couldn't feel the pain, it flung the black blood-covered blades away. It didn't seem to notice how its hands were smoking and burnt where it'd touched the kindjals. It spoke, and a teal Guide box popped up, instantly translating its gravelly words. [**Damn mist witch. I'll kill you. Again.**]

My brows rose. So it was finally going to talk to me? I thought we were going to do this whole thing silently. I pointed my kindjal at the bleeding monster. "What do you think about the strength of the current intelligent species now?"

The orc spat at me.

I sidestepped the phlegm. "Unlike you, we aren't weak enough to become monster slaves. I'll make sure of that." I Warped behind it and attacked.

It lifted its arm and blocked my first swing with its thick arm bracer. By the time my next attack landed, it had its sword in hand. Unfortunately for the red orc, it wasn't just my immediate attacks it had to deal with. The two floating kindjals closed in and joined the fray, and every time there was the slightest opening, one of my four blades snuck in.

I could see why it had been titled the leader. Even against my endless assault, it was able to keep up. But slowly, between the constant slashes, my Warping, and Merging with the mist, I started to shave its substantial HP down a hundred points at a time. If its natural defense weren't so damn high, the attacks would do more damage, like with the other red orcs, but I didn't have time to complain. I was able to dodge most of its attacks, but each time one landed, I dropped a larger percentage of HP.

Slowly, I took the lead of the fight, but I wasn't in a hurry to end it. This was what I wanted. It was just like when I was fighting Blake. I didn't want it to end so easily. That horrible monster inside me wanted this moment to go on. Wanted this damn red orc to know what it felt like to be the victim.

The more HP it lost, the tighter the red orc's thick black brows pinched together over its red eyes. The fury in its blood-colored pupils slowly changed to disbelief. And fear.

It swung its massive sword at me. It was so wounded that its movements were sluggish enough for me to easily duck under the attack. I sliced across its massive chest with both kindjals, leaving two long, burning, bleeding slashes. When the monster bent over in reflex, I kicked up and smashed the heel of my boot into the underside of its jaw.

The lead red orc was knocked right off its feet. It smashed to the ground, flat on its back, dust and debris puffing into the air around. The red orc didn't have time to recover. I waved a hand, and four solid blocks of mist smashed down on its limbs, pinning it to the ground. I was sure it was enough to hold it down for now, but I didn't know how long.

The orc yelled in pain as its feet and hands were flattened in awkward angles.

For a couple seconds, I just breathed heavily as the toll of the fight caught up to me. There were still two other red orcs to deal with—one caught in a dome and another pinned under a mist block, but the thick poison around them was already doing considerable damage. Slowly, I walked over to the leader pinned on the ground.

I had lain in almost that exact same position the last time I was in Vapria, knowing I was going to die. Knowing I'd let my family down. It felt good to have the roles reversed.

I reached down. My hand easily passed through the solid mist as I jerked the huge, red sword from the orc's broken fingers.

It snarled up at me. [**You will die, detestable current intelligent species.**] Black blood leaked from its twisted mouth as it spat out its gravelly, harsh language.

"Been there, done that," I replied softly, lifting the sword that was almost taller than me up over my head. "If I could, I'd laugh at you right now. Give you a taste of how it feels to be sport for someone else. But I don't really think this is funny. Gratifying, yes, but not funny."

I stabbed the sword down into the lead red orc's heart.

CHAPTER 32

An hour later, I stood on top of a building staring down at the rectangular Roman-like palace in the middle of the city. The tall green fires between the columns illuminated the thick mist, making the already eerie scene feel completely ghastly. With the low light of the cloudy sky and the mist combined, the crumbling building definitely looked haunted.

Regen had done its job. I was completely healed and whole, but my body was still covered in dried black and red blood. Since it wasn't night yet, my armor, Her Resistance, hadn't been restored yet, so it was riddled in cuts and tears. It still gave the same defense buffs, so I was fine, but as usual, I looked like a mess. Kinda sad, considering I'd just upgraded the armor only hours ago. I'd cleaned my face and hands with wet wipes as much as I could, but I wasn't going to spare any water to do a better job. Staying hydrated was more important.

There were close to a hundred red orcs inside the palace, much fewer than the last time I was dragged in there; I didn't want to spend the effort to figure out the reason why. But even these smaller forces still presented a challenge. Charging in there with just my sword wouldn't work. Killing the lead red orc had given me a confidence and EXP boost, but not enough to take on that many monsters and the orc king at the same time.

In theory, the reason why the lead red orc had been in its position was because it was the second strongest, so the only S-ranked monster in there should be the orc king, since it was the Boss. I just didn't know the levels of the monsters rallying in the palace. And yes, I'd say rallying. While I had been waiting for Regen to finish my healing, I'd watched several groups of orcs hurry back to the palace, and not one had exited ever since. Apparently, the mist covering the city and the fact that they had only found broken buildings when they went searching for the leader's group had really freaked them out.

Now, how to settle them as effectively as possible? I needed to save all my MP for the Boss fight—which hopefully, I was strong enough to win. Just taking on the lead red orc, who was a low-level S monster, had been taxing enough.

I tilted my head to the side, looking at the palace with its rows of columns in front. There weren't any windows on the sides that I could remember.

I wonder...

Lifting my hand, I created a barrier around the whole palace. Then I flooded the inside with as much Poison Fog as I could.

A loud explosion of angry, alarmed roars came from inside the building. I couldn't help but wince as my sensitive ears rang. One particular roar was the loudest of all. Just the power behind the howl was enough to shake the building.

A wry smile stretched across my face as my heart did a somersault. That one had to be the Boss. Could Kesstel shake a building with just a roar, too? I just couldn't picture him howling like that.

I probably shouldn't have thought about something like that when I was about to get in a Boss fight.

Something very powerful hit the ceiling of the barrier in the back of the palace. The immense pressure sent a jolt through my body and lifted the hairs on the back of my neck. My attention focused on that point, and a 3D image of the building popped into my head. I could see more than half of the red orcs slowly collapsing to the dirty ground. Whatever their levels were, they were obviously lower than mine and greatly affected by the poison. Several of the stronger orcs hit the walls but couldn't break through my barrier. Which was a good thing. The longer they were in there, the higher the chance that they would become poisoned. Once they did, it was just a waiting game, since there wasn't a cure.

The orc king stood on the platform in the back of the throne room, growling up at the ceiling and waving its six-foot sword. It had to be the one that attacked my barrier; I was sure of it. The scantily clad female red orcs were on the ground around its gaudy, abused throne, either affected by my poison or by the backlash of the king's attack. Either way, the orc king obviously didn't care. It held its giant sword and jumped toward the roof above it like an arrow.

Damn, that would break my shield. To keep the integrity of the whole barrier, I opened a hole right where the orc king was headed. The Boss swung its sword and smashed it right into the ceiling.

An eruption of powdered, dingy white marble and tan tile bits blew into the air, raining down onto the rest of the ceiling tiles. Inside the cloud of dust, the orc king landed on the roof and looked in my direction.

I didn't even flinch as I met its red gaze, although my heart flipped a couple times. The Boss was just as intimidating as the last time I'd seen it, a full head taller than the other red orcs and dressed in a black robe which revealed its massive, muscular chest. A thick braid fell from each temple while the rest of the black dreads were loose. It gripped a giant red sword in its beefy hand like it was light as air.

Even so, I wasn't going to show how nervous I was, no matter what. Not this time. Instead, I closed the hole in my barrier so other red orcs couldn't get out.

The orc king didn't seem to notice. Instead, its lip lifted in a growl. **[Witches aren't allowed in my city. Die.]**

A reckless sneer pulled at my lips. "This city belongs to Goddess. You are the ones trespassing. You go and die."

Holding onto the devil-may-care attitude was the only bluff I could muster to keep my hands from shaking. Even though it was one-on-one right now, the odds were still against me. The orc king was still seven levels higher than me, and I didn't know if it had any special abilities due to its Boss status.

Its ugly, square face twisted in a snarl. It disappeared from where it was standing—the only warning I had.

If I hadn't had my mist, I wouldn't have been ready. Even with that cheat, I still barely had my kindjals up in time to block the Boss's powerful attack. Its sword struck mine with enough force to fling me back, right off the building. I flipped over and landed on the side of a building half a block away with bent knees. The wall took on the rest of my momentum and cracked nearly in half. In one second, over three hundred of my HP dropped from a blocked attack.

Damn!

I Merged with the mist half a second before the orc king's sword smashed right where I had been standing. The entire side of the building fell to pieces. I materialized behind the king and slashed at its throat, but it jerked to the side, and my kindjal sliced across its shoulder. The monster twisted around to backhand me, but I Warped out of range in the nick of time.

I materialized closer to the palace. As long as Mist was activated, the barrier shouldn't dissolve, but I didn't want to risk the other red orcs getting out.

The Boss followed me like a shooting star. Twisting in the air, I cast Mirror and Telekinesis at the same time, before the orc king's huge sword smashed into the two floating kindjals. A jolt of pain twinged my brain from the encounter, and I lost a hundred HP, but I refused to falter.

Instead, I angled the floating blades and directed the attack to the side, since going head-on against the Boss's strength was too much. A small opening in the orc king's defense appeared when its inertia sent it past me, and I sank my right kindjal into the huge, red ribcage. Its torso was so wide, the tip of the short sword didn't even exit on the other side. The handle was ripped out of my fingers, the force spinning me around.

The orc king roared in pain and landed on a tiled rooftop thirty feet away. Its beefy hand yanked the kindjal from its side, leaving a bleeding, smoking hole. The monster twisted as if to throw the sword away, but the kindjal disappeared from its smoking grip. It jolted in shock, then jumped out of the way when my two floating kindjals closed in for the attack. It deflected the blades and came at me again.

I Merged with the mist a second before the massive sword smashed down where I was, destroying the whole building. I moved to the side, ready to attack, but the orc king turned in my direction before I solidified. It could obviously tell my general location when I was Merged with the mist, but it couldn't seem to pinpoint exactly where. Instead, it swung its sword in a wide arc, covering a large space. I would have been caught in the attack if I'd been a second faster in solidifying my body.

[+1550 EXP]

[+1600 EXP]

The windows didn't pop up in my vision, but I was aware of the added EXP. For a second, I was confused where it was coming from, then I remembered the red orcs I'd left in the Poison Fog.

The two floating kindjals shot at the orc king, distracting it enough for me to consolidate my body. I activated Feather Step and shot at the Boss, employing Quick Hit. I got several good hits in before the orc king regained itself enough to send me flying with a punch that took off 1500 HP. I landed on a neighboring rooftop and turned just in time to dodge and counter his next attack.

A series of grueling exchanges followed in quick succession. Slowly, I was bleeding the Boss's HP dry while trying my best to stay out of range of its devastating attacks. I used all my abilities and skills as I switched from one style to the next, trying to catch it by surprise enough to land a killing blow. Unfortunately, even my best efforts to get away from its attacks still ended in HP loss for me.

What helped was the stream of EXP—slow at first, but then the numbers started to fly—that I got from the red orcs dying in the palace.

[**You have Leveled Up!**]

The sudden boost of strength and health was much needed. Still, it wasn't enough to give me the advantage.

The wear and tear of the fight started to affect both me and the orc king. Still, neither of us was going to give up. All the buildings around the palace started to collapse one by one as our fight moved about, but no matter how intense it got, I was conscious of directing most of the orc's formidable attacks away from the palace. Since I was getting tired, my barrier was becoming compromised. Luckily, the red orcs inside were getting weaker too, so they couldn't break out yet, but a solid hit from the Boss would most likely break the whole thing.

[**You have Leveled Up!**]

"Ha!" I yelled as I kicked off the last remaining wall and shot at the orc king. My right eye was burning from the blood that leaked into it from a nasty cut on my forehead, but it didn't influence my ability to zero in on the Boss.

The monster swung its sword, perfectly timed to intercept my attack.

I Warped just before the bloody red metal touched me. The sudden lack of resistance threw off the orc king for a second, and at that moment, I appeared on its shoulders, ready to take off its head.

The Boss lifted its hand just in time and grabbed the blade. No matter how much the monster's red skin burned black, its viselike grip didn't budge.

I gritted my teeth, grabbed my crystal blade with my left hand, and tried to force it into the orc king's throat. There was so much black and red blood on its bare shoulders that my boots nearly slipped off as I used my whole body to brace against its back and pull the sword back into me. The huge monster twisted its body around, trying to throw me off, but I was determined to hang on. The floating kindjals closed in, forcing the Boss to use its sword to defend against them.

The monster's hand shook, and slowly, my kindjal bit into its throat, releasing a trail of black blood.

The orc king suddenly threw itself back into the wall twenty feet away.

I wasn't able to get out of the way fast enough and was smashed between the dingy marble and the Boss. All the air slammed out of my body. At least one rib broke, and a metallic bloody taste filled my mouth as I coughed for breath. A System warning popped up as my HP dropped into the red.

Dimly, I was aware of something breaking. It wasn't something I heard through my ears, but a feeling I had. It took me half a second to realize it was the sound of the barrier cracking—I'd been thrown right into the city palace. The shield shattered, and all the Poison Fog inside flooded the surrounding area.

The orc king whipped around, ready to backhand me.

I Warped out of the way and appeared thirty feet away, in the plaza in front of the palace; it was the most intact place in the vicinity. I staggered back a step and stood as straight as I could as another System notification let me know that my MP had also dropped into the red. Every inch of me was bloody or bruised, and I could feel the swelling on my right knee from a series of recent attacks.

The orc king bent over, breathing just as hard as I was. Its black robe had been so shredded that the orc king had discarded it a long time ago, revealing a loincloth just like the lead red orc's. The Boss's red skin was just as covered with cuts as mine, even though its skin was its armor. It was also favoring its right hip, and now its left hand was sporting a large gash from my most recent attack.

Its ugly voice distorted in a snarl. [**You will . . . die.**] If it weren't for the System's translation, I wouldn't have even noticed it was saying any words.

I puffed a breath, dimly aware of the red orcs moving inside the palace. "You first."

The orc king's eyes widened. Its dark red pupils suddenly began to glow a bright blue, and the ugly expression on its face relaxed to a blank slate.

A jolt of surprise shot down my spine. What was that? Did the Boss have a berserk stage when its HP dropped too low? I'd only heard theories, and this was my first time fighting a Boss. It could happen. But right now was a bad time to take on a berserker Boss.

[**+1650 EXP**]

[**You have Leveled Up!**]

I was shocked again as a new sense of power filled me. My HP and MP grew out of the red into the yellow as my numbers increased. My heavy, battered body felt just a touch lighter. It wasn't a big boost, but it was enough to help me last a little bit longer. Just a bit longer.

I wasn't going to die now. Not when I had finally reached my goal of becoming an S-ranked Hunter.

CHAPTER 33

The orc king stared at me with glowing blue eyes, such a freaky pop of color against its red and black skin. I had gotten so used to its brutish anger, the sudden calm was alarming.

I brandished my kindjals, two in my hands and the other two floating at my sides, ready for the next attack.

[You should already be dead.] The orc king spoke, its gnarly voice almost smooth. [How are you still alive, Goddess?]

My eyes widened in shock. The more I stared at the strange Boss, the more I found it weird. This was the same monster I'd been fighting the whole time, wasn't it? It hadn't changed into a different being, had it? Was that even possible? I didn't know how to answer the question. I wasn't Goddess, and I didn't think anything good would come from me talking to him, anyway. This was way past the flinging insults at each other stage.

[Answer me!] the Boss yelled, staring right at me as if it knew she was in me.

Suddenly, it jerked and grabbed its head with a wail. Its eyes flickered between glowing blue and the normal bloody color.

The instant it showed weakness, I attacked. My floating kindjals shot at it at the same time I Warped behind its form. The orc king turned and blocked my attack, throwing me back with a manic swipe of its sword. It kept swinging in a circle and knocked the floating kindjals away.

In that second, I Warped right in front of it and activated Mist Blade. My right kindjal immediately extended ten feet and impaled the orc king right through the heart.

It froze mid swing, a look of shock on its ugly face.

The floating kindjals appeared and stabbed into its sides, crisscrossing inside the massive chest. Blood gushed out of the Boss's mouth, but it still wasn't dead. With a yell, I lunged forward and swung the remaining kindjal in my hand.

The orc king's head thudded to the ground five feet from where its body dropped. Its wide eyes stared at me, the blue light fading slowly until it was the orc king's normal face.

[**+10,000 EXP**]

Breathing heavily, I walked up to the body and extracted my kindjals from it. I stabbed down where the energy crystal was, and the Boss's body exploded into little lights. My pained groan echoed in the desolate square as I bent down and picked up the drop orb left behind. And the orc king's sword. My Items Bag was nearly full with all the stuff I was collecting in this world alone.

[**Obtained King's Crown.**]

Goddess gasped, her breathy voice right behind my ear.

I jumped and whipped around, my kindjals at the ready. There was nothing behind me. "What?" I muttered in a gravelly voice. God, even talking hurt right now. "What's wrong?"

The crown . . . the circlet . . . she whispered in a stuffy voice. *How did it get here?*

"Huh?" Just as I was about to open up my Items menu, the ground started to shake.

Alarmed all over again, I looked around. Kesstel had said that once a Boss was killed, that world fragment vanished. Was the world disappearing right now?

In the distance, I could see the mountains which circled the remnants of Vapria start to dissolve, like leaves directed by a blower. It wasn't fast, but it was obvious that the world was starting to fade away. What would happen if I didn't get to the portal in time?

You are also a Boss of this world, and I still have some control of it, Goddess said. *Vapria won't disappear until we leave the world. But that doesn't mean you should linger too long.*

The huge double doors to the palace swung open, and several red orcs holding weapons came out. They were trying to act big and tough, but they were heavily poisoned. One of them couldn't even stand straight and had only a third of its HP left. Their gazes locked on me in surprise.

Apparently, they didn't expect to see me alive. Did they think they could give moral support after their king had won the fight? Too bad for them. They didn't even have time to recover from their shock before my floating kindjals shot through their chests. In less than ten seconds, they all exploded into little lights.

I didn't have a lot of time—even without Goddess's warning, I could see the world fragment was slowly wafting away—but I'd said I was going to clean out Goddess's city. And there was no way I was going to walk away from all that EXP.

My aching steps were slow as I walked up the wide stairs to the palace. Last time, I was terrified out of my mind. Now, even though I hurt like hell, I felt completely calm as I stepped into the massive dark room. Green fires dimly lit the place, casting green highlights on the red orcs still inside. Half of them were already dead, the other half were either weakly on the ground or hugging the walls. They no longer looked at me like I was a toy for their entertainment. They stared at me like I was death incarnate.

I was okay with that.

The floating kindjals at my sides shot out, aiming at all the energy crystals. Twenty minutes later, I walked out of a completely empty palace two levels higher.

I didn't have any more black blood on me—that all disappeared when I destroyed their energy crystals—but my armor was still covered in my own. I didn't have time to rest either, judging from the increased speed at which the world was disappearing. Because of mental strain, I canceled Mist.

"I want a nap," I muttered as I Feather Stepped over the rooftops toward the hill on the outside of the city. I couldn't say that the meditating I'd done while cultivating here had been very relaxing. "And food." When was the last time I ate?

In the streets below, a multitude of different kinds of monsters rushed into the now mist-free city, fleeing from the collapsing edges of the world. Either they didn't notice me or they were simply too panicked to care, but they left me alone while I ran the opposite direction as them.

Fine by me. I was too tired to deal with anything else right now, easy EXP or not. Not when the clock was ticking down. Goddess had said the world wouldn't collapse until I left it, but I didn't trust the parasite to not make things difficult.

I frowned as a thought came to me. "Goddess, was that another person possessing the orc king in the end?" I asked. "It seemed like it was suddenly a different person. Who was it?"

I don't know, she whispered back. *I also think something happened to that disgusting creature. But because I'm anchored to you, I couldn't tell where the soul that possessed it came from. It was like puppet strings descended from the sky and attached to it.*

"Hm." Well, waiting here wasn't going to get me any answers. It would just get me caught in a black hole.

I leapt past the last building in the city and landed at the base of the hill. The portal's small black arch stood like a lonely paper cutout against the cloudy sky. My lips pulled in a frown. "Goddess, you said this portal isn't the Las Vegas Portal, right?"

That is correct.

"Do you know where it is?" I jumped up the hill and landed in front of the portal.

No. But you should be able to use the mist to find it. As long as it's in a place that has access to air, the mist should be able to get inside. If not, well, with how long you've been gone, I should think the expedition team would have found it by now. There was a slight hint of disappointment in her voice.

I blinked. "Wait, how long have I been gone?"

It took you a week to absorb the extra energy, and another five days to cultivate the mist. Plus one more day to clear out the city, so . . .

"Thirteen days?" I gasped.

It's only been four days on Earth, Goddess said like that solved everything. *But I can tell that boy is starting to make trouble even from this distance, so you better get back now.*

Boy? What boy? My eyes widened in alarm when I understood what she was talking about. "Kesstel? Is that who you're talking about? What's he doing?"

Getting anxious.

"Ah." Anxiety and power didn't really go together that well.

I turned around and took one last look at the city as it wafted away like snow in the wind, disappearing into the cloudy sky. I knew it wasn't the real world, just a relic the parasitic planet had made, but to me, this was Vapria. I hated this place, but it was still my beginning. And also the place where I'd gained the ability to keep me and my family alive. I was grateful for that.

I faced the portal and stepped through it. In theory, it should take me back to the same place, but I didn't actually know if that was true. I'd never actually witnessed a portal successfully bringing a person back. I was unconscious the first time I left Vapria, and the Josu Portal disappeared with Kesstel still in it. Not very encouraging.

Usually, when I went through a portal—like the Gate—it only took one second, like stepping into a room. There was just a little disorienting pressure at the doorway, then it was done, and I was in the new place. That was how it was when I went into Vapria, but that wasn't how it was going as I left. Was it different because I'd killed the Boss? Or maybe because I was the new Boss coming out?

Instead of an instant thing, the portal was like a long dark tunnel. I slowly walked along, each step like wading through heavy, waist-high snow. Intense pressure resisted every step forward, but at the same time, I could feel that there was nothing behind me to retreat to. As soon as my foot lifted up, whatever dark or invisible path under my feet disappeared, along with everything behind me.

Vapria was gone. I could feel it inside my soul, as if a hole had opened up in my heart. Behind, there was nothing but a black void. And every step I took shortened the portal to where it used to be.

Goodbye, my beautiful world, Goddess whispered.

I'm sorry, I thought back, since I didn't dare open my mouth. I could breathe, but I didn't know what was in the air.

So am I.

Her tone implied she didn't want to talk anymore, so I let her be.

Slowly, I became aware of words drifting around me. I couldn't understand them at first, like they were just a muffled whisper behind a pillow. But the more I walked, the clearer they became. It was . . . two men talking?

"You c . . . stay . . . ere," one guy said, his voice fading in and out.

The other guy responded, his words too muffled to understand.

"I'm . . . orry, but you need t . . . help," the first guy insisted.

" . . . ou're wrong," the second guy said.

My eyes widened, and my heart flipped as I recognized that cold voice. Kesstel!

"Really? An E alone in the middle of this godforsaken place for four days? She's dead, dude. Get over it. You knew this was going to happen when you brought the poor girl. I mean, look at Price's team. At least they found the bodies."

Hang on, I knew that voice, too. Who was it? The flashy S Hunter from the party before we left. What was his name again? Trevor? Taylor? No, Tyson. Right, it was Tyson.

"She's not dead," Kesstel insisted.

"Huh. How do you figure that?" Tyson drawled.

Silence followed. I frowned, straining my ears as I continued to trudge through the black tunnel. I couldn't see anything around me; I just hoped I was walking in a straight line. I had been using their slowly crescendoing voices as a gauge, but now that they weren't saying anything, I was left alone in the black void.

"Kesstel?" I called out, but my voice fell flat, as if it didn't go an inch past my face.

No one responded.

Finally, Tyson sighed in frustration. "How long do you plan on sitting there, waiting?"

"Until the world collapses," Kesstel replied evenly.

"God, man. Right now is not the time for your warped sense of humor." Tyson groaned. "Ss are supposed to encourage the public, remember? You can't talk like that."

"It's true," Kesstel said.

The pitch black in front of me started to change. Slowly, it lightened in color to a soft gray circle. Encouraged, I tried to walk faster, but even though my legs were now moving at a trot, it felt like I was still advancing at the same speed.

I kept running.

"Sure, man." Tyson muttered something else under his breath that I couldn't catch. "And if she's alive and doesn't come back before the end of the world, huh? What then?" He threw it out like a challenge.

"Then I go look for her."

A small smile curled my lips. Oh, this guy. How could anyone say something like that with just a flat, emotionless voice? But it made his words even more precious, because they were obviously his real feelings.

I reached out to the light gray circle. My fingertips touched a smooth, soft surface, and the gray suddenly receded, opening a three-foot hole in the visually flat space. On the other side was a sand-covered mound of debris. I ducked through the hole, my boots grinding sand into the broken concrete road, and straightened up, facing a massive pile of brick, steel, wood, and sand that rose like a small mountain above me. I'd thought I'd come back to the hotel's pool area. So where was I?

I turned and finally caught sight of a familiar landmark—the RV resort with the empty minute-size pool. I glanced between the RV resort, the huge pile of debris, and the road I was suddenly standing on, comparing it to the mental map I had of the area. This mountain of debris was . . . the hotel casino? What happened to it?

Two figures appeared on top of the debris. Kesstel, with Tyson close behind.

"W-What?" Tyson gasped. "A portal?"

Kesstel simply jumped down to me. He wasn't wearing armor, just designer shorts, a navy-blue T-shirt, and hiking boots.

I glanced at the small black portal at my side. Its edges were already wiggling and collapsing. Within a second, it had shrunk to the side of a platter, and a breath later, it was gone, forever erasing Vapria from existence.

Kesstel landed in front of me and immediately reached out as if I wasn't a disgusting mess. I lifted my hands—to hug him back or hold him off so I didn't get him dirty, I didn't know. I never got the chance to decide.

Before we could even touch, he flinched away. In a flash, he jumped back ten feet and stared at me with wide eyes.

I blinked at him, completely baffled. "Are you . . . okay?" I asked.

Kesstel's eyes started to faintly glow bright blue.

Jynn Devhro

Rank S		**Level** 92	
		EXP to Next Level	12,569
HP 1515/15,696		**Stat Points** 6	
MP 165/6681			
Strength 155 (+40)		**Agility** 148	
Magic 141		**Perception** 142	
Constitution 148 (+40)		**Intelligence** 133	

Skills	Abilities
Throw	True Mist
Critical Hit	Feather Step
Quick Hit	Regen
Mirror (Improved)	Stealth
High Jump	Poison Fog
Float	Mist Blade (Enhanced)
	Merge
	Warp
	Telekinesis

CHAPTER 34

The orc king's glowing blue eyes popped into my mind. I froze, staring into Kesstel's own glowing, bright blue eyes. It wasn't the first I'd seen his eyes glow, but nothing good ever happened when they did. Most of the time, it happened because he was angry. Right now, it felt like an instinctive response of one predator meeting another.

Kesstel's aura fluctuated, wisping around our feet, disappearing, then swirling back, as if it was trying to break out but he was holding it back. The pressure was heavy on my tired body, but I wasn't incapacitated by it like before.

Kesstel's face tightened in a frown, and he stepped forward, reaching out to me. His movements were slow and taxed, like he was pressing them through wet cement.

I didn't know what had caused this reaction, but I understood he wasn't trying to hurt me. If anything, he was fighting against something that was trying to force him to reject me. It hurt my heart just seeing him struggle like that.

I reached back, unimpeded. The dirty gloves on my hand disappeared, stored back in my Items Bag, and I took his hand. As soon as our skin touched, the tension in his body lessened, and his aura settled. The glow in his eyes disappeared.

Kesstel wrapped his arms around me and pulled me into a tight hug, mess and all. His shirt was soft under my cheek, his heart beating reassuringly in my ears. He rested his chin on top of my head. "You are so much stronger now . . . that's good. Don't disappear on me like that again."

It took me a second to recover from the shock of him suddenly wrapping around me like this. The hot sun on his skin smelled so good; a million times better than the stench of red orcs. My hands snaked around his waist to grip the back of his shirt as I leaned against him. I didn't even realize I'd been so tightly strung until that moment, when I could finally relax. "Sorry. I wasn't expecting it to take that long either."

Kesstel hummed in response.

"Oi, that's enough lovey-dovey stuff. Especially when I don't have a squeeze right now." Tyson appeared and tapped my shoulder. "Hey, little girl, did you really just come out of a portal?" While Kesstel was dressed in casual clothes, Tyson wore an open white shirt and black leather pants under an open red mage robe. A large red pendant rested against his bare chest, matching the magic stones glinting on his belt and ear stud. The whole design was as flippant as his personality.

Kesstel scowled and brushed Tyson's fingers away.

Oh, right, he was here too. I'd been so focused on Kesstel, I'd forgotten about everything else. My cheeks heated and I stepped back. "Ah, yes. That was a portal. But it's not the Las Vegas Portal. That's still out there."

Kesstel let me go but didn't back too far away. He frowned at the pile of rubble where the hotel used to be. "So that wasn't the portal we've been looking for?" Even he sounded surprised that there were two. "That must be why they can't pinpoint where the Las Vegas Portal is. Between the monsters and the second portal, it must be throwing off the detectors." Kesstel focused on me. "Did you do what you needed to do?"

A wide smile spread across my face. "Yes."

Tyson threw his hands up in the air. "Hold up. An E just came out of a portal. There's something majorly wrong with that." He paused, peering over my head. "Where's your rank?"

I blinked at him then looked over my head instinctively, even though no Hunter could see their own name title. Weird. Tyson was still two levels higher than me, so he should be able to see my rank.

Your rank has become moot, so I thought it wasn't needed anymore, Goddess supplied.

Well, I was going to do something about that, I thought back. *I just didn't plan on house hunting so soon—*

Kesstel grabbed my arm, startling me out of my thoughts. "What was that just now?" he demanded, his eyes intense.

I froze, shocked. Was he talking about Goddess? He shouldn't be able to sense when she talked to me, right?

"Ah, what?" Tyson asked, completely confused.

Is it because he's a Boss? I thought I was hiding enough to not be detected.
Goddess sounded just as perplexed.

As soon as Goddess spoke, Kesstel's brows pulled together. His hand
twitched on my arm, but he didn't tighten his fingers to hurt me. "What
is *that*?"

My mouth parted, then closed as I tried to figure out what to say.
Could I tell him what was going on yet? Even if I could, I didn't want
to bare my soul right in front of Tyson. I was sure he meant nice, but he
wasn't one of my trusted people.

Tyson looked between us, completely baffled. "Okay, now I've offi-
cially gone from third wheel to roadkill. What the hell is going on?"

I swallowed and plastered on a smile for Tyson. "Ah, it's nothing."

For a second, Kesstel looked like he was going to argue. Instead, he let
me go. After all, he knew there were things I couldn't talk about.

I glanced at the pile of rubble towering over us. "What happened to the
hotel?" It couldn't be more obvious that I was changing the subject. I just
hoped the men let me.

Kesstel's lips thinned. "Nothing important."

Tyson snorted. "Nothing important, my ass. This guy here"—he thrust
a thumb at Kesstel—"threw a fit when we couldn't find your body, so he
decided to take apart the whole thing piece by piece to make sure. And he
hasn't moved since."

Kesstel scowled. Was it the desert sun, or were the tips of his ears pink?
His face smoothed into a lordly expression as he looked at me. "You look
like you need a break." It seemed I wasn't the only one who wanted to
change the subject quickly.

That was an understatement. I nodded. "A shower, some food, and a nap
sounds great." I frowned down at my body. Two weeks without a bath was just
gross. The physiological shadow alone was enough to make me uncomfortable. My hair didn't feel oily—probably thanks to Goddess—but no matter
what she had done to keep me clean while I was cultivating, I was sweaty and
bloody now. The hot sun definitely wasn't helping with my smell.

"Right. We'll finish talking after that," Kesstel said. He waved his hand,
and the camper appeared on the street not far away. He tilted his head and
shot a look at Tyson. Everything about his manner screamed "Go away"
to the other man.

Tyson gaped at him. "Hey, no." He crossed his arms across his chest and
glared. "My job is to bring Kesstel back to the party. Knowing you—both
of you, actually—if I let you out of my sight, you're going to disappear like

usual. There's still a lot we need to know about this little girl coming out of a portal. And if there's another one out there, any information you have about it." For once, he looked ready to fight tooth and nail for his opinion.

My lips pursed to the side. Everything he just said was true. Well, to a degree. There was a lot I couldn't tell them about the Vapria Portal, but there was some stuff I could. As a member of the expedition, I did have an obligation to help find the Las Vegas Portal—which I completely planned on doing. I just wanted to clean up and have a nap first.

"We'll find you later," Kesstel told Tyson, his tone unyielding.

I shook my head. "No, it's okay. It doesn't matter where I sleep, as long as I can." Even if there were people around, as long as Kesstel was there too, I should be able to actually get a good shut-eye. Then again, I was tired enough, I could just lie down right here and pass out.

"And she needs a healer," Tyson added, trying to coax Kesstel.

Ah, yeah. It did look like I needed one, although Regen was currently working on me since I was standing still. My HP was going up, but it didn't do much good to my tired mind.

Kesstel glanced at me. Even though I'd never told him, Kesstel was observant enough to know I self-healed. Still, his expression was considerate, asking if I really wanted to go back and find a healer.

The healing part didn't matter as much to me, but since we'd been gone for four days—me in the portal and Kesstel refusing to budge at its entrance, from the sounds of it—we really should check in with the rest of the expedition team.

I nodded to the side in a "let's go" manner. It didn't really matter where we talked, since he could put a barrier around us no matter where. As long as he wanted it, no one was ever going to eavesdrop on our conversation. For that matter, my mist barrier could do the same; it just wasn't invisible like his.

Kesstel shrugged. "If that's what you want." He waved his hand again, and the camper disappeared back into his Items Bag. "Let's get you back to camp." He scooped me up into his arms.

I was getting so used to him doing that that I just naturally rested a hand on his shoulder. "I can run by myself, you know," I muttered. "I bet I can even keep up with you easily enough now."

A proud smile curled his lips. "That wouldn't surprise me, but you obviously need a rest."

I glanced down at where I was held against his chest. Dried brownish smears spread across his navy-blue shirt. "I'm making your clothes a mess. Sorry."

"It's not important," he said. "I'm more concerned that it's obviously all your blood. You got . . . hurt a lot." His eyes narrowed as his aura wisped around his feet once more.

Kesstel leapt forward, starting to run. The air rushed by me, cooling down the midday sun's heat, and the buildings turned into different shades of tan which blurred past in an afterimage. Slowly, I relaxed more and more, until it was hard to keep my eyes open. I never thought I'd be so content to be in a deserted desert city, but I guess it mattered who I was with.

Tyson caught up, sprinting alongside Kesstel, and glanced at me. His flamboyant red robe trailed behind him like a cloak. He was using some sort of magic item to keep up with Kesstel, but I couldn't tell what exactly. "What did you mean that wasn't the Las Vegas Portal?"

I blinked away the sleep that threatened and glanced at Tyson. "Just that. There were two portals in Las Vegas. The one I came out of was a little side one I stumbled across." Completely on purpose. "The actual Las Vegas Portal, the one which caused the earthquake and sank the Florida peninsula, is a different one." I paused. "But I did find out that the red orcs aren't related to the Las Vegas Portal."

Kesstel looked down at me. "You found the portal with the red orcs?" His voice was a little tense, his brows pulled together.

I nodded. "But I don't think they're going to be a problem anymore. Their portal collapsed." I was vague enough that Tyson wouldn't get what I actually meant, but from the way Kesstel's eyes narrowed, he understood.

"Did you . . . meet any Blood Mists?" he asked softly.

Instinctively, I knew he wasn't asking about the Blood Mist monsters; he was asking about the Warriors of Mist. Just like me, Kesstel was using roundabout ways to talk while Tyson was on his heels.

I paused, then shook my head. "There are no more."

"What's a Blood Mist?" Tyson demanded.

I glanced at him. "A ghost monster. A very scary one."

Honestly, as sad as it was for Goddess, I was glad there weren't any Blood Mists on Earth. With the abilities I now had, if they were taken and warped by a monster, Earth would fall just as fast as Kathar did. I would have never had the chance to even be born.

Tyson skipped a step. "A ghost monster? An astral type? Those are a pain in the ass without a mage. Where did you find one of those?"

Kesstel glanced over his shoulder at Tyson. "We'll talk once we get back. That way she doesn't have to repeat the same thing twice."

CHAPTER 35

The expedition team had set up camp in a golf course in the western part of the Las Vegas area, technically in Spring Valley. The dead green stretched between clusters of ruined houses, dry trees, and empty pond holes. It would have been a great place to golf before it fell to ruin, but as it was, it fit right in with the rest of the apocalyptic scenery. What it had going for it was a lot of open space around the circle of campers, giving the Hunters plenty of warning in case monsters showed up.

It was the middle of the day, but most of the expedition team was at camp. And it wasn't just the Eden team—the Redding and Quebec teams were there, too, all sitting or standing in the middle of the circle.

Kesstel landed just outside the ring of campers and set me down. Tyson hurried ahead and disappeared into the camp.

From inside, I could hear voices rising and falling.

"It has to be somewhere! We know for a fact there's a portal here," a woman argued.

"According to the readings, yes," a man argued back. "But we've been all over this city already, killed all the monsters, and still haven't found it. What if it was a Portal Burst? It opened, caused an earthquake, dumped a ton of monsters, and closed?"

Kesstel motioned to where the heated words were coming from. "Since they're busy, take a break. You can report when they're done." He took his extra-large camper out, then opened the door for me.

My gaze locked on the mess I'd left on his shirt. "You should change first. You'll only take a portion of the time I will."

From the camper circle, a low male voice marked by a thick French accent broke through the heated voices. "But the readings indicate that the portal is here. Also, we have not cleared all the monsters; new ones keep showing up every day, so there must be a portal. We cannot leave until we know for sure."

"About that," Tyson's voice cut in. "I have some more information there. Or rather, I know someone who does."

Kesstel and I both froze. We both turned our heads at the same time and looked toward the suddenly loud group of people. I couldn't help but sigh. I just wanted to get clean and eat something first. Was that too much to ask?

"Tyson," a familiar man said over the noise, although I couldn't peg his voice. "I thought you were going to bring Noble back?"

"I did," Tyson replied, obviously having fun. "And a surprise."

I glanced at the open camper door, debating. Should I just hide in there and wait for this all to blow over first?

Kesstel nodded inside with a knowing look. "No one would blame you."

I snorted. "Yes, they would."

Kesstel crossed his arms over his chest. "I'd like to see them try."

I couldn't resist rolling my eyes. "You should stop bullying people, your lordship. It's bad for your image."

He smirked. "As if they'd say anything to my face."

If they weren't dead before they finished arguing, they'd be on the ground cowering in fear. After all, everyone knew how terrible Kesstel's aura was. It wasn't just that he was an S rank; he was also a Boss. By definition, his very presence made prey submit—in other words, anyone weaker than him. Which was everyone.

I paused as a thought came to me. Did the same thing apply to me now? The idea that people would collapse at my feet wasn't a very comfortable one. I always kept my aura hidden because I was pretending to be an E, but what would happen if I didn't hold back?

My thoughts were interrupted when the crowd of Hunters moved around the campers to Kesstel and I, with the leaders of each city in the front.

Healer Laurel Harris gasped, and Blood Sword stiffened with surprise, their eyes on me. Miranda, at his side, scowled, while the rest of the crowd muttered to their friends in shock.

"I thought she was dead!"

"Where has she been this whole time?"

"I never thought an E could last that long alone. Heh, tough chick."

Jonovan pushed out of the crowd and walked up to me. "Jynn, thank god." His voice choked up. "I thought you were . . . " He took a breath and regained his calm demeanor, although he still frowned. "Independent streak or not, you can't just go out by yourself. Even Kesstel was worried. I was trying to figure out what I was going to say to your sweet sister." He ignored the way I flinched at his words and reached out his hand to my shoulder. His golden magic soothed away the last of the aches that Regen hadn't healed yet.

Almost immediately, Jonovan's fingers flinched away from me. His serious eyes widened as he stared into mine. He already knew I was stronger than a year ago, but he must have noticed I was even more powerful now. His mouth cracked open. Instead of saying anything, he licked his lips and continued to heal me. He, at least, had enough tact to not yell my secret out to the world.

Meanwhile, Kesstel was talking with Blood Sword. "Like I said, she's not dead."

The S-ranked Hunter shook his head in shock. "Then where has she been this whole time?"

"She came out of a portal." Tyson popped up like he couldn't wait to spew juicy gossip. A crooked smile spread across his flashy, handsome face. "I saw it with my own eyes. Apparently, there was a portal by that hotel where Price's group was ambushed. This little girl came out of it, and the portal disappeared." He looked like he couldn't be more delighted to fan the flames.

In the back of the crowd, President Price stiffened. His aura flashed in agitation, and his square face turned to stone. If looks could kill, I'd be ten feet under.

At his side, Penny and Mark shifted, examining me as if to make sure I was actually alive. Both of them looked completely normal, as if what had happened the last four days didn't matter.

I couldn't decide how I felt seeing them still alive. I mean, I did purposefully save them. Since I did it, I wanted my plan to succeed. At the same time, I didn't really care if they died. But since I'd helped save them, I hoped that meant they weren't going to try and take revenge on me. Neither of them were looking at me with the same hatred Price was. Instead, they looked just as conflicted as I felt about them.

The tall Quebec female leader looked at me, a frown on her handsome face. "Did you really just come out of the portal?" she asked, her accent so thick it took a second for my untrained mind to comprehend what she said. It was also a novel idea for a very strong stranger to talk to me in such an unbiased tone. After all, it was common knowledge I was a "leech."

As soon as she spoke, the rest of the crowd hushed and listened, heeding the natural leadership aura she possessed—which had nothing to do with the intimidating vision she made in full armor.

"Yes," I replied. There was no reason to hide it now.

"What happened in there? What did you do?"

My mouth twitched as I debated for a second before going for broke. I waved my hand. The twenty-six orc weapons I'd collected appeared on the ground in a pile, the orc king's giant red sword on top. "I was orc hunting." That was all they needed to know. "Since you didn't believe me last time, I thought I'd bring back more. Maybe I should have brought back an orc head, too."

Violet, standing behind Blood Sword, let out a fangirl scream. "Oh my god! Look at them all!" She elbowed Blood Sword. "Can I go touch them? *Please* let me examine them."

The rest of the crowd was just as stimulated, whispering to each other. Armorers in the group shifted in fascination, trying to edge closer to the pile of crude-looking weapons.

Miranda folded her arms and stretched a smile on her angular face. "Oh my. That does look impressive. Where did you find them all?"

I rolled my eyes. "In the portal. I just said that."

She giggled, acting like she was on a stage. "How is that possible? An E goes into a portal and survives. It's the funniest joke I've ever heard." Her eyes softened as she turned her smile to Kesstel. "Really now, Mr. Noblé. I didn't know you had such a sense of humor. It must have been hard pulling all this together under our noses."

Kesstel didn't even look at her. As if he never heard a thing, he walked over and picked up the orc king's blade. He handled the six-foot sword like it was a twig as he lifted it, feeling the weight, then he paused and brought the blade closer to his face. It was hard to see because of the color of the metal, but the dried blood on the edges matched the dried blood which covered my body. My blood. Thankfully, Hunters had the ability to bleed like a cartoon character and still walk it off.

Kesstel's eyes flared as he scowled. His fingers tightened on the handle.

I tapped his tense elbow. "Don't break it." That was my keepsake from the battle. Proof I wasn't a weakling anymore.

"The Boss's weapon?" he asked quietly.

I nodded, ignoring the odd looks that came my way from the other Hunters.

Kesstel tsked under his breath. "I should have been there. There was no reason for you to get hurt like that. You didn't tell me you were going into a portal." He shot me an accusing look.

I shrugged. "I actually did try to message you, but I was interrupted, and the option never presented itself again." In order to appease him, I didn't mind stretching the details a bit. I did try to call him, although I never planned on letting him come with me to Vapria. It was obvious Goddess didn't want him around.

Miranda's face screwed up, obviously annoyed that we had both ignored her.

"Quiet," the Quebec female leader snapped at Miranda before she could make a racket. "Petty squabbles can wait until after."

Miranda gaped at her. "I do not squabble, Hunter Fortin."

That's right, I remembered. The Quebec Hunter's name was Mila Fortin, and the equally severe man at her side was her husband, Logan.

Mila scoffed under her breath while her husband leveled me with his narrow gaze. "Where is the portal?" he asked, his voice low and thick with an accent.

I shook my head and waved my hand dismissively. "The portal I just came out of isn't the Las Vegas Portal." I was starting to feel like a track on repeat. "It was a Portal Burst"—controlled by Goddess—"that opened up and drew me in. When I came out, it shut after me." They didn't need to know the whole of what had happened. I couldn't tell them, anyway.

My words were met with surprise.

Blood Sword frowned. "How do you know it wasn't the portal we're looking for?"

I pursed my lips, trying to figure out how to proceed. In the end, I flat-out lied. "When I was coming back to Earth, the tunnel I went through was long. It wasn't instant, like the Gates. I could see there was another tunnel right next to me going to the same place I was. I think that's the actual Las Vegas Portal."

Tyson hummed over the noise of the other people. "Is that really how it works?"

"Yes," Kesstel backed me up. "That's exactly how it works."

Hm, I was mostly just making stuff up. The tunnel I'd walked through was too dark to see anything.

"I have a way of finding the Las Vegas Portal," I added. Another wave of disbelief rose up, causing me to frown. I simply talked over them, completely ignoring the questions that were practically hurled my way. "It's an ability only I have," I announced. Then I laid down my terms in the next breath. "But first, I'm taking a nap."

"I thought you didn't know how to Track," Charlie Moon exclaimed.

I looked away, feeling a little guilty. "It's not a Tracking ability. It's different. But I should be able to find the portal." I waved my hand, and the pile of orc weapons disappeared back into my Items Bag.

Violet, the armorer, let out a discouraged gasp. "Wait! What are you going to do with all of those?"

I paused, surprised by her question. I didn't really have a purpose for them. I'd collected them mostly because it was becoming a habit, and I wanted to make a statement for the Hunters. Okay, make a statement for Miranda. I guess I was petty like that.

But I didn't actually need them. They were terribly made, so I would never use any of them.

"About that." I took the Boss sword back from Kesstel, "I'm going to donate a couple to research, but I think I'll sell the rest." I tapped at the red blade with a finger before I stored it in my Items Bag. That particular blade and the lead red orc's weapon were mine.

Violet suddenly threw her hand in the air. "I'll pay a hundred thousand!"

Her words shocked me, and I was completely floored as other Hunters started yelling out higher prices. In seconds, there was an impromptu auction happening.

Hang on, I thought we were worried about the Las Vegas Portal. Where did this come from? "Um, I'm not going to do anything until we get back to Eden," I said to the excited Hunters.

Without waiting another second, I fled into the camper. All the noise outside was cut off once Kesstel's barrier shut over the trailer.

CHAPTER 36

By the time I woke up, it was dark outside. It felt good to wear normal clothes after being in my armor for so long. Granted, my armor was super comfortable, but it was nice to have a change of pace. Kesstel's barrier was still in place, so it was quiet. Quiet enough to pay attention to the very important item the orc king had dropped.

I sat cross-legged in my bed area, staring at the familiar, intricate circlet in my hands. It was the exact same one that every ruler in Vapria wore.

"How did the orc king drop this?" I asked Goddess. "King Terre was wearing it when he turned into a Blood Mist."

I don't know, Goddess answered back. *Technically, it should have been that Katharian who acquired it when he killed the Blood Mist form of my young King Terre.* There was a slight bitter tone to her words. And acceptance. *As much as it hurts my heart to see this circlet, I'm glad you are the one who has it now. You are, after all, the last of my children. It only stands to reason that you wear it. It's not only the symbol of my ruler—it's also the symbol of the leader of my warriors. Which you are.*

My lips curled in mocking amusement. "Well, I'm the only Warrior of Mist."

She chuckled. *That too.*

Gently, I rubbed my fingers along the smooth white gold lines of the circlet, feeling the bands of metal that bent and twisted around each other. Then I circled my finger around the fingernail-size diamond in the middle, where it would rest between the brows. The diamond was clear, but the middle swirled, like there was mist trapped inside the stone. Just like my kindjal.

I concentrated on the circlet, and a title bar popped up. [**Her Supremacy: The symbol of kings, the chosen official of Her Holiness. Significantly improves MP. +40 Magic.**]

"Her Will, Her Defiance, Her Supremacy," I slowly said the names of my kindjal, my armor, and now my circlet. "A matching set?"

Yes. You would have gotten the circlet when you got the other items, but I didn't have it. Her Will is an extension of me, so it returned to me when my people fell. Her Resistance was created anew for you when I merged the System into your body. Since the armor was created by me, the kindjal won't cut it. It took so much effort making armor with my depleted strength, I couldn't remake a circlet. After some time, I concluded it was better to simply improve ourselves instead of clinging to past relics, so I abandoned the idea of recreating the circlet. She paused. *But I am glad it was returned.*

Still, I didn't know how I felt about walking around with a crown on my head. There were hundreds of people who were better at being in the spotlight. Miranda, for one, who proudly showed off her circlets. Yes, multiple. She had a different one for every mage robe—and I hadn't seen a single repeat outfit yet.

I just hoped that people didn't think I was trying to one-up her when I showed up with this. I definitely wasn't princess material, but I couldn't *not* wear the circlet. Not only was it important to Goddess and who I was now, it was too good of an item to let rot in my Items Bag.

I felt Kesstel's presence and instinctively put away the circlet, like I was hiding a big secret. A second later, he softly knocked on the door beside my bed.

"Come in," I called.

He opened the door and stepped in. After the door shut, he stopped and examined me. "You only slept for eight hours. You can sleep longer."

I smiled and shook my head. "I'm good."

He nodded then sat on my bed. A moment later, he flopped onto his side and threw an arm over my legs as he half curled his body around me like a big cat. "They've decided not to look for the Las Vegas Portal until morning. Even though everyone here has good eyesight, they don't want to put themselves at an accidental disadvantage by rushing into a night battle."

The weight of his arm around me felt so natural.

Funny. Not too long ago, just being near him set my nerves on fire.

I leaned back on the wall and shifted to a more comfortable position. "That makes sense." Gently, I slid my fingers over the grooves that defined the muscles in his arm. "When you collapsed that portal, it caused a worldwide Gate Surge. But everything was normal when I came out."

"Nothing happened," he agreed with me. "I thought the parasite would throw a temper tantrum, but I was disappointed."

I wrinkled my nose. What a casual way to describe such a terrible thing. A giant planet looming over us, ready to eat the planet we were standing on, was nothing like a toddler. "I'm not. Gate Surges are bad—especially worldwide ones."

He shrugged. "That is true." But he didn't sound like he cared all that much. "I actually came back to ask about something else." He leaned up on an elbow so our faces were almost level. "Who did you bring back from the portal with you?"

So he really could feel Goddess. "How do you know?"

"I can't feel it all the time," Kesstel said, frowning, "but I can feel a presence around you occasionally. I thought it was a mistake at first, but there's definitely something attached to you. Whatever it is, it automatically triggered my attack mode when you first appeared." There was no relenting in his tone. He wasn't going to let me out of this conversation.

I'm going to tell him, I informed Goddess. *At this point, there isn't a reason not to.*

He is still a parasitic Boss, Goddess argued.

As soon as she spoke, the blue in Kesstel's eyes sharpened like blue diamond blades. His fingers flexed on my hip and released before he hurt me. "That. What is that?"

I trust him, I told Goddess. I reached out and brushed at the pale blond hair that fell on his forehead, using soft actions to relax him. "You've noticed that I get stronger when I kill a monster," I started.

He somewhat relaxed his body and stared at me with undivided attention. "Yes."

"Well, there's been someone helping me get stronger. She—not *it*—is the soul of the world the Warriors of Mist came from. Every time I destroy an energy crystal, she purifies the energy in it and uses it to make me stronger." The whole time I spoke, I kept waiting for my voice to suddenly cut out. It never happened. It felt so good to finally talk about what was happening to me; like a weight had been lifted off my shoulders. I was surprised that Goddess let me tell him. I had a feeling she wouldn't let me tell anyone else about her, but at least I could tell Kesstel. "When I went to the remnant of that world, she came back with me. Apparently, you can feel it when she talks to me."

His eyes flared in surprise. "You've been possessed by the spirit of a world?"

I paused, a little taken aback. "Ah, yes. I guess that's technically true. I never thought about it that way, but she is attached to me." I frowned, trying to think of the right way to explain it.

He scowled and sat up. "I don't like this. Having another being inside a body is dangerous."

I could say the same thing about him, Goddess responded in my mind. *There's no saying when this Katharian Boss will lose his mind.*

Kesstel frowned. "I take it she just spoke?"

I winced. God, having them argue with each other when they couldn't even communicate was complicated. And I didn't want to be the translator. "Ah, yes." I lifted my hands, trying to use them to get my point across. "But the fact is, she's not going to hurt me. And she's not actually possessing me. The System that's helping me get stronger is a part of her, so I'm more like an anchor for her soul, instead of a body she's using." Did that sound any better?

No, Goddess added unhelpfully.

"Whether or not you like it, it doesn't change the fact that she's attached to me and that she's the reason I'm stronger. She's the one who's taught me how to be a Warrior of Mist and everything else I know about fighting. I need her, and she needs me," I stated. "What's done is done."

Kesstel didn't look impressed. "Bringing her over here was probably not the best idea. I don't know how the parasite will react to another world's soul here. If I have such a strong reaction, I'm sure the parasite will, too."

I shook my head. "There wasn't much of a choice. She needed to move from that fragment world before she was destroyed. Just like you."

He paused, thinking about my last words. Then he shook his head, obviously still not pleased. "She didn't have to possess you, though. She could have attached her soul to a rock you could have kept in your pocket. After all, that's what she used to be attached to—a planet-size rock."

A rock! Goddess shrieked in my head. *My Vapria—a rock!*

I pressed a hand to my suddenly aching head. "Kesstel, try to be a little nicer. She did just lose her planet. She's also the reason you can go back to normal when you touch me. Her power is purifying the energy inside you, so you're benefiting from her, too. Besides, I like this configuration." I took a breath and tried to take control of the conversation. "Anyway! Goddess is going to help us find and defeat the parasitic planet. Even if you two don't like each other, you both have the same goals, and we're going to work together, regardless."

Kesstel scowled. "She doesn't like me?" There was a challenge in his tone, almost like he was asking what was there not to like.

I rolled my eyes and poked his knee next to mine. "Who likes being bad-mouthed like what you just did? Not to mention, there's the whole Blood Mist thing. Honestly, it's complicated between you two, and it puts me in an awkward situation because you're both important to me. And I need both of your help to save Earth. Please, get along."

Kesstel pursed his lips. "I don't like the idea of being spied on when I'm with you."

I don't have a reason to trust him alone with you, Goddess said. *You're the last person I have left. Everything I have, I'm betting on you. I can't comfortably leave you vulnerable to a Boss.*

I've already killed a Boss, I reasoned back. *It's not like I'm powerless.*

Yes, you killed one Boss. But truthfully, this Katharian is stronger than that disgusting creature. I can't even tell how strong he is. Even though you're an S, I don't have confidence that you can handle him in a fight, Goddess explained.

I frowned. One of the things I wanted the most was to stand on equal ground with Kesstel. Proof I had the right to be at his side. I thought I'd finally achieved that, but now, it suddenly felt so far away. If Goddess couldn't tell how strong he was, how many more steps would I have to take to reach him?

"You said," Kesstel muttered, "we were both important to you. But who is more important? That Goddess or me?" For once, he wasn't looking at my face. Instead, he stared at a spot just past my left shoulder. His fingers tightened on my hip.

I blinked in surprise at his expression. Not in a million years did I think I'd ever see him sulk. "Huh? I mean, you're both important in different ways, so I don't even know how to answer that question."

He shook his head. "But who's more important?"

His insistence baffled me. "Why?"

He reached out and snagged my hand, holding on like he was afraid I was going to float away if he let go. "Because you are my everything." He finally met my gaze. Even though he was still scowling slightly, his eyes were earnest, and his ears were pink on the top. "But I'm not your everything. I have to share you with your family, Miss Emma, and Miss Wilks. Even though I understand and try not to get in the way, it makes me . . . insecure." His mouth twitched, like he was swallowing a fly for admitting it. "The only time I feel you're focused wholly on me is when we're alone. And now, even that can't happen."

I stared at him, completely at a loss on what to say. But since he was baring his soul, it was only fair that I did too. "I'm sorry. I didn't mean to make you feel that way." I tapped my fingers on my thigh, wondering what to say. "I guess, I also feel a little insecure. I sometimes wonder . . . how you actually feel about me. If I'm your everything by choice. Or if that's a condition imposed on you because the energy I get from Goddess enables you to actually feel emotions. Like you don't actually like me, but you imprinted on me because I was the only option."

It was something that had been on my mind a lot as soon as I noticed our relationship was getting closer and closer. Especially since I was more than halfway . . . in love with this man. But it was scary, thinking that I was falling for an illusion created by something he couldn't control. It was pitiful, and I didn't want to be that person.

Suddenly, I couldn't look into his face. I didn't want to see the moment he realized that what I said was true.

His fingers brushed through my loose hair, tucking it behind my ear so it didn't block my face. "It's true that right now, I can only feel emotions around you. But I met many people before this condition happened, and I've met many people since. And I've never felt like this for any of them. I can't even say exactly what it is about you that draws me. Just everything about you is wonderful, from your bravery to your absolute loyalty for your loved ones, and it just feels right when we're together."

My heart stuttered to a stop then pounded a million miles per hour, and a blush burned my cheeks.

His finger hooked under my chin and tilted my face up so I could look into his intense blue eyes. "One thing I know is, my feelings aren't forced. If I wasn't naturally attracted to you, I would have continued to treat you like a friend, like in the beginning. Somewhere along the way, those feelings changed to more. It would be easier if those were still my feelings. I wouldn't be going in circles in my mind, wanting to be closer but worried about frightening you away."

His thumb brushed across my lips, soft as a butterfly. "It took me so long to love someone, I just want to be selfish and hide you away so no one can take you away from me. But I'm trying to hold back because I know

I can't do that. I just want, whenever we are alone, for you to concentrate only on me. I want to be the only one in your eyes, if only for a moment."

He leaned down and gently rubbed his lips on mine.

My mind exploded into fireworks. All my attention was focused on his warm lips. The feel of his large hand cradling my head. The feel of his heart pounding his chest under my palm. I barely even heard him when he whispered, "Please?" against my lips.

"Yes," I responded and kissed him back.

CHAPTER 37

——

Blood Sword looked surprised when he opened his door and saw me standing there in the dark. Then he caught sight of Kesstel beside me, standing just out of the light glowing from inside his camper. "Noble. Miss Devhro. I didn't think I'd have the pleasure of seeing you again until morning."

Was that a polite way to say it was midnight and he wanted to go to bed? Since he wasn't in pajamas and I could tell there were several other people in his camper, I decided I didn't have to be so polite. "I need to talk to you about something. Some information I found while I was in the portal."

Blood Sword stiffened in surprise. "Is this something all Hunters need to hear?"

I nodded. "Everyone should know about it."

Kesstel shrugged. "You can decide after you hear what she says."

I scowled at him. "They should all hear."

"It's not the first time you've tried," he reminded me. "They didn't believe you then; they won't now."

Blood Sword pressed his lips together, and he nodded over his shoulder. "Why don't you come inside, and we'll talk? I hope you don't mind that Laurel and Jonovan are here, too." He stepped to the side and motioned us in.

The camper wasn't big. Even though Blood Sword was technically the head of the whole expedition and the go-between for the other cities' Hunters, he still only had a ten-foot camper. As nice as it was, with all the bells and whistles, it was still only intended for one person. Five people was simply four too many. The small table was already taken by the two healers, the mugs in their hands releasing a nutty coffee aroma. Blood Sword shifted around me and Kesstel, then offered us a cup. When we declined, he picked up the third mug from the table and sat on the twin bed next to it.

I glanced at the cups. Apparently, they didn't intend to sleep any time soon. Then again, did caffeine affect top-ranked Hunters like a normal human? Well, no. With their enhanced bodies, a Hunter would have to down a lot of coffee to get a zing. Even most medicines, which were very rarely needed, had to be adjusted according to a Hunter's rank.

Jonovan nodded a welcome. "Evening. Or is it time to say morning yet?"

Kesstel shrugged a shoulder and leaned on his right hip. "Still evening. Some people should be sleeping still."

I pursed my lips and chose not to respond. Kesstel was still a little disgruntled that I broke up our cuddling to come talk to another man—specially to talk about a subject he felt was pointless to warn people of.

Laurel smiled and waved. "Hello, Noble. It's nice to finally talk to you, Miss Devhro. I've heard a lot about you lately."

I smiled back. "Ah, yes. Hi."

Was it just a healer thing to have calm eyes that looked like they could see into your head?

On second thought, no, I'd met too many other healers who didn't—especially Pink from the Rainbow Brigade. But Laurel and Jonovan looked like they were cut from the same cloth, with the same steadfast expression. Just seeing them reminded me of the bottle of Dreamer cure in my Items Bag. I couldn't wait to get back to Garden City and hug my mom again.

"Since you're here," Blood Sword said, "I want to ask some questions first."

I glanced at him and nodded. "As long as I get to say what I want to say, too."

"Fair enough." He nodded before looking into my eyes. "When did you Reawaken?"

I blinked and habitually shifted close enough to feel the heat from Kesstel's chest. I wasn't trying to hide that I was stronger; I just didn't expect Blood Sword to shoot so straight.

"No E could do what you've done," Blood Sword explained and motioned to the table with the healers. "Jonovan has also disclosed to me and Laurel that you are stronger."

Kesstel stiffened and tilted his head to the side, staring at the healer. "It's against the law for a healer to disclose another Hunter's personal information without permission."

Jonovan frowned and nodded, admitting his mistake. "Yes. It's a breach in the Personal Information Safety Act, but I felt it was important for the leaders of this mission to know. That way, they can plan and act accordingly. I hope you will forgive me, Miss Jynn."

I nodded, understanding. Even if it was against the law, the Hunter's Association wouldn't do anything to the second-best healer in Eden. At most, he would pay a fine and get a slap on the wrist. Since he didn't go around telling everyone in sight, I wasn't too concerned. After all, no E could have walked out of a portal.

"It's okay," I responded to Jonovan then looked at Blood Sword. "I actually Reawakened a while ago," I admitted. "But my Reawakening was a little different from most Hunters. I didn't get my strength all at once. It's slowly increased over time." I paused. "And I'm still getting stronger."

Laurel hissed in a surprised breath, and Jonovan stiffened. Blood Sword frowned, his thick brows pulling together. "How strong are you right now?"

"S ranked," I responded, bubbles of excitement popping in my chest. It still didn't feel real. Hell, nothing that had happened in the last couple days did.

"And still getting stronger," Laurel said in amazement.

"Good Lord," Blood Sword muttered under his breath. "How is that possible?"

I shook my head. "It's a unique thing that only I can do. I can't even tell you why or how it happened; I just know it does." That was about as specific as I could get.

"It happened that time you were unconscious for four days, didn't it?" Jonovan asked. He frowned and twisted his mug in his long fingers. "That's about when you stopped coming to get healed."

I nodded. "Yes. I didn't want to tell anyone because I didn't want to become a lab rat." And I couldn't tell them, anyway. Nothing good would have happened with people constantly following me around.

Blood Sword slowly nodded. "Yes. I can see why you came to that conclusion." He glanced at Jonovan. "No offense, but it wouldn't be the first time medical scientists have ignored human rights when trying to discover the secrets of Hunter evolution."

Laurel shrugged. "True. But those were mostly criminals. What human rights did they have? Still, I know several crazies who would love to get their hands on someone who keeps getting stronger. Maybe they could create something that could improve everyone." She looked at me, considering.

Kesstel rested his arm on my shoulders. "But no one else will know about it outside of this camper. Right?" There was no asking in his tone. It was a flat-out order, accompanied with a warning flicker of his aura.

Laurel smiled as if he'd told a bad joke. "She's an S now. Even without you there, who is going to make her do anything against her will? I think she was wise to hide until now."

Jonovan nodded his agreement. "Even with laws in place, the number one rule of Eden is the strong are always right. If she doesn't want to be experimented on, she needs to be strong enough so they can't make her." He paused. "As it is, we'd already decided we weren't going to disclose anything about her Reawakening outside of the three of us."

Blood Sword took a drink. "But she still should change her registration information when she gets home."

I shrugged. "I was already planning on that." Unfortunately, it meant I was going to be homeless until I found new housing. Since so many Hunters had shown interest in the orc weapons I'd picked up, I was confident I'd be able to get into a nice house now. But until everything was settled, I would be caught in limbo.

"Now," I started before anyone else could talk. "There's something I want to talk to you all about." I took a breath. "Earth is dying. In fact, it's almost dead. When that happens, the whole planet is going to collapse into a cloud of dust, and we're all going to die." Since Blood Sword had played straight ball with me, it was only fair I threw it back at him. And this way, there was no way they could misinterpret me.

My words were met with silence.

"You said . . . you found this information in the portal you were just in?" Laurel was the first to react. Her words were hesitant and slow.

I nodded. It was close enough to the truth, at least. "Yes. The Gates are controlled by a giant interdimensional monster that's trying to eat Earth. That's what all this is about. The Gates, the monsters, the Hunters, the Dreamers—*everything* is caused by this monster. And it's winning. Big time."

It was the same message I'd put in the Hunter forum every month, only to get kicked out for thirty days again and again—after waves of people hurled abuse at me. I was starting to think there were people who were counting down the days with me just so they could dance the same steps online. This time, I hoped that something positive might happen because I was talking to influential people face-to-face. The Association's President and Mr. Wilks had shut me down before I could get to the main problem, but maybe I could get one of these three to understand if I started with the main threat first.

I was doomed to be disappointed.

Jonovan frowned. "Miss Jynn, I thought I warned you away from—"

"This doesn't have anything to do with the cult!" Agitation shot through my veins in an instant. I wasn't one to lose my temper—in fact, I think I let go of too many things for my own good—but in the face of the same thing over and over again, I was tired of accommodating people. "It absolutely has nothing to do with that horrible Epson. I should know! I was the one who provided the clues to take him down. He was a murdering, thieving con man. That's it."

Jonovan stiffened and frowned. Did he remember the clue box I'd left outside his office door? And how they never did find the person who ruined the last assembly the cultists held?

Fog rolled over the floor, several inches thick, and curled around everyone's feet—and with it, my S-ranked aura. The three S Hunters were fine, but Jonovan's face paled. Still, I didn't try to rein it in. If this was what it took for them to take me seriously, I'd use it.

I motioned to the sky, trying to indicate the invisible ginormous monster up there. "But this, *this* is different. It's true! *I've seen it with my own eyes*. The earthquake that happened when the Las Vegas Portal opened was part of an attack which caused Earth's soul to fall unconscious. In literally less than a year, the planet we are standing on will shatter like a glass ball, and *we'll all die*."

Turning into a monster was nearly the equivalent of dying. Kesstel was a miracle, and that might be one reason why Goddess resented him, too. If he could stay human, why couldn't any of her people?

Kesstel wrapped his arm around my shoulder and leaned close to my ear. "Calm down first," he whispered.

I frowned, then leaned into his warm chest and took a breath to settle the emotions raging in my heart. The mist receded, returning to me. The three Hunters watched it with shock on their faces. Unfortunately, the thing they were most interested in was my mist, not my words. Damn.

"Earth's soul fell unconscious?" Kesstel asked, the only one who took my words seriously.

I nodded stiffly. "Yes."

He hummed under his breath. "That's unfortunate."

Impulsively, I grabbed his shirt and pulled him down until he had to look at me. "No, that's the wrong thing to say. I need you to help me save Earth. I can't do it alone. I need you. This is your home, too, because it's my home." I stared into his blue eyes. "Please. Help me."

At first, he was quiet, but then he sighed. A small, losing smile touched his face. "Okay. I don't believe anything will change, but I could never deny you when you finally ask me for something. Like you said, it's my home, too."

A warm, sweet feeling spread in my chest, making me feel light as air. It was the first time he accepted that Earth could be his home. The first time he said he was going to fight for this planet. Maybe he wouldn't try to make finding the parasitic planet a suicide mission. If we were alone, I would have hugged him. Only, I wasn't daring enough yet.

Instead, I leaned forward and rested my forehead over his beating heart. "Thank you."

"You honestly believe this," Blood Sword muttered, seriously observing me.

I smoothed out the wrinkles in Kesstel's shirt and turned back to the other three. "It's all true. I've been trying to tell people for months, but no one will believe me."

"Still, think of how insane this sounds. World souls and interdimensional monsters?" Jonovan said. "It sounds like something from a book or what crazy people would say."

"Thirty years ago, did you believe someone would be able to heal a broken leg with magic?" I challenged him. All three of these Hunters were normal people before the Gates appeared, but Jonovan was the only one whose history I knew a little about. "Thirty years ago, if someone told you that one day you'd be fighting monsters in the skeleton of Las Vegas, you would have thought they were crazy. Now look around you." I opened my arms, inviting them to do just that.

His lips twitched, but he didn't deny it.

"The reason that is true today is because of the interdimensional monster that's attacking Earth." I was so used to calling it a parasite, it was odd calling it something else. But I had a feeling that *interdimensional monster* would have a greater impact on these Hunters. "It's filling Earth with monsters and energy crystals from its own body to weaken Earth enough for it to eat our planet's soul."

"Now you're saying that energy crystals are part of the problem, too," Blood Sword said. "You know that nearly everything on Earth is powered by them, don't you?"

I nodded. "Yes. But that doesn't make them any safer."

Kesstel tapped his fingers on my shoulder as he added, "You call it clean energy, but what it is doing is releasing the para—interdimensional monster's magic into Earth's atmosphere and choking the soul of the planet." He shrugged. "I told you all this seven years ago, and you didn't take it seriously then. I've always found it funny how determined you all are to destroy your planet."

Laurel pursed her lips and asked Kesstel, "What were you going to call it before you changed the name?"

"I've always thought of it like a parasite," Kesstel admitted. "Interdimensional monster might be accurate, but it acts like a parasite."

I nodded.

The three Hunters looked at each other. Various degrees of emotions were displayed on their faces—disbelief, concern, caution, confusion. None of them looked sold, but they weren't completely rejecting my words, either.

Blood Sword frowned. "There's a lot that you've said, and we're going to need some time to process. I'm . . . not saying you're wrong, per se. But there's a lot that needs to be thought through."

I nodded. "I understand." It was a small step, but I'd take it.

Blood Sword put his obviously cold coffee on the table. "Then I think we'll end the talk here and say good night. We're planning on looking for the Las Vegas Portal at eight in the morning. Get some rest until then."

Kesstel and I bid them all goodnight and left.

As we walked through the dark to our camper, I reached for Kesstel's hand. Just before our skin touched, I noticed two people hanging out just outside the inner ring of campers.

I looked over to see Penny and Mark step out around a trailer.

Penny hooked her thumbs in her black studded double belt and nodded over her shoulder. "Let's talk. Alone."

CHAPTER 38

K esstel grabbed my hand, intending to walk away. "Let's go."
I pursed my lips and put on the brakes. "Just a second. This won't take long." Did I really want to talk to her? Well, a part of me did. Mostly, I wanted to know what happened after I left them on the parking garage.

I rubbed my thumb over the back of Kesstel's hand to appease him, then let go and followed Penny and Mark away from the campers.

A week ago, I might have been a little nervous to be alone with these two A Hunters, but I didn't have the same reservation now. Maybe it was sad—just one sip of power, and I was already getting drunk on the confidence that strength gave me. I just needed to make sure I didn't go overboard on it. No matter what, I wanted to stay me.

The two night watch Hunters didn't say anything as we left the ring of campers and walked closer to the silhouettes of the ruined houses around the dead golfing green, till we were far enough away that the average A Hunter wouldn't overhear us if we talked softly.

What was left of the dead vegetation crunched under my shoes, and even though my body was nearly weatherproof now, I could still feel the dry heat the clear night sky couldn't kill off. I thought deserts were supposed to get cold at night, but I guess the ground got so hot during the day that it still couldn't cool off now. Yuck.

Penny and Mark stopped walking and faced me. Mark was slightly scowling, an expression I knew well on his face, but Penny was simply staring at me with open curiosity.

She planted a hand on her hip and leaned to the side. It was the first time I'd seen her without her usual high ponytail and thick black mascara around her almond eyes. It made her look a little more approachable and less fantasy gothic. "The other day at the hotel. You were there, and us three were the only ones who made it out alive. Did you save us?" she asked in her thick accent.

I pursed my lips, debating on answering. I could say yes and hold it over their heads. They were highly ranked and highly regarded in a strong guild, so I could get some good benefits from them. At the same time, it was also admitting I was there and might know how Blake died. Which was practically saying I did it. Which I did and didn't do. Right now, there was a lot of gray area I could work around. If I admitted to anything, I'd be pulled one way or the other.

"We just wanted to say thanks," Penny said, not waiting for me to answer.

I blinked at her in surprise. "Ah, you're welcome?" I puffed out a breath and shook my head, completely unsure of where to go now. "Is that really why you called me out here? To thank me? I thought you hated me?"

Mark tsked under his breath. "To say that we hate you is overkill."

"We'd have to care enough to hate you," Penny added, as if that made a difference.

Well, it was nice to know I'd been tormented for months by the whims of someone who didn't actually care.

Penny waved a hand. "Both of us should have died against that giant spider. All we know is that we both passed out in the battle—which should have killed us—but when we woke up, we were safe below and surrounded by our team. Blake and Jed were dead, and your body couldn't be found. When you came back alive, we could only assume you did it. Although I don't know how you got us off the building." She folded her arms, as if everything was a fact she was a hundred percent sure about. "We might have a messed-up history, but we are grateful to you, anyway."

"Did you kill him? Blake, I mean," Mark asked.

I frowned at him. "How about we do an info exchange?" I suggested. "You want info from me, and I want some from you. Let's exchange."

The other two glanced at each other. I could tell they were having a full wordless conversation with just their eyes.

A moment later, Penny nodded to the side. "Sure."

"Blake got caught by the spiders," I said, not going into details. I didn't wait for them to pick at the plot holes before I fired off a question that had plagued me for months. "Why did you send so many hitmen after me? If you didn't care, why didn't you stop after the first?"

Mark's brows rose on his forehead. "The one who cared was Blake. How many did he send after you?"

I frowned. "A handful or so. You don't actually know? I thought you two were his henchmen or something."

Penny scoffed. "Babysitters. The term was *babysitters*."

Mark scowled at her and cut in. "She means retainers. If we had been in charge of it, you would have died the first time someone came your way. We aren't idiotic enough to use junkies instead of professionals. We knew Blake was trying to sneak something; we just didn't know what until a week ago. He was using his own pocket money to hide it from President Price, so the ass went cheap."

I stared at them. Was this really the way they should talk about someone they knew really well who had just died? "What did I ever do to him, anyway? We barely even talked. Why did he fixate on me so much?"

Mark tucked his thumbs into his pockets and shrugged like he didn't care. "Blake got everything he ever wanted. Anything that didn't go his way, it disappeared. First, you were an E who had the audacity to talk in front of him, then you had the audacity to not die when he wanted you dead. And then his own cousin, who gave Blake everything he ever wanted, started to cater to you. Why wouldn't he hate you?"

Was he dissing Blake or me or everything in general?

"Nearly tore apart his room when I told him you were still alive," Penny added. "How did you get out of that portal, anyway? It closed right after we came out. That's what I've always wanted to ask you."

My lips pursed as I tilted my head to the side. "I don't know. I actually died in there, then woke up in the Eden hospital. That's it."

"The hell?" Mark muttered in surprise.

Penny elbowed his side. "Told ya she was weird."

I could say the same thing about them. "Here's another question for you. Why did you even follow Blake if you didn't like him?" It wasn't like they'd been singing his praises this whole time, but they sure had been dedicated to doing his dirty work.

Penny shrugged. "It paid hella good. Since my parents are trying to repopulate the world by themselves even though they're broke, I have a lot of mouths to feed and bodies to clothe." She bumped Mark with her elbow. "He's just killing time and getting rich in the process."

I felt someone approaching seconds before I heard a deep male voice say, "Apparently, I paid you too much."

I turned my head as President Price walked up to us, his body movements tight and his hand fisted at his side. This was the first time he wasn't either in a suit or armor in front of me—he wore ball shorts and a shirt—but he still looked ready to fight.

Mark arched his brows. "I think we were paid the right amount, President. We were the only ones who lasted over the years. That's merit enough. It's not like we killed Blake."

Penny's relaxed stance stiffened.

"Then why is he dead and you aren't?" President Price demanded. "I paid you to make sure he didn't stop breathing before you." He glared at the two people in his guild. I couldn't tell if he was actually grieving or not. Maybe he was just an angry griever. "What are you going to do now that your cash cow is dead? Did you team up with this insect to make your life easier?"

My mouth twitched, and I glared at him. Was I keeping my aura so reined in that he didn't notice I was stronger than him?

Mark's brows pulled together. "We nearly died trying to keep him alive, President. We can't be responsible for what happens when we're unconscious."

Price snorted. "Excuses." He glared at me. "Then you tell me, how did my cousin die? These two said you were there. Why are you alive and not him? Tell me what you did, and I won't drag your little friends or family down with you." Everything about his bloodthirsty countenance screamed he was lying.

My eyes widened as my heart twisted painfully. In all this time, no one had ever threatened my family like that. Fury boiled in me so fast, all I could do was ugly laugh at his disgusting joke.

"Ah, you wanna know what happened?" I was so angry, my words were as loose as my emotions—angry enough to lie just to stab salt into Price's wounds. "After his babysitters were gone, Blake cried in fear and ran away. It was his own fault he didn't watch where he was going and fell into the hole with all the spiders below."

President Price's beefy fists tightened until they visibly shook. "Bullshit."

I gave an exaggerated shrug, as if I didn't care. "Believe what you want. But he was perfectly alive before he fell into that hole." The fact that I was the one who put him in there was going to come with me to the grave. I hoped that it burned Price for the rest of his life. My eyes narrowed maliciously. "I find it ironic, though."

When I didn't finish my thought process, President Price spat out, "What?"

"Do you know what spiders eat?" My lips curled up as I tilted my chin up. "Insects."

President Price's narrowed eyes flared in fury. With a roar, he punched at my face like a freight train.

I grabbed his fist with my right hand and directed his inertia to the side. He flew past me, and I twisted and kicked his back—hard. The whole exchange lasted a split second. Price flew across the ground for nearly thirty feet before he hit the ground and skidded another twenty feet. My toes tapped on the ground, and I shot after him, tailing behind until his back smacked into a house with enough force to crack the wall.

I landed crouched over him, one foot on his burly chest and the other on the ground at his hip. He still hadn't caught up on what happened when I rested the tip of my kindjal against his trachea. If he moved more than a centimeter, he was going to bleed.

His Adam's apple bobbed as he stared up at me in shock and disbelief.

There was no mirth at all in my face as I leaned over him and released my aura. Thick mist settled around us like a weighted blanket, smothering him. President Price's square face turned ghostly pale in the moonlight. "If you ever threaten my people again, I'll rip you apart piece by piece," I stated. "Any peep, any mistreatment, if I hear anything at all, even if you didn't do it, I'm coming after you. You and your bitchy cousin have made my life hard enough, and I'm itching to retaliate."

Unfortunately, Emma was in his guild, and if I killed him now, it would throw off the balance between the guilds. I didn't know how it would affect Emma, since she had a signed contract with Stone Mace. Some contracts could be years long or face a heavy fine if broken.

Price licked his lips as if he was trying to think of something to say.

My eyes flared as I felt an attack coming from behind me—but it wasn't aimed at me. I didn't move a centimeter as a familiar sword shot past, the wind from it ruffling my hair.

Price screamed in shocked pain. He obviously was trying not to move, but even so, the tip of my kindjal dug into his throat enough to draw blood. The bottom half of his right arm flopped to the ground, cut off at the elbow.

CHAPTER 39

The blue steel sword that cut off President Price's arm embedded into the wall and sent fissures all the way to the roof, raining down bits of stucco dust.

Price kept screaming. Whether it was from shock or pain, he was loud.

Mark and Penny swore in surprise behind me. They must have followed us after I kicked President Price across the golf green.

Standing up, I turned to face Kesstel as he walked past Mark and Penny. The two Hunters jolted in surprise, as if they hadn't even realized he was there.

I nodded at the arm on the ground. "A little exaggerated, don't you think?"

"He attacked my person, so I removed the part that offended me. I think I went a little too easy on him, don't you think?" Kesstel tossed the question back at me before turning to the whimpering Price. Casually, Kesstel reached out and jerked his weapon out of the wall, leaving a considerable hole. With a controlled flick of his wrist, the edge of the pretty bastard sword rested on Price's cheek, indenting the flesh but not cutting. Yet.

Price froze, not even breathing to keep from losing more than just an arm.

"Jynn is too nice for her own good. She gave you a warning. I'm not as nice. You might as well bury yourself with your cousin when you get home, while you still have the money to do so." His oppressive aura leaked out, targeting Price like a drill and making his already pale face ghastly. Kesstel flicked his wrist again and smacked the flat of his pattern-welded blade against Price's head. The president toppled to the ground, disoriented.

Kesstel stood up and looked at me. "Done?" His sword disappeared.

I nodded and glanced at the two standing like statues behind us. "Done."

Mark finally woke up and pulled an elastic tourniquet band out of his Items Bag. With a stony face, he dropped to the ground next to the bleeding man and tied the band around what remained of the bloody limb.

Penny walked over and looked down at the arm lying on the ground. "Should I take that with us?" There was no urgency in her expression. Either she had too much experience with scenes like this, or she just didn't care. Both were possible.

Price gasped for breath and moaned in pain. "Get me . . . a healer!"

There were two healers I knew who could grow Price's arm back. I'd personally watched Jonovan grow back body parts—without him, I would have an odd number of digits. And I knew Healer Laurel also could; I just hadn't seen her at work yet. There were probably other healers in the camp who could as well, or else they wouldn't be on the expedition.

Mark hoisted the moaning Price over his shoulder. "Let's go," he said to Penny. He paused to glance at me before they walked away.

I watched them go. "What are you going to say when Blood Sword gets mad at you?" I looked up at Kesstel. "Maiming each other is against expedition rules," I reminded him, feeling completely hypocritical. My kick to Price was passable, since it wasn't enough to seriously damage him. And Blake . . . well, there weren't any witnesses, so that was that. Kesstel cutting off someone's arm was entirely different.

He smirked and took my hand. "Price attacked first. I was simply defending my partner. There are witnesses to validate the order of things. What are they going to do to me?" He guided me to walk side by side back to our camper. "None of them can beat me. Or will they try to ground me? They've been hounding me for days to act. They aren't going to make me sit on the sidelines now."

I hummed under my breath. Everything he said was true. "I did have the situation under control, you know."

"Yes. But I was still too angry to hold back." He brushed his thumb against the back of my hand, appeasing me just like I did earlier to him.

My heart skipped a beat. In order to distract myself, I glanced up at him. "Are you really going to take away his money?"

"Yes." There was no hesitation in Kesstel's voice. "You should have told me he was the one who kept sending those killers after you."

I shrugged. "It was actually his cousin, and that's not a problem any-more," I said before following with my other thought. "Do you even have the ability to attack Price like that? It's a lot different than just stabbing him with a sword." I couldn't imagine being able to bankrupt a person, especially someone who owned a guild. It sounded way too complicated.

Kesstel smirked, his eyes narrowing. "I've been on Earth for nearly eight years now. I have connections and subordinates set up where I need them. You can't stand on top of the masses if you're only strong in one aspect." He glanced up at the half moon over our heads. "I didn't know how long I was going to be here, and I wasn't about to let myself fall into an uncomfortable position again. I'd learned from past mistakes. I agreed to babysit Miss Wilks for that period of time, but it also allowed me to infiltrate the Association's structure. All information that goes into the Association also crosses my desk. Knowledge is power, and the right power can smother another person. Easily."

My fingers tightened around his. I knew one world had attempted to experiment on him when they found out he was an alien. Were the other times that hard, too? "Did you have a hard time in the other worlds?"

"Not really," Kesstel admitted. "It's easier to accept things when you don't have emotional reactions. Since I couldn't get mad or feel betrayed, it didn't affect me as much. It was just another thing happening to me. But once was enough. If I didn't learn, I'd be an idiot." He made it all sound so easy. From setting up a network in the Association to jumping around from planet to planet.

I smiled in defeat. "I don't think I could do what you do. Not in a mil-lion years."

Kesstel stepped forward and opened the door to our camper before motioning me inside. "Obviously. You haven't been taught to. I spent my life in Kathar learning how to gather and manage information, where to apply the right pressure to get what you want." After I stepped in, he followed me up and shut the door. "It's actually easier here, since every Hunter falls over themselves when they realize I'm an S. Because strength is key in Eden, I don't have to worry about opposing political parties and making sure that everything is balanced for the economy to run smoothly."

"But there *are* politics here," I reminded him. "There's a balance in the guilds' power. Even though the ranking changes often, it doesn't mean that it isn't important. And if one guild gets wiped out suddenly, hundreds of Hunters will be affected. And the people who are attached to them." I sat on my bed and looked up at him. "Emma belongs to President Price's guild."

Kesstel's mouth twitched in displeasure. After a second, he sighed and leaned against the cabinet. He crossed his arms in front of his body and stared me down. "So you're saying you don't want me to do anything to President Price. After everything that he's done."

I paused. My fingers drummed on my thigh while I thought. "No, it's not really that. I'd love to see Price get his just deserts. I just don't want the Stone Mace guild to fall apart. Emma's in a good group, but I don't know what will happen if their guild collapses. I'm sure they'll try to stay together; unfortunately, that might not work out if they join another guild as a team. And I hear that forming a guild is tough. Small guilds don't get the opportunities that large ones do."

"Noted." Kesstel held out his hand, and a small bag of dried cherries appeared in his palm.

"What does that mean?" I asked as I took the cherries. I popped one in my mouth and paused before slowly chewing the tart fruit leather. "I like the sweet ones better," I muttered, eating some more.

"Tart ones are better before bed." Kesstel took some out for him and started to eat them. "It can help with sleep."

Oh, right. It was still bedtime, even though I didn't feel tired. That's what I got for sleeping the day away. "When did you become such a dietary guru?" He spent more attention and money on my snacks than I did on my whole day's worth of food. Even after I'd said I didn't need it, he still kept it up.

"Since I met you," Kesstel replied, completely deadpan. "I didn't know it was so hard to keep a young lady healthy until I met you."

I couldn't help but laugh. "I didn't know someone could care so much about my health until I met you." I chewed some more cherries. "Were you like this with your family too?"

He paused then shook his head. "Not until the end. My father was that way with my mother—he tried every day to spoil her rotten until she got mad. I used to sit back and mentally shake my head at him, thinking that he was being silly. But I understand why he did it now." His eyes softened, and a smile curled his lips as he obviously relived the moment. "It wasn't until I started losing family members one at a time and resources became scarce that I began to pay more attention to my family's physical well-being. When it was just my youngest brother and I left, I realized I'd be alone if he was gone. I tried my best to make sure he was as healthy as me and kept him out of harm's way so I wouldn't lose him too. In the end, I watched him turn into a monster before my very eyes. And when an intelligent species from the next world cut him down, I didn't even flinch because I couldn't control my own body. Couldn't feel the emotional pain. Even though a part of me was screaming in my mind."

My heart hurt listening to his story. I didn't even know how I'd handle something like that happening. Then again, he couldn't control how he reacted, anyway. I set my dried cherries aside and stood up. My arms wrapped around his waist, and I leaned my head on his chest, listening to his heart under my ear.

"You're not going to lose me," I said quietly. "You don't have to be alone now." I paused. "Neither of us do, now that I'm strong enough to follow wherever you go. I'm going to be there for the rest of your life, and you're going to be there for the rest of mine." I smiled up at him. "Deal?"

He smiled softly and kissed my forehead. "Deal."

"Ah," I muttered as I thought of something. "We're not going to Siberia. I hope you haven't bought any snow gear yet."

"No?" Kesstel shifted and sat us down on my bed.

I leaned against his side. "No. Goddess said that there isn't a portal open to the parasite right now."

"Is that so?" As soon as he heard her name, Kesstel looked less than pleased. "Does she have an idea when one will open?"

I shook my head. "But she should be able to tell when it does. When her world collapsed, a giant Scorpion Man monster appeared through a portal. Then her world fell apart," I said thinking. "Maybe the portal to the parasite doesn't open up until right before the world collapses."

"A giant Scorpion Man?" he muttered slowly, as if thinking of something.

I noticed the change immediately. "Does that ring a bell?"

He blinked out of his thoughts. "Yes. A giant Scorpion Man appeared before one other world I was in fell apart."

"Hmm. Maybe there's a connection?"

"Maybe," Kesstel mused. "What it means is that we can't attack the parasite until right before Earth falls, if that's when the portal between the two opens up." He met my eyes. "Which is a bad thing for Earth. After Earth is damaged to that degree, it might not ever recover, even if we kill off the parasite." He paused. "If the parasite is dead and Earth still collapses, we won't be able to travel to another planet to survive."

CHAPTER 40

The morning alarm in my System went off at 8:00 a.m.

The first thing I was aware of was the feeling of a man's arms around my body. I couldn't help but frown, disoriented. Even though this was my bed, it didn't feel like it because I was pressed against Kesstel's bare chest.

I shifted, trying to get out of his hold.

His muscles instantly tightened, resisting my movements, then he opened his arms and let me sit up. His eyes cracked open lazily. "Good morning."

I sat up and adjusted my large pajama shirt, which had slipped to show my left shoulder. "Good morning." Even though we weren't on an intimate level, just waking up in the same bed was enough to blow my mind. Morning light streamed through the open divider curtain, perfectly illuminating the scene. My face was hot as I looked away, and my finger drummed against my knee, trying to relieve the awkward energy bubbling in me.

The corner of Kesstel's lips curled up in amusement. He reached out and brushed my hair behind my ear. I jumped and shot to my feet, and he grabbed my arm to keep me from hitting my head on the low ceiling. A full smile spread across his face as he patted my head like I was a puppy before he stood up and stretched, his pajama pants riding low on his hips.

My face went up in flames at the sight of the perfect male body I'd been snuggled against all night long. With a quick movement, I swiped the curtain closed. From the other side of the divider, I could hear Kesstel chuckle under his breath. Stupid jerkface.

While I waited for my heart to slow down, I changed into my dark-gray under armor.

On the other side of the curtain, I could hear the sounds of Kesstel moving around and getting ready for the day. Not long after, the door to the camper opened. "I'll be waiting outside," he called, then the door shut.

I peeked out of the curtain at the empty camper. How many women would love to be in this position with Kesstel? And yet I was too embarrassed to look at him properly. I hadn't had any trouble last night when he grabbed me and we lay down to sleep. It was just seeing him in the morning light which changed things. I was so lame.

After using the bathroom, I put on my black leather armor. As soon as I was done strapping my hip satchel on, a faint glowing oval appeared at chest level. The circlet, Her Supremacy, formed in the light.

Instinctively, I reached out and caught it as the light faded and gravity took hold of the crown. I held the circlet and turned it this way and that. It had changed. Some of the intricate twisted metal had been removed, and the misty gem which rested between the brows was smaller. It was still beautiful, but a little plainer.

I thought you'd be more comfortable with something simpler, Goddess explained.

"Oh," I said slowly. It was true I didn't like to stick out, but . . . "Can you change it back? I appreciate you thinking about me, but this is an important symbol of your people. It's looked the same since it was made, and it should stay that way."

Yes. I couldn't see her, but I could feel her warm approval in that one word.

The circlet glowed again and changed back to its original version.

I took a deep breath and put it on. I shouldn't be nervous putting on a crown, but it felt so official—and, well, dorky—putting it on.

As soon as it touched me, the rest of my armor started to glow. I looked down in surprise as the design changed. Before, my armor had been dark colors and more low-key in appearance, functional and somewhat feminine. It stayed the same shape, but a silver design which matched the circlet appeared over the wide sections down my sides, on the rims of my boots and arm bracers, and on the triangular half skirt around my hips. Other silver accents appeared on the chest plate and shoulder guards.

"Cool," I muttered, examining my new armor. "Maveric is going to flip. I bet I go through another round of him trying to weasel out who the maker is."

You could just tell him you made it yourself, Goddess suggested.

I laughed. "Yeah, no. No one in their right mind would believe that." Finally ready, I went outside.

Like usual, our camper was not in the party's circle and was faced away from the others. Even the noise was cut off because of the barrier Kesstel had placed around our unit. It was like we were the only ones on this dead golf course.

Kesstel sat on one of two chairs set up facing the abandoned houses, holding two plates with easy to-go breakfast food. His eyes locked on me, a frown on his brow. "Ah, that's what I felt," he said as he examined my new armor. He stood up and walked over. After passing me a plate, he ghosted his fingers over the circlet without actually touching it. "It looks beautiful on you."

I shifted the plate in my hands. "Normally, I don't wear this kind of thing, but it's important to Goddess."

Kesstel slipped his hand down the hair of my ponytail. "You should. It looks great on you. The whole armor does. My mother used to wear a circlet a bit like this sometimes. The way she'd twist her hair up and around it was beautiful. If I could, I'd show you how, but I have no talent with women's hair."

I smiled, appreciating the thought. "Sounds pretty."

We sat down on the chairs and started to eat, the sun getting hotter with each bite. In the daylight, the pathetic state of the city was blatant. "Not the best of views," I muttered, taking another bite of my blueberry muffin. If I was alone, I'd fill my stomach with just enough to hold on till lunch. But Kesstel was all about high calorie meals. "*You need energy to burn energy,*" is what he liked to say to me, the (silly) health nut.

"Agreed." He rested his empty plate on his knees and glanced at me. "Almost ready?"

I nodded and shoved the last bite in my mouth before taking his plate and throwing both away. "Oh, I wanted to ask if you had any empty slots in your Items Bag?"

He looked at me in interest. "You've picked up that many—what did you call it?—drop items in the last couple days?"

I nodded. "My bag is so full I had to stop picking them up." There were some valuable items I wasn't about to bring with me. I tried to sort my Items Bag and throw out the useless stuff, but there were some things I just couldn't gauge. What if I threw out something that was actually really valuable simply because I was ignorant?

"We haven't been collecting trophy items this whole time, so I have a lot of extra slots." Kesstel's blue steel breastplate appeared in his hand, and he started to put it on.

I stepped up and helped him buckle it. Everyone else, including me, was in full armor, and this man still walked around in just pants, simple but top quality knee and shin guards, and a long-sleeved tunic with a breastplate, arm bracers, and gloves. Then again, his bare skin was stronger than any armor he could put on.

Once that was done, I transferred eighty percent of my drop items over. I could have given him all of them, like he suggested, but I felt bad using him as a pack horse.

"It seems like everyone is ready," Kesstel noted, slipping his gloves on. "Tyson is pounding on the barrier now."

Because of the effectiveness of Kesstel's shield, I couldn't hear a thing. Suddenly, I couldn't help but wonder . . . was I strong enough to break it now?

I looked at the broken houses a short distance away. I could feel the barrier, but I couldn't see it, since I didn't own it. Curious, I called a kindjal to my hand then threw it as hard as I could. The sword shot like a blur twenty feet before it suddenly stopped. I couldn't hear it, but I felt a crack in the barrier as my kindjal stabbed into the invisible wall. It was just an inch deep, not enough to actually break it, but I felt a wave of pride in that. I was catching up to Kesstel in strength.

He looked at me and lifted a brow in question. "Is there a problem?"

I shook my head while I retrieved my kindjal back into my Items Bag. "Just curious."

He hummed under his breath as he waved his hand and vanished the whole camper.

On the other side, Tyson stood in his red robes with his arms folded, looking impatient. Behind him, the rest of the expedition's Hunters were talking to the leaders, obviously getting instructions. Tyson's mouth moved, but we still couldn't hear what he was saying.

Kesstel's barrier disappeared, and the noise of the crowd finally reached our ears. The last of the campers were being put away, leaving a large crowd in a dusty field.

"That's not fair," Tyson said, waltzing up to us. "You get a quiet little lover's retreat, and I'm stuck listening to every snoring train all night."

"You have your own camper," Kesstel commented.

"But it's not soundproofed," he complained. "With my hearing? I might as well be in the same room." He shuddered. "Eh, the thought just grosses me out. You're a melee Hunter, Noble, and I'm the mage. Why can you make soundproof barriers and I can't?"

I frowned at Tyson. Well, he had a point. A Skill Stone could enable Tyson to make one, but that was only if he had access to the right Skill Stone. Only a handful of those were found in Eden's Gate every year—at least the reported ones. And that was with tens of thousands of Hunters going into the Gate every day. There were unreported Skill Stones—like the one which gave me Stealth—but they were just as scarce.

Still, this flashy guy was beyond me. I didn't know what to say around him. "We should go."

The rest of the expedition Hunters were gathering around Blood Sword and the rest of the S leaders. Tyson walked over to stand with them, but Kesstel stayed with me. When we joined the group, the closest Hunters edged away with uncertainty. And not all of it was aimed at Kesstel; I was getting my fair share of odd looks. I'd done too many weird things; I was starting to make an impression on them. Whatever it was, as long as I wasn't a punching bag, I could handle that. Given the wary stares, even though my aura was hidden, they didn't look ready to test me.

When Blood Sword saw that everyone was here, he cleared his throat and drew everyone's attention. "Good morning," he called out. "I know we have scoured the whole city already, but because we haven't found the portal, we're going to go back over it again." He ignored the dozens of exasperated sighs and glanced at me through the crowd. "Hopefully, it won't take long for us to find it. We've already been through the city metropolis once, so most of the monsters have been slain. All that's left are the ones that have spawned overnight."

Out of the corner of my eye, I saw Penny shifting to whisper to Mark at her side. They stood on the edge of the crowd in the back, slightly away from everyone. On the other side of Mark, President Price stood in full armor. His square face looked like he was sucking on a sour lemon, although his arm was healed, as if it had never been cut off. He glanced at me out of the corner of his narrow eyes, obviously visualizing my death.

In a flash, Kesstel turned and swung his arm out. A long dagger covered in his blue magic shot like a shooting star at President Price. Penny and Mark stiffened as the dagger went past them, the magic surrounding the blade leaving scratches on their chest plates even though it didn't actually touch them.

Price didn't have a chance to dodge the attack. Last night was repeated all over again as Price screamed in pain and the bottom half of his arm dropped to the ground. He clutched his bleeding limb and bent over, groaning and panting his distress.

The rest of the Hunters all gasped and jumped back, trying to get away from the angry S god.

Penny and Mark looked down at Price, obviously wondering what they should do.

Even I was a little confused. I glanced up at Kesstel's face, trying to figure out what was going on in his head. Kesstel didn't look angry, actually. He was quite casual as he stood there and gazed at Price apathetically.

Normally, Kesstel and I were on the same page . . . but he also didn't normally cut off the same person's arm twice in a row.

Jonovan stepped out of the crowd and walked up to Price. "Kesstel, what is this?" he asked as he reached his golden glowing fingers out to heal the man.

"I wouldn't waste your magic," Kesstel advised. "Every time I see that arm, I'm going to cut it off."

Jonovan paused and gaped at Kesstel.

Price turned his head, a look of horror, pain, and disbelief on his face.

The rest of the Hunters muttered in surprise and backed up even farther. None of them wanted to get tangled up with a person whom an S god had condemned. That one sentence was enough to ruin at least half of Price's connections as soon as word got back to Eden.

Blood Sword jumped over the group of Hunters and landed beside Kesstel and me. "Noble! What is the meaning of this? Didn't you get a copy of the expedition's rules?" Angry veins were popping on his forehead, but he still managed to keep his voice somewhat reasonable.

"I read them." Kesstel shrugged. "His hand offended me. So he doesn't need it anymore." He made his logic sound like it was normal. "He should be grateful I didn't kill him."

I looked down and worked hard to keep the smile off my face. I shouldn't smile in this situation, but Kesstel's caring for me was touching. After all, he was being unruly this time just for me.

Blood Sword sputtered in disbelief. "We are on a dangerous mission. We've already lost twenty of the best Hunters in North America. We need every able body we can get. Without his arm—his sword arm—he's as good as dead."

Price's face paled even more. Sweat beaded on his broad forehead and dripped to the dry ground. He turned his head and stared at Kesstel with wide, desperate eyes. "M-Mister No—"

Kesstel folded his arms and tilted his head, leveling Blood Sword with a look, and spoke as if Price hadn't said anything at all. "That's not my problem. He's welcome to grow it back as often as he wants, but every time I see it, I'm going to take it off. I was already taking the guilds into consideration by not killing him. Any more is his good or bad luck."

I bit my lips and shifted a little closer to Kesstel. He really did listen to me last night.

Jonovan glanced at Kesstel, then reached out. A golden light encircled the bleeding stump on Price's arm. The bleeding stopped, and color started to come back to Price's face, but his arm didn't grow back.

The pain was going away, but Price was still staring at his severed limb with an appalled expression.

Mila Fortin stepped forward. "This is unreasonable," she said.

Kesstel cut his gaze her way.

Healer Laurel grabbed Mila's arm and pulled her back. "Don't get involved," the healer advised softly, though I could still hear her over the mutterings of the crowd. "It's not worth it. The people who offend Noble rarely live that long. He was already being considerate to not flat-out kill him."

Miranda, at their side, paled. She glanced at Price as if finally realizing that could be her someday.

Mila's husband, Logan, frowned in amazement. "Just how strong is he, that he can behave like this, unchecked?" His already severe face tightened as he looked at Kesstel.

"Strong enough to do whatever he wants," Healer Laurel muttered. Apparently, she and the other Eden Hunters were still smarting from Kesstel's berserk rampage which happened weeks ago. "No one can stop him. Except that girl at his side."

All the S Hunters focused on me like I was a wondrous, mythical creature.

I sighed. Seriously, they were blowing it way out of proportion. Kesstel only listened to me when he wanted to. All the other times, he usually just steamrolled right over me. I looked at Blood Sword. "I'm ready to go whenever you are."

CHAPTER 41

L as Vegas was shaped a bit like an oval with a tail, roughly twenty miles wide and thirty miles long. My mist only spread ten miles wide, so it was best to break it down into six sections, which was how I found myself standing on the middle of a large bridge in the northwest part of the city over an obviously used-to-be-busy road labeled 95 filled with abandoned cars. The cars on the bridge had already been cleared off by the Hunters so everyone could comfortably fit in the space, not that they actually needed that much room. Some Hunters simply enjoyed throwing as many cars as they wanted off a bridge just for fun.

Even so, they still didn't dare get too close to me and Kesstel. But that was the least of my worries. I looked over at Blood Sword, who was standing in the space between me and the other Hunters. "I don't know how long it's going to take me to search every space. The portal could be as small as the doorway of a house."

The rest of the party didn't even have to be here. They could be dealing with monsters or even waiting at camp while I looked. They wouldn't be needed until I found the portal, but the leaders had agreed that the whole party should stay together, since they didn't know what was going to happen when the portal was found.

He nodded. "We understand."

Basically, my audience wasn't going away anytime soon. Well, might as well let it all out now.

Walking to the middle of the bridge, I lifted my hands like I was holding an invisible ball. Mist pooled between my palms, swirling and condensing into a sphere as I pushed more and more power into it until it thickened and looked nearly solid.

The Hunters a little ways away shifted, muttering to each other and trying to figure out what I was doing.

Kesstel stepped up to me and glanced down at the ball. For a split second, his eyes glowed bright blue before the color settled down. "That magic is really not compatible with the parasite," he commented.

I smiled at him. "But it's useful. Do you think we can end this today? I'm ready to go home and heal my mom."

Kesstel smiled, a challenge gleaming in his eyes. "We can try."

I spread my hands out wide. The mist ball exploded like a bomb, rapidly expanding faster than I could run. It filled up the bridge and spilled over onto the road below, washing up the rocky hills and into the residential and business areas around the converging roads. My mist was thirty feet tall and thick as soup as it spread out, reaching as far as I could push it. I was instantly aware of everything it touched; every person, every tiny bug, every monster that turned and fled as it rolled out.

The Hunters gasped in shock. They knew I was going to use magic, but I never told them what kind, just that it wasn't going to hurt anyone.

"Is this fog?" Tyson asked in disbelief. He lifted a hand and waved the mist through his spread fingers.

Another Hunter from the back of the crowd gasped out, "The Josu Ghost! She's the Josu Ghost!"

Other Hunters piped in, voicing their surprise.

Meanwhile, Healer Laurel sighed and shook her head. "Goodness, I want to study that girl so bad," she muttered.

Jonovan looked at her. "What do you mean?"

Laurel motioned to me. "We've been looking for the Josu Ghost for months. Researchers are dying to figure out how she manifested a new magic system. Noble was smart to keep her hidden at his side until now. The last mutant magic system they found died only a couple months after they got their hands on him. Reports say he went insane and started attacking people. All the cleanup crew found were mutilated bodies and several loose monsters." She shrugged at Jonovan's horrified look. "That was about ten years ago. Human life had even less value then, remember? Granted, most people at the lab still hold that mentality. Science over survival, you know."

A chill went down my spine at the casual way she so easily wrote off a person's life. Then again, I had done the same thing with Price just an hour ago. The difference was, *I* could have been that person in the lab under the knife of the too-eager scientists.

"So noisy," I whispered, closing my eyes.

When I was by myself, I didn't have to worry about distraction, but since I wasn't going to get some quiet time anytime soon, I got down to business. Even though my mist hadn't fully spread out, I started to scour where it had reached, searching every nook and cranny for the abnormal feeling of a portal.

Finally, my mist stretched out to the full ten miles. I was still busy searching the northern section when I felt something off in the southeast. That funny feeling was the only impression I got before it turned into a full jolt of alarm.

My eyes opened wide, and I stiffened.

The whole city creaked and groaned as an earthquake rippled through the ground in waves nearly two feet tall. Thousands of buildings collapsed, exploding dust and sand into the air, creating a dry cloud which settled over the city.

I flung my hand out a second before the ripple reached our bridge. A thin barrier appeared under everyone's feet, and in the same movement, I lifted everyone up. The Hunters startled in surprise and cursed, but they didn't have time to react more before the bridge they were standing on collapsed.

"Calm down," I called to them, then ignored their noise and concentrated on controlling the dust that polluted my mist. Really, I hated this dry stuff; it infected my mental map, like watching a TV with a grainy, unfocused screen. But it wasn't as bad to deal with now. Since I was stronger, I could force the dust to the ground until my mist was clean again.

"Convenient," Kesstel said, tapping his toe on the barrier under his feet. "Mine doesn't do this. Once it's set, it's set."

"Mine's a little pliable," I admitted. "From what I understand, as long as I can think it, I can make it. And change it how I want it."

I concentrated southeast—the earthquake's epicenter.

"What's going on?" Blood Sword demanded. "I can't see a damn thing." He wasn't the only one complaining about his lack of vision. "What did I just feel?"

Yeah, he wouldn't be able to; not with how thick my mist was right now. All the Hunters were probably blind right now. Everyone except . . . I glanced over at Kesstel. Sure enough, he was staring southeast.

"I think I figured out why you couldn't find the portal," I told Blood Sword.

The crowd finally stilled, listening for my response.

"Why?" Blood Sword asked.

"It's underground," Kesstel answered.

Because of the nature of the mist, I couldn't see the portal, but I could feel the magic and almost angry energy radiating through the ground there. It was the same reaction Kesstel had had when I walked out of the Vapria Portal. A large section over there was blatantly rejecting my mist, like one vicious predator reacting to another.

"Where is it coming from?" Logan Fortin asked. Like the other S Hunters, he obviously felt the sudden surge of magic in the air. And like all the others, he couldn't seem to pinpoint where it came from.

"The airport," I answered him, not too surprised at his confusion. After all, Kesstel and I were different from them. It made sense that we'd feel the portal more strongly. To make it easier for the Hunters, I thinned the mist enough so they could see, but didn't take it away.

Maybe I shouldn't have done that—they had a whole new shocked reaction when they realized the bridge they used to be standing on was over fifteen feet below their floating feet.

I glanced at them, just waiting for someone to stupidly fall off the barrier. It wasn't big, with a barely five-foot lip around the group. The ground was still rolling in ripples about a hundred feet apart—something the Hunters could finally see.

I looked up at Kesstel. "Do you think you can reach it? Digging isn't really my expertise."

Kesstel lifted a brow. "Are you treating me like a simple laborer?"

I grinned wide and patted his shoulder. "There's nothing simple about you, but yes."

He snorted and brushed his hand along my hair, careful not to let it get caught in his glove. "Only for you."

Another magical surge came from the airport, like a magic geyser. Loose gravel and dust was caught up in the movement and exploded into a mushroom cloud two hundred feet high. Another large earthquake rippled out then stopped moving just like that. The dust cloud slowly settled to the ground, falling over the tipped-over airplanes and abandoned cars. It was too still, especially after that violent activity. The other Hunters noticed the oddness and went on high alert.

"What do you feel?" Blood Sword asked me and Kesstel, his voice a blaring horn in the stillness. He wasn't turning over leadership, but he'd obviously figured out that Kesstel and I were a step ahead when it came to whatever was going on.

I glanced at Kesstel, the portal expert.

"Trouble," he responded, as if that helped.

The ground gave another rumble, but it didn't come from the airport like before. The tremor spanned the entire land below us, rattling the already compromised vehicles. Another wave of buildings collapsed, filling the air with noise and dust.

"There's going to be nothing left of the city by the time this ends," I said. I could tell there was a threat surrounding us, but I couldn't locate it. Instead of recklessly jumping into danger, I stayed up on my barrier and waited for it to show its ugly head first.

"There's going to be nothing left of the world if this keeps going on," Kesstel muttered. "If we close this portal, is another one going to open? Then another and another? What are we going to do about the ones that exist outside of this country?"

"I don't know." I didn't have an answer to that very real potential problem, but right now, the most pressing question was, what was the problem under my feet?

Suddenly, thousands of pillars broke out of the ground. Dirt, sand, concrete, gravel, dead grass—it didn't matter what was in the way, the ten-foot dirt-colored pillars still surged out of it.

It wasn't until the pillars started to move that I realized I was wrong.

They weren't pillars—they were worms.

CHAPTER 42

The worm monsters wiggled around, obviously upset by my mist, but they didn't go back into their holes. They had no eyes or noses, just wide mouths on top of their heads which opened and closed in agitation. Two rows of needle-sharp teeth, like a shark, filled their mouths. I could smell their decaying stink from here.

Kesstel hummed under his breath. "Well, I've seen worse." Though his nose wrinkled in disgust.

My eyes narrowed as I stared at the thousands of monsters that wiggled all over the ground, barely five feet between each one. "This is the second time I've seen them."

Only, the ones I saw while tailing the red orc were level forty-five. These worm monsters, called mega annelids, ranged between levels seventy-eight and eighty-six. Nearly twice the strength.

Was it because I agitated the portal? Most likely. My mist bothered Kesstel, so it must work on other things the parasitic planet controlled.

"What is that?" Jonovan asked, trying to peer through the thick mist to make out the things wiggling just under our feet.

I drew the miles of mist cloud back to me then thinned the water vapor platform enough so the other Hunters could finally see what I could.

More than a few people jumped and gasped once they realized they were standing on an invisible sheet over open, toothy mouths. The mega annelids wiggled and chomped their mouths open and closed, fast.

"My god," Blood Sword muttered, looking around. I didn't know if he was talking about the thousands of monsters or the fact that eighty percent of the city's buildings—including all the huge casinos it was so proud of in the past—had been reduced to a pile of rubble.

One of the worm monsters couldn't resist the temptation of food anymore and rose higher into the air, reaching over fifteen feet tall.

I maneuvered my mist and locked a ring around its head. The monster instantly writhed and squirmed, knotting and twisting its body, but it couldn't pull free of my hold. Curiously, I lifted the mist block around its head, pulling the monster from its hole. My brows were pinched together, bewildered, as it just kept coming. In the end, twenty-two feet of disgusting worm hung in the air. As soon as its tail was free of the ground, it swung out, smacking into other mega annelids and hitting the bottom of the platform we stood on.

I turned to the shocked Hunters and motioned to the gooey, writhing mess dangling ahead of me. "They respond to the vibrations from movement on the ground, and they're fast. Concrete and other hard surfaces are like water to them," I explained.

Slowly, the shock of the situation went away, and I could see the Hunters settle into battle mode one by one.

"Their weak spot is just below here." I turned and threw my kindjal at the monster, three feet below its head. My blade sank into the worm's slimy, soft flesh just above where the energy crystal was. It instantly scrunched up its body, curling around the short sword. "Cut off the head or take out the energy crystal—it's up to you."

"The portal is that way," Kesstel added, pointing into the distance over the heads of thousands of worm monsters. "The Las Vegas airport." He glanced at me. "From what I can tell, it's large."

I nodded. I couldn't get a good read since my mist couldn't permeate the ground, but I knew for sure it was wider than a house. As for how it worked with being under a layer of dirt, well, we would just have to see when we got there.

"Jynn and I are going to the portal," Kesstel said. "You're welcome to join us if you can."

Tyson scowled. "What about all the monsters in the way?" he asked, motioning at them with disgust.

Kesstel snorted. "What about them?" His sword appeared in his hand, the blue-and-silver steel glinting in the harsh light.

A small smile pulled at my lips as Kesstel's arrogant confidence bled over to me. The knowledge that I was finally there, finally able to stand side by side with him in a battle, was like a shot of adrenaline.

I held out my hand, and the kindjal still stuck in the monster's neck returned to me. As soon as it touched my skin, it multiplied into four swords. I took one in each hand while the others slowly drifted around me, ready for my command, a pale light gleaming from inside each crystal blade.

Kesstel tilted his head and smiled, looking into my face. "Pretty."

From the crowd, Miranda gasped. "I thought she was a melee Hunter? How can she do magic?"

At her side, Mila rolled her eyes. "She's also an E. Does anything we used to think about her apply anymore?"

I chose to ignore their words, instead pointing at the group's feet. "You have thirty seconds before what you stand on disappears. I'd find solid ground before then or try not to look like an idiot in front of your teammates when you land." That was all the free information they'd get from me.

Deeming my part on the team done, I looked toward the airport where magic was still spilling into the atmosphere, like clear smoke rising up from a geyser. I could feel it when my mist was there, but this was the first time I'd seen the parasitic planet's magic with my own eyes, not just its effects. Like smog, the miasma pooled over the city, both clear and colorful at the same time, random rainbows that flashed as the magic rippled, then disappeared as the magic smoothed out.

This must have been what Kesstel had been seeing all this time, I realized, remembering how he'd sometimes stop and look around when he gauged how much longer Earth had. Maybe it was a good thing I couldn't see it all this time. It would have been too nerve-wracking, and at least I could do something about the magic pollution in front of me now.

"Let's go," I said. The mist bridge shot out of the platform, forming a straight line in the direction of the airport, ten feet above the broken ground.

I jumped down and sprinted across it, my kindjals following behind. The first monster that exploded was the one I still had strung up in the air. It was completely powerless as I slashed it in half, my blade cutting through like a warm knife through butter. Their skin wasn't actually that easy to cut; it was just that my weapons were that superior. Unfortunately, it gave the impression it wasn't hard for the people watching me, but I couldn't dwell on it for too long before I engaged the monsters around me.

The two mega annelids flinched when my mist touched them, snapping their mouths open and closed as they flailed around. The monsters didn't have eyes, and I wasn't touching the ground, so their movements were random, as if they were trying to figure out where I was. I didn't give them the time. My floating kindjals took care of one giant worm, while the other fell by the swords in my hands.

The monsters exploded into little lights, accompanied by the notification I'd gained more EXP. Two drop orbs fell onto the mist I was Feather Stepping on. While I twisted and sliced the next monster in half, I waved a hand and brought the drop orbs to me. As soon as they touched my skin, they instantly went into my Items Bag.

The mega annelid lunged at me, moving like a pale, fleshy blur. Before I had the chance to move, a blue-and-steel bastard sword flashed and lopped the monster's head off. Kesstel appeared above me and kicked the head away before it could fall on me. And with it, the monster's energy crystal.

My mouth twisted as I watched the head shoot a hundred feet away until it smashed into the side of the broken building. Definitely not worth going to get right now. The sad part was, because I didn't destroy the energy crystal, the monster's carcass didn't disappear. It slumped to the ground in a disgusting fleshy pile, spewing black blood like a hose. I grimaced as some of the blood splashed onto my legs, but I didn't do anything about it—I was already attacking the next monsters in my way. The blood on me gave away my location, making the monster's attacks more accurate. A little trickier, but I was still able to handle it.

It was a dog-eat-dog environment. As soon as a worm slumped over, the monsters around it would lunge at the still-twitching body and start ripping chunks off, creating a massive feeding frenzy.

In Kesstel's case, every move he made attracted monsters. Not only did he have their blood on him but he also left a lot of severed bodies, neither of which fazed him. Every creature that came within swinging distance died with the same casual flick of his wrist, just like the monster before it. A faint smile spread across his face, and his blue eyes faintly glowed as he fought like the god of death, cutting down monsters in the blink of an eye.

He never strayed too far from me, just enough that our fighting styles didn't conflict with each other, but close enough that he would sometimes jump over and assist me in a kill. At the same time, I'd pay enough attention to him to destroy as many energy crystals as I could from the monsters he cut down. If there was an obvious drop orb I could get, I'd snatch it up, but for the most part, I stopped bothering with collecting them. There were just too many, and I was busy.

The group of Hunters and the sounds of their fighting faded behind as Kesstel and I plowed through the mega annelids toward the airport.

Kesstel quickly figured out the convenience of running on my mist and often used it. He was so fast and so deadly.

I didn't want to be left behind in speed or monster count—not that I was actually counting. I just wanted to make sure that every time he killed one, I did too. It didn't take long for me to fall into the rhythm, moving around monsters and slicing the kindjals around like beams of death. Tiny white lights exploded everywhere I went.

Slowly, Kesstel and I began to develop a technical understanding of how the other person moved, and adapted our own fighting styles to adjust around each other. I'd shoot a kindjal over and pierce the energy crystal of a monster that was going for his back; he'd appear at my side and take care of the excess monsters before I could get injured. Most of our fights were still separate, but there was enough crossover to say we were actually tag teaming. We were both covered in blood, but outside of a few scratches, none of it was our own.

Because of the mega annelids' habit of eating their dead—or anything else that moved—it would have been easy to get stuck in one place for a long time, but Kesstel and I never lingered long. We did, however, leave a long trail of dead worms in our wake, which led to other monsters wiggling in to get a meal. The whole thing was just gross.

We were both breathing heavily by the time we reached the airport.

Behind us was a mass of wiggling giant worms, but the large stretch ahead was as still as a graveyard. Rusty airplanes and shuttle buses were tipped on their sides, scattered across the runways of broken concrete like a child's messy playroom. The airport building was in a pile of rubble, with only a couple steel-frame structures protruding out. It was easy to tell where the portal was because the mega annelids created a near perfect circle around it. For whatever reason, they wouldn't go over it.

The only movement at all on the place was the thick miasma which seeped from the dry ground. My mist collided with it like oil and water. Just the thought of stepping into that stuff left an unpleasant twist in my stomach.

I pushed out with my mist, trying to force the magic away from our location. It resisted and countered, but slowly, it moved away until Kesstel and I had a comfortable five-foot circle to stand in.

A low, muffled rumble echoed out from under the circle of dirt. Another earthquake rippled out, rocking the ground below the barrier we stood on.

Sorry, I thought briefly to the Hunters several miles behind us, still fighting on the ground.

Kesstel pointed his sword at the smooth ground. "I think here's a good spot to start digging." Before I could agree or disagree, he jumped off my barrier.

CHAPTER 43

K esstel grabbed the handle of his beautiful sword with both hands and lifted it over his head. Bright blue magic spread from his fingers down to the tip of the blade, leaving a stunning arc in the air as he dropped to the still ground. He landed on bent knees, his sword sinking two feet into the earth.

In a flash, the blue magic cracked through the dry dirt and spread like a burn scar from his location, tearing to the other side of the calm circle. Kesstel shifted and changed the grip on his sword. With a grunt, he swung his blade up like a shovel. His blue magic exploded in a tidal wave, hurling the dirt, planes, cars, and anything else in its way into the air.

I thrust out a hand and sent a wave of mist over the debris in the air— and with it, a solid barrier to push it out of the way. A small mountain of stuff landed on the wiggling monsters on the other side of the airport, burying anything in its wake, monster and building alike.

"Your digging is a lot more effective than mine," I muttered. An understatement, considering he'd cleared the whole airport of literally everything in one swing. "Good job."

Kesstel jumped back from the small island of remaining dirt and landed by my side. "Thanks."

We stared down at the flat black portal nine feet below the surface of the earth. It rippled like a black pond, as eerie and big as a Gate. It was even more disturbing because it wasn't a Gate. It meant there wasn't a Gate Vale or barrier to prevent the monsters from entering Earth; they could just freely exit whenever they wanted. As for how, given the worms, it wouldn't surprise me if there used to be holes in the dirt which were dug daily to allow the monsters out.

"Let's go." Kesstel bent his knees, ready to jump down.

You shouldn't go in there, Goddess suddenly said.

I paused, also preparing to jump in with Kesstel. *Why?*

As soon as Goddess spoke, Kesstel's eyes narrowed in displeasure. He shifted to a standing position and stared at me, waiting.

That cursed parasite knows I'm loose. And stronger. It can't get to us here on Earth yet, but the remnant planets and the tunnels between them are controlled by that horrible being. We would be at its mercy in that remnant world, with possibly no way out. Even with your Katharian, there's no guarantee we could make it back to Earth any time soon, Goddess explained. *You should avoid going into portals until we find the one leading to the parasite.*

My brows rose high on my forehead. It made sense. *What about fighting in the Gate? How am I going to get stronger without destroying energy crystals?*

That will also be dangerous. If you can conceal your presence, it might be okay, she reasoned slowly. *Remnant worlds are most sensitive to foreign beings, as opposed to Gates, which are a melting pot of many different things.*

I nodded slowly and looked up at Kesstel. "I can't go into the portal." My finger tapped my thigh in frustration. The portal needed to be closed, but I didn't want Kesstel to leave me and go in alone. I wasn't a weak little girl anymore. And what if he got lost in there again?

He paused then bobbed his head, easily accepting my words. "I should have thought about that before as well." He lifted his hand and held it over the portal, as if he could feel something. "The Boss is just on the other side." His eyes narrowed as he smirked. "Pathetic thing can't figure out how to get out." He looked at me, the thrill of battle in his eyes. "Since we can't go in, it's only proper that it comes out to greet us."

My eyes widened at how easily he applied my restrictions to himself.

Right, we'd promised we would go everywhere together now. I had no idea what he was planning, but that hardly mattered. His mood was infectious enough that my own lips curled. "Right. It's only polite."

He pointed to the middle of the portal. "Would you make me something to stand on right there, just above the portal? So I don't accidentally fall through."

I waved my hand. The small misty platform had barely appeared where he wanted when Kesstel jumped over to it. His jump was so long and fast, it almost looked like he was flying.

Landing, he bent down, resting his hand on top of the black surface of the portal. As soon as he touched it, it started to ripple like a disturbed pond, but it didn't affect the ground around the portal, or even the wiggling mega annelids. Meanwhile, Kesstel's power jolted through the portal's area, the black ripples almost taking on a pale blue color at their tips.

I noticed a couple worms getting too close and turned. One of them attempted to lean over the edge of the platform I was on and take a chunk out of my calf. I frowned at the ugly, gaping mouth and flung a kindjal at it. The sword stabbed through its toothy mouth, down its throat, and punctured its energy crystal. The monster exploded into lights, while the kindjal was already on the move to the next monster. Ten seconds and three dead worms later, I turned back to Kesstel, just as I felt a sudden shift in the magic around the portal.

A spiderweb of blue magic cracked across the portal, starting from his hand and spreading all the way across the black surface. Kesstel's lips hooked up, and he jumped from the platform back to where I was standing. Hooking an arm around my waist, he took us back into the air. "We should step back."

The portal pulsed like paint on a beating drum, the sharp blue peaks pulling at the black surface.

Just as Kesstel's leap reached its peak and we started to fall, I created something for us to stand on. As soon as our feet landed, the portal surged up, bowing over thirty feet in the air. Suddenly, it split open.

The monsters from the portal were huge worms, but the Boss was a centipede-like monster. Two hundred feet long and over twenty feet wide, thousands of angular legs rippled at its side as it flew through the air. Thirty-foot-long antennae wiggled around the front of its head, flicking and moving around before setting to our general direction. The huge mandibles on the sides of its huge mouth twitched as its mouth opened and closed, revealing pointed teeth taller than me. Every section of the body was plated in a rust-colored exoskeleton, the appendages only a couple shades lighter. On top of its head, two black eyes focused on us.

"Ugh," I whispered as a chill went down my spine. I'd seen a lot of monsters, but this one just looked gross. I'd take the nasty, mucus-covered worms over this. I couldn't even tell why; there was just something horrible about watching the thousands of legs on its long body and the unnatural way the antennae moved.

Or it could be the fact that it was two hundred feet long, flying, and an S-ranked Boss.

"Still seen worse," Kesstel muttered as he let go of my waist.

"I don't envy that," I responded.

The Boss volpoda arched in the air and drove at us, fast as a freight train as its thousands of feet rippled. Kesstel jumped right and I dove left. The Boss plowed straight between us and chomped down on the spot where we were a second ago, the sound of its jaw slamming shut sharp and loud enough to make my ears ring.

I twisted in the air and lashed out, a ten-foot Mist Blade growing over the crystal end of my sword as I swung. My attack hit against the armored joint of a passing leg but reflected right off the exoskeleton, the rebound throwing me off-balance. I gritted my teeth as I tipped backward, but I took control of the flip and landed on a mist barrier.

At the same time, Kesstel attacked the Boss on his side. The monster grunted and arched higher into the sky, avoiding the bright blue magic of his attack. A plate-size chunk of a leg's exoskeleton dropped to the rippling and boiling black ground below.

Without its Boss, the portal pulsed, sending black spikes ten feet into the air. All at once, it compressed on itself and began to shrink, like a black hole eating itself. In a minute, the huge portal shrank to the size of a basketball court. It left a near perfect circular crater in the ground in its wake, the dry dirt it revealed completely smooth. The black hole kept shrinking until it disappeared entirely.

In the distance, something . . . screamed.

No, I couldn't even call it a scream because I couldn't hear any sound. It was a *feeling*. An awareness. Something was happening somewhere in the west. It wasn't a call, because it wasn't inviting me, but I couldn't help feeling like it was directed at me. Whatever it was.

A shadow rested over me, knocking me out of my distracted thoughts. I turned to see the volpoda diving straight down at me, hungry mouth open.

Kesstel appeared in front of me and swung his sword. A blue magical tidal wave burst out of his weapon and crashed into the Boss. Its mandibles closed around its mouth and eye area as it curled its head down, and the blue magic hit the volpoda right in the middle of the armor plate on its head before deflecting off into the blue sky. The Boss's dive angled away, and it shot right by, the drag of air turbulence pulling at my body and whipping my hair in my face.

Kesstel landed next to me. "You don't have time to get distracted by the parasite's tantrum," he said, his gaze locked on the Boss as it took a wide turn over the whole city, obviously coming back at us.

I was high enough in the air to see that wherever the volpoda's shadow touched, the mega annelids would duck back into their holes. Given that they ate their own kind, I was sure the same thing applied to their Boss. The Hunters were several miles away, still fighting the giant worm monsters. For whatever reason, the Boss didn't even indicate it was aware of them. It seemed to be focused on Kesstel and me, which was probably for the best.

I flicked a glance at Kesstel, paying attention to his words. "Are you saying that what I just felt was the parasitic planet?"

He jerked a nod. "It didn't like that a portal closed."

My eyes widened. "Did it start a Gate Surge?" With so many of North America's top Hunters here, a Gate Surge would be bad. Especially a global one. I glared at the thick magic in the air, shifting and flashing rainbow spots as the volpoda flew through it and disturbed the miasma.

"Possibly," Kesstel replied. "We won't know for sure until we get back. Either way, there's nothing we can do about it."

But my family was in Garden City. For the first time, I wasn't there to protect them. Unease bubbled in my chest. I finally had a cure for my mom—I couldn't let anything bad happen to them now.

I took a breath and forced it down. Kesstel was right. I was getting too distracted.

"I can't cut through its exoskeleton," I said. "How did you damage it earlier?"

"It's weakest between the plates," Kesstel noted. "And a little around the edges of the plates. That's where I shaved off a small piece."

I nodded. So aim for the joints. Got it. "I'm going to flood this place with mist. I hope it's not going to be a problem." I wouldn't be able to fight to my fullest until I did. I was holding back because I didn't want to inconvenience Kesstel, but I couldn't do much until I did.

Kesstel jerked a shoulder in a shrug. "Do what you need to do." As the Boss drew closer, a smirk hooked his mouth. "I'll do me."

"Deal."

CHAPTER 44

Mist spread out across the city like a low-hanging cloud; for Kes-stel's sake, I didn't poison it or make it too thick. Besides, I had a feeling that my mist wouldn't impede the volpoda much. No matter where it was, one antenna always pointed at me and the other pointed at Kes-stel—even when it was on the other side of the city.

As soon as the Boss entered the mist, I Warped onto the back of its head where one armor plate overlapped with the next one. The wind was thick with the stench of the gigantic monster, and its body was slick with a clear liquid which leaked from between the plates. The moment my feet touched the shell, the Boss arched its head, almost bending at a ninety-degree angle. I was forced to step back as the top plate rubbed on the one I was standing on, like a razor over a smooth surface.

Even though the exoskeleton was thicker than my hand, its edges were razor thin and laid together perfectly. When it arched its back like this, there were no openings I could slide a sword into. At least not directly facing me.

The exoskeleton over the Boss's underbelly, so impenetrable when it was straight, slightly parted to accommodate the Boss bending backward. As soon as the gaps spread, my floating kindjals stabbed into the slits. Unfortunately, Mist Blade only applied to the sword in my hands, not the ones flying around me. A two-foot-long sword wasn't that effective against a twenty-foot-thick monster, but if I needed to bleed this monster apart one HP at a time, then that's what it took.

The monster shuddered, the pieces of its exoskeleton rubbing against each other. More clear, stinking liquid leaked out from between the armor plates and dribbled down the tiny grooves in the armor till it oozed over and around my boots. My stomach twisted, and I wrinkled my nose. If only the smell were the worst part. The traction between my boots and the Boss's back was instantly gone, and the wind ripped at me as the volpoda streaked through the air, sliding me farther and farther back. It was hard to stay in the center so I didn't slip from one side to the other.

Suddenly, the two antennae arched back toward me. I jumped back, just out of reach, as the tips touched each other. An electric explosion boomed so fast and hard between the antennae that I didn't have time to react. The electricity rippled all the way down the Boss's body, crackling along the liquid lines covering it, and shot through me from the liquid on my boots, adding to the spark created by the antennae touching. The explosion was so bright that it almost overshadowed the sun.

I was blown right off the Boss's back, twenty percent of my HP blasted off just like that. A dull ringing echoed in my ears, muffling the sound of air rushing by as I fell limp through the air. I vaguely understood I needed to do something, but my muscles were all still seized up from the shock wave, and my mind was fuzzy. I was simply a doll flung from a skyscraper.

Jynn! Dimly, I recognized Goddess' voice, but I couldn't seem to respond to it.

Strong arms wrapped around me, and I was anchored against a wide steel breastplate. Not the most comfortable position, but I felt safe.

The gray haze clouding my vision slowly receded, just in time for me to see the volpoda's ugly, open mouth closing in.

Kesstel swung his sword and sent a blue tidal wave of magic at the gigantic centipede. The Boss ducked its head down and deflected the magical attack with its exoskeleton into the ruined buildings to the north. Dirt clouds exploded into the air, and piles of rubble were flattened wherever Kesstel's power landed.

Kesstel touched down on one of the few remaining standing buildings, his eyes following the volpoda as it arched through the sky. "Are you okay?" he asked.

I took a breath and nodded slowly. The ringing in my ears was already starting to go away, and I could finally feel my limbs and fingers again. I pressed on his chest, and he set my feet down. "That's one helluva electric shock." It had blasted 4000 HP points off in one go, worse than any attack the orc king had done. At least I had Regen. My HP hadn't had time to climb back up, but I could at least move.

Kesstel glanced at me and rubbed his gloved hand gently over my cheek. "Don't let that happen again." He didn't tell me not to go back or suggest that I hide while he fought alone. He just wanted me to be more careful.

Even if I wasn't careful, I knew he had my back.

"Yes. You watch out for it, too. That thing's a lot faster than I thought."

He hummed in agreement. "I'm having a hard time getting high enough to attack it before it moves on. I can't run on air like you. I'd like to just blast it out of the sky, but I'm worried about hitting you." We both turned our heads and looked up as the Boss closed in again. "Ready to jump back in?" he asked. "Can you make it arch once more? I was too far away last time to do anything."

"Sure," I replied, immediately understanding what he wanted.

"When you do, get out of there as fast as possible," Kesstel warned.

I nodded and grabbed his hand. "Come on." I jumped sixty feet up, Kesstel an inch behind me, matching me height for height, then I created a block for us to stand on, just on the bottom of the mist cloud.

The volpoda entered the mist again, aiming to swallow us.

"Let's do this," I muttered before Warping.

I landed on the back of the Boss. As soon as my boots touched the section behind its head, I turned and Feather Stepped down its body, sure to avoid the clear goo.

The volpoda instantly arched its head back, the antennae reaching and just about to touch. At the same time, I felt Kesstel's power surge.

I Warped to the far side of the mist cloud, hoping that half a mile was far enough out of the way. I landed on a mist block and turned just in time to see a massive wave of Kesstel's bright magic shoot up from where he stood, growing bigger with each foot it ate up. The blue magic, nearly fifty feet wide, hit the volpoda just as its antennae touched. The two magics exploded together, creating a ball which engulfed half the Boss, the white-yellow and bright-blue magic fighting for dominance.

The light was so strong, I couldn't look at it. Even when I closed my eyes, I could see a glaring afterimage. The shock wave from the explosion ripped through the air, painfully displacing my mist. A second before it hit me, I knelt down and grabbed onto my block. The mist around me was knocked away, but I forced the solid stuff I was on to stay still, feeling like a giant hand was trying to squeeze me into a ball on all sides. It came and went so fast, I was left a little disoriented once it was gone.

Breathing slowly to settle my rattled nerves, I opened my eyes.

The blue-yellow tiny sun in the middle of the city's sky began to fade. The long shape of the volpoda dropped to the ground, landing with an earthquaking thud and sending a huge dust cloud into the air.

Kesstel was still on the pedestal I'd made for him, but he was bent over and breathing hard. That attack must have taken a lot out of him.

Unfortunately, it wasn't enough to kill the Boss.

The volpoda rose out of the dust cloud and arched its body, the mandibles in its mouth flailing in the air with a silent roar. Its thousands of feet stabbed into the ground as it jerked and writhed, streams of black blood flowing from between the armor plates on the first half of its body—the plates which had opened up before Kesstel attacked. Electric bolts flared all over its body as it thrashed around, frying the mega annelids that were attempting to flee from it.

I Warped over to Kesstel and quickly collected the large mist cloud overhead back to me, leaving the block we were standing on. "You okay?" I rested a hand on his arm.

He nodded. "Fine." His gaze zeroed in on the Boss below, blazing like blue fire. "Ready to kill it."

I agreed. "See you in a minute." I jumped forward and arched down toward the huge monster. Mist exploded out from me and fell over the Boss.

The volpoda jerked, the water vapor obviously agitating it more as I Warped just to the right of it. One of its legs had been blasted right off, and several other limbs were missing plates of exoskeleton. My attention was drawn to the small chunks broken off from the main body, oozing black blood and creating small gaps in the once impenetrable armor.

Most of the black liquid that pooled on the ground was coming from the stomach area, right where Kesstel had attacked. I couldn't—or shouldn't, at this point—get under the Boss to see what the underside looked like, but I could take advantage of what was available.

A split second later, I Warped on top of a leg and stabbed my long Mist Blade into the tiny gap between the armor plates. The exoskeleton was nearly impossible to stab through, but as soon as I got past that, the inside of the Boss was like poking melted butter. There was practically no resistance.

The volpoda convulsed, a wave of lightning crackling down its body. I wasn't standing on any ooze, which was the medium for the attack, so the shock wasn't strong enough to force me off. The leg I stood on jerked, and the surrounding legs thrashed, attempting to stab me. The body quickly turned and rolled up, trying to catch me in the middle of it. I Warped away before it caught me, landing on the ground twenty feet away, all four kindjals out and ready to find more holes in its armor.

The antennae lifted, reaching out toward me. Before they could touch, I encased the tip of the right one with a mist block and slammed it to the ground. The other antenna sparked, but there was no massive electric explosion because they couldn't touch. The volpoda's mouth opened in a soundless wail as it jerked its head, trying to get the antenna free. Inch by inch, it started to slip out of its confinement.

Careful of the other antenna, I landed on top of the stuck one. The Mist Blade shrunk down to the kindjal's normal size, and I slid it between the armored layers that made up the appendage. As soon as it was in, I activated Mist Blade, and with a *crack*, the end of the right antenna broke off.

The volpoda thrashed its giant head, its mandibles jabbing out at me. I lifted my kindjal just in time and blocked the attack, but it was still strong enough to make my boots slide back on the pool of black blood I stood on. Tiny lightning arcs danced all over the Boss's body; I couldn't tell if it was on purpose or not. The only thing I knew for sure was that they were half as strong as before. Cutting the antenna must have affected its lightning magic somehow.

A small arc of lightning ran down the mandible to me. Before it could touch me, I Warped to its other side.

The Boss turned its head, trying to attack me. It stabbed its many pointed feet at me, swung its head, and lashed out with its mandibles. Every time it stepped down, the ground shook in a mini earthquake. I Warped from one place to the other, slashing at the joints when I could. My flying kindjals shot around its legs, searching for weak spots to jab into. Unfortunately, I was on the move so much, I couldn't find too many good spots to attack. There were just too many appendages and parts I had to dodge. I thought the Boss would be slower on the ground. Guess I was wrong.

While it was focused on attacking me, Kesstel appeared on the volpoda's head and stabbed his sword down into its black right eye. The Boss flung its head back so fast that Kesstel was thrown into the air, but he twisted and landed cleanly on its back.

Kesstel glanced at me, our eyes connecting for just a split second.

I understood what he wanted immediately.

I Warped in front of the Boss's vulnerable chest, finally getting a good look at the bleeding underside. Kesstel's magic attack from earlier had blasted a three-foot hole in the exoskeleton, exposing the white muscly flesh on the inside. Without the outer armor in the way, I could finally see where the energy crystal was—slightly to the right of the hole, directly behind the neighboring armor plate.

Without hesitating, I stabbed my Mist Blade into the still-bleeding opening at an angle, reaching for the energy crystal.

The volpoda withered violently. Its pointed legs convulsed and curled in, clawing at me, but I refused to budge. My eyes widened, and a circular mist barrier appeared around me. The sharp tips of the armored claws hit the bubble and stopped just feet from my back. Furiously, it stabbed and gouged at the mist, but it couldn't puncture more than an inch into it.

I gritted my teeth against the force it inflicted on my barrier and hung on to my sword. Tiny little lightning jolts pulsed from the black blood leaking down my arms and through my body, but I refused to let go. Even with my ten-foot blade wiggling around inside the Boss, I still couldn't reach the energy crystal. I was two feet too short, no matter how hard I pressed my hilt against the small opening. But that didn't prevent me from stirring up the monster's insides the best I could.

The Boss violently dropped to the ground, not because it was injured enough or out of energy but because it obviously wanted to crush me under its colossal weight.

I gasped, watching the huge body get closer and closer to me as if in slow motion. All the thrashing and wiggling from the Boss had caused the mist around it to thin, but I should still be able to Warp out of here. It just depended on if my barrier was connected to the rest of the mist, or if it was currently isolated.

Even so, I was reluctant to leave this spot—I was so close to the end goal.

Kesstel appeared beside me, lifting his hands and catching the weight of the volpoda. He grunted, his knees bending, but he forced the gigantic centipede's body to tent around us.

Several of the Boss's legs stabbed at him, so I quickly expanded my barrier to cover him, too.

I was grateful for him trying to protect me, but now we were both caught under this thing. I might be able to Warp out, but I couldn't take Kesstel with me. I refused to leave him behind, and I didn't know how his movement worked. Could he even get out if I did?

The Boss continued to stab at my barrier as it pressed down on Kesstel. Tiny electric jolts arced between the gigantic centipede's body and ours, each one shaving off chunks of HP. The constant zings were almost more nerve-wracking than they were painful.

I gritted my teeth and put more strength behind my Mist Blade, trying to open the hole wider to get my arms deeper.

Suddenly, something exploded on the volpoda's right side. The monster jolted and eased up a bit. From the small gap between its legs, I could see the expedition Hunters sprinting closer.

CHAPTER 45

Hunters swarmed the volpoda on all sides, like ants on a worm. The sounds of steel on hard exoskeleton and bright flashes of magic polluted the air, coupled with yells and curses, and it didn't take too long for them to realize they needed to attack the joints between the armor plates.

Meanwhile, the volpoda jerked and attacked in kind. Its thousands of legs lashed out at the Hunters, but with them working together, it couldn't move very much. As soon as it attacked one Hunter, another one took advantage to attack on the other side. Even so, it was a hard fight, and the weaker Hunters kept needing to fall back to get patched up by the constantly working healers.

Although the small bursts of lightning which covered the volpoda were considerably weaker, they could still render an unsuspecting Hunter numb and defenseless for a couple seconds if it hit him or her at full strength, leaving them perfectly vulnerable to being stabbed by the sharp end of a leg. At least three Hunters were lost before they figured out how to stay away from the largest lightning arcs.

Kesstel and I couldn't dodge the lightning, still stuck under the volpoda. My barrier did help dull the constant jolts, but it only made them manageable, not go away. It obviously wanted to attack the Hunters fully, but it seemed reluctant to let Kesstel or me up. It also hadn't attempted to fly since Kesstel knocked it down and I broke the antenna. I didn't have the time to consider why; I was too busy trying not to get squished, stabbed, or electrocuted.

Kesstel wasn't too much better than me. Sweat dripped down his forehead, and his arms trembled as he kept holding the Boss up over us. While

I wasn't the one holding it, I could feel the weight of it pressing down on my barrier. It was heavy as hell, especially when it was moving around like it was.

"Come on!" Leader Charlie reached out through the gaps between two legs, obviously trying to assist us. She didn't seem to notice the strong arc of lightning which scrambled like a freaky bug along the bottom of the volpoda toward her.

Thrusting out my hand, I sent a small mist block at her. She was hit directly in the chest and thrown back fifteen feet just as the lightning reached for her. A small yellow line touched her fingers as she went back, but most of the attack missed her. A split second later, a leg stabbed down where she used to be, the dry ground cracking under the force. Because of the mist, I could see that Charlie landed next to a group of healers, dazed but okay.

The thick dust in the air permeating my mist made it hard to breathe. I looked at Kesstel, blinking sweat out of my eyes. I was starting to lose feeling in my arms from stabbing up at an awkward angle for so long. "I can't reach the energy crystal. We need to take this plate off or something."

He nodded then looked at the group of Hunters directed by Blood Sword to our right. They'd been trying for a while to get us out, but nothing they did made the volpoda move. Even with my sword in it, it obviously thought we were better under it than free.

"Attack the head!" Kesstel yelled. "Use magic!"

Blood Sword glanced at Kesstel and nodded. I couldn't hear what he said to the other Hunters, but seconds later, S-ranked mage Tyson led a large group of mages—with several melee Hunters to protect them—to rush the head. A mass of magic exploded on the volpoda's head, and colors flared and blended as magic hit other magic, mixing into a rainbow wave of power almost as big as the lightning bomb the Boss had set off.

I winced as the shock wave smacked right into us, threatening to blow away my barrier. Kesstel shifted until he was between me and the explosion.

The volpoda shuddered like an earthquake, then it reared back, lifting its head thirty feet in the air.

I didn't even take the time to draw a relieved breath. Immediately, I let go of my sword and flipped around, bracing my feet against the slippery white flesh of the Boss and gripping the razor-sharp edge of the armor plate with my hands. With the same thought, Kesstel mirrored my position. We didn't even need to count out loud before we both gripped the edge of the shell and pressed up with our legs as hard as we could. Black blood and clear liquid crackling with lightning dripped around my hands and smeared the bottom of my boots, but I refused to let go.

I grunted as the armor plate resisted us, trying to stop our movements.

"Ha!" Kesstel and I yelled at the same time with a burst of power in our legs.

CRACK!

The whole armor plate broke away from the Boss's body. The volpoda jerked and froze, as if in a silent scream, and every single mega annelid in the whole city wiggled violently in their holes, responding to the Boss's reaction. It caused the ground to tremor, making the Hunters around us stumble.

I was suddenly free-falling. Narrowing my eyes with determination, I let go of the armor plate and twisted in the air. The kindjal disappeared from inside the volpoda and appeared in my hand again.

Kesstel pushed the twenty-by-ten shell out of the way and Double Jumped back up to the Boss. He swung up, his blue steel sword gleaming in the harsh desert light as he slashed through the thick white meat above him, leaving a considerable gap.

My toes touched the ground, and I instantly launched back up with all the power I could muster behind Feather Step. The blade in my hand grew to ten feet long as I rocketed up toward the gap Kesstel had just cut. My toes tapped on his shoulder. He fell down and I shot up, using him as a springboard to put more power behind my attack.

My Mist Blade sliced right through the white flesh all the way up to the hilt. I came to an abrupt stop with enough force to make the Boss's long body bend. At the same time, my sword shattered the monster's energy crystal.

The volpoda exploded in millions of tiny lights.

[+45,000 EXP]

[You have Leveled Up!]

[You have Leveled Up!]

Suddenly, I was free-falling again. This time, I didn't bother to control my movements. Instead, I went limp and fell right into Kesstel's arms. Three drop orbs fell down not far away. I waved my hand and drew them to me using Telekinesis.

"Oh my god," I moaned, breathing hard. All traces of the volpoda had disappeared, but I could still feel the phantom shocks coursing through my muscles. It was enough to make my head ache as much as my body.

"I thought that thing was never going to die." Now that I could finally breathe, I pressed on Kesstel's chest and made him set my feet down. He had to be as tired as I was.

"That armor sure was a pain in the ass," he agreed. After helping me stand, he rested his arm across my shoulder and leaned some of his weight on me. A fair exchange.

The rest of the Hunters were either busy cursing with shock from the Boss disappearing right in front of their eyes, lying painfully on the ground being treated, or checking on their teammates. Another group created a ring around the Hunters and the battleground, keeping the mega annelids back. Five bodies were lined up on the side of the busy group, covered in blankets.

I watched the Hunters move around us like worker ants. "I'm glad you were here," I said softly to Kesstel. Without a doubt, I would have been a lot more hurt without him. Not to mention, I didn't know if it was because Kesstel's attitude affected me or if I was just relieved to not be alone anymore, but I wasn't nearly as nervous about this fight compared to others. Even though this fight was the hardest one I'd ever experienced.

He nodded. "It's been so long since I fought side by side with another, I forgot how enjoyable it was."

A battle-worn Blood Sword walked up to us, leading a small group of people behind him. "Are you okay?"

He hadn't even finished his question before Jonovan stepped around Blood Sword and motioned for me to step away from Kesstel. Even as a healer, he hadn't come out of the day's fight unscathed. There were multiple rips and bloodstains on his blue robes, and his long brown hair was lopsided and tangled. It was the most disheveled I'd ever seen this mellow man. "Where are you most hurt?" he asked, even though his hands were already glowing gold.

I shook my head. "Nowhere in particular; just aching all around. That lightning was no joke."

He nodded and proceeded to give me a full checkup. There wasn't any nagging or smothering concern as he went about it, just a steady, immovable calm. Jonovan had seen the battle. Maybe he could finally accept that I wasn't the same weak little girl anymore.

In the meantime, Blood Sword was talking with Kesstel. "Since you are the leading information source on everything that doesn't make sense— what the hell just happened? Where did that monster come from? I've never seen a monster that strong outside of the Gate."

"That," Kesstel said, his voice flat like it usually was when talking to anyone but me, "was the Boss of the Las Vegas Portal."

Quebec's Logan Fortin lifted his thick eyebrows high on his sweaty forehead. "The Boss we needed to kill to close the portal?" Exhaustion thickened his French accent. Just like everyone else, he was covered in black and red blood. There were countless scratches on his black steel armor, and his left arm bracer was completely missing. "How did the Boss get on Earth?"

"I brought it out." Kesstel shrugged at the other people's shocked faces. "It was better for it to come out of the portal instead of all the Hunters going in. A portal isn't like Earth or the Gates. At least we'd have a home turf battle instead of being at the mercy of an alien environment."

Blood Sword scowled. "That was a dangerous gamble. What if it got away? An S-ranked monster could wipe out the human race by itself."

Kesstel tilted his head to the side, frowning. "A worthwhile gamble. Every Hunter here was willing to lay down their lives to make sure it didn't get away. I sure as hell wouldn't have let it go, especially since I brought it here. I figured it was less of a risk than the whole expedition going into the portal and risking the chance of getting locked inside it when the Boss died. How would North America fare if half its best protectors disappeared?" He didn't bat an eyelash as he lied straight to Blood Sword's face. The only reason why he didn't go into the portal was because I couldn't go in. It had nothing to do with the other Hunters. In fact, they weren't even in the equation when we set up the battle plans.

Kesstel left his words hanging and turned to me. "Are you better?"

"Yes." I smiled, impressed despite myself. It was a pretty convincing argument, considering it was probably all made up on the spot. As it was, the originally disapproving faces of Blood Sword and the other people stiffened as the possibilities flashed through their minds. They obviously didn't know what to think about it all now.

Jonovan stepped away from me and lowered his hand as the golden glow faded. "All better. Now let me look at you, Kesstel."

He waved his hand. "That's not needed."

My lips pursed, but I didn't object. Healers could discover a lot about the physical state of the person they were healing. If Jonovan was able to tell that I'd leveled up so high, he'd be able to tell that Kesstel wasn't from Earth, either. Kesstel probably never used a healer, which was just as well. He was mostly indestructible, and he healed naturally, just like me.

Jonovan wasn't ready to give up. "That's not right. I can see with my own eyes that you have injuries." He motioned to the tears in Kesstel's clothing.

Kesstel reached up and opened wide the gaping hole in the shoulder of his under armor. Then he wiped away the smear of black blood, revealing his pale skin. He was perfectly intact underneath, without even a bruise. "None of it is mine." He said that, but I knew for sure that some of the blood on his body was his. It was just the same color as the monster's blood, so it was impossible to tell what was what.

That knowledge made my heart ache.

Jonovan hummed but didn't have room to argue anymore.

"What happened to the Boss's body?" Blood Sword asked, unwilling to let Kesstel go just yet. "It turned into a million lights. It is dead, right?" His face pinched in a scowl. "It didn't teleport somewhere else or anything?"

"It's dead," I assured him, drawing everyone's eyes to me. "I killed it for sure."

I wouldn't have been able to get the EXP unless it was dead.

In the past, I wouldn't have gotten any EXP from it because I'd fought with other Hunters—a way which forced me not to lean on others and take the easy way out, since I needed the energy absorbed from the monsters through the kindjal to make me—and Goddess—stronger. But now that Goddess was with me, that didn't matter as much anymore. Although I could feel a bud of power buried in my soul that she was keeping in reserve for herself, for the most part, our powers were shared.

I waved my hand toward a clear patch of dirt not far away. The volpoda's empty exoskeleton—one of the drop items from the battle—appeared in a pile, the huge pieces thudding disjointedly together. It was so sudden, several tightly strung Hunters actually brandished their weapons at the mountain of monster carcass. Even though I was ready for it, it was creepy to see the empty husk of the Boss's head lying there on the side, the eyes nothing but gaping black holes.

Tyson, who was closest to the head, actually jumped in shock, his hand encased in fire and ready to blast. "God! How did—what . . . ?" His face wrinkled in distaste at the huge exoskeleton skull as he kicked it with his toe.

It wasn't just the complete exoskeleton that I got from the drop orbs, either. I also got five gallons of the clear liquid the volpoda secreted, and an orb full of crackling lightning. What I was supposed to do with those, I didn't know. I didn't mind handing the exoskeleton over because it was fairly a spoil of war. Even if it was a short time, everyone had a hand in fighting the volpoda, and some even died for it.

"Where did you get that?" Jonovan muttered in shock.

I glanced at him. "Um . . . a special ability? Never mind."

As if that wasn't shocking enough, how was I going to explain the liquid and lightning orb? Especially the lightning orb. Magic stones were common enough, but a glass ball holding a bunch of lightning? Nope. I didn't even know if I could touch it without getting blasted. In theory, I should be able to, but I wasn't ready to test that without rubber gloves. I'd wait to handle those without an audience, thank you very much.

After all, Kesstel deserved half the money from them.

To distract Blood Sword, who was getting ready to talk, I activated an item transfer to him. He immediately focused on the Guide screen that popped up in front of him, requesting that he accept the volpoda carcass.

I smiled slightly and nodded toward the pile of exoskeleton. "You should keep that. You'd know what to do with it more than me."

"The portal is gone," Kesstel added. "So monsters will stop filling up the area. All that's left are the ones that haven't been killed yet. A large part of the previous monsters have probably already been eaten by the worms." He glanced at me, gauging my reaction. "Jynn and I will start working on them. You can join us when you're ready."

I frowned at him. "Are you rested enough?"

"Of course." There was no room to argue with the confidence in those two words. He looked around the ruined city, nothing but piles of rubble, sand, and dancing worms. "There's nothing to worry about anymore, is there?" he asked Blood Sword. "I can move freely now?"

The Hunter accepted the item exchange and nodded at Kesstel. "It's not like you can accidentally bury the portal anymore."

Kesstel looked at me and jerked his chin in the direction of the closest mega annelid. "Shall we?"

Without any restrictions, Kesstel could use his magic to get rid of dozens of monsters in one swing. I was going to have to work out hard to keep up. A smile curled my lips as a challenge lit in my chest. "You bet."

CHAPTER 46

Two days later, all the surviving Hunters met at the junction in North Las Vegas where the original expedition had split into groups nearly two weeks before. When we first stepped into Las Vegas, the party was a hundred strong of the best Hunters. Only seventy-eight walked out of the city.

A group of buses were waiting to take us back to St. George. From there, each Hunter would fly back to their respective cities. There was also a large cleanup crew waiting. The original plan was that the expedition team would kill all the monsters and close the portal, then a cleanup crew would come in to collect the valuable parts remaining on the monster carcasses. The money from the parts would go toward financing the expedition, among other things the Hunter's Association handled. How the cleanup crew was going to be able to get most of the valuable monster leftovers now that they were buried under rubble and sand . . . well, that wasn't my problem.

It did make selling my drop items a little harder, since I technically wasn't supposed to collect them, but if I didn't touch the drop orbs, they would simply disappear and leave nothing. It was a waste—and I'd already left a lot behind. Nor was I going to collect the orbs then toss the items away for someone else to pick up. It just meant that I most likely wasn't going to use Maveric to sell my items this time. Reputable dealers asked questions and followed the law—not really all that great for handling hidden matters. But Maveric could still help me sell all the orc weapons I had.

Or, I thought while glancing at Kesstel sitting next to me, *this guy could help me.* But all that would have to wait until after my mom woke up.

I knew things were going well, really. Earth was shakier than ever, but I felt a moment of peace and accomplishment right now. We'd dealt with the most pressing threat and closed the two portals, killed thousands of monsters, I was an S-ranked Hunter, and now Goddess was here to help find the way to the parasitic planet. With Kesstel and I finally able to work together, it felt possible.

Things were going to work out. I sure as hell was going to make certain they did.

I turned away from the window as Las Vegas fell into the distance behind us. Even though the portal was closed, there was still a thick layer of magical miasma over the city boundaries, like a semitransparent smog. How long was it going to take for that to go away?

Humming under my breath, I leaned my shoulder against Kesstel's arm, getting comfy for the trip back to the airplanes.

Not everyone in the bus shared my moment of relief. A heavy atmosphere of exhaustion hung thick in the quiet bus. When we first came here, everyone was raring to go fight monsters. Now, they just wanted to go home and relax. A and S Hunters fought the toughest monsters in Gate Vale daily, but that was mostly between 7:00 and 10:00 a.m. Two weeks of constant fighting for ten plus hours would wear anyone out.

Blood Sword and his party of leaders were especially tense. Their fingers were flying across the texting boards of their Guide screens, their body language stiff. They were also passing around a file of papers. What were they stressing about now?

Kesstel shifted a little to make it more comfortable for both of us and wrapped his arm around my stomach without taking his eyes off his Guide screen. The fingers of his left hand flitted across the blue screen as he opened up files and paused to read. "Ah, I thought so," he muttered.

I blinked out of my thoughts and glanced up at his blank blue screen. Sadly, no matter how much I stared at it, I would never see what he was reading. "What?"

"When the portal closed, it set off a worldwide Gate Surge," he said softly, still reading the screen. No matter how quietly he spoke, it would never be low enough in a silent bus full of super humans.

The entire bus erupted in shock and disbelief. Multiple people jumped to their feet and others started yelling, demanding to know what was going on. The driver was taken by surprise, and the bus swerved on the road.

Above it all, Healer Laurel jumped to her feet and demanded, "How did you find out?" Her exclamation only incited people more, since she'd basically confirmed what Kesstel said.

I sat up and turned with wide eyes to him. "W-What?"

Then I paused, thinking about the weird feeling I had when the portal closed. Kesstel'd said it was the parasitic planet, then I'd been so distracted fighting the Boss and cleaning after that I'd completely forgotten about it until now. How could I have forgotten about it like that?

My hands jumped up into my hair and gripped the strands hard. "What happened to Garden City?"

Oh my god. I left my family defenseless. Half the best Hunters in Eden came on this expedition. Without them, how was Eden going to handle a Gate Surge? How many monsters got into Garden City before they were stopped? Were they stopped at all? Was that why Blood Sword and his people were acting so tense? What about other Gates?

Kesstel reached out and gently untangled my fingers from my hair. "The city suffered, but it's still standing." As soon as he spoke, the rest of the people went silent.

Multiple eyes turned to Blood Sword, looking for an explanation.

He cleared his throat and stood up, drawing everyone's stares. His face had leaned out in the last couple weeks, and there were stress lines on the sides of his mouth and eyes. "I was going to wait a little bit longer to tell you. Two days ago, while we were fighting the Boss of the Las Vegas Portal, a worldwide Gate Surge took place." Even though we'd just heard it, hearing the second confirmation was still unsettling. It left no room to doubt it was true. "Multiple cities were destroyed across the world from both the Gate Surges and several earthquakes which went off at the same time. We have lost communication with Japan, Australia, and all the African continent. There are multiple other countries that are currently evacuating as we speak."

The more Blood Sword spoke, the tighter I squeezed Kesstel's hand. He didn't pull away, simply sat there and let me try to pinch off his fingers. "Oh my god," I whispered. That was so many people. "What happened to Garden City and Eden?" I demanded, lifting my voice to be heard over the shocked muttering. I glanced at Kesstel.

Blood Sword was the one who answered. "Since so many of our top Hunters were involved in Las Vegas, our people took a heavy hit around the Redding, Quebec, and Eden Gates. We were fortunate to not suffer from another earthquake at the same time. It took ten hours, but they were finally able to kill off all the monsters that exited the Gate in each city."

My chest tightened painfully. Ten hours was a lot of time. A lot of damage and death could be done in that amount of time. Was my family okay? It was already bad enough that I'd left them before the condo was settled. What if they weren't even alive when I got back? Then what did I do all this work for?

Kesstel tightened his arm around me, and he pressed his lips to my hair, but I barely felt it.

"Eden was heavily hit before the Wall around it was broken through in C District and the monsters entered Garden City. The total death toll is in the several thousands and still climbing." Blood Sword kept talking, but my attention was shot by the messy thoughts which exploded in my mind.

C District. That was on the other side of Garden City from where my family lived, but it wasn't too far from Mom's hospital.

I pulled my cell phone out of my Items Bag and stared at it. We wouldn't be within range of a working cell tower until the plane landed in Garden City. It was useless to even look at it. Still, I couldn't resist clutching it in one hand with Kesstel's arm in my other.

The bus and plane rides were silent. No one was in the mood to play around or relaxed enough to nap. It was the second time I'd ever been on an airplane, but there were no excited bubbles in my stomach as we took off. I just wanted to get home to check on my family.

They had to be okay. They had to be. They were on the opposite side of the city from where the Wall broke, and the hospital had been successfully protected. But it was still possible that they had been out doing errands or something when it all happened. If they were out of the house when the Surge occurred, and transportation shut down for it, they could have gotten caught in the fight if they weren't able to find a place to hide.

Just the thought made me nauseous.

The airplane circled the cities as it lowered to the airport runway. I wasn't the only Hunter pressed against the windows, trying to get a good look. Eden had never suffered this badly since it had been built.

The Hunters' city had taken a lot of damage, which was to be expected. After all, it was designed to keep the fighting contained inside. C District and E District were practically totaled. D District was pretty beat up, more than half of the buildings inflicted with damage in various stages. A District had suffered some damage, but since the buildings were better

constructed, the damage was less. Still, at least fifteen percent of the buildings showed damage. The least destroyed District was the Guild District.
Dozens of construction crews were clearing the rubble along with thousands of Hunters.

Blood Sword's voice came over the intercom. "The Hunter's Association
wants everyone to check in at the Association building. Most guild members
are residing inside their guilds at the moment, since most of the housing in
Eden has been destroyed. Those who don't have guilds to go to are temporarily living with family in Garden City if possible, or staying in hotels. Monster
count in the Gate is pretty low right now, so most of the Hunters are being
instructed to assist in cleanup." He paused. "Not fun, but this is our home.
There's going to be a lot of rebuilding, and everyone is expected to pitch in.
More information will be given when you check in at the Association."

While he talked, my eyes were glued to Garden City. From up here,
I could see the wreckage trail from the breached Wall in C District
spreading out into Garden City. It was shocking to see, especially since
the human city had still been trying to recover from the first earthquake.
How many more people had been killed, injured, or left homeless? Tarps
and tents were stretched out in the streets, with people bustling around
between them.

As soon as the plane touched down, I took my phone out of flight
mode and stared at it. Who should I call? There was only one way to call
my family's apartment—a landline. What if it was damaged?

Kesstel tapped my shoulder and directed me to exit. All of our luggage
was in our Items Bags, so we didn't need to pull anything down from the
storage bins, but we were in the second row, and there was a line of anxious people behind me. I absentmindedly followed him out and down the
staircase attached to the plane.

As soon as my foot touched the ground, my phone vibrated and indicated I had a voice mail from yesterday from an unknown number.

My heart flipped, and I stepped to the side so the Hunters behind me
could exit. My fingers were shaking as I opened the voice mail and put the
phone to my ear.

"Please be okay," I whispered. "Please, please be okay."

Kesstel stood at my side with his thumbs hooked in his jeans pockets.
I must be affecting him because his body was tense as he watched me.
Blood Sword beckoned to him, but he just waved him away.

Aunt Mina's tired voice sounded in my ear. "Hey, baby girl." She paused
to take a deep breath. "A lot of things have happened since you left. Some

good . . . um, like, like the condo's foundation isn't as damaged as they thought. We should be able to move in soon. All your hard work is paying off." She took a shaky breath as her voice turned nasally and thick. "I know that you're a long way away right now. And that you're doing a lot of dangerous stuff and shouldn't be distracted but . . . but I just thought you needed to, to know that yesterday . . . "

The phone slipped from my numb fingers as the rest of her message echoed in my blank mind.

Kesstel caught my phone.

I didn't even glance at him as I turned on my toes and sprinted toward the hospital like my life depended on it.

CHAPTER 47

I couldn't count how many times I'd stood in this room full of washed-out colors and smelled the strong hospital sanitizer. Thousands. Tens of thousands. Every other day since I was ten until I became a Hunter, then it went down to once a week or once a month at my most desperate. The first time this room changed was a month ago, when one of the four women Mom shared the room with passed away.

Now it'd changed again. But in a way I never thought possible.

I didn't even know what I felt as I stared down at Aliya in the white bed. Numb. If I had to pick a feeling, that was it. So shocked, scared, horrified, grief-stricken, that it all jumbled into one colorless emotion which settled over me, chasing away everything else. It didn't seem real. Like an illusion caused by the most horrible monster ever.

That couldn't be my sister with her hair smoothed over the white hospital pillow. Her eyes were closed, face slack and peaceful, as if she were just asleep. As if at any second, she'd open her eyes and shout, "JK!"

But that was only if you overlooked the breathing mask covering most of her face. The IV drip that was tapped on her hand. The wrinkle in the cover where the feeding tube lay on her stomach. Her information sprawled across a whiteboard hanging over her bed. The constant beeping machines she was attached to, slightly off beat from Mom's just one bed over.

My vivacious sister, who'd hugged me so tightly the morning I left for Las Vegas, was just like all the other Dreamers now.

My knees nearly gave out. I subconsciously took a step back, away from the terrible sight, as I forced my body to stabilize.

Uncle Carl, who stood with my crying aunt next to me, reached out and rested a hand on my shoulder. In the short time I'd been gone, he looked like he'd aged ten years. Puffy black bags rimmed his tired, red eyes. His skin was sunken, and the gray was more prevalent in his unkempt hair. His hand on my shoulder trembled, his bony wrist sticking out of his winter coat.

"Your aunt and I were at work when the Gate Surge happened. We were scared, but when we heard where the path of destruction was, we thought it was okay. Aliya." His voice choked. He stopped, swallowed hard, then kept talking in a shaking voice. "Aliya was at a friend's house studying for a test, not far from home. When your aunt called, she said she was okay. By the time we got home, it was dark. Since the lights were off, we assumed she was staying at her friend's house, but she wasn't there when we called. She'd left before dinner. After searching other neighboring houses for a while, we found her unconscious on the little walkway on the side of our apartment."

Aunt Mina, who looked just as aged and neglected, gasped out a sob. " . . . 'ya . . . Aliya . . . " How long had she been crying like this? From how raw her voice sounded, a long time.

Uncle Carl kept talking, his voice cracking. "She's okay, just unconscious. A . . . Dreamer." Water pooled in his eyes.

I stared at him, processing what he'd said and not at the same time. I should be crying, too. I understood that, and some tiny part of me felt guilty that I wasn't. I just couldn't feel enough yet. Maybe that was a good thing, I thought, staring at my broken aunt and uncle. I needed to be strong. For them.

Yet, I could feel something inside me starting to crumble under the weight of this room.

That future, that dream I'd been doggedly striving for, the one thing which always kept me going. It was me and my sister together as Hunters, killing off the last of the monsters which remained after the parasitic planet was dead. It was being able to go home and see my mom smiling as she finished making a family dinner, with Kesstel on his way. It was knowing my aunt and uncle were not far away, enjoying their own quiet evening.

A future where my family got together, laughing and loving. All of us were healthy and whole. No fear of dying at any second. No stress about money. No confinement to a hospital bed. No . . .

Nothing. There was nothing now. That dream was gone.

I only had one antidote to the Dreamer's disease. And there were two beds with my loved ones in front of me.

I gripped my hip satchel as my breathing came faster. *No, calm down.* I had to stay calm. Dreamers were people who couldn't handle the magic which spilled out of the Gates. My magic was different, but I couldn't take the chance. There was still a desperate hope that Aliya would simply wake up if the magic pollution went away. I couldn't make it worse now.

I turned to the door a second before a knock sounded. I wasn't surprised when a doctor walked into the room and shut the door. I could never remember his name, but I recognized his gait as his soft-soled shoes slapped the hall floor. He looked at the three of us, a concerned and polite expression on his thin face. "I'm glad everyone is here now. I have a couple questions, especially for Miss Devhro.

"In the last two days," the doctor started in an even though exhausted voice. "Along with all the injured patients from the Gate Surge, there has been a sudden large influx of Dreamer victims. In fact, the numbers for both afflictions are almost equal."

I jerked in shock. My hand drifted until I touched the back of Aliya's still hand.

"The numbers are so high, frankly, we don't have the space or amount of equipment to handle them all. We've even contacted instacares and doctor offices to board the ones we can't fit." He motioned to the bed behind us. "Because you have a contract with the Hunter's Association, Mrs. Devhro will be kept until the contract runs out in four months. All requests for extensions are being denied. We have to make room for the new victims who still have a chance to wake up. You can attempt to transfer her, like what we talked about before, but I must warn you, the sudden influx of Dreamers was not an isolated incident. Hospitals all over the world are suffering from the same circumstances we are." His words were even and slow, as if he'd rehearsed this speech a hundred times. Given the situation, he probably had.

My body went cold. I could feel mist bubbling up inside me, reacting as the dull blanket over my emotions started to shed away, piece by piece. A sharp spike of grief washed over my body. I pulled my fingers away from Aliya's hand to prevent myself from accidentally hurting her.

The doctor reached into the pocket of his white coat and pulled out a sealed petri dish. A familiar red fish-scaled bracelet rattled inside as he held it up. Light caught on the fanged snapper scales, flashing a fiery opalescent ripple.

I frowned at it and subconsciously touched the matching bracelet on my own wrist.

"As we processed all the recent Dreamer victims, we noticed a pattern. Ninety-two percent of them were wearing an item which emitted magic waves." The doctor motioned to the bracelet. "Miss Aliya Devhro was wearing this when she came into the hospital. Although the magic coming from this is very weak, there is still magic on it." He pointedly looked at my wrist. "We have concluded that it is made with fanged snapper scales. Do you know where she got it from?"

My body started to tremble as I understood. "I-I gave it . . . to her." My voice broke as horror flooded my mind.

Aunt Mina gave a great sob and sank to the ground, pulling Uncle Carl down with her. Their noises were just muffled sounds in the background of the panic dominating my thoughts.

I gave it to her. I personally made the item which helped my sister fall unconscious.

I didn't even think anything of it. I was just so happy to give her something nice. It was our little secret: matching charms, proof that things were going in the right direction. And when she became a Hunter and came to Eden, I was going to give her a better gift. Make her life better.

At the time, I didn't know it was dangerous for her. I didn't know it was the parasitic planet's magic which caused Dreamers. And when I found out, I didn't even think about the bracelet I'd made for my sister a month prior. It shouldn't have mattered anyway, since she was going to become a Hunter. And it was the parasite's magic which made Hunters. Aliya always sounded so sure she was going to be a Hunter; she was even counting down the weeks until she became one. I just assumed she was going to be one, too.

I never thought . . . I'd spent my whole life trying my best, bleeding blood and sweat, to make sure my sister was happy. I never thought I would be the reason my most precious person would be dying.

My knees nearly gave out, and I tipped back toward Aliya's bed. My eyes widened in horror. No, what right did I have to stand by or even touch her? My bracelet, my hip satchel, and the pendant from my birthday were made with the parasite's magic. What if I hurt her more by being here? What about Mom? Was I making it worse for her, too?

In a flash, I moved to the other side of the room, as far as I could from the people on the beds. I gripped the pendant hanging around my neck as I pressed my back against the wall. My eyes were wide, breath coming short and fast. The dam around my emotions and self-control crumbled with every gasp I gave. Mist pooled around my feet, threatening to break out and flood the city.

No, I couldn't let that happen here. Control. I needed control. I was stronger than this. I had to be stronger. Strong enough to control my emotions. Strong enough to protect my loved ones.

But I was the one who put her in the bed.

No, Goddess said softly in my mind. *It's the thick magic in the air from the Gate Surge.*

But she's been wearing that bracelet on her skin for months, like a slow poison, I thought back. *If she hadn't, she might have been strong enough to withstand the magic.*

Goddess didn't argue back. After all, the facts were undeniable.

Aunt Mina suddenly clutched her chest and started to gasp for air.

"Mina!" Uncle Carl grabbed his wife in shock.

The doctor rushed over and dropped to his knees in front of her, pulling out a walkie-talkie and starting to order for assistance. My mind was too jumbled to understand what he was saying.

I flinched back, pressing harder against the wall, trying to get away from the people who were my world. "No, I didn't hurt her." My voice trembled. "I swear, I didn't."

My family was already so broken. How were we going to recover from this? What if they broke more than this? With all this going on, how were my aunt and uncle going to handle their physical and mental challenges? Even if the parasite went away, how was anything going to go back to the way it was?

Uncle Carl was talking fast to the doctor. " . . . another anxiety attack." He paused and looked up at me as a horde of nurses entered the room and swarmed Aunt Mina. "It's going to be okay, Jynn. Calm down." For a second, he looked like the strong man who raised me. The one who, when Mom became shut in this room, stepped up and tried his best to give his nieces a happy childhood. "Your Aunt Mina, me, your mom and sister, we are going to be okay," he said over the nurses talking. "Why don't you step out and calm down? I'll call you later, and we can talk more."

My chin shook, and I bit my lips hard to make it stop. I looked at Aunt Mina, watching as her breathing started to slow and she started to respond to the group of medical personnel around her. I wanted to get closer, but I was too scared. What if I hurt them? I could already feel my control slipping with each wave of terrified guilt that crashed over me.

Without a word, I Merged with the mist at my feet. The people gasped and screamed in shock as I dissolved into smoke right in front of them. It just made me feel worse. Like a monster.

I fled out the door, the thin water vapor slipping over the heads of the people and down the hall to the closest open window.

The air was thick with magic pollution. It fizzled and rejected the mist which housed my essence as much as I rejected it. Desperately, I looked around. I didn't know where to go. The E Hostel had been flattened. It felt wrong to go to my family's apartment when they were all here. But I couldn't stay in the hospital.

Most of it was my fault.

My chaotic emotions sparked my magic like a bomb. The mist I was in expanded, forming a huge, thick cloud. Desperate to get away from the hospital, I lifted higher in the air until the mist could spread across the sky without touching the building.

My body condensed inside until I knelt in the air, with my face buried in my hands. The cool water vapor drifted around me, gently brushing against me in soothing strokes. I knew it was Goddess trying to console me, but I didn't respond.

All I could do was curl into a ball, tightening every muscle. My eyes burned like they were full of lava, but I refused to let the tears fall.

Even Goddess' voice was muffled as she talked to me. I couldn't seem to understand what she was saying.

"Jynn?" Kesstel's voice broke through the thick shell encased over me.

My eyes cracked open as I instinctively responded to his voice.

"Jynn, let me in." His voice sounded so smooth, so gentle. Like an anchor in the storm raging in my mind and heart.

Slowly, my hands fell away from my face.

He stood on top of the hospital, staring up at the tightly shut mist ball around me. He could break it open if he wanted to. Instead, he stood there in jeans and a button-up shirt, waiting for me to respond to him. Just like always. So patient, so steady.

How did he know that I needed him right now? No matter what or where, he always knew when I needed him most. He'd protect me from everything—even these emotions which smothered my reason. I was safe as long as he was there. I didn't have to hold in my emotions. I couldn't hurt him or cause him to leave me.

My hand trembled as I reached out to him.

He jumped up and skillfully passed through the barrier I'd opened up for him. He knelt on the mist block I was on and reached for me.

I leaned into his chest and clutched his shirt. As soon as he touched me, all the tense fear and self-hatred dissolved, leaving bone-aching, weary grief.

He didn't try to ask what was going on or hound me with words. He simply held me close, like I was a glass figurine he desperately wanted to protect. Right now, I didn't want words. I just needed him to be here.

My eyes closed as I listened to his steady heart. It was reassuring, but it also reminded me of the two beeping machines in the hospital room below. The ones that controlled my mother's and sister's lives.

My eyes cracked open as my hands tightened on the soft cotton in my fingers. "I know . . . "

Kesstel bowed his head over me, waiting for me to continue.

"I know I have to be strong." My voice cracked. "But . . . can I take a break?" My voice hitched, forcing me to swallow hard before I continued my slow, thick words. "I'll be strong again tomorrow. Strong enough to fix everything that's wrong. I promise. But right now . . . I'm so tired."

So tired of the emotional roller coaster. So tired of keeping all my emotions bottled inside. So tired of fighting. So tired of trying so hard only to watch everything fall apart again.

Kesstel's lips pressed into my hair. "Go ahead. I've got you as long as it takes. Until you're ready to stand on your own again."

The tears burning in my eyes spilled over and seared a trail down my cheeks until they were soaked into Kesstel's shirt. I never knew I needed this permission. But as soon as I heard it, it was like a ten-ton stone was lifted off my shoulders.

All the emotions from years of trying to be strong rained from my eyes. Tears from when my mom fell unconscious. From watching my aunt and uncle ruin their health for my sake. The disappointment of being the weakest Hunter in history. The pain and fear as I struggled to survive. The relief of finally turning my life around, only to watch that hope shatter into pieces. And knowing I accidentally had a hand in it.

The horrible realization that I was going to have to choose to save either my mother or my sister. No matter what I chose, one was going to stay in that hospital room. And if Earth collapsed too soon, the first to die would be the Dreamer I left behind.

The more I cried, the tighter I held Kesstel. Held onto my harbor in this gale of emotions.

All the while, he cradled me in his arms and pressed soothing kisses to my hair.

CHAPTER 48

I didn't remember crying myself to sleep. When I woke up the next morning, I recognized the bedroom decorated in navy and shades of gray. Kesstel's spare room. Several decorative pictures were missing from the wall, as well as the vase that used to hold a couple fake white ball flowers and twigs.

Some part of me knew I needed to get up, but I just lay there in the bed. I felt like a lifeless doll. If it weren't for the warm covers, I might have assumed I'd frozen in place. For the first time in a very long time, I didn't get a notification of daily tasks from the System. My phone on the bedside table flashed a message from Uncle Carl, saying that Aunt Mina was okay, and Mom and Aliya were still stable. I stared at my phone for a while but couldn't bring myself to call him back. Not yet.

When I dragged myself out of bed to wash my face and change in the bathroom, I found all the missing decorations from the guest room. They were in pieces in the garbage can, probably a result of the disasters which kept plaguing the city.

Kesstel's house was empty, aside from me. I thought I'd feel more nervous walking around his huge, expensive home, but I wasn't. Maybe it was because it smelled like him—a comforting, rich smell. Maybe it was because I couldn't seem to feel my emotions properly yet.

After such a big cry for the first time in ten years, I felt mellow. Like a leaf floating on a still pond. Moving had kick-started my mind, but I wasn't in the grips of hysteria.

I walked barefoot to the kitchen, noticing other changes in the house as I moved. Most of the lamps were gone, as well as the large art piece which used to hang over the fireplace. There was a crack in the bookshelf, like it had taken a tumble, but it was still there. Probably because there was nowhere else to put the stuff it held if it was gone. Kesstel wasn't really a just-pile-it-on-the-floor kind of person.

A box of assorted muffins and a slip of paper sat on the marble kitchen counter, set in plain sight. I slipped onto a stool and reached for the box. Since I knew they were for me, I took out a lemon crumble muffin without feeling guilty and took a bite while I glanced at the note. Kesstel's handwriting was as neat and sharp as a steel blade.

Jynn,

I went to report to the Council. They probably won't shut up until I do. They want a full report of everything that went on in Las Vegas. They also insist that you turn all the orc weapons you have over to them in the name of research for the betterment of human society. As if they have the right to steal your hard work. I'll make sure they spit out a good price.

Take a break and rest. If you need me, call.

Kesstel

It looked like I didn't even have to worry about selling the weapons or dealing with an auction. I should be glad, but I didn't feel anything at all.

My fingers played with the partially eaten muffin for a minute before I set it aside and laid my head on the cool stone counter. In the quiet house full of Kesstel, I finally felt like I could think about what was going on. Finally felt like I could cope with the horrid joke my life just became.

I'm glad you finally calmed down, Goddess said quietly in my mind. *You were so hysterical, I couldn't even get through to you.*

"Hm," I hummed out loud. No one was around to hear my one-sided conversation, anyway. Not to mention, I wanted—no, *needed*—to voice my thoughts. It felt like it was the only way I could turn this tangled mess in my mind into something tangible. "I'm sorry I ignored you yesterday."

I understand. I've also seen my hopes and dreams fall apart in front of my eyes.

Those words alone were enough to make my eyes burn with more tears. God, I thought I had cried myself dry by now. I gritted my teeth and turned my face to press against the cool marble. I couldn't start crying now. One night of feeling hopeless was enough.

Now, I had to do something about it.

"I . . . I don't know what I should do," I whispered. "How do I choose between my mother and my sister? My mother was my hero. The coolest, most amazing person I've ever met. Everything she did, the effort she put in for me and Aliya, taught me what love and perseverance is. I wouldn't be who I am today without her." My voice broke. I took the time to lick my lips and rein in my thoughts before they ran rampant again. "Then there's Aliya. She's the biggest reason why I tried so hard my whole life. Every time I hit the bottom, I never gave up because if I wasn't there for her, no one else would be. And I wasn't going to let her be alone. I couldn't give up on myself because I couldn't give up on her. She was the future I tried so hard to make happen."

My head tilted to the side so I could press my aching temple to the stone, as if it were a magic cure. "Do I choose the woman who has had a life already and who has been unconscious long enough that she won't live another couple months? Or do I give up on her and choose the girl who just started life? But there's still seven years before she'll be pushed out of the hospital. That should be enough time to isolate the vaccine from Mom's blood and create a cure."

I didn't really need Goddess to answer my words; I wanted to hear the options. Luckily, she seemed to understand that and stayed silent even though I knew she was listening.

The tiny, intricate bottle appeared in my fingers. I twisted it this way and that, watching the small amount of liquid inside slide around. It was such a miracle when Goddess gave me this cure. It was the answer to my desperate prayers; a blessing I couldn't be more grateful for. Now, it almost felt like a curse in my hand. A reminder that I had to choose to kill one of my loved ones.

"How long do you think it would take them to isolate the cure in someone's blood?" I whispered.

I could tell, from the thick magic which hung over the land as far as the eye could see, there wasn't a lot of time left before the parasitic planet struck. Once it appeared, the first people to disappear and become parasite food were the Dreamers. Since they couldn't handle the parasite's magic, they couldn't become monsters. Outside of their life energy, they would be useless to the structure the parasite had developed.

Too long, Goddess replied simply. *Not only would they have to isolate it, there's a chance the ingredients inside the cure could change from their original state once it makes contact with human blood. That would add more time. If everything was peaceful, it would be fine. But now . . .*

"But right now, they would be able to remake the cure," I said, watching the morning light coming through the kitchen window gleam off the bottle. "They could mass-produce it. You said that Earth has all the ingredients to make it. The scientists should be able to do it. Right? Then both of them could wake up."

A small bud of hope bloomed in my chest.

It is possible, given that the ingredients' data is stored on their computers. If not, they would have to search across the globe and match the ingredients. Just like that, my hopes were crushed under the heavy boot of reality. *You won't have time to search for ingredients anymore. I'm attempting to stabilize Earth with my presence, but that can only go so far. Even more pressing, that loathsome being now knows I'm here and is obstructing my help.*

"So, what you're saying is that I'm going to be busy soon? How so? Extra monsters and whatnot?"

I couldn't guess the mind of that foul creature. I just know it loves to torment those who oppose it.

"Sounds fair," I muttered, a chill spreading in my chest and stilling the conflicting emotions in my heart. Right now, I felt reckless enough to almost look forward to the parasitic planet attacking me. Since I couldn't go to it, I could only wait until it came to me.

Then I planned to hurt it as much as it'd hurt me. Until it went away forever.

It was at that moment I realized I couldn't give up on my dream of having a whole family. I couldn't pick and choose which piece I wanted. The puzzle would never be complete if one piece was missing. There wasn't a lot of time. But until the world ended, I was going to keep going as if tomorrow was going to be okay.

Because I was going to make it okay.

I will remind you, that vial is the only one I had. Just one dose. Once it's gone or some is taken out, there is no replacement. No one will wake up, Goddess added.

My fingers jerked. I put the bottle away before I could do something stupid like accidentally crush it in my hand. "I understand."

The muffins Kesstel left for me looked amazing, but food sounded disgusting. I carefully wrapped up the one I'd started to eat and put it and the rest of the box inside the fridge for later. I flipped Kesstel's note over and sprawled a short message saying I'd be back.

Once that was done, I locked the door behind me and took in a deep breath of chilly fall morning air. Then I turned into a mist cloud and flew over the buildings, headed to Gate Square and the giant black arch that loomed over the city.

Most of the buildings within two blocks of Gate Square were destroyed. Construction workers and Hunters wearing temporary neon orange vests milled around the piles of buildings. They were digging things out of the wreckage and loading piles of debris into dump trucks. Some construction crew members and weaker Hunters used machines to help move stuff. Stronger Hunters simply picked up sections of brick walls with their hands and dropped them into the awaiting vehicles. I paused, watching a petite woman hoist a broken metal L-shaped office desk bigger than she was tall and toss it into the dump truck like it was a piece of foam. She slapped her gloved hands together to get the dust off and reached down to grab another large piece of broken furniture.

The only buildings which remained mostly untouched were the Hunter's Association and the Eden Hospital. Both of them had very strong barriers around them, but even with that, they showed some damage. Understandably, they were also the buildings already being fixed up. Kesstel was in the Association building right now, but I turned to the other side of the Square and landed in front of the hospital.

I converged my body back together and drew my mist back inside myself. I'd made my decision, only now that I was here, I couldn't help but second-guess myself. What if . . . they used up all of this dose without being able to recreate it? Then both my mother and sister would be doomed—and it would be my fault for giving the cure away. Was I really doing the right thing, gambling their lives away like this?

The glass front doors slid open, and a pair of Hunters came out.

I blinked out of my thoughts and stepped around them. Before the doors slid closed and I lost my nerve, I hurried inside. It felt a little odd being in the hospital. There was a period of my life where I was here once or even twice a day. Now, it'd been so long since I was in here, I almost felt like a runaway finally coming home.

My mouth twitched at the absurd feeling, and I walked to the front desk. For the first time, I didn't know the name of the woman sitting there.

She looked up from her computer. "What can I help you with?" Her eyes flicked over me, taking note that I wasn't hurt. A puzzled, polite smile settled on her face.

"I need to talk to Healer Jonovan."

Surprise flashed across her face. "Oh, well, it's a busy time right now. It could take a long time . . . " She tapped on the keyboard as she spoke.

"I could set you up for an appointment next week? How does Monday sound?"

I shook my head. "It has to be today. Tell him that Jynn Devhro needs to talk to him about something important." I motioned to a cluster of beige chairs next to a wilting plant. "I'll wait for his reply."

CHAPTER 49

Thirty minutes later, a nurse guided me to Jonovan's office. I already knew where it was, but it was policy. She tapped on the door and waited for the man inside the office to respond before she opened the door and let me pass.

I thanked her then shut the door in her face. Privacy was a habit I doubted I'd ever get over.

Jonovan sat behind his desk, hands crossed and resting on the wood in a relaxed manner. He smiled at me, looking just like when I met him over eighteen months ago. His pale brown hair fell over his left shoulder and white mage robe overtop of his business casual dress. "Good morning, Miss Jynn. I wasn't expecting you to visit me so early. I was told it was important?"

I took a breath and sat down in one of the chairs before his desk. "You once said that you were involved with making the cure for the Dreamer's disease." I looked into his eyes. "Are you still part of that team?"

He blinked in surprise. "Yes. Although, there wasn't much advancement in its development while Healer Laurel and I were away. Things will get back on track once the labs are cleaned up from the earthquake."

My brows wrinkled. "Do you think you will find a cure?"

He nodded, his gentle handsome face tightening with determination. "We will. Is that all you needed to talk about?"

I bit my lips and stood up. My hand floated over the expensive wood for a second before a small, intricate vial appeared. My fingers rested on the pretty lid. Everything in my body was screaming to grab it and run. No matter what, I could at least guarantee that one of my loved ones would live. I'd worked so hard for this cure, and now, I was just giving it away with no proof that I was doing the right thing.

Instead, I forced my fingers to lift. My hand shook as I drew it back to my side, and my movements were stiff as I stepped back and sat down again.

Jonovan watched me. He didn't know what the vial was, but he could obviously see how I was struggling just letting it go.

"This"—I took a deep breath—"is the cure for the Dreamers."

His eyes widened as his jaw went slack. He focused on the vial like it was the most precious thing in the world. "Are you sure?"

I nodded. "I got it while we were in Las Vegas. It's the cure. The only one on Earth."

"Are you giving this to me?" he asked. His hands twitched as if he wanted to grab the vial that rested between us.

As soon as he moved, my body tightened, ready to lunge forward and swipe it away from him. Instead, I threaded my fingers together and fisted them in my lap. Hopefully, he couldn't see how white my knuckles were. "Yes." The word was like jagged glass on my tongue. "But I have some requirements."

He reached out and gently picked up the vial. He didn't notice my body stiffening because he was so focused on the cure. He lifted it into the light and watched the light reflect on the bright liquid inside. "It's pretty." He lowered it and gently put it back on the desk. "What requirements do you have for me?"

"Do you promise you'll recreate the cure?" I pressed, my hands shaking in my lap. "You have to promise me, or I'll take it back right now. That's the only dose in existence. If you take even a part of it and can't recreate the formula, it will be useless. I'd rather take it back and use it now."

"Did . . . something happen?" he asked slowly. "I know that your mother is a Dreamer, but . . . " He left the sentence hanging.

"My sister," I said softly. "Three days ago, right after the Gate Surge."

He bowed his head briefly. "I'm sorry to hear that. From how you used to talk, I assumed she'd be a Hunter."

I nodded slowly. "I did, too. That's actually requirement number two. The first two people to get the completed cure are my mother and sister. I don't care if you only manage to make three cures and people are offering millions of dollars. The first two who get it are my family." There was no mercy in my voice.

I wanted to be a good person, but not at the expense of my family. In the end, I wasn't really fighting to save the world or to save humanity. I had a conscience, but I wasn't a saint. I was fighting to protect my family because they'd die if Earth fell. It might be sad that I was putting the lives of four people over the lives of billions, but it was the truth. And I didn't feel sorry.

Jonovan hummed in agreement. "I understand. What else did you want?"

I paused. I didn't have any other demands. As long as my family woke up, I didn't care what else happened. I shook my head. "That's it."

He smiled softly. "I'll make sure you are fairly compensated."

I blinked at him. "Huh?"

He motioned to the vial in his hands. "This little bottle is worth millions, if not billions. There were over five hundred million Dreamers in the world before the sudden influx a couple days ago. If each dose only costs a dollar, even that would be no sneezing matter. But I can tell you now that each dose will be a lot more than a dollar. It's only fair that you are properly paid for your efforts in waking those people up. Without your work, we wouldn't have the chance to."

A bitter smile spread across my face. It was just too painfully ironic, really. I'd struggled with money my whole life, to the point where there were days that I only ate one meal and wore clothes which were falling apart, even relying on Henry to get that meal sometimes. Still, I'd pressed on because I needed to.

Now, it felt like money was raining from the sky. Between the items in my Items Bag, the orc weapons, and now the Dreamer cure, I suddenly found myself practically rolling in money. And it all meant nothing to me. I couldn't jump up and down with glee and laugh out loud like a nutcase because the very reason why I wanted money to begin with was in a hospital bed on the other side of town. What was the point of having money now? To pay for medical bills?

I'd trade every penny, go back to wearing rags and starving every day, if only Mom and Aliya would open their eyes.

"Okay," I whispered. "I want the benefactors, if something happens to me, to be my mother and sister, then my aunt and uncle. Can you help me with that? I don't have the faintest clue on what to do. I don't even care if you take a commission fee."

He shook his head. "That's not needed. I'm happy to help. Ecstatic, almost." A smile bloomed across his face. "Holding this in my hand, I finally have hope in waking them up. Thank you, Jynn. From everyone that will never even meet you: thank you for your sacrifice." His smile turned businesslike. "Let me write a rough outline of what you want first.

I'll contact you tomorrow with an update. You aren't the only one eager to wake up their loved ones. I promise, I'll wake them up. Starting with your family."

I trusted him to keep that promise, which was why I'd brought the cure to Jonovan. I trusted his ethics and honesty. There were only two other Hunters—Henry and Emma—whom I knew were moved for the greater good and not just power. The difference was, Jonovan had the status to uphold his word.

Even with that mindset, I still couldn't decide if I had done the right thing as I stood outside the hospital a short while later.

My chin tipped back as I looked up at the looming black Gate—and the rippling air around it. It reminded me of the heat mirages I sometimes saw on hot pavement in the summer. Unfortunately, it didn't have anything to do with fast-moving air and everything to do with magic leaking out of the Gate. It wasn't like this two weeks ago. The tasteless, scentless, nearly invisible miasma was all over the city.

As much as I blamed myself for Aliya, now that I wasn't freaking out, I understood that the real cause of her becoming a Dreamer—and Mom's condition—was because of this magic. Nothing I did or could have done could do this much damage.

I looked at the working people sweating in the chilly fall air, cleaning up the mess around me. I should help too, but there was something I needed to do first. Since Aliya couldn't wear the bracelet I'd made for her, I should give her one she could.

I already knew that E District had been totaled, so it didn't surprise me when I saw that the hostel was nothing but a pile of rubble. Even the new gym in the back was mostly destroyed. From the gaping hole in the front, I could see blankets and tarps stretched out inside as temporary housing. How long it would take for them to get out of it and into real accommodations, well, E District was very low on the list of things to be fixed. Always had been, always would be.

What did surprise me was how few people were cleaning up the rubble. There were over twenty-five people who lived in the building. Only six Hunters were there now. Two held shovels, dumping scoops of debris into the waiting wheelbarrows the other two people were holding. Another two were picking through the mess. Where was everyone else? They couldn't have been assigned to another cleaning site, could they?

I recognized all of them from months of passing in the halls or dining room, but I didn't know any of their names.

One of the scavengers in the middle of the pile suddenly jumped to her feet and waved a beat-up dirty tin can in the air. "I found it! I think I found the location of the food storage from the kitchen!" Her voice was shrill with excitement. "There's still unbroken cans!"

The other rummager awkwardly hurried over the pile toward her while the two men holding shovels rushed over, using their shovels like paddles to go faster. "No shit?!" one of the men yelled in excitement. "Let's cook some now!"

They were excited to find a can of food buried under a building while I'd turned away gourmet muffins because I wasn't in the mood to eat. Strength really was everything.

Just the mention of food brought up a glaring problem. I walked to the closest Hunter holding a wheelbarrow and caught his attention before he could join them. "Hey, where's Henry?"

As surprising as it was to see so few people working here, the most surprising thing was not seeing that short, round-faced old man busily bustling around. I'd never been in this building when he wasn't here.

Since he was the one in charge of the hostel, did he need to go to the Association building for some reason? He couldn't be at the hospital. Because of the wonders of healing, very few Hunters spent extended time in there.

The guy used the back of his dirty hand to push at the sweat streaming down his face, leaving a black streak on his burnt tan skin. He looked at me like I was insane. "Where have you been? Look around you. Henry's dead."

CHAPTER 50

He's dead?" I muttered, shock crashing through me. I stared at the piles of debris around me, but what I was really seeing was the last memory I had of Henry.

He stood in the middle of the kitchen, eyes narrowed as he smiled at me. "Ah, Jynn girl. Taking part in a secret government mission, huh? Well, no matter how tall the mountain is, it cannot block the sun. Take care of yourself and stay away from the wrong people." He patted my shoulder and passed me a bag of snacks for the plane ride.

That same Henry, the one who'd cared for me like a grandpa since I stepped into this city, was gone?

"How can you not know?" The guy holding the wheelbarrow snorted.

My brows pulled together, and my eyes burned, but I didn't let myself cry. I'd done way too much of that lately. I swallowed the lump in my throat. "I wasn't in Eden when it happened. I just got back."

He paused, his brows rising high in surprise. "Well, you're one lucky shit. I wish I could say the same." He scowled and motioned to the people scavenging around the debris. "We're the only ones left in the hostel. Most of us went to Gate Square to fight. The hell with that; it was a massacre. Then the monsters started crashing through E District. Leslie"—he motioned to the woman who was excitedly pulling out cans of green beans—"was here when it happened. A bunch of two-headed earth trolls attacked the hostel. That stupid old man"—his hands tightened around the handle until his knuckles were white—"actually tried to fight them. He was just an old man with a limp. What the hell was he thinking? He should have just run away like everyone else. Of course he was gonna die." The guy's voice was so thick that he stopped talking. I couldn't tell if he was angry at Henry or grieving or both.

I nodded slowly, accepting the reality. I was used to people dying. It was an occupational hazard of being a Hunter. But I honestly never thought Henry would die before me. I thought he'd grow old and die a natural death, still helping people in the hostel.

"Anyway," the guy grouched and jerked his head toward the rest of the people. "If you wanna eat, you have to help dig it out. The Association hasn't sent food since the Gate Surge, and who knows when we'll get more. You should be glad I'm willing to let you have any at all. Most weaker Hunters are already starting to fight over food." He left the wheelbarrow and joined the other Hunters.

I stayed still, thinking about everything. The more I saw, the more I couldn't help but thinking about the pictures and stories from when the Gates first appeared. The apocalypse that wiped out half the human population. Was that happening again? Was there even going to be a human population to save before long?

I blinked out of my thoughts and jumped over to the other Hunters, careful to control my moves so I didn't freak them out. I didn't care much to help them, but I knew if Henry were here, he would have. There were more pressing things on my mind, but I still stayed and helped them dig out all the usable food we could find. They didn't notice when I stealthily moved the heavier pieces of metal, wood, and brick out of the way to make it easier for them. Frost had collected in the shaded spots, making a couple Hunters complain about the cold, but we kept working anyway. An hour later, they were happy with the pile of food we'd transferred to the partially collapsed gym.

While they excitedly started a fire to feast on the spoils of our work, I went back to the rubble. My room had been in the northwest corner of the third floor. When the building fell, my stuff could have been scattered around, but I chose to start in roughly that spot, digging for the safe that had been in my room. I should have moved my stuff out of it before I left, but I didn't think anything would happen. Sure as hell not this.

I grabbed a four-foot piece of carpet and pulled it aside, dragging all the debris on top with it. I wasn't winded or even tired, but I could feel certain muscles start to complain. My body was built for fighting, not construction work. It required a whole new set of muscles that didn't get used often.

I took a drink out and tipped my head back. While I wiped my mouth, I glanced at the ground . . . and paused.

The drink vanished from my hand as I crouched. Carefully, I extracted a picture from a pile of wood bits and the twisted remains of a computer.

The worn frame was broken, and what glass was left was in tiny shards cutting into the picture behind it, but I could still see the happy faces of the family that Henry missed so much.

My chest squeezed tight just looking at his face and knowing that I'd never talk to him again. At the same time, seeing this picture, I didn't feel so sad anymore. Henry had waited for years to rejoin his family. Now he finally had.

I painstakingly cleaned up the picture and glass as best I could. I didn't have a way to fix the frame—out of the ever-growing list of miscellaneous things I kept in my Items Bag, tape wasn't one of them for some reason—but I pushed it back together until it was presentable. Slowly, I walked over to where Henry's garden was. It was mostly covered in junk, but there was still a half-smooshed white flower peeking out. Kicking the rubble away until the flower was free, I bent down and propped the picture up behind it.

I didn't share Henry's beliefs, but I'd seen him paying homage to his family a couple times when he thought no one was watching. Since Henry's family was gone, he'd never get a funeral, but at least I could do this much for this wonderful man. I took two small candles out of the expedition Items Bag I still had, lit them, and set them next to the picture. Not knowing what else to do, I simply knelt down in front of the photo and bowed my head.

"What are you doing?" Leslie came over, bringing with her the smell of warm corn. She held a can in one hand and a spoon in the other. The can must have been hot because it was wrapped in cloth. She stared at me with curiosity while possessively clutching her food.

I motioned to the picture. "Giving him a funeral. It's the least I could do, after everything he did for me."

She bobbed her head and shoved a scoop of corn in her mouth. She chewed for a bit, then asked around the pocket of food in her mouth, "Why did you come back? If you were hoping to scavenge a fortune, you picked the wrong place. The Association took all the safes they could find when they dropped the dump truck off." She scowled at the vehicle.

I blinked at her. "The Association took all the safes?"

She bobbed her head and swallowed her bite. "Yeah. The property of dead Hunters without family belongs to the Association. They're sitting on a gold mine right now. You think they're gonna let it get stolen away? We got to keep ours, since we were here at the time."

I glanced at the makeshift home in the gym. "I thought they were providing housing for the Hunters who lost theirs. Hotels and stuff."

Leslie shrugged. "For the stronger Hunters. They ran out of room for people like us. The Association said they'd work on finding us housing soon, but I wouldn't hold my breath. Especially before all this mess is cleaned up." She nodded at the broken hostel then looked pointedly at the men around the campfire behind her. "These guys are alright. At least I know them. Better than a bunch of people I don't."

I hummed in thought. It sounded like my safe was most likely with the Association right now. At least I could check there before I dug through a whole building. It was more travel time, but it could save me a lot of use-less digging. After I found my safe—and my mother's bracelet inside—I'd come back and help clean up the hostel. I'd lived there with these people for a year. I didn't have that much attachment—if any—to them, but I could do that much before I walked away forever.

In the end, I left them all the leftover camping gear the Association gave me for the expedition to Las Vegas. Because I'd stayed with Kesstel the whole time, the only thing I'd used was the camping chair, and even that was very lightly used. The E Hunters were excited and hoarded the items—one-person tent, chair, small pots and pans, firewood, campfire griddle, and other odds and ends—into the gym. While they moved, I could feel eyes staring at us from a distance. Other Hunters looking for a quick grab to make their lives easier. Whether the E Hostel Hunters were able to keep the gear I gave them, well, that was up to them.

I'd just entered Gate Square, heading to the Hunter's Association Head-quarters, when I noticed a familiar face in the mass of Hunters in the square. Some were working, others waiting outside the Association build-ing, and some looked like they were simply taking a break and talking.

I couldn't resist sighing in relief before I called out to her. "Emma!"

Emma paused midstep, falling behind her team and turning in my direction. They were just like everyone else in the city, wearing junky work clothes and covered in sweat and grime. Emma's dark hair was pulled up in a messy bun, and there was a dirt smear on her cute face.

Her eyes lit up as soon as she finally pinpointed me. "Jynn! Oh my goodness! You're alive!" She ran over and threw her arms around me hard enough to make me step back.

I hugged her just as tight. Thank god, at least one of my special people was safe. I was starting to think I was going to lose everyone.

She started talking a million miles per hour. "I was so scared! I couldn't get a hold of you! Miss Bethany said you were on a mission for the Association, but that could mean a bunch of things. Then the Gate Surge and all the monsters. So many people died. When I couldn't get a hold of you, I thought . . . I thought . . . " She choked up and sniffled hard. "But you're okay!"

I patted her back soothingly as her team walked over to us. "I'm okay. I'm glad you are too." After she calmed down a little, I stepped back and greeted the rest of them.

They all muttered a greeting except for the new guy, Russel. He just frowned at me, obviously still confused as to how to class me.

Mason gave me a smile. "It's good to see you."

"What the—" Billy muttered, staring over my head where my title bar would be. "Where did your rank go?"

I paused, not surprised that he was the one to point out what I didn't want to talk about. "I lost it."

"The hell? How do you lose something like that?" he demanded.

I pointedly looked at Emma and changed the subject. "Are you guys helping with the cleanup? How damaged is your guild?"

There was an obvious mood change in the whole team, ranging from upset to sad.

"Is it that bad?" I wondered aloud. I thought the guilds didn't get too damaged.

"Well, it's not really the state of the building; it's the state of the guild," Mason explained. "President Price is, well, not right in the head right now. I heard he took part in an Association mission and lost a bunch of money and Mr. Hans, his cousin. He was missing an arm when he came back, and even though the arm was fixed, I heard he's become paranoid. He's lashing out at everyone. Even his right- and left-hand men, who were his cousin's bodyguards, left the guild."

"If you ask me," Kip, the mage, huffed, "the President has it out for us. I swear he's making our team do all the worst jobs. Even lower-ranked teams are getting better treatment than us."

Emma bit her lips. "We thought we'd look around and see if there are any other reputable guilds taking team recruits right now. There are a lot of empty slots in guilds right now, you know? So a lot of guilds are recruiting to boost their numbers so they can jump in rankings."

"Or maintain them," Healer Morgan added.

I nodded slowly. The rest of the city was in shambles—with Hunters digging food out of ruins—and the guilds were still playing politics. Ugh. But I couldn't help paying attention.

"So Price started bullying you?" My head tilted to the side, thinking. I'd warned him not to touch my people. What an idiot. "It sounds like he really doesn't want to keep his arm, huh?" I muttered to myself. Kesstel wasn't the only one who could take it off. Or should I take off more?

Emma's eyes widened. "What?"

Mason frowned. "Do you . . . know how he lost it?" He paused. "You just came back from a mission. Were you on the same one?"

There wasn't a reason to deny it, so I nodded.

Billy let out a low whistle. "How did you manage that? What happened?" Curiosity burned in his eyes, ready for dirt to fly.

I pursed my lips. "Price and Blake pissed off the wrong people—two S Hunters." That was all they needed to know.

The whole team gasped.

"No way," Emma muttered. "That's so stupid!"

"It sounds like we really need to leave," Mason said softly. "I'd hate to get caught in the backlash, especially if it damages our reputation, too. We have a good team, and there are several other guilds interested in us. We were just seeing who would give us the best offer."

The team nodded in agreement.

"Are you going to join a guild yet, Jynn?" Emma asked. "You're so skilled and knowledgeable. I don't know why you haven't yet."

I smiled and shook my head. "Nah. I have a partner, and that's all I need."

She blinked. "Who?"

"Kesstel Noblé."

Kip choked in shock with the rest of the team. "The Noble? You're partners with the Noble? How is that even possible?"

I smiled at her then glanced at Mason. "The two people who left, were they Mark and Penny?" The last time I saw them with Price, the tension in the air was palpable.

Mason seemed surprised that I asked. "Yes."

Under his breath, Billy muttered, "Tight-lipped as usual."

I snorted and looked at him to retort.

All of a sudden, my chest tightened almost painfully as my whole body screamed in alarm. Instinctively, I threw up a mist barrier around us.

A sudden pulse of magic detonated from the giant black Gate in the square. The magic rippled through the air and ground, vibrating everything like a blaring subwoofer without noise. Hunters were thrown off their feet, and glass rained down as every window that hadn't been broken yet shattered.

The magic hit my dome barrier and pushed it across the ground five feet, taking the whole group with it. The pressure was so immense that my knees almost gave out. Emma and her team were flattened, even with the barrier buffer.

"What's going on?" Emma screamed with the rest of the shocked Hunters in Gate Square.

The magic coming from the Gate let up, but the black arch started to warp and twist. At the same time, a siren rang out in the air.

"Another Gate Surge!" Mason yelled in horror. "How is that possible?"

Suddenly, the sky dimmed. The bright sunlight faded, and an eerie red tint colored the world.

Shocked, I tilted my head and stared at the cloudless blood-red sky. "No . . . "

CHAPTER 51

The whole city was dyed red as the sky changed colors. At first, there was a frightened hush that hung heavy in the air, then the screams started echoing out.

"The sky!"

"What happened?"

"It's like the Gate at night!"

The Hunters were alarmed, but the screams from Garden City on the other side of the Wall were near hysterics. They were so loud, I could hear them all the way from Gate Square. Made sense, really. The humans had no idea what actually happened in the Gate. They were kept to their safe little lives for a reason—to prevent the mass hysteria I could hear going on right now.

Emma pushed up to her bleeding hands and knees, rubbed raw from sliding across the concrete when the Gate destabilized. "What's going on?! What happened to the sky?!"

My chest tightened so hard that I could barely breathe as panic set in. No, I wasn't ready yet! I hadn't found the portal to the parasite. Kesstel and I hadn't set up a solid plan of attack. My family was falling apart, and I hadn't fixed it.

But my thoughts didn't change anything as the sky grew more and more red. Just like what had happened to Vapria right before it was destroyed.

It's begun, Goddess whispered.

A roar broke through the Hunters' panicked yells as monsters started to spill from the Gate. They rushed at the unprepared Hunters, ready to start feasting.

Instinctively, I threw out my hand. A pool of mist swallowed the Gate and sealed the monsters inside, who hit my barrier and attacked it with everything they had, some stopping inches from horrified Hunters.

I gritted my teeth at the immense pressure it put on me, but I refused to let them go.

Some Hunters started to slap their armor on as fast as possible, ripping off awkward clothing that was in the way, not bothering with under armor before slapping their armor plates over their street clothes. It was a frenzied mess, but when death was right there, growling at you from the other side of a transparent barrier, nobody cared much for privacy. Other Hunters were too shocked to do anything. They just kept looking from the red sky to the endless stream of monsters filling the mist barrier again and again. There was so little space now, and the monsters were so agitated, that they started to attack each other.

"What are you standing around for!" I yelled at the people still lying there. "Get ready!" I couldn't hold this forever. Every time another monster came out of the Gate to join the pile, it was like another ten-pound brick was placed on my shoulders. There were hundreds, if not thousands of monsters in there—it was a lot of pressure. I still had to get my own armor on.

Here, Goddess said.

My circlet appeared in the air, floating just above my hands. Well, it wasn't the first time the System had pulled something out for me. Only, I needed more than just the circlet. It was pretty and boosted my magic, but I needed to protect my body, too.

Still, I turned my hand and took the circlet out of the air. As soon as I touched it, it disappeared. Faster than the blink of an eye, my street clothes were gone, and I was wearing my under armor and armor. They were just there, complete with the circlet around my head.

Since when was that an option? I thought in shock, trying not to get too distracted from the barrier. That could have saved me a lot of time in the past!

Since right now. I thought you might need a shortcut at the moment, Goddess reasoned.

Very much so. Thanks, I thought back.

Kip, who was in the process of buttoning up her baby-blue mage robe, paused and blinked at me. "How . . . "

I tilted my head back as I felt Blood Sword, leading a group of S

Hunters, come up behind me. The rest of the Hunters hurried past, but Blood Sword and Healer Laurel stopped at my side.

He reached out to pat my shoulder, but his hand ran into the small dome still surrounding me and Emma's group. He glanced from his hand to the Gate and the monsters piling inside. "Are you the one doing that?"

I nodded.

He jerked his chin down in a sharp nod. "Good job." He turned and faced the crowd of Hunters. "At the ready!" he yelled.

Hunters already dressed—or at least mostly dressed—hurried into formation around Gate Square. Since Emma's team was in roughly the right position, they didn't try to move, staying inside the dome I hadn't taken down yet.

Weapons started to appear.

I gritted my teeth and attempted to push the monsters back into the Gate. There was so much resistance, it was like trying to move a mountain with my bare hands. I puffed out a breath, then caught Blood Sword's attention before he could join the rest of the S Hunters on the front line. "Where's Kesstel?" I asked. He wasn't with the other Ss who walked by, and I couldn't feel him in the crowd.

Blood Sword pursed his lips. "The Council is still questioning him about the current turn of events." He glanced at the red sky, his face darkening.

I snorted. "It's a little too late for that. They should have listened when there was still a chance to do something about it. This is the end of the world. If there is a tomorrow, it'll be a miracle. If the Council wants to change anything, they need to get off their asses and fight with the rest of us."

Emma, and anyone within hearing distance, paled. "What?" She gasped.

Blood Sword frowned. "I hope you're wrong."

The side of my mouth curled up in a bitter smirk. "I'm going to do everything I can to prove me wrong, too."

I gritted my teeth as a group of A-ranked lichs came out of the Gate. They pressed on the mist barrier, their ghostly hands slowly inching through my resistance. A sharp pain stabbed in my temple. Ruthlessly, I blocked around their hands then snapped those blocks up. The lichs wailed, a high-pitched shrill, as their hands were broken right off. The limbs would grow back, but it at least relieved me of the pressure for now.

"Hurry!" I yelled at Blood Sword.

Suddenly, another magic pulse exploded—but this one wasn't from the Gate in front of me. It came from the wilds on the other side of the walls around Garden City.

The magic crashed through Garden City, smashed into the Wall around Eden, then washed down into Gate Square. Everywhere it rolled across, people were flattened, and untethered things were sent flying. If it weren't for the dome around me, I would have been thrown off my feet like the rest of the Hunters. Even the Ss were taken down. Emma was groaning from the heavy aura and pressing against Mason as he tried to protect her.

The magic ripple crashed into the mist barrier around the Gate. I yelled in pain as fractures split around the shield, but I refused to let it fall yet. Every Hunter was on the ground right now. They were dead if I let the monsters out. My head pounded painfully.

Gasping, I turned my eyes to where the magic came from.

On the other side of the city, a black arch rose in the air, bigger than Eden's Gate. It stood like an onyx tombstone against the red sky.

Blood Sword scrambled to his feet. "Oh my god. Another Gate?"

The new Gate rippled. A pair of humongous pincers, at least fifty feet long, emerged from the black arch, followed by the gigantic face of a man, his wide, bare torso, arms with clawed hands, and then the rest of his body—his scorpion body. He was at least a hundred feet tall and over two hundred feet long. Every time one of his clawed eight feet stabbed into the ground, it set off a small earthquake.

My eyes widened as I recognized the Scorpion Man from the day that Vapria fell.

Both cities were deadly silent, everyone petrified at the sight of the monster which made the volpoda look like a weak little worm. Just the Scorpion Man's aura was enough to make the few E Hunters near me shiver with fear.

The Scorpion Man tipped his head back, opened his mouth to reveal small pincers hiding inside, and roared loud enough to make my ears hurt from here.

Blue Guide screens popped up in front of every Hunter.

I blinked at the teal translator screen in front of me containing one word.

[GODDESS!]

Kip gaped at her screen. "Did . . . did that monster just say a word that translated?"

The Scorpion Man roared again, and another screen yelling "Goddess!" appeared.

Instantly, I knew what was going on. My power came from Goddess, and seventy percent of the mist I had stored in me was from her palace on Vapria. Because I was holding back the monsters in Eden's Gate with my magic, the parasitic planet had been able to locate us. Now, it'd sent something to take care of us.

I was scared. After all, I'd personally witnessed what this Scorpion Man Boss had done. But more than being scared, I wanted revenge. Revenge for Goddess's people; revenge for mine. I wanted to protect my family, who were in the defenseless city standing between me and that horrible Boss.

I turned my head and locked eyes with Blood Sword's wide ones. "Are you ready? I'm going to let the monsters out now." I nodded toward Eden's Gate. "You take care of those. I've got that one." I jerked my chin at the Scorpion Man, who still roared.

Blood Sword collected himself and frowned in concern. "Are you sure?"

Ignoring Emma's protests, I nodded. "Of course. After all, it's calling for me."

I glanced to the far side of Gate Square. I couldn't see Kesstel, but I could feel him waiting at the crumbling Wall around Eden.

"We'll go with you!" Emma instantly volunteered without even asking her team. The rest of them paled but didn't actually argue.

A soft smile touched my mouth as I looked at her. If this was the last time I would see her, I wanted it to at least be with a smile. "No. That monster will kill you all without a doubt. Stay here, where you can make a difference. Protect the people, and live while doing it."

She shook her head. "But you're just an E. I have to protect you."

I laughed and shook my head. "I'm grateful that I met you. Truly. You were my first true friend since I became a Hunter. I'm grateful for you and your team." I glanced at all of them. "I hope that we all get to see each other again. If we don't, then thank you. And goodbye."

Before Emma could object, I canceled the dome around us then jumped up into the air and landed on a mist block.

Blood Sword took my cue and ran to the front line. "Ready!"

"Now!" With a sigh of relief, I let go of the barrier around Eden's Gate.

Monsters spilled out and ran right into the weapons waiting at the ready for them. Steel flashed, magic exploded, and monsters roared among the screams of Hunters. Soon, the whole Gate Square was a bloody mess. The monsters were relentless, and the Hunters were desperate, putting extra energy behind every attack. It was enough to bring the fighting to a stalemate.

They have to be fine, I told myself as I turned away. There were bigger things I had to deal with.

I focused on the giant Scorpion Man still roaring for Goddess and marching toward Garden City. Kesstel jumped up next to me. For the third time since I met him, he wore full armor.

He fell into step with me, not even bothering to ask if I'd make my blocks big enough for him. He just assumed I'd naturally do it, which I did.

"That's the giant Scorpion Man you were asking me about, huh?" Kesstel asked, frowning at the monster as we quickly closed in. There was nothing relaxed about him at all. He regarded this creature to be as big of a threat as I did.

"Yes."

"You still want to save this planet?" he asked, glancing up at the red sky. "Right now is the time to slip away into a portal without any backlash."

"We have to save it," I insisted. "It's my home." I glanced at him. "That means it's yours too, right?"

His face softened for the barest of seconds. "Yes."

My kindjals appeared in my hands as I glared at the Scorpion Man. "Then let's save it."

CHAPTER 52

The Scorpion Man stabbed his clawed insect feet into the ground, leaving ten-foot-deep holes in the ground with each step he took toward Garden City. He was so big, he didn't take too many steps before he was looming over the buildings.

The cannons attached to the walls around the city, which hadn't been used in over ten years, fired. Cannonballs exploded when they hit the Boss's chest; only, he didn't seem fazed at all. The cannons weren't meant for something like that gigantic monster, but they didn't stop. There wasn't much else they could do. The mage guards stationed on the walls attacked with their magic, but it was like a fly headbutting a door.

The Scorpion Man swiped a huge pincer out and took out an entire section of wall in his way, taking the cannons and Hunters on it with the chunks of bricks. He threw his head back and roared loudly. [**GODDESS!**]

Kesstel and I closed in fast, silently sprinting over the city on mist blocks. Our steps were perfectly in sync, a smooth, steady rhythm which calmed me even in this situation. If I'd been alone, I would have been more rattled. With Kesstel at my side, the only emotions I felt were burning revenge and a determination to protect my family. I just hoped they were okay.

As we reached the edge of the city, I lifted my right hand. A wall of mist rapidly grew ahead of us, and as soon as it was a hundred feet tall, I thrust my hand out. The mist wall shot at the Scorpion Man, the whole thing becoming solid right before it reached him. It rammed into the creature, pushing it back thirty feet and out of reach of the city.

Open shock flashed over the Boss's ugly face.

Kesstel and I landed on a floating mist cloud at the edge of the city ninety feet in the air so we were face-to-face with the Boss.

I glared at him and tilted my head, acting more cocky than I felt. "You don't have to yell so loud. I'm right here."

The Boss's solid black eyes flared, his gray lips curling in excitement. He looked ready to eat me. Then he noticed Kesstel standing beside me, and he snarled, the pincers inside his mouth sliding out of the corners of his lips and snapping—a morbid thing to see happen to a mostly humanoid face.

It was, without a doubt, the reaction of one predator to another.

My lips wrinkled in distaste at the sight. I pointed my kindjal at the Boss. "There are already two Bosses on this planet. Three's a crowd."

"So die," Kesstel finished, pointing his own sword, matching my movement.

The crimson sky high above us started to wrinkle. Suddenly, the heavens split open. On the other side of the jagged rip was a giant blue crystal planet looming in the void of space. A heavy pressure settled over everyone's shoulders, as if gravity had doubled in strength. The image vibrated slightly, like it wasn't quite solid, but it didn't make the obvious threat any less menacing.

A horrified hush fell over the city. Even the screams from Garden City stopped, and the sounds of fighting from Eden quieted, as if everyone was too scared to make a noise. As if the slightest whisper would drop the blue crystal planet onto Earth.

My chest tightened in fear, but I refused to let it take over. My eyes narrowed on the parasitic planet, finally seeing a place to channel all my wild emotions. Now that I had a target, a calm settled over me as my mind shifted to battle mode.

The Scorpion Man's face suddenly relaxed into a sneer, and it rumbled a growl. [**Such arrogance for such an insignificant being.**] His eyes began to glow, the same color of blue as the planet hanging over our heads.

I blinked, taken aback by the sudden change. Then I realized that the Scorpion Man wasn't talking to me. It was focused on Kesstel.

[**I made you. Do you really think you will ever be free?**]

My eyes widened.

Oh my god, the parasitic planet was talking to us through the Scorpion Man. It could do that? Suddenly, I remembered the orc king and how his eyes had glowed, too. Was that what was happening?

Kesstel glared at the Boss, his own eyes starting to glow bright blue. The same color as the monster he was staring down. "You created your own grim reaper. Congratulations."

The Boss snorted with amusement before looking at me. Or in my direction. I could tell he wasn't really seeing me but the aura around me. [**You should have stayed where you were, Goddess. You changed nothing; just the location you will die.**]

A transparent, slender hand wrapped around mine, holding the kindjal with me. Out of the corner of my eye, I could see Goddess's silvery hair floating around me, and her white dress dancing around my feet. Instantly, I knew her image had overlapped mine, but she hadn't completely smothered my appearance. We were just standing together, one human and one ghost, occupying the same space.

Kesstel's hands tightened on his sword, but he didn't react otherwise.

"I will not let you touch my family," I grated out.

"*I will not let you touch my people,*" Goddess said at the same time, our words overlapping just like our bodies. For the first time since I came to Earth, I could hear her words with my ears, not just in my mind.

"You will pay for what you have done to Earth."

"*You will pay for what you have done to my world.*"

"All the pain and suffering you have inflicted on us, I will give it back."

"*All the pain and suffering you have done to me and mine, I will give it back.*"

"*Prepare to die,*" we said together. The crystal blade in our hands started to glow, as if confirming our promise.

The Scorpion Man's glowing eyes narrowed, then he threw his head back and opened his mouth wide. The pincers inside wiggled around as if laughing, but the sound coming out of his throat was more like a growl. He looked back at me, obviously amused. [**You said those words before, obnoxious pest.**] He snarled, referring to when Vapria collapsed. [**This time will be no different; only, I won't keep you alive after I crush you to pieces.**]

The blue light disappeared from the Boss's eyes. He roared loud enough that I felt it in my chest, but this time with no words, like a monster, and swung his huge hands at us—fast.

Goddess's image vanished as she retreated into me.

I Warped just as the claws reached me.

Kesstel jumped up, out of the way, and I lost sight of him.

The hand smashed into the mist block we had been standing on. The tinge of pain flashed in my mind, but I refused to let the block disappear. The Boss gripped the box as if confused about the sudden solid obstruction.

Landing on its arm, I sprinted at full speed up its length all the way to his shoulder while summoning all four kindjals. The Boss turned his head, furious at how fast I was, and those disgusting mouth pincers snapped at me, so fast they looked like black blurs. I used my two floating kindjals to deal with the mouth things as I jumped at the Scorpion Man's face and slashed. He tilted his head to the side just in time, and instead of cutting his eyes, my blades left two long gashes along its cheek.

As soon as the black blood touched my glowing blade, Goddess gasped. *This energy crystal! It's connected to the parasitic planet! I could use it to make a portal!*

My eyes widened in shock. I was momentarily distracted, and instinctively glanced down to where the Boss's body changed from a man into a scorpion. There, in the middle of his stomach, was a faint glow indicating where the energy crystal was.

In that split second, the Boss grabbed at me. I twisted in the air, slipping away from the first hand, but couldn't get out of the way fast enough to escape the second one. Before he could squeeze me in his huge hand, however, I turned into mist. The clawed fingers filtered through the fog and clamped shut, but while I still took damage, I wasn't dead.

Quickly, I slid through the wrinkles in his gray skin then condensed on top of his fist. All four of my kindjals stabbed down into his hand, two on top and two at the palm. I was aiming for the tendons and cords of blood vessels, but I didn't do as much damage as I wanted before I was suddenly airborne and rocketing toward the ground. Gasping, I gained control of my fall and slowed the speed with Float. As my body turned weightless, I twisted around and landed on a mist block thirty feet from the ground, breathing heavily.

From this angle, I had a good vantage point of what Kesstel was doing. While I had been attacking the Boss's face, Kesstel had gone after the scorpion body. I could tell its exoskeleton was hard, but there were still cuts and holes along the huge expanse.

Kesstel was constantly on the move, avoiding the clawed legs jabbing at him, but the most concerning part was the long tail tipped with a ten-foot stinger, which stabbed fast as lightning. Even with his amazing speed, Kesstel still had trouble dodging the attacks. Every time one missed and stabbed into the ground, the dry dirt exploded as if it were a bomb, and a pool of yellow liquid filled the hole. From the trails of smoke that wiggled up from the pools, and the strong acidic stench I could smell from here, it wasn't hard to guess that the liquid was very dangerous. Kesstel was forced to be just as defensive as he was offensive—not something he did often.

As I watched, the curved stinger stabbed down at Kesstel.

I shot my two floating kindjals to where the stinger was heading. At the same time, Kesstel dodged then Double Jumped right over my swords as they flew like beams of light. The stinger stabbed into the ground, thrashing the small vegetation there, and an explosion of dirt sprayed in the air. The kindjals shot right into the middle of the dust cloud and stopped with a *crack*.

The Boss roared, lifting his tail up. Two glowing swords stuck out of the bulbous part of the stinger, trails of yellow acid leaking from the holes and covering the blades. The acid clung to the metal and crystal, causing steam to float up. The damage caused Mirror to deactivate, and the floating kindjals disappeared, leaving two leaking holes behind.

Kesstel landed next to me, breathing just as heavily.

"I need the Boss's energy crystal," I said, pointing to its location. "Goddess thinks she can use it to get to the parasite."

Kesstel's eyes widened before they narrowed in a challenge. "Gift wrapped, or can I leave it bloody?"

He could talk like that in a situation like this? I snorted, watching the Boss focus on us again. "I'll be happy with whatever you give me."

"This is where you should act coy and ask for the stars," Kesstel responded. He swung his sword and sent a tidal wave of blue magic at the Boss's torso just as the Scorpion Man reached for us with both his hands and the huge scorpion pincers. Apparently, Kesstel was really determined to get that energy crystal.

To keep out of Kesstel's way and distract the Boss, I went after the scorpion body.

CHAPTER 53

The Boss lifted his giant front pincers, using them as shields against Kesstel's magic.

While Kesstel's magical attack charged toward the Scorpion Man's torso, I used the thin mist I'd spread across the whole area and Warped to the other side of the Boss, where the stinger attached to the tail. I was already swinging before my body was fully congealed. The ten-foot Mist Blade slashed right where the two pieces of exoskeleton met and sent a spray of black blood flying as I sliced through the soft flesh.

The Boss jerked in pain, and his front pincers shifted ever so slightly—but it was enough. Half of Kesstel's powerful attack hit the wide pincers, leaving not even a scratch on the hard exoskeleton. The other half crashed into the Scorpion Man's fleshy torso, causing an explosion which made him stumble back. The light faded, revealing gaping holes in the gray skin that rained down pools of black blood to the ground.

While it was still reeling back in pain, I Warped to stand in front of Kesstel and lifted my hands. As soon as I appeared, he paused, stopping whatever attack he was about to do. Thickening the mist around the Boss's human body until the monster disappeared from normal eyesight, I turned Mist into Poison Fog. Hopefully, the Scorpion Man was hurt enough for the poison to take effect. I was an S Boss, too, but the Scorpion Man was still six levels higher than me.

My brows tightened together as I tried to force the poisoned mist against the bleeding wounds. Unfortunately, I could see the injuries already starting to heal, and a thin layer of skin was starting to stop the bleeding.

I tsked under my breath and retracted the Poison Fog from everywhere except around the head. "Be careful of the head," I warned Kesstel. "I don't know if that mist will hurt you or not."

"Noted." He softly brushed his left finger—his right hand was covered in blood—around the shell of my ear and flashed a soft smile before he jumped back into action.

I rolled my eyes at him, but a smile was tugging at my lips.

Still, I couldn't help but wonder if he was flirting right then and there or if being so close to the Scorpion Man—who was apparently closely tied to the parasitic planet—was affecting Kesstel, and he needed a touch to calm himself down.

The Boss lunged at me, giant pincers snapping.

I watched the attack come as if time had slowed down. At that moment, I became distinctly aware that I was standing right in front of Garden City. I could feel people's lives behind me moving around in the wreckage of the collapsed wall, yelling to each other in panic or reassurance. There were even a few brave Hunters talking about jumping in and fighting. If I dodged now, at this angle, the Boss's attack would hit Garden City again. Who knew how many more people would die?

A mist block appeared behind me to act as a brace as I lifted my kindjals. The pincer, five times my size, hit my blades. Gritting my teeth, I forced it to stop, my arms shaking painfully and my legs aching under the pressure, but I refused to move.

The second pincer closed in. Quickly, I sealed the first one in mist then jumped up and swung my kindjals in a quick one-two hit as hard as I could to deflect the attack. The claw was forced up, swiping right over the buildings just inside the city wall. The structures shook from the pressure, but none of them fell.

At the same time, Kesstel let out another massive magical attack on the tail and back feet. The Boss grunted in pain as his hind legs nearly gave out. I took that opportunity to create another mist wall the same size as the Boss and thrust it at him. The mist wall smashed into the Boss. His weakened legs gave out, and he was forced back away from the city a hundred feet before he dug in the claws on his feet and flung his arms out as he roared, breaking my mist wall apart.

The Boss looked livid.

I winced at the sting in my mind from him crushing the wall, but it wasn't that important. The wall had served its purpose, so I didn't need to hold on to it. Gripping my swords, I summoned new floating kindjals and jumped back into the battle.

It was like the Scorpion Man had entered a berserk stage. His movements, which were already fast, grew faster. He snapped with his pincers, slashed and grabbed with his hands, and jabbed with his scorpion tail as we exchanged blows. Blood was flying on both ends, and although the Boss had a humongous amount of HP, Kesstel and I were working on whittling it down.

Once the Scorpion Man's HP reached fifty percent left, the Poison Fog anchored to his head finally kicked in. Unfortunately, the Poison and Bleeding effects only lasted for five minutes before the Boss's healing ability took the negative effects away. His healing ability wasn't intense, but it was enough to make things difficult.

I was losing HP too, and my MP was dropping like a leaking cup. Still, I kept the monster away from Garden City while dealing as much damage as I could. The battle got so intense, I couldn't even spare a moment to pay attention to the situation of the collapsed wall or hear what was happening in Eden.

The land in front of the city was riddled with giant pits, puddles of corrosive goo, and battle scars from the fight. All the foliage had been uprooted or trampled to dust, leaving just a mess of dirt around us. The main interstate to and from Garden City had been reduced to rubble.

The Scorpion Man roared and swung his hand back at me.

I was just a hair too slow to react; the back of his huge hand smashed into my whole body.

All I could do was gasp as I saw stars while all the air was slapped out of me. Every cell in my body instantly screamed in pain as I was shot down to the ground like a fly swatted from the air. The gray haze which covered my eyes faded away just enough for me to see the ground zooming up toward me. I tried to right myself so I wasn't headfirst, or use mist to catch myself, but I was still too disoriented. Neither my body nor my magic seemed to obey me.

Just before I hit the ground, Kesstel appeared under me, wrapping his arms around my limp body and cradling my head, stopping my fall inches from the ground. His chest was puffing with effort, and sweat dripped from his forehead into his tired face. His scratched steel armor was covered in black blood, but I couldn't tell what was his and what was the Boss's.

I gasped for air as Regen began to work its magic on me, taking away the dizziness. Unfortunately, there wasn't much it could do about the fatigue or my low HP until the battle was over. My heart hadn't even settled before I felt another large attack coming.

Kesstel dropped me flat to the ground as he turned, his sword up to block the attack. I landed on the dirt just as the stinger on the Boss's tail collided with Kesstel's sword. Sparks flew as the stinger was deflected off its original course, but it wasn't enough to fully defend against the attack.

My eyes widened as the stinger punctured Kesstel's stomach right through his armor and stabbed through to the other side.

Kesstel yelled and bent over in pain, but stayed where he was. In front of me, like a shield.

"Kesstel!" I screamed in shock.

I'd never seen him hurt like this before. This was Kesstel, the strongest being I knew. One of my most precious people; the man I wanted in my life forever. How dare that creature hurt him like that in front of me?

Don't touch him! The words screamed wildly in my heart as cold fury settled in my mind.

I Warped from where I lay and appeared above the stinger.

"Hah!" I yelled, stabbing the ten-foot Mist Blade down into the stinger with all my might. The semitransparent blade cracked through the exoskeleton and sank down into the fleshy bulb, then with another crack, the blade reappeared through the bottom. The stinger was pulled from Kesstel's stomach just as I nailed it to the ground with my Mist Blade.

Kesstel groaned and stumbled back, holding the heavily bleeding hole in his torso. His face was pale, and his hand shook as black blood stained his armor. He bent over in pain but still kept his head up, eyes narrowed and ready for another attack.

Everything in my body screamed to go to him. He got hurt protecting me. I needed to make sure he was okay. I could see how injured he was; I just needed to know if he could heal from it. If I needed to find a healer, to hell with Kesstel being outed as a Boss or not.

Only, I couldn't. The fight wasn't over yet. I couldn't take Kesstel and leave. Garden City would be totaled before I found a healer good enough to help Kesstel.

The Scorpion Man screamed, trying to pull its stinger away, but my Mist Blade had it pinned.

Frigid fury burned in me. My thoughts stilled to a deadly silence as my body began to act by pure, ruthless instinct. Six solid mist blocks appeared around me—only, they were different from any I'd ever made before. They were shaped like spikes, their tips needle sharp before they spread to three feet wide and twenty feet long.

I turned to face the Scorpion Man, sweeping my hand out at him.

The semitransparent stakes shot at the Boss like giant bullets. He lifted his pincers to protect his torso, but the spikes pierced right through them and into his fleshy humanoid body. The Boss roared in agony, grabbing at the spikes with his hands to pull them out, but his clawed fingers slipped right through the mist, all while blood gushed from the holes that couldn't close.

I jumped high in the air and Floated above the scorpion body, but I wasn't idle. More mist spikes appeared around me, thirty feet long and sharp. I started raining them on the scorpion body, nailing it to the ground like a bug on display. I deliberately targeted the joints between the exoskeleton plates. If the first spike didn't break through, another one immediately followed until a hole was created and the Boss's body was speared through.

He tried to dodge at first, but after the second spike, he lost a lot of his mobility. The Scorpion Man was stronger than me by six levels, but he was overwhelmed by my furious and vicious assault.

Make it feel the same pain that Kesstel felt. That thought dominated my mind as I sent spike after spike down. My head pounded from the excessive use of magic, but that hardly mattered. When I was content that the Boss couldn't move anymore and his HP was low and red, I Warped behind him right where the glow of the energy crystal was.

I lifted my right hand, and one more mist spike appeared above my hand, five feet wide and twenty feet long.

The Scorpion Man turned to me, his face tight with pained anger. He reached for me, obviously wanting to crush me in his huge hand.

Before he could touch me, I launched the spike at where the gray human body turned into a scorpion. His pincers were still pinned to his body, and his hands weren't fast enough to stop the attack. The spike pierced the blood-slick skin and sank into the Boss's body five feet before it suddenly stopped. He stiffened in pain.

I immediately lunged after the spike and landed on the blunt end with my feet, kicking it with all my might and will.

With a grueling pop, the spike pierced all the way through the Boss's body. The tip came out the other side, and with it, a ten-foot-long oval energy crystal.

CHAPTER 54

The giant energy crystal dropped to the ground with a *thud*. It was so heavy that the ground sank almost a foot under it.

The Scorpion Man collapsed and landed with a small earthquake, his body contorted oddly from the mist spikes which stretched him across the ground. I didn't have to check to know he wasn't breathing—a pond of black blood pooled around his body, getting bigger by the second. My nose wrinkled in disgust at the sight.

With a wave of my hand, I canceled the mist spikes. The Boss's body slumped in a gross pile, and for the first time since I got the System, I didn't get any EXP for killing the monster.

The huge portal the Scorpion Man came out of, a half a mile to my right, started to wrinkle and shake as it began to collapse.

I gasped. *No! We needed that portal! That was the way to the parasitic planet!*

Kesstel took a couple steps toward it, his face tight with pain and a hand pressed over the hole in his right side.

It's okay, Goddess said. *That actually doesn't lead to where we want to go. That giant insect wasn't kept on that abominable being, so this portal doesn't lead to the parasite.*

The tension drained out of me. All I wanted to do was flop on the ground and not move. I was dead tired, and a migraine threatened to pound my brain to mush, but I turned and hurried to Kesstel. "It's okay," I told him, gesturing to the portal. "It's not what we want."

He didn't question me, simply stopped moving and watched the portal collapse into nothing. Another earthquake rippled through the ground, but there was nothing we could do about it. Kesstel's jaw tightened as he withstood the shaking. He wasn't bent over as much, which meant he was healing, but I could tell he was still hurting a lot.

The earthquake had passed by the time I landed at his side. I was so tired that my knees almost gave out, but I forced them to stay strong. The aftereffects of the adrenaline from the battle caused my fingers to shake as I reached for his hand covering the hole in his armor. "Are you okay?"

He nodded stiffly. "A little disgruntled, though." A wrinkled smile stretched across his face.

I blinked up at him in alarm. "Why? What's wrong?"

His eyes softened, as if he thought I was funny. "I was supposed to get you the energy crystal. Not sit back and let you do it alone."

I scowled at him. "The hell with that. I'm not some weak little woman who needs a big, strong man to solve all her problems."

I bent down, trying to examine his wound while taking a couple medical sanitizer wipes out of my Items Bag. Quickly, I ripped open the packaging and cleaned off my hands. When that was done, I carefully peeled his fingers out of the way and started to clean off Kesstel's wound. It was hard, working around the armor, especially since I was trying not to hurt him. I did what I could.

Kesstel breathed a soft laugh and let me touch as much as I wanted. "I know," he said, responding to my words, "But I want to do it, anyway." His damaged breastplate disappeared, revealing a black stained undershirt.

I hummed under my breath as I tore the hole in the shirt wider to get a better look. Thankfully, he wasn't so hurt anymore. A thin stretch of skin was already spreading over the wound, so it wasn't bleeding anymore—it just looked awful on the outside. He was healing so fast, it would be a waste to use any more medical equipment on him. Instead, I concentrated on cleaning the blood off around the wound.

I sighed in relief then looked up at him. "But I am grateful for everything you've done for me. And I would have been seriously hurt if you hadn't caught me. Thank you."

He hooked my chin with his fingers and guided me to stand. Before I could ask what was wrong, he dropped a short kiss on my lips. "That's how you say thank you." A wet wipe appeared in his hand, and he softly started to clean the grime off my hot cheeks.

"Oh," I whispered, letting him do as he pleased.

"Are you okay?" he asked as he started to clean my forehead.

I nodded and glanced toward the sister cities. Most of the people were digging through the rubble of the collapsed wall, obviously trying to find any survivors. Others were peeking out from around the wall, some even snapping pictures on their phones.

I wrinkled my nose at them. "Do you think they'll ever get what's going on? I mean, look at the sky. Or just look around you. Everything is tinted red right now. Who in their right mind would be taking pictures at a time like this?"

Now that I wasn't in the middle of a battle, I could hear the sounds of fighting going on in Eden. It obviously wasn't over yet, but it didn't sound like it was coming closer, which was good. That meant the Hunters were being able to keep the monsters inside Eden. According to the rules, Kesstel and I should hurry and join them, but that was not going to happen any time soon.

"Ignorance is bliss," Kesstel muttered. He turned his head and looked at the Scorpion Man's energy crystal on the ground not far from us. "Your Goddess said that she could use that to get to the parasitic planet?"

"Yes. But . . . " I trailed off and glanced at his wound. He wasn't the only one with low HP.

He knew what I meant. "We should heal up first."

I nodded and looked up at the rip stretching across the red sky. It was important to get to the parasitic planet as soon as possible—the Gate Surges wouldn't stop until we did. Not to mention that that damn planet was trying to break into our atmosphere.

But Kesstel and I were both more than half dead. It would be idiotic to go in this state. Who knew what was going to happen up there?

He waved his hand, and two camping chairs appeared next to him. Then he pulled his shirt off, revealing the large patch of angry red skin that was still healing. It took up most of the right side of his stomach, and although I hated seeing him hurt like that, it was good that it was on his right.

Kesstel's energy crystal was on the left side of his torso.

He took a couple water bottles out of his Items Bag, passed one to me, and poured the other over his head and body, washing away the blood.

Inspired, I dumped my own water bottle over my head and body. As much as I hated wet armor, it felt wonderful to feel all the blood leave my skin.

Kesstel's lips twitched. "I meant for you to get a drink. You have to be thirsty." Another bottle appeared in his hand, and he offered it to me.

"I am. Thanks." Taking it, I then waved my hand at his body. The water clinging to him converted into mist. Since it was still stained with blood, I guided it away from us.

Satisfied, I offered him a water bottle from my own Items Bag. He smiled and took it. "Thank you."

Happy though still tired, I dried myself and sat down to heal up.

The alarm sirens wailed in Garden City, coupled with the sounds of the battle from Eden. The tear in the red sky grew bigger, and the image of the parasitic planet on the other side continued to solidify. Some of the Hunters from Garden City's patrol wanted to come out to us, but my mist was still spread out over the battle site, and even though it wasn't in barrier mode, the Hunters seemed reluctant to go into it. It was just as well. I didn't want them to mess with anything until we dealt with the energy crystal.

I kept looking in the direction of the hospital. As much as I was dying to go see how damaged the building was from all the quakes or if my mom or sister were hurt during them, there wasn't time. I needed to rest and heal up. My cell phone didn't have a signal either. A quick glance proved that the building where the phone tower sat on had collapsed sometime today.

Ten minutes later, Kesstel was dressed in a blue tunic and his spare breastplate, the one he usually wore. Neither of us were completely healed yet, but we were both eager to go.

We walked up to the huge energy crystal. The dead Scorpion Man's head was just ten feet away, vacant eyes staring right at it, but I ignored it as much as I could.

Press Her Will against it, Goddess instructed.

Press, not stab, huh? I thought as I took the weapon out of my Items Bag. The pure crystal blade started to glow, the mist inside moving rapidly. Wherever the light touched, it seemed to push away the red hue staining the world, reverting things to their natural color.

A half a step behind me, Kesstel's hands twitched, but he didn't do or say anything. Was he still disgruntled that Goddess was talking to me, or was he reacting to the kindjal?

I didn't ask. Instead, I reached out and pressed the tip of the glowing sword to the energy crystal.

At first, nothing happened. Then the light from the kindjal started to slowly spread into the energy crystal. Like multiple snakes, the white light wormed through the inside of the blue energy crystal. Everywhere it touched, the faint blue glow changed to Goddess's silvery white light.

A heavy pressure settled over the land from above.

I winced at the feeling and looked up at the red sky. Inside the gaping hole, the parasitic planet seemed to tremble.

Kesstel grunted and put his hand against his left side, over where his energy crystal was.

Alarmed, I looked at him. "What's wrong?"

He nodded. "It's fine. Keep going."

That wasn't the answer I wanted, but it was probably the best I was going to get at the moment.

Cracks split over the surface of the Boss's energy crystal, webbing out until they covered the whole giant oval. White light pierced through the cracks, shining like an oblong moon. All at once, the outside casing of the energy crystal shattered, the jagged pieces evaporating into tiny white lights that rose into the air and faded away into nothing.

At the same time, the body of the dead Boss—and everything related to it—exploded into the matching white lights and faded away.

What was left was a glowing ball of white light, the size of a basketball. It drifted over to me.

The kindjal disappeared from my hand by its own will. Instinctively, I reached out and caught the ball. It never actually touched my hands; the glowing light simply floated three inches above my skin, but I could feel the immense power pulsing from it. Unlike the magic from other energy crystals, I didn't feel a strong sense of repulsion from it. Instead, it felt like a warm morning sun. Soft and fresh. The kind of balm that heals the soul.

Kesstel, on the other hand, took a slight step away. His face, which normally showed his natural emotions around me, was blank as a stone as he stared at the light in my hand. Even so, I could see the unease in his blue eyes.

A ripple of silver shimmered in front of me. Goddess appeared across from me, her transparent body with her constantly moving long hair and dress faintly glowing like a ghost. She smiled gently and lifted her hands until they rested under mine, as if helping me support the light ball. I couldn't feel her physical touch, but I could feel the warmth of her hands on mine.

"Ready?" she asked, the word ringing in my ear. Instead of her normal, gentle-looking self, her face was tight with fierce determination.

CHAPTER 55

Goddess pressed up on the bottom of my hands and lifted them in the air, raising the ball of light high. When it was higher than my head, she lowered her hands. Subconsciously, I lowered my hands too. The ball of white energy stayed where it was.

Goddess flicked a glance at Kesstel, her lips tight. She still didn't approve of him, I guessed. Focusing back on me, a determined smile hooked her pale pink lips. "This is what we've been looking for all this time."

She reached out a delicate finger and tapped on the energy ball.

At first, nothing happened. Then the ball started to shrink, the energy condensing tight like a white black hole. Small sparks of silver exploded inside, like little flowers. All at once, the ball of light burst like a firework, spreading out and growing larger.

My eyes narrowed in reaction to the brightness, but I didn't look away. It felt so warm, like a heat lamp in the dead of winter. So cozy. I could stay in it forever. I did, however, notice Kesstel as he angled his face away from the light. After all, the root of his power was the parasitic planet. Did this light make him uncomfortable?

With that in mind, I reached out and hooked his fingers with mine.

His fingers curled around mine in a firm but gentle hold.

The light spread out, slowly creating a silvery-white glowing arch about seven feet tall. It looked just like the portals, only a different color. Just like with the ball it came from, everywhere its gentle light touched, the red stain from the sky vanished, this the only naturally colored location as far as the eye could see.

Goddess drifted around from the back side of the white portal, reaching out to me. "*Let's go. It's long past time for my people to be avenged.*"

"And to save Earth, your new home." I looked to Kesstel. "Together."
He gave me a quick nod.

I took Goddess's hand with my available left hand. As soon as our skin touched, she disappeared, leaving only a small wisp of mist where she used to be. I felt her presence settle in the back of my mind.

Then Kesstel and I stepped into the light, hand in hand.

My stomach lurched as if someone had put a hook around my waist and yanked it. Kesstel's hand tightened on mine until it was borderline painful, but I was squeezing his just as hard.

I was completely blind, just like when I'd walked through the portal between Vapria and Earth. The difference was that back then, it was pitch black. Now, it was so bright that I could barely keep my eyes open. My feet touched solid ground as something pulled me, urging me forward.

Goddess had control of this portal, so I felt confident as I walked, dragging Kesstel behind me. He was a little more hesitant, as if he didn't know which way he should go, but even so, he let me guide him.

It was completely a case of the blind leading the blind. I couldn't tell if we were walking down a narrow passage or an open field. We could be walking in loops, for all I knew. All I could see was white. All I felt was Kesstel's hand, the solid surface under my feet, and the feeling directing me where to go.

Either way, there was no turning around.

Maybe I should be scared. I was going to an alien world with no clear way home, and I was going to be facing a whole planet with an unknown amount of power. Strong enough to eat other planets. I didn't even know if I could breathe up there, for that matter, but somehow, I wasn't scared.

As long as I held Kesstel's hand, I would be okay no matter what happened.

But whether or not I was okay, I couldn't fail. It was literally the end of the world if I did. This was our only shot. There would never be another Goddess to attempt to poison the parasitic planet before Earth died.

Instead of worrying about it, I threw all my emotions into my determination to win. Determination to survive with Kesstel and see my family on a healthy Earth.

The bright light started to fade. I still couldn't see where we were going, but I wasn't blinded by it anymore. A dark arch came into view not far ahead. Because everything was white around it—if the floor, walls, and ceiling existed at all—it looked like the dark arch was floating.

Our strides picked up pace. As safe as it felt in the portal—at least for me—there was something we needed to do.

Kesstel pulled me to a stop in front of the arch. When I looked up at him in question, he wrapped his arms around me. "I'll protect you. I promise," he vowed, burying his face in my shoulder. "No matter what happens. So stay safe. Always think about your safety first, and don't recklessly get hurt. I know what all this means to you. Believe me, I understand more than you think. I'd have gladly thrown away my life to save Kathar. And I'll gladly do it now to keep you safe."

I smiled and hugged him back. "I'll protect you, too. It's not just Earth and my family that's important to me." I brushed my lips on his warm cheek. "You are, too. So, so much. I . . . I love you, Kesstel."

Some people could say words of love at the drop of a hat, but for me, I could count the number of people I'd said them to on one hand. To my family, it was easy to say. But those three words with romantic inclinations held the weight of the world to me. My parents had only said those words to each other. For them, as high school sweethearts who struggled through an apocalypse and the rebuilding of a world with each other, those words were lifelong binding.

And I viewed them the same way.

Kesstel's eyes softened as a smile spread across his handsome face. "I love you, too. I never thought I would be able to feel that emotion again. I cannot even express how grateful I am that I met you. After so many years, I thought I was going to exist alone forever. Exist, because there was nothing to live for. Now, you are my something. My everything."

I rose on my toes and kissed him, hot and heavy. If I was going to die on the other side of that gray portal arch, I wanted to do it with his taste on my lips. If we survived, well, I'd find another excuse to kiss him again. Or I wouldn't even need an excuse; I'd just do it.

All too soon, we stepped back at the same time. Maybe we shouldn't have stolen even this little bit of time, but now that it'd happened, I realized how much I needed it. Needed to hear his emotions and tell him mine. I wasn't planning on dying now, but there was no guarantee.

Hand in hand, we walked through the gray portal.

I didn't know what I was expecting to see on the other side. Maybe an alien control room like in sci-fi films? With smooth desks and angular, uncomfortable chairs all made out of blue energy crystals. Or maybe a giant floating head, like in the movie with the little girl and that Toto dog.

I, at least, expected to see a person. After all, Goddess had a humanoid appearance.

I was disappointed in all aspects.

We stepped out into a flat, barren land, the smooth ground made out of solid blue crystal. There weren't any hills, mountains, or lakes, nor were there any cracks or imperfections in the blue crystal at all—a gemologist's dream. I couldn't see any light source in the sky. Instead, the light came from the center of the planet, its blue light glowing from underneath my feet. There were no clouds overhead, just a dark, red-tinted sky. Floating in that void were hundreds of near see-through globes. Each orb had a piece of land inside, the remnants of planets that the parasite had already eaten. They hung like mini stationary moons. It would be kinda pretty if the reason wasn't so horrifying.

Directly overhead was a huge fissure in the dark-red sky, mirroring the one in Earth's atmosphere. On the other side was Earth, looking close enough to touch. From here, I could see how the originally blue, green, and tan planet from the pictures in schoolbooks had changed. Most of the continents had changed shapes as pieces of land fell into the ocean. Over twenty percent of the remaining land was stained black. These weren't even the parts where nukes had been dropped twenty years ago, trying to kill the monsters when they first appeared. Something else was causing the discoloration. Whatever it was, it looked horrible.

It all just proved how damaged Earth was.

Taking a shaky breath, I focused on the planet we stood on. The only landmark I could see for miles around was a cluster of tall, slender crystals grouped together in the distance. They stabbed into the sky, their edges sharp and unforgiving.

"Every planet has a heart," I whispered to Kesstel. Something about the still, silent atmosphere prompted me to subconsciously lower my voice. I didn't know how the parasite interacted with people—did it have a humanoid body at all?—so I didn't know if it had ears to hear me. Or maybe it didn't need ears at all. "That must be the parasite's." I motioned to the tall crystals.

That is correct. I did try to get you as close as I could, Goddess explained. *The rest of the distance will have to be on your own feet.*

Thanks, I thought back, stepping forward.

BOOM!

In an instant, the entire terrain changed. Millions of crystals exploded out of the smooth ground, stabbing at us with their sharp, angular tips.

Luckily, we were able to react at the same time. The crystals chased our feet as we rose into the air. Twenty feet. Forty feet. Sixty feet. How much higher were these crystals going to rise up? At seventy feet, I reached the top of my High Jump and plateaued. Kesstel grabbed my waist and pulled me with him when he Double Jumped, boosting us higher. Still, the crystal chased us up.

Suddenly, I became aware of the fact that this whole planet was made of energy crystals. The same crystals Goddess didn't want me to touch. The same stuff that turned people into monsters when it got inside them. What would happen to me if I got some inside me?

We needed to get this over quickly, before either of us got hurt.

My eyes narrowed as I focused on where the parasitic planet's heart was. The crystals attacking us were so tall, the heart was covered up. If we were going up, we weren't going to be able to get closer.

I tapped Kesstel, giving him a heads-up, then jumped away from him and activated Feather Step. At the same time, I Mirrored my kindjal and pooled a cloud of mist around me. Since there was no liquid on the planet, the mist was pulled directly from my internal stores. As soon as it came out, the light from inside the crystals around us flickered brightly. The parasitic planet obviously didn't like the water vapor.

My two floating kindjals orbited around me once, then shot out, slicing off the sharp tips of the crystals closest to us. I landed on the flattened tip and sprinted ahead, toward the heart of the planet. Kesstel followed a step behind me, managing to move on before the tip resharpened to a blade.

The crystals were still changing, trying to stab us. As soon as we started to move forward, sharp branch-like sections exploded out of the tall crystals around us. The needle-like offshoots were tenacious as they reached for us.

New crystals grew out ahead of me in various angles, blocking my way and stabbing at me. I twisted and cut at them, leaving a trail of shattered crystals behind me.

Kesstel didn't have as easy of a time. His sword couldn't cut them, so he was forced to simply dodge around them as we ran. His power attack could break the ones ahead of us, but they grew back at a faster rate than from my attacks, and it took so much energy from him that it became counterproductive. He tsked in annoyance, but there wasn't much he could do except stay on my tail and move before the crystals were able to reform.

I had my hands full trying to clear a way forward. I just had to hope that he could keep himself safe.

Suddenly, Kesstel pushed me from behind. "Careful!" he yelled, then grunted in pain.

His shove sent me several feet ahead, where I landed on the side of a crystal, slicing off the sharp tip as I turned to look at Kesstel. My eyes widened in shock.

He stood right where I used to be, an inch-wide crystal offshoot stabbed right into his side.

CHAPTER 56

H is face was tight as blood dripped down the crystal, staining it black. The crystal was barely wider than my kindjal. It didn't look like a killing move—and nowhere near the magnitude of when he was stabbed by the Scorpion Man—but it still must have hurt.

"Kesstel!" I gasped. It was shocking to see him so blatantly injured, never mind being stabbed in the stomach twice in one day. It was a testament to the difficulty of the opponents we were facing, and the likelihood of not being able to walk away from it.

I swung my kindjal and broke the crystal stabbing into Kesstel. Small pieces fell from the broken edge and shattered against the larger crystals which continued to reach for us. With a swing of my arms, the two swords in my hands and the two floating above broke all the crystals around us.

Kesstel grunted and gripped the stub sticking out of his stomach. His eyes narrowed as he pulled the sharp shard out of his body. With a look of disgust, he threw the blackened piece away. He didn't even watch as it shattered into pieces ten feet away.

"Are you okay?" I asked.

I only had time to spare a quick glance at him before I had to focus on the assaulting crystals. They never seemed to stop. Then again, I was on the body of a parasitic planet that could control monsters. Why wouldn't it want to kill me?

"I'm okay," Kesstel replied, though his face was still wrinkled in annoyance. "If only these were monsters." He glared at the crystals. "Then I'd actually be helpful." He glanced at me. "Let's get this over with."

I nodded. With him following behind, I cut through the crystals and raced toward the heart of the planet again.

Angle to the right, Goddess spoke. *You're off course.*

I immediately followed her instructions. *You can tell which way to go?*

With the crystals growing higher and higher, and them being all the same color and mostly the same shape, I was starting to second-guess the direction I needed to go. I had a faint feeling that one direction was more dangerous than the other; an instinct that I shouldn't go that way—so of course that was the way I went. The most dangerous place, the heart of the parasitic planet: that's where I wanted to go. Only, that feeling was vague enough with all the action going on around me, it was hard to focus on it and go in the right direction.

Yes, Goddess replied.

Guide me, I said, swinging my swords.

The crystals around me shattered in thousands of pieces in a dangerous yet dazzling display as the light from inside the planet reflected off the millions of surfaces, causing them to flash a bright blue. The small shards bounced off the barrier I'd put up around me and Kesstel. It didn't do squat for the stabbing crystals, but it kept the pieces I broke away. I didn't want to risk getting an energy crystal in me. Even a tiny shard could be dangerous.

While we ran, I kept an eye on Kesstel. In theory, being stabbed by an energy crystal shouldn't affect him. He was already a monster, so he couldn't change into one again. Still, the fact that his wound was leaking black blood was concerning. Kesstel's healing ability should have healed that cut by now.

"We're almost there." Fatigue from constantly breaking the crystals was starting to wear into my voice, making my words breathy.

After we got to the heart crystals, I just needed to stab the kindjal in them. From there, Goddess would take over. I didn't know what was going to happen after, but for now, I was just going to focus on what I did know. I needed to get to the heart of the parasitic planet.

Behind! Goddess yelled at the same time I felt the attack aiming at my back.

I twisted around, my kindjals automatically reaching out to block the assault.

Sparks flew as blue-and-silver patterned steel smashed into the misty crystal blade. My arms shook from the force of the attack, but that wasn't the thing that blew my mind.

"Kesstel?" I whispered in shock, eyes wide.

As much as my mind instantly rejected the idea, it didn't change the fact that what I was seeing was real. The pressure against my blades trying to overpower me was real. It really was Kesstel who had attacked me. But . . . not a Kesstel I knew.

His handsome face was blank. Not the normal, apathetic stone face he showed to everyone else, but truly blank, as if there wasn't anything in his mind. His arms shook, like mine, as he gripped his sword with both hands and pressed against me. From the angle, if I hadn't blocked him, he would have cut my head off. His irises were glowing neon blue, bright enough to put the glow from the parasitic planet to shame.

But what surprised and horrified me the most was the second glowing spot on his left torso, right under the original glow of his energy crystal.

There was a second crystal inside him.

"Kesstel!" I yelled, trying to get him to react to me. Goddess's power stored in my body had always fixed him before. It should work now, right?

I was wrong. His only reaction was to break the hold I had on his sword and attack again. He slashed at me with deadly intensity, all while the planet's crystals stabbed at me. Instinct took over my body. The floating kindjals broke the crystals as my right blade directed his sword to the side. My left blade flicked out at him, counterattacking.

The crystal sword cut through his breastplate like butter, slashing diagonally across his chest. Black blood gushed out of the long, shallow cut and spattered on the blue crystals growing around us. From the gap in his breastplate, I could see the edges of his skin around the cut start to turn burnt black. Just like the red orcs. That had never happened before.

I froze, shocked all over again. My chest squeezed painfully until my lungs burned for air and my heart ached. *Oh my god, I cut Kesstel. Badly.* In all the time I'd been with him, I'd never hurt him before. I didn't mean to. I really didn't. It was just a reflex I developed when fighting against something that wanted to kill me.

"Kesstel!" I gasped. "Wake up!"

The second energy crystal. Was that why he was acting this way? If I took it out, would he go back to normal?

I glanced at the glowing spot. It was right next to his original crystal. Would I be able to take one out without damaging the other? He was so much stronger than me. Could I take it out while he was trying to kill me?

The light in his eyes flashed brightly, then the blue from his irises spread until his whole eyes glowed blue. Just like the Bosses who the parasite took over. Kesstel's face was still blank, but a sneer pulled across his lips.

"I told you." Kesstel's familiar voice was flat and cold, unlike anything I'd ever heard before. If I hadn't watched his lips move, I wouldn't have believed it was Kesstel talking. "I created him. I can have him back whenever I want."

Moving too fast for normal eyes to see, he went from in front of me to attacking my side. I blocked his attack, but as soon as I moved to counterattack, I hesitated. I . . . couldn't bring myself to make Kesstel bleed like that again. It didn't show on his face, but I knew it hurt. I'd watched his HP drop from the strike.

My fraction of a second hesitation was just long enough for Kesstel to sweep out his leg between the two kindjals floating around me. His foot caught me squarely in the stomach. Hard.

Nauseous pain vibrated from my core down my legs to my toes and up to the roots of my hair. I grunted and fell back five feet. Dozens of crystal spikes stabbed out of the blue pillar behind me, attempting to impale my back. Just before I hit the sharp tips, I Merged into mist and reappeared over Kesstel's head. The moving crystals were noticeably slower now, probably because the planet's consciousness had shifted. It made it easier for me to handle them, but I absolutely hated the reason why.

It was hard to tell which one ached more: my stomach or my heart. Either way, I glared down at Kesstel as I Floated ten feet above. "Get out of Kesstel's body!"

He cocked his head to the side, making Kesstel's white-blond bangs fall into his face. "I don't actually enjoy being crammed inside such a tiny body. It's very restricting. And being forced to use a verbal language is too limited. All the more reason why you should bow down and accept your place in the food chain." He rotated his right shoulder as if he was testing out the limbs. "Now that you ruined my last chosen body, I need a new one." He leveled me with a dead look, a mean smile on his face. "Might as well use the body that would cause the most damage."

My eyes widened. Since we'd killed the Scorpion Man, the parasitic planet had purposely targeted Kesstel? My teeth ground together painfully. "Get out!"

He laughed in my face. "Although annoyingly tiny, this body has more power than the last one. And—" He lifted Kesstel's sword. Blue magic flared from his hand and spread up until the whole blade was encased in it. "Its advantages at the moment are amazing. He's going to feel every bit of pain you inflict on him. So, Warrior of Mist, what are you going to do?"

He swung his sword, the magic on it like a blue blur. I dodged out of the way.

On and on, he chased me as I jumped, slipped, and twisted out of the way. My four blades did a lot of damage to the sharp crystals around me as I moved through them, but not once did I attack Kesstel.

I just . . . couldn't.

I couldn't hurt him. Not again. If I could get to the heart of the planet, I wouldn't have to. I could stab Her Will into the heart, and then hopefully, the parasite would become injured enough to let go of Kesstel.

You're getting farther away from the heart, Goddess warned.

I already knew that. The possessed Kesstel had put himself between me and the heart. I was fast enough to keep from getting hurt, but at the expense of him driving me away.

Jynn, you have to do something. You can't just dodge. You have to attack back. Force your way through, Goddess urged.

The blue magic flashed as it swung past my shoulder, so close that I felt the afterburn of it. I winced and sidestepped another attack. *I won't hurt him,* I argued back. Kesstel was my partner, my . . . my most important person. He didn't want to hurt me. It was only because of the second energy crystal that he was acting like this.

You have to do something, Goddess reasoned. *We're so close; you can't give up now. Earth will collapse if you do. Your family will die or turn into monsters. The more energy you burn on fighting him, the less I'll have to deal with the parasite. It's true that I've kept some power in reserve, but that's because I absolutely need it. If you use it to fight the Katharian, I might be powerless to kill the parasite.*

Kesstel swung his sword and sent a tidal wave of magic at me. Desperately, I Warped out of the way. I wasn't able to go far. The atmosphere here rejected my mist, so I wasn't able to create a large pool to move freely in. I dodged the attack, but the mist that was hit evaporated, making my cloud that much smaller.

I understand what this man means to you, Goddess spoke. *But there's never been a monster with two energy crystals before. It's possible that his consciousness is already gone, and the parasite is just moving his empty shell.*

CHAPTER 57

The horror of her words caused me to pause. Kesstel was . . . already gone?

My gaze locked on Kesstel, watching as he rushed to close the distance between us. How could she even say that when I could see his body moving? See the veins lifting on his neck as he moved to attack me again. There was blood pumping through his body; a zombie wouldn't have physical reactions like this.

It wasn't just my eyes that rejected the possibility; everything in my heart and mind screamed in denial. Kesstel wasn't so weak that he'd die just like that, his soul slipping off into oblivion without a fight. The parasite said that Kesstel could feel all the pain I inflicted on him. It might have been lying just to dig at me, but I was going to take its words as truth.

He's not dead, I told Goddess with conviction. *I refuse to believe that he is. As long as I take that other energy crystal out, he'll wake up.*

Maybe. Maybe not. It might kill him, Goddess said. *Not to mention, the crystals are so close together. I don't know how you can destroy one without damaging the other.*

I can do it, I thought, resolutely. There wasn't an option not to. He was too strong for me to get around. As long as Kesstel was standing, the parasite would force me away from the heart. Maybe my voice could get through to Kesstel, but I wasn't banking on that. If I wanted to have any hope of destroying the parasite, that second energy crystal needed to be removed.

Kesstel attacked me again.

I turned and met him head-on. Both blades flashed bright, his blue and mine white, when they collided. I could feel the parasite's magic stabbing and burning as it tried to overpower the misty magic in the kindjal. It felt disgusting, like a million tiny bugs trying to burrow into the crystal blade and poison the pure mist inside.

This wasn't just a contest of physical strength. Each power struggled to overthrow the other—Goddess's power against the parasitic planet's.

Vile creature! Goddess roared in my mind.

A sharp spike of magic pulsed from the kindjal, sparking a massive magic blast as the two powers collided. Kesstel and I were thrown in opposite directions. I gasped as the residual magic washed over me, making my whole body sting. Still, I twisted in the air to avoid the sharp crystals trying to stab me. My toe tapped on the side of one, and I shot back after Kesstel. Now that I'd decided to win this fight, there was no more time to hesitate.

"Resisting is useless!" he roared and swung horizontally at me, trying to cut me in half.

I ducked and dipped right under his attack. My back sizzled from the blue magic still emitting from his blade, but I swung out, aiming to his left. The tip of my sword caught his side, puncturing his breastplate and slicing out toward the crystal. Unfortunately, he shifted fast enough that I was off mark. The bleeding cut was four inches too low and to one side, missing the second energy crystal.

It was barely more than a scratch to him, but knowing I was the one who did it, my heart instantly bled. If Kesstel's cuts were like the red orc's, the power of the kindjal not only burned on touch; it repressed his healing ability. I needed to take him down, so it benefited me, but it was going to be very painful for him.

The hard angle on Kesstel's elbow smashed into my back as I shot past, just to the left of my spine. Pain exploded in my body as a rib popped. The force of his move threw my balance off, and I lurched toward the crystals below. At the last second, I Warped out of the way of the sharp points and appeared ten feet over his head.

Kesstel pressed his hand to his side then looked at the blood on his fingers as if it was interesting. "I didn't think you'd attack him. Humans, more than other intelligent beings I've devoured, have an idiotic habit of getting attached to things." He looked at me with his glowing eyes as he rubbed his wet fingers together. "Or have you become so drunk on power that you'll even attack your own?"

I gripped my swords and got ready to attack. "If you won't get out of him by choice, I'll beat you out of his body."

He sneered. "It actually wasn't hard to take over this being's mind," he gloated, as if talking about a funny secret. It was so bizarre to see. No matter how his mouth moved in humor, the upper half of Kesstel's face stayed emotionally blank. "All he needed was a little push to realize his deepest desires, and he tumbled off-balance enough for me to step in. Would you like to hear his true thoughts? You might find them . . . enlightening."

My eyes widened. What did that mean? A bad premonition twisted in my gut. I gripped my swords, ready to attack.

The blue light in Kesstel's eyes reduced back to his irises. For the first time, I could see a clear emotion on his face. Determination. He was finally a Kesstel I recognized; the same face I'd seen hundreds of times. He tipped back his head, eyes focused on me, and his mouth pressed in a tight line.

My muscles instinctively froze, pausing the attack.

That slight pause was enough for Kesstel to reach out and grab a long shard of energy crystal growing by him. With a jerk of his wrist, the shard broke off, creating a foot-long weapon. In a flash he was at me, wielding his bastard sword in one hand and the energy crystal in the other.

The parasite's attacks were heavy, each blow like a mountain determined to smother me, and full of magic. But this two-handed assault from Kesstel was completely different. He used very little magic, instead relying on speed and muscle strength. The sudden change of pace was hard to adapt to, but I did my best. After all, I was finally fighting a style I knew. I'd never fought him before, but I'd seen enough of his moves to keep out of the worst of his attacks.

Every single one of his slices, stabs, and cuts were acts of desperate fury, as if his very life depended on it. But the heaviest emotion of all was a deep sadness that laced every move. He desperately wanted to attack me, but it pained him so much that his eyes were wet. Still, he didn't stop.

The longer we fought, the more his wild emotions bled into me. My heart hurt so badly that my eyes burned.

"Stop, Kesstel!" I yelled, one hand blocking his sword, the other deflecting the energy crystal he was determined to stab into me.

It was becoming more and more clear that he wasn't actually trying to kill me. He was trying to stab me with the energy crystal. I was fast enough to block all the crystal attacks because I was most concerned about them. As a result, I was taking damage from his sword. But as much as each cut burned when the blue magic tried to poison me, it was the best choice I could pick, given the options—his sword, the energy crystal in his hand, and the continual onslaught of surrounding crystals.

Kesstel was taking on just as many injuries. My floating kindjals were hard pressed, keeping the ever-growing crystals away from me, while my hands worked just as hard. Most of my attacks were aimed at his left side, but I'd come to understand that I needed to wear his HP down to accomplish anything.

Kesstel shook his head, finally responding to my words. "No. I can't stop."

A small seed of hope bloomed in me. He'd finally responded to me. Goddess was wrong; he wasn't dead yet. And if he was responding to me, that meant the parasite's control was weak enough for him to break out of it, right? "Kesstel, please stop. Don't let the parasite control you."

He shook his head, his expression twisted as if confused. "No. No. I have to." He focused on me. "Don't resist me!" he roared, lunging at me.

His vicious swipe caught my kindjal just above the guard and knocked it painfully out of my hand. He kept moving forward, using his whole weight to tackle me in a desperate act.

Shocked, I was thrown off-balance and fell back against the wall of crystals growing behind me. Quickly creating a cocoon of solid mist around my body, I hit the crystals, stopping my fall. They stabbed at the barrier, trying to puncture through, but I hardened the shell.

In front of me, Kesstel's sword disappeared into his Items Bag, and he used both hands to grip the long shard and stab it into the barrier, aiming at my stomach. The tip hit my shield and stopped, Kesstel's hands shaking with the force he was using to keep pressing.

My eyes widened as I threw every ounce of power I had into the barrier. The floating kindjals winked out of existence as I used their energy to fortify the mist. Kesstel was a higher level than I was, so my barrier wasn't going to hold up against him for long. With energy crystals in front and behind me, I couldn't let it fall.

"Kesstel! Stop!" I yelled. "You're going to kill me!" My whole body was shaking, both from the hundreds of injuries that heavily depleted my HP and the effort it took to hold up the barrier against the two forces.

He shook his head again. Sweat was dripping down his tortured face. "No, I'm not. I just have to . . . I just have to . . . " He groaned in pain but didn't stop pressing the crystal at me.

A thick stream of blood leaked from his left side, all from injuries I'd put there. Twice I'd managed to catch him in the right spot, but both times, I hadn't stabbed deep enough to reach the second crystal. I was so scared of hitting the original one, I pulled out before the blade was two inches deep each time. I felt like I was unintentionally torturing him—and it was torturing me.

"Listen to me, Kesstel," I tried to reason. "I'm Jynn. You have to stop." Maybe if I touched him, I could help clear his head. Only, I didn't dare lift the barrier.

The question was, if I took my attention off the shield long enough to Merge with the mist, would it be fast enough to escape before Kesstel broke in?

"No. We have to be the same!" Kesstel insisted. His hands shook, the edges of the shard in his hands cutting through his gloves as he pressed it against my barrier. The tip of the crystal slowly edged a half an inch into the shield.

My heart jumped at the sight and his words. "What do you mean, the same?"

He made a frustrated sound. "We're different. As long as you don't have an energy crystal, we could be separated." He looked into my eyes. Tears pooled in his eyes, and his eyebrows were tipped up in desperation. "I've lost all my other loved ones. I can't lose you, too."

CHAPTER 58

His words broke my heart. The tears I'd been fighting off pooled in my eyes. My tired hands shook as I reached out to his tortured face. His sweaty hair was a mess, he was covered in blood, and his eyes were glowing like a demon, but he was still so annoyingly bred-to-be handsome. All I wanted to do was soothe all the pain away. Heal all of his wounds and reassure his insecurities until he never thought of them again.

But I couldn't.

My hands touched the cocoon around me. I could easily push through it, but I didn't. No matter how much I loved him, I couldn't help him right now.

"If you put that crystal in me, I'll die," I tried to reason. It was the only thing I could think of right now, since I couldn't break the barrier. Not with the sharp crystals pressing up below and behind. I glanced at the foot-long crystal dagger in Kesstel's hand; the one he was trying to push through my shield into my stomach. "If that goes in me, if I don't die, I'll turn into a monster. Then you'll be all alone again."

I hated using his insecurities against him, but I needed to do something for him to let up enough for me to move. I could already feel my shield starting to slip. It wasn't going to hold on much longer. I had to do something soon.

Kesstel shook his head wildly, like a vicious beast instead of the noble gentleman he usually was. "No. You won't die. I won't let you. We'll be Bosses together, concurring wherever we go. If you go insane, I can control you until your mind comes back. You're strong enough; you won't be out of control forever. Then I won't be repelled by your magic anymore."

He pressed harder on the crystal, his arms shaking from the effort. It slipped another fraction of an inch into the barrier. His bright eyes bore into mine, pleading. "Then I won't be alone anymore, and you'll never have to know how it feels to be lonely."

Oh god. I thought my heart couldn't hurt more. I was wrong. "You're wrong, Kesstel," I said slowly, as if a throbbing, painful hole wasn't burning my brain from the crystal being pushed through my mist. "If that thing touches me, I'll die. With the way my magic is, there's no way I'd turn into a monster. I'll instantly die. Then the parasite will win. You've worked for so long to get revenge. Are you going to throw it away now?"

"No. No!" he insisted. "You won't . . . I won't . . . " He paused as if confused, like a blind man desperately groping for a hand in the dark.

That pause was all I needed. I Merged into the mist and rose to the top of the oval barrier. The instant my full attention was taken off the shield, Kesstel broke through. The sharp, blue energy crystal stabbed forward with enough force to cause sparks to fly and the shard to break when it hit the larger crystals on the other side. Luckily, I was incorporeal enough that the stab went right through my body. There was still a burning sting which knocked a couple hundred HP out where the crystal touched the mist of my body, but it was nothing compared to what turning into a monster would feel like.

I zoomed up until I wasn't trapped anymore. If I could spread my mist out more, I could Warp to a safe place every time I was in a jam, but I couldn't force out more than a ten-foot circle. The atmosphere in this awful place was too strong. If I put more effort into it, I might be able to force a wider radius, but concentrating on Kesstel was much more important from a staying-alive perspective.

As a mist cloud just barely above the growing crystals, I turned and finally located the heart of the planet. As soon as I locked onto it, I rushed forward, leaving Kesstel behind. I needed to get there, needed to destroy this parasite.

For Kesstel, for my family, for Goddess, and for Earth.

A tidal wave of bright blue magic spilled through the crystals and rushed toward me from the side. Startled, I converged into a human and jumped back just in time to escape the attack. The magic crushed the crystals into each other, and they exploded, shrapnel flying everywhere. My hand thrust out and created a barrier a split second before the fragments hit me. They thudded against the solid mist and fell to the depths below. Even with the shield, the repercussions of the magical attack were enough to affect my HP.

"Well, did you find it enlightening?" Kesstel's dead voice asked, the tone so bland for a man who was closing in on me like an arrow. The blue glow in Kesstel's eyes had spread until it consumed his whole eyes again, indicating that the parasite was in control. He'd replaced the broken crystal with a new one, glowing and ready to stab me.

Great.

My teeth gritted together. I hated the parasite to a whole new level. It'd never occurred to me that I would be fighting against my loved one, but I couldn't hate Kesstel—just the being controlling his body. Since it was Kesstel's body, I couldn't take my hate out on him, and breaking the crystals didn't seem to make me feel better. Nor was it giving me any energy or EXP.

"Not that it matters anymore," the parasite controlling Kesstel said before I could respond. "In the end, you and that weakling Goddess cowering inside you will return to me." He swung his sword at me.

"Not weak," I replied, deflecting his attack, trying to make his own inertia take him to the side. It worked, except he lashed out with the energy crystal, aiming at my side. I twisted, the crystal missing me by centimeters, and kicked his back to make him go past. "Just waiting," I finished as Kesstel landed on a crystal ten feet away. Despite the casual way he was standing, I knew my kick hadn't been a light little love tap. "Waiting for the right time to kill you, you disgusting parasite."

I glared at him, acting like my body wasn't on the verge of collapse. In my vision, my HP was flashing red, and my MP was pretty low. I knew Kesstel wasn't that much better, but the parasite wouldn't care about the state of the body it possessed. This fight had been going on for too long; at this point, we could both die up here.

Throughout the whole fight, I kept track of the rip in space above. It continued to grow, and Earth on the other side was getting closer and closer. I could only imagine how much damage Earth was taking while Kesstel and I fought.

I needed to end this fight. Now. No matter how it ended.

All four of my kindjals came out. In a flash, I lunged at Kesstel, trying to beat some sense into him. If I didn't stop him soon, I'd have to try and kill him.

"Kesstel, you have to wake up," I half begged. "You're strong enough to beat that monster out of your mind."

My right kindjal slashed at his chest, always hatefully aiming for the left side. He blocked it with his sword. Quick as a flash, I lashed out with my left hand. He used the crystal shard to block that attack, but he didn't have enough hands to stop the floating kindjal that flew by and caught him across his back.

His body shook in obvious pain, but the being controlling him didn't so much as grunt. The growing crystals exploded around us, trying to stab me, and Kesstel's sword twisted against mine, leaving a long cut all down my right arm.

I hissed in pain as another wound was added to the long list of injuries I was sporting now. Still, I kept fighting because my life depended on it. Neither of us stopped, our moves going so fast they'd be a blur to outside eyes. Every time my kindjal struck Kesstel's glowing blue sword, a bright flash would spark off as the two magics resisted each other.

With a flick of his wrist, Kesstel knocked the kindjal out of my almost numb right hand. I gasped, suddenly knocked off-balance and vulnerable. A gasping yell was ripped from me as Kesstel's sword sank into my unprotected right side in an explosion of searing pain. The blue magic coating the sword instantly attacked my insides, trying to ruin my body from the inside out. I was in so much pain, my body froze.

A System message popped up in the corner of my graying vision, obviously an automatic command coded into the structure. [**Your HP has dropped dangerously low. Please seek medical assistance immediately.**]

The growing crystals behind me shot up, trying to take advantage of the situation to stab me too.

Jynn! Goddess screamed.

My floating kindjals suddenly reacted outside of my control, spinning like a tornado around me and shattering anything that came near.

From the small space in the back of my mind where Goddess and her extra magic resided, a rush of power spread out—the power that Goddess had set aside to poison the parasite with. Its warm strength filled my body, soothing the mind-numbing pain. The kindjal still in my left hand lifted up, directing my whole arm with it, and prevented Kesstel's crystal shard from stabbing my shoulder. The feeling returned to my body and mind, and I took over my weapons again.

That extra power had been held back for a reason. I was grateful to Goddess for using it on me, but if I used too much, how was Goddess going to kill the parasite?

Kesstel prepared to jerk the sword from my side. Instead, I grabbed his hand and kept it in place. When he jerked back, trying to loosen it, I lunged forward with his movement, keeping a death grip on his hand. He was caught off-balance and fell back. At the same time, the two floating kindjals shot in from each side. I felt the air move as they brushed against me, angling in. Kesstel was so distracted by my strange grappling moves that he didn't notice.

Until the two kindjals stabbed both his sides with tremendous force.

Letting go of his hand, I pushed him with all my might at the same time. The combined force threw Kesstel backward, ripping his sword painfully out of my body. His back smashed into a dense cluster of tall crystals, and the kindjals stabbed right through his stomach and into the cluster behind, effectively nailing him in place.

I followed a breath behind. The right kindjal appeared in my hand as I thrust it into his left side, right where the second energy crystal glowed.

Kesstel lifted his sword up, but he was a half a step too slow to block me.

The misty blade sank into his body, gliding through the openings I'd previously cut. Four inches in, there was a slight resistance as I hit the second energy crystal.

Kesstel's eyes widened as his mouth gaped open in obvious agony.

The crystal shattered, and the kindjal stabbed the rest of the way through his body until it embedded itself into the cluster behind.

Kesstel slumped like a broken puppet, his heavy-lidded eyes like blank blue glass.

CHAPTER 59

In an instant, all the crystals turning the entire planet into a pincushion disappeared, leaving the surface smooth as glass. They didn't shatter or lower back into the glowing ground; they simply vanished—even the ones that Kesstel was pinned against by my kindjals.

He dropped like a lifeless doll, plummeting forty feet below. As he fell, the three blades in his body vanished.

I dove after him, catching him just before he hit the ground, but the movement wrenched open the still bleeding wound in my stomach. The pain was so intense, I couldn't control my mist very well. The vapor pooled under my feet softened my fall but broke apart before I could fully stop.

I landed heavily, Kesstel's weight pressing on me as if I wasn't an S Hunter—I was that weakened. I tried to set him down carefully, but I didn't have complete control of my war-torn body, and both of us flopped to the ground, him on his side and me on my back beside him.

I panted for breath, trying to regain my strength. Tears, hot and blinding, leaked from the corners of my eyes. I couldn't seem to stop them, and honestly, I didn't want to. They dripped to the blue stone surface, next to the pool of Kesstel's blood which continued to grow.

The rip in space loomed overhead, revealing Earth on the other side. In the short time I'd been on this parasitic planet, the black spots on Earth that I'd noticed earlier had grown bigger. I didn't know what they were—most likely contaminated places where the parasite had a strong hold. Either way, the black spots weren't natural. I had a good view of North America, and I could see they weren't near Eden, but it was only a matter of time.

Instead of feeling panicked about Earth, I kept my attention here on this silent planet around me. Everything was still; even the glow coming from inside the blue crystal planet was dimmed. The only sound in my ears was the slow heartbeat of the man next to me. The one that was getting slower with every beat.

My body shook as I pushed onto my knees. My trembling hands reached out and smoothed his messy hair out of his face. "Goddess? Is Kesstel . . . " I couldn't bring myself to finish the question.

I wanted to hear her say he was okay. That he was just sleeping. But I had eyes and ears. I could see the blood leaking from him and hear his heart skipping beats. One of my tears dropped onto his cheek. Carefully, I brushed it away, feeling his cool skin against my hot fingers.

The two energy crystals were so close together. She sounded a little breathless. After all, she'd used some of her own power to keep me alive. The question was, had she used too much? *You nicked his original energy crystal when you destroyed the other one. I didn't steal the energy from the original crystal, but it doesn't change the fact that it was damaged.*

His energy crystal was damaged. It would have been better for him to be stabbed in the heart. He could heal from that. But there was no way to fix a broken energy crystal.

And I did it with my own two hands.

More tears slipped down my face as self-hatred boiled inside.

Jynn, you have to hurry, Goddess urged. *The parasite is only momentarily stunned. Right now is the best time for us to attack its heart. I don't know how long we have.*

"Yes," I agreed with her. Gently, I touched Kesstel's cool cheek. "I'll be right back," I said as if he could hear me.

My legs felt like jelly, but I pushed up to standing. Pain pulsed from the hole in my stomach, making me groan and bend over. I pressed my slightly numb right hand, still sporting the deep cut from Kesstel, against the hole as I looked around for the heart of the planet.

In front of me was a small silvery white arch in the distance—the portal me and Kesstel had taken to get here. Even though it was half the size it was before, it was impressive it'd survived the battle.

Behind me, closer than I thought they would be, was the cluster of crystals which signified the heart of the parasitic planet. I didn't think I'd gotten that close, but they were only thirty feet away. If I hadn't been so focused on Kesstel, I would have seen the six-foot tall pillars right away. The crystals were glowing, just like the main planet, but every once in a while, there was a small flare of light, almost like a heartbeat.

For some reason, that pulse angered me. It wasn't just that it belonged to the parasite. It wasn't fair that this heartbeat was getting stronger while Kesstel's was getting weaker.

Fury powered my body as I marched up to the cluster of crystals. Red and black blood that had collected on the bottom of my boots smeared the pristine glassy surface as I walked, but I couldn't think of a better accent for this damn place. This planet shouldn't be pretty enough to belong on a fantasy magazine. A disgusting being like this deserved to be dripping blood, drowned in the life liquid it stole from all its victims.

As I came up to the heart of the planet, I held out my right hand. Her Will appeared in my grip. The silvery handle shimmered brightly, without a single trace of blue reflecting on it, as if it rejected the glow from the planet. The mist inside the clear blade swirled around anxiously. I gripped the handle.

For the first time, Goddess's magic, which was always so prevalent on the kindjal, didn't soothe my aching soul. Even though the blade was flooding with her warmth, my heart was too distraught to feel it.

Stopping in front of the crystals, I lifted the kindjal high over my head. Goddess's power poured into the clear blade. The silvery-white light it always emitted intensified until it was like a star shining in my hands. Her light collided with the blue glow coming from the parasite's crystals, casting a harsh light on them.

Time for your retribution! Goddess yelled.

"Die, you damn thing!" I screamed and stabbed the kindjal into the first crystal with everything I had. *Die for all the lives you stole. Die for Earth. Die for my family. Die for Goddess. Die for Kesstel. Die for me!*

Like cutting butter, the shining blade sank all the way to the hilt. Because of the clear quality of the blue crystal, I could see right through it. The light of the mist blade intensified, chasing away the blue light and turning the energy crystal clear. Like a mass of writhing snakes, Goddess's white power seeped from the tip of the sword and burrowed through the blue heart crystal, eating away the dim power of the parasite.

All at once, the blue glow pulsed, bright and strong. It forced Goddess's power to stop, and even started to push it back.

My eyes widened as the blue light changed from a pulse to a steady glow. *The parasite woke up already? No!*

Goddess groaned in my mind. *Not strong enough . . .* The white ribbons of power twisted and pulsed, trying to pierce through the blue light.

The smooth stone under my feet shivered, tiny little points ghosting across the surface and collecting in some areas before fading back down. Like the precursor to more growing crystals. Damn.

I'm sorry, Jynn, Goddess apologized gravely, her voice trembling with effort. *I need all my power back. I don't have enough without it. I just hope it's enough.*

My eyes widened as I realized what she meant. Then a small smile curled on my lips. "It's okay," I whispered softly.

After all, all my power was originally hers. I was more or less a container—a delivery girl. In the beginning, when I first got the System, I was treated like a tool; a means to accomplish an end. And I had viewed the System the same way. A means to use to get what I wanted. Somewhere along the way, I'd learned to trust the System, and it also started to treat me better. We'd come a long way from the morning I woke up in the hospital. Long enough to sometimes forget the original reason why the System was made to begin with.

I'll make it okay, Goddess promised. If only she sounded more sure of herself, I might have believed her.

My hand around the handle of Her Will began to tingle, and like a leaking sink, I could feel my power start to drain out from my grip, funneling into the kindjal. My heavily battered body became heavier, my legs going from already trembling to fully shaking. I could almost feel my levels dropping with my power, all being sucked away.

The idea barely popped into my head when the System menu popped up, displaying my stats.

Jynn Devhro

Rank	S	**Level**	94
		EXP to Next Level	39,205
HP	1512/16,706	**Stat Points**	6
MP	205/7108		
Strength	163 (+40)	**Agility**	150

| Magic 143 (+40) | Perception 144 |
| Constitution 150 (+40) | Intelligence 135 |

Skills	Abilities
Throw	True Mist (10 mi)
Critical Hit	Feather Step
Quick Hit	Regen
Mirror (Improved)	Stealth
High Jump	Poison Fog
Float	Mist Blade (Enhanced)
	Merge
	Warp
	Telekinesis

As I watched, the numbers on my EXP section started to go down, like a countdown clock. As they went down, my levels dropped accordingly.

Level 94 . . . 93 . . . 92 . . . 91 . . .

After all the work I'd gone through to go from level one to ninety-four, I thought I'd be more upset to feel them deplete. Strangely, I wasn't. I'd gathered all this energy to protect my family. And that's what was happening now. With the parasite dead, they would be safe.

The more my power drained into the kindjal, the brighter Goddess's power grew. With renewed fervor, it attacked the parasite's blue magic and cut through.

Level 45 . . . 44 . . . 43 . . . 42 . . .

My EXP wasn't the only thing going down. So was my HP and MP. It was staying at the same percentage, I think, but the numbers were adjusting accordingly. Each time the numbers dropped, the injuries covering my body ached all the more. The hole in my side wasn't bleeding anymore, but it wasn't closing, either. My Regen was tied to my power. Since I was getting weaker, the healing effect was, too. I pressed a hand over the large injury, but that didn't seem to make it feel better.

The bright white power dug through the waist-high crystal, almost reaching down into the actual planet. Once it touched the parasite's whole body, Goddess wouldn't be cornered anymore. She could spread out and attack more places at once.

Level 11 . . . 10 . . . 9 . . . 8 . . .

Suddenly, the whole planet let out a blindingly bright blue pulse of magic. It swallowed up Goddess's magic in an instant, and the kindjal disintegrated in my grip, vanishing to a puff of mist that slipped through my powerless fingers.

I didn't even have time to gasp before I was thrown back twenty feet, landing hard on my back and rolling to a stop. Coughing for air, I pushed up and looked around.

I'd flown far enough that I was back at Kesstel's side. He was still limp, but the collar on his torn blue tunic shifted as his chest moved in shallow breaths. It wasn't much, but he was still alive.

The portal we had taken to get here had disappeared at some point. Either Goddess took back that power too, or it was blown to pieces from the parasite's power pulse. Either way, there was no way home now.

The heart of the parasitic planet was glowing so bright, I couldn't look at it fully without my eyes hurting. Try as I might, I couldn't see a bit of white in those blue depths.

We . . . lost?

I couldn't feel the System inside me at all. There wasn't even the tiniest bit of Goddess's magic in me, and I couldn't contact her.

All I knew was Kesstel was dying . . . and so was I. The wounds that had stopped bleeding were reopened when I was tossed in the air like a rag doll from the parasite's burst. It didn't matter that I wasn't injured at all in the actual attack; I was going to bleed out my last remaining 11 HP here on a vicious, alien planet.

My hand shook as I reached out to Kesstel. It hurt to move, but I pulled his right glove off, revealing his slightly dirty, pale fingers. His whole body was stained by the blue light coming from the planet below and the harsh red light from the rip in space overhead. Without Goddess's cleansing power, I was colored the same.

With a groan, I flopped onto my back. The glove on my own hand disappeared before I gently pushed my fingers through Kesstel's still ones and threaded our fingers the best I could. It wasn't perfect, but it was the best I could do.

It was so soothing, feeling his cool skin on mine.

I looked up at Earth as it grew closer and closer. As the rip in space grew bigger and bigger.

"It's been about twenty years since a human has seen Earth like this," I said, talking as if Kesstel could hear me. My rough voice sounded terrible, so maybe it was better that he couldn't. "There used to be astronauts circling Earth all the time, but when the Gates appeared, there wasn't a way to communicate with them. Never mind sending food or trying to get them back to Earth. People on land were too concerned with their own lives; no one took the time to care about the ones stuck up in space, you know."

The brightly glowing crystal surface under me started to ripple. Every once in a while, I could feel the tiniest point, as if a crystal was trying to grow and stab me.

Still, I continued to stare up at Earth. Well, Earths. Double vision blurred the globe and overlapped the images, but I focused as much as I could on where Eden would be.

I should be more upset than I was right now. I should be burning with furious determination. Angry that my HP was dripping out of my body one blood drop at a time. Instead, I felt at peace. I'd done everything I could. I literally couldn't do anything else for my family.

If by some miracle Earth did survive, they'd be fine without me. I trusted Jonovan to make the cure and wake up my mother and sister soon. As hard as the grieving process would be, after it, they'd be comfortable for the rest of their lives with all the money from the cure.

If Earth didn't survive . . . well, they'd be dead too.

It was funny, really. I used to get so mad at how Kesstel planned to make this a suicide mission. I talked on and on about going home and living together after. So naive. But at least there was one promise I could uphold.

My vision started to blur as the rims turned gray. Instinctively, I tightened my fingers around Kesstel's. "I promised, didn't I?" I whispered. I didn't have the energy to talk any louder. "That I'd go wherever you go, Kesstel." I couldn't smile, but I wanted to. "Heaven or Hell . . . I'll never let you feel alone again."

I wanted Kesstel to be the last thing I saw, but I couldn't see anything— just gray. I didn't even have the energy to tilt my head. The last thing I heard was his heartbeat.

Slowly . . . slowing . . .

CHAPTER 60

M y eyes cracked open. Gradually, I became aware of a bright glow over my head. I blinked several times before my vision cleared.

Goddess's face came into focus. Her thick silvery hair rippled in an invisible wind around our faces as she leaned over me. Her lips curved up in a gentle smile as her silvery eyes framed in thick black lashes narrowed affectionately. "Good morning, sleepyhead."

I blinked at her a couple more times. "Morning?"

She smiled wider. "Ah, I suppose it's actually afternoon right now." She reached out and gently brushed my hair back, like I was a child.

I was curled up with my head on her lap. Her legs were tucked under her, long white dress fluttering around us like her hair. She was sitting on . . . nothing?

My eyes widened and I sat up . . . only to gasp in shock.

We were floating in space, surrounded by a clear bubble. The Earth and the moon floated in the void before us. Earth's rich colors—blues, greens, and browns—were bright against the star-studded black background. There was no glaring red rip in the sky, and even most of the black spots it had sported when I last looked at it were gone. The only ones left were the ones that humans had put there with nukes, trying to get rid of the monsters. Earth looked so serene, slowly turning in peaceful silence.

"It's still there," I whispered. "It didn't collapse." I turned back to Goddess. "I mean, we are still alive right?"

She laughed. "Yes. We are. We were successful, although it took some time. That's why it took so long for me to wake you up." A seriousness touched her gentle smile.

That was when I noticed what was behind her. The parasitic planet floated there. It wasn't blue anymore, but white. It was also smaller than it used to be, barely larger than the moon. It was like a beautiful giant diamond, shimmering against the starry blackness of space. The hundreds of remnant planets caught in clear orbs and chained to the parasite were gone. If I was alive, then the parasite was dead, and this was its leftover body. It didn't pose a threat anymore, but my mind was still trapped in my last moments on that planet.

I looked around frantically, my whole body shivering uncontrollably. "Where's Kesstel?" My voice broke, and my throat started to burn. "What happened to him?"

I'd stabbed him. No, it wasn't even just stabbing; I'd practically killed him. My clothes were clean now, but I could still feel his slick blood on my skin. "I didn't . . . he didn't . . . " My throat closed before I could choke out the rest of the sentence.

Goddess frowned and waved her hand.

Kesstel appeared, floating horizontally in a bubble next to us. His clothes were clean, like mine, and all traces of injury were gone. Even his armor had been repaired. But his eyes were closed, his thick lashes dark on his pale cheeks.

I lunged at him, propelling myself forward. My bubble moved with me, and Goddess came with it. As soon as the edges touched, they merged, creating a larger bubble which encompassed all three of us.

I stopped at Kesstel's side, my heart squeezing painfully. My fingers shook as I reached out and touched his face, something between a gasp, a sob, and a sigh bursting out of my mouth when I felt his warm breath on my skin. Unable to stop myself, I grabbed him, hugging his head to my chest and holding his broad shoulders tight.

He was breathing, but his body was limp in my arms.

"What's wrong with him?" I asked Goddess, my voice still shaking.

"Sleeping." Goddess floated over to my side, her dress and hair ever moving. "I didn't have a way to send you back to Earth or heal you while I was wrestling with the parasite. So in order to protect both of you, I put you in suspended animation."

I nodded. I'd kind of already guessed that. Gently, I brushed Kesstel's soft hair off his forehead and traced his handsome features. "How long were we asleep?"

"In the parasite's dimension, it's been fifteen years. Although I was able to intercept its communication and connection with the Gates on Earth after a week, it took me five years to subdue and eradicate the parasite. After winning, I fell asleep for seven years to regain my energy and integrate fully into the leftover shell of the parasite." She let out a small laugh. "I never thought I'd possess the body of the being that tried to kill me. But I need a new planet—I can't stay in you forever—and there are free materials just sitting there."

She smiled at my shocked face, assuming I was reacting to her story. "I had to wait for three more years to wake you up from the suspended animation I placed you in. We were in the other dimension still, and I had no way of providing you with bodily needs. Yes, a god can make whatever they want, but that's only if the right atoms are there. Those three years were spent figuring out how to get my new planet within Earth's gravity without damaging Earth or my own new planet."

She glanced at the white globe with fondness. "I was able to create a barrier around my planet which locked-in its own gravity so it didn't mess with Earth's. For now, it will be just like another moon. As long as my people and the humans stay friendly with each other, I don't mind staying here. If not, well, there's still room in the life belt around the Solar System's sun to move my planet to."

I gaped at her, still stuck on her first sentence. "Fifteen years?"

Oh my god. My family! They must have thought I was dead! I could tell by looking at my hands and body that I looked the exact same age as when I closed my eyes—nineteen. But everyone else in my family would have aged fifteen years, all the while thinking I was dead. What were they going to do when I appeared?

She nodded to the side. "Although it's only been five years on Earth."

I swallowed hard and nodded. That was a little better. Sort of. Still, my heart hurt at the grief they must be feeling. My arms tightened around Kesstel. Even though he was unconscious, I still found myself seeking him for comfort. Idiotic maybe, but I couldn't resist.

Goddess smiled gently and touched my head. "Silly child," she whispered lovingly, even though she looked younger than I was. "Everything will be alright."

I looked at her helplessly but didn't push her hand away. Just like the first time I met her, I couldn't resist the instant love I had for her. "What happened on Earth while I was asleep? Do you know?"

"Of course I know." She laughed like I'd made a joke. "I am now the owner of the energy crystals. Every single one is my eyes and ears on Earth. I hear every conversation, see every interaction."

My brows wrinkled as I tilted my head to the side, thinking. "That sounds awful." I could think of a number of situations I'd never want to overhear.

She waved her hand. "It's always been that way for me, ever since my children were created. In fact, those many long years when all I heard was silence were unbearably excruciating for me. I was so lonely." She tapped her finger to her mouth and gave a hopeless shrug. "But those situations you're worried about, I also choose to ignore. The information I collect is a bit like a radio on Earth. I can choose to change the channel at will, and even mute it in the back of my mind."

I shook my head. It still wasn't my cup of tea. I never wanted to know that much about anyone.

Well, that might not be exactly true, I admitted as I gently brushed Kesstel's silky hair.

"All the Gates and portals on Earth collapsed the day after you disappeared," Goddess explained.

I looked up at her, listening intently.

"As I said, I intercepted the signal between the parasite and them as fast as I could. A week on the parasite ended up being about a day on Earth. Without the parasite's command, the Gates became unstable, then the parasite pulled back its energy to fight me, which stopped its invasion on Earth. In that precarious moment, I was able to weaken the bond between Earth and the other dimension. Although the two dimensions weren't separated completely, it caused all the holes between them to close."

She shifted over to my side and folded her legs under her as if sitting. Her big silvery eyes stared down at Earth with me. "The monsters that had already exited the Gates were still on Earth. The Hunters did a good enough job dealing with them, but there aren't many Hunters or humans now."

She hummed under her breath.

"Since all energy crystals are controlled by me, I removed the most dangerous monsters from Earth. The rest have been weakened, both physically and magically. Just like the Hunters. Monsters are now acting like normal animals. Some are even breeding, though their offspring don't have energy crystals and are weaker because of it. Earth's animal population has almost become extinct, and it will be some years before science is advanced enough to clone the DNA they saved from the original animals. These new monsters will most likely replace them in the meantime."

I blinked at Goddess. "What happened to the Hunters?"

She glanced at me. "Their power came from the parasite. It was sifting out the humans who were most likely to make the best monsters once it ate the planet. Now, the power that was supplying them has been cut off. About four years ago, all Hunters lost half their strength. E Hunters are pretty much glorified humans now."

I lifted my left hand up to my face and turned it this way and that. I didn't feel any different. Or I should say, I didn't feel any weaker, even though I'd lost nearly all my levels before I passed out. I felt just as strong as I did before we left Earth—an S Hunter.

Out of curiosity, I cast Mist. The thin vapor pooled around my hand, lacing in and out of my fingers like ribbon.

Goddess reached out and poked the mist with a slender finger. It swirled and created a misty round diamond, its pointed pavilion hovering above my fingers. Like the white crystal planet behind it, light shone from the inside. "Of course, that doesn't apply to my children. I will not send them down there without the means to defend themselves."

I tapped the diamond with my thumb. It spun around like a top, the inner light reflecting off each perfect facet.

She shrugged. "They're not my children. Why should I waste the power meant for my children on them? Humans were not originally designed to house magic; it was injected into them from an outside source. But since they are there, the genes that have mutated will, of course, be passed on, although they will weaken with each generation. I imagine in a thousand years or so, the Hunter gene will be completely gone. If Earth's God gives it back to them when he wakes up, then that's his choice."

"I guess that makes sense," I muttered and waved away the mist diamond. Instead, I hugged Kesstel closer.

The people on Vapria had had magic, but they'd been peaceful. It was actually the time before the Warriors of Mist—before magic was given to the people—when they were war-torn. But since Goddess had been physically there to maintain peace, there were no wars after the people had magic. Humans didn't have that supervision. I mean, just look at the brutal caste system that was created after Hunters came into the picture.

"I am still supporting the humans," Goddess continued. "Since Earth's God will still remain unconscious for maybe another millennium, I am the one preventing the world's functions from stopping or falling apart. I have also kept the energy crystals on Earth and continue to provide them with energy to power the human world—clean energy, so that the

Dreamer's disease has been eradicated with the help of the cure you so graciously provided."

My eyes widened, and my fingers flexed harder than I meant on Kestel's arm. My hand shook as I reached out to grab her hand. "Then my mother and sister . . . " My voice broke.

I couldn't tell what emotion was bubbling in my throat, cutting off my words. Excitement? Doubt? Anxiety? I wanted to know, but a small part of me didn't want to hear. My mother had been a Dreamer for so long, and I didn't know how long it had taken for the cure to be developed.

She turned her hand and grabbed mine in return. "It's okay. Healer Jonovan upheld his side of the deal. He figured out the disappearance of the Gates was connected to you, and he passionately fought to ensure your family was taken care of as compensation. Three years ago, your mother and sister woke up."

CHAPTER 61

My hands shook as I covered my mouth with one hand and gripped Kesstel tightly with the other. "It worked. Oh my god, it really worked."

Even as I gave the cure to Jonovan, there'd been a part of me that believed I'd sentenced my family to death. Hearing that they were awake seemed too good to be true.

"They woke up," I whispered, still trying to process it. My gaze locked on Earth below, where Eden would be, as if by looking hard enough I could actually see them. Such wishful thinking.

Goddess nodded. "Your mother is still going through light physical therapy, but she can walk and maintain a normal life. Your sister has completely recovered. She's going through nursing school and plans to intern in Healer Jonovan's hospital. He made quite an impression on her."

I looked up sharply. "Intern in Jonovan's hospital? But Aliya's a human." Now that Goddess was powering the energy crystals, I wasn't worried about Aliya getting hurt by magic. Well, not by the kind that would put her in a coma.

Goddess nodded. "Yes. Now that the Gates are gone and Hunters are weakening, the two societies are merging back together and creating a new normal. The strong caste system that Hunters followed has lessened considerably as a result, since they have to consider humans now." She paused. "Without Gates, a lot of Hunters were displaced, especially since normal weapons like guns now work on monsters, not just Hunter weapons. Most of the powerful monsters near civilizations have already been eliminated. Now, Hunters can either get a normal job, join the military, or leave the cities to reclaim the lands abandoned when the Gates first appeared."

I bobbed my head, both listening to her and not listening to her at the same time.

They are okay, I thought. Excitement bubbled in my stomach, and I couldn't hold back the laughter that burst out. "Mom, Aliya . . . they're okay!" Giggling like an idiot, I hugged Kesstel tight. Ah, I wished I'd been there to see them open their eyes. Still, it was better that they'd woken up then, rather than waiting for me to get home.

But it wasn't just that they were awake. Kesstel, Goddess, and I were still alive. We did it. We survived, and it sounded like Earth was on the upswing.

Brimming with happiness, I let go of Kesstel with one arm and reached out for Goddess, initiating a group hug. It didn't matter that Kesstel and Goddess were like water and oil and I wasn't a touchy person, I squished us all together anyway, all the while laughing like a broken record.

"We won!" I yelled, my voice echoing in the bubble that surrounded us.

Goddess chuckled softly and hugged me back. Gently, she kissed my hair like I was a child. She tapped Kesstel between the eyes once with the tip of her middle finger then disappeared from my arm and reappeared sitting next to me.

Kesstel's eyelashes fluttered.

Instantly, all my attention was locked on him. I touched his face, gently tracing his cheekbone. "Kesstel?"

His eyes opened. As out of focus as they were, I couldn't be more excited that they were his normal baby blues. No more scary glowing. No more dead, glazed expression.

He blinked, and I could see his consciousness waking up, focusing on me. "Jynn." His husky voice cracked, out of use, but it was like his whole world hung on that one word.

An almost painful smile spread across my face as my heart squeezed so tight I could barely breathe. There was still a wealth of guilt plaguing me from almost killing him, but I was just so happy to see him back to normal, I couldn't resist leaning down and pressing a hard kiss on his mouth.

Since there was an audience, I pulled back way too soon. "I'm so sorry I hurt you," I whispered, pressing my forehead against his. "I didn't want to. I just couldn't figure out how to make you stop."

He reached up and threaded his hand through my loose hair, cradling my head, as he wrapped his other arm around my waist. "I hurt you first," he whispered, regret thick in his voice. "After I promised to never do so.

I'm sorry, too. I could feel my body moving, and no matter how hard I tried to stop it, it wouldn't obey. Even . . . attacking you . . . with the energy crystal.

"It's true, there is always that insecurity, but I'd rather die than inflict you with the same thing I've gone through."

"I know. You'd never intentionally hurt me," I agreed, smiling into his eyes. I was too happy to do much else. Besides, Goddess was sitting right behind me. "And neither of us will ever have to be lonely again, because I'm never going to leave you, and you're never going to leave me."

His worried expression smoothed out to a smile. He kissed me again, his lips clinging to mine. "Jynn. My Jynn."

"My Jynn," Goddess interjected, her soft voice like a cold bucket of reality.

Kesstel's smile thinned a little. He sat up, still holding onto me like I was a lifeline. "*My* Jynn," he corrected, tipping his head in a challenge. Unlike before, he wasn't straight up hostile like he was facing an enemy. Probably because he wasn't being influenced by the parasite anymore. But it was still an argument he wasn't willing to let go.

I sighed, trying to gather enough energy to care about their ridiculous spat.

"Well, technically, both of you are mine. So there." Goddess lifted her chin into the air as if she had won.

Kesstel stared at her in utmost confusion.

For a second, I was lost. Then I realized what she meant. My hand spread over Kesstel's left side, where I'd almost killed him. The wound was gone, but I could still see the tiny glow where his energy crystal was.

"Your life, Kesstel, is tied to your energy crystal. Even though that horrible being is gone, there's no way to take it out without killing you. However, I'm the owner of the energy crystals now," Goddess announced, a gentle, playful glint in her eyes. She smirked right into his face. "So you are now mine. *My child.*"

His lips parted, but even he looked at a loss for what to say.

I turned my head to hide the snicker which threatened to erupt. I wanted to ask him how he felt about that, if he felt the same instinctive adoration I felt for Goddess. I could tell he wasn't as guarded as he was before with her, but did he feel anything else? However, I didn't think he'd answer that question right now. Not that it mattered, really. Since she could hear everything around the energy crystals, she was going to hear his response when I asked later, anyway.

But he didn't need to know that right away.

"Your . . . child?" Kesstel asked.

She nodded smartly. "Right. My child. Jynn is my first child, my Warrior of Mist. You, Kesstel, are my child as a human with an energy crystal inside him. One of a kind. The only one that will ever be. Your energy crystal and life span has been tied to hers," Goddess explained to him. "You're still an S Hunter, with her, but you're no longer living outside the times of the Earth. Meaning, you will start to age as a normal S Hunter now. As powerful as you are, when Jynn dies, you will die."

He nodded, accepting her decision without so much as a tiny pause.

I was the one who had the hang-up. "Why? I don't think that's fair."

Goddess shook her head. "He might start aging now, albeit very slowly, but it doesn't change the fact that he's a being who shouldn't even exist." Her tone was naturally soft, but she didn't even try to soften the blow of her words. "No matter how he ages, his energy crystal will prevent him from dying. This is the best solution. It's just as well, since you will need his help in the future."

I frowned. "With what?" I was strong enough; I didn't need a babysitter or bodyguard.

Goddess laughed like she knew what I was thinking about. "It's actually something he was naturally gifted at, before his planet was destroyed."

Kesstel's arms tightened around me for just a second, revealing the shock that didn't show on his face.

Goddess waved her hand in the air. The side of the bubble that surrounded us and kept out space—and provided us with air, most likely—swirled and shimmered, the mist catching in the sunlight. A rainbow of colors flashed before they merged and created an image. It took me a second to figure out I was staring at a picture of a cave somewhere in the mountains on Earth. It didn't seem all that exciting; it was just a rocky cave surrounded by green trees, probably about ten feet tall, twenty feet wide, and pitch black inside.

"The energy crystals on Earth are not everlasting," Goddess explained. "Just like the original ones, the power inside them will run out, like a battery. Since the Gates are gone, and the monsters who possess energy crystals are lessening, Earth will run out of them in a matter of several years. Humans have adapted to using them so much, I expect them to have another energy crisis."

My eyes widened in understanding. Kesstel nodded, easily accepting her explanation.

"Since my children will be living on Earth until my new planet is finished, I refuse to let them go through that suffering. I have implanted a large vein of energy crystals in this cave. It's for your—my children's—use. You can distribute it for income. Keep it for your own convenience. Whatever you do, it's your choice. As long as my children are in control of it, I will continue to replenish it forever."

My eyes widened, finally understanding why I'd need Kesstel's help. I knew absolutely nothing about business. When I was growing up, most of my attention was on odd jobs and studying to be a Hunter just in case. The idea of being part of a business was laughable, never mind heading a billion-dollar business like controlling the world's main energy source.

But Kesstel had been raised as the heir to a duchy. Before he became the deadly Hunter he was today, he'd been trained to juggle businesses and manage lives. Even when he was just planning on temporarily staying on Earth, he'd still set up an information collection gig.

Kesstel hummed in interest. "That vein is the only energy crystal source in the whole world? There will be a lot of people who'll want it."

Goddess waved her hand in dismissal. "The moment someone other than my children takes control over it, I will remove it from Earth and let the humans suffer their original fate. The energy crystals aren't there for humans; they're there for my children. Even a thief sneaking in at night will leave with a pocket of empty air." She smiled at Kesstel as if challenging him. "I trust that you can maintain control over it. After all, there are no Hunters higher than a C on Earth now. If you can't watch over a little hole with such an advantage, I chose the wrong helper for Jynn."

He lifted his chin, accepting that challenge. "There will be no trouble."

I grabbed his hand and held it tight. I was a little overwhelmed with the daunting task ahead of me—it wasn't going to be as easy as poking something with a pointy sword—but I wasn't going to back down. Especially since I wasn't going to be doing it alone. I'd always done well in school in the past, so I should be able to learn what to do. "We can handle it."

Goddess nodded, satisfied. "Remember, this vein will be the backbone income for all my children to come. It is there to sustain you financially. Your power, which I have not lessened, is there to protect yourself with. But my children are not meant to be the dictators of Earth," she stressed. "Anyone who tries to become a tyrant will be reprimanded by me. We are simply visitors until I've finished remodeling this planet to sustain life."

She motioned to the diamond-like planet behind us. Even though it was all the same color still—white diamond—on closer inspection, the beginnings of oceans and mountains were there. Massive cracks divided the surface, creating massive sections that collided and pushed against each other, forming those dips and rises. Tectonic plates?

Even with the slow aging of an S Hunter, I would never live long enough to see what it would look like when it was done. It was a little saddening, but not crushing. I'd probably be too busy in the future to even think about it. After all, I had no idea what would happen when we got back to Earth.

I instinctively knew that the crystal vein wasn't near Garden City; just a vague, general knowledge that I would know exactly where to go to find it. Now, whether it would be livable around the vein . . . well, I'd like to think Goddess wasn't mean enough to send us to the middle of nowhere.

Still, I was itching to get back to solid ground. I did like talking to Goddess face-to-face, though. But I could tell that something was different, now that she wasn't in the back of my mind anymore. The System was still there, as was the Pearl embedded in my temple, just without her in it. Even so, I believed I could talk to her anytime I wanted.

But what I wanted most was to see my family. I had Kesstel back; now, I needed to hold my sister and mother, too. And check on how my aunt and uncle were doing.

Goddess smiled like she knew what I was thinking. "Well, that's all the instruction you need for now." She placed her hand over mine and Kesstel's joined one.

A blinding light flooded my vision. Instinctively, I closed my eyes and held Kesstel tighter. His own arm tightened around my waist, anchoring me to his side and smothering what little space there was left between our bodies. For a moment, we were weightless. Then my feet touched the ground, and I stumbled forward a couple steps as gravity finally grabbed me for the first time. If it wasn't for Kesstel, I might have tripped and fallen. Instead, I blindly followed his stride forward.

My eyes cracked open, and I looked around as we stepped out of the bright light. It took me a second to figure out where we were because the huge black arch was gone. It wasn't until I spotted Eden's hospital and the Hunter's Association building that I realized where we were—Gate Square. The very large open expanse of pavement looked the same as before, only there was a large plaque in place of the Gate covered in tiny writings—a memorial. All the other buildings around were different from the last time I was here, probably because they were ruined in the last battle.

Directly behind me was a fifty-foot-tall white arched portal—the thing we'd just walked out of. Unlike when the parasite's portals or Gates appeared, the area didn't show any damage from its appearance, but the hundreds of people walking around the buildings, whether shopping or visiting the hospital or Association building, stopped and turned in our direction. Sounds of shock, despair, and wonder filled the air. Some people—obviously Hunters, although they were dressed in casual or business clothes—drew weapons and got ready for battle. Other people, with less survival instincts, pulled out phones and started to take pictures.

I straightened up. Kesstel's arm slid from my waist around my back until he could lace our fingers together.

Goddess floated behind Kesstel and me, her long hair and white dress fluttering, looking breathtakingly beautiful. She rose until she was ten feet in the air, a gentle smile on her face. "I am Goddess." Even though she didn't raise her voice, I knew without a doubt that everyone in the whole city, if not the whole world, could hear her soft words.

She opened her arms then lifted them, drawing our gazes to the sky. The white moon hung in the blue afternoon sky. Behind it, the bright blue sky shifted and warped until another moon appeared behind, a little whiter and bigger.

The people around us gasped.

Even my own eyebrows lifted at the sight. I knew it was going to happen; I just thought she would wait longer before she revealed her planet body.

Kesstel glanced at me, and I knew exactly what he was thinking. *Things just got a little more complicated.*

"I am the owner of the energy crystals that power your civilization," Goddess explained. "And I come in peace."

People spilled out of the buildings, running to get a good look at us and the second celestial body in the sky. People in suits from the Association building pushed to the front of the crowd—I even recognized some of them—but no one dared to cross the line into the square. Those who were in it before we appeared had retreated.

Whispers flew through the air.

"Look at her! She's gorgeous! Am I seeing things?"

"I think she might actually be a real goddess!"

"Wait! Isn't that the Noble?!"

"Hey, I know that girl! She's from that video from five years ago! I thought she died!"

Under so many gazes, all I could do was hold my head high and grip Kesstel's hand. As much as I hated being the center of attention, I couldn't hide from this.

Goddess lowered her arms, presenting me and Kesstel. "You owe my children a great debt. It was their actions, along with mine, that vanquished the monster and collapsed the Gates that were ripping Earth apart five years ago. They have now returned, and I would have you treat them with the respect they deserve." She was polite, but it was clear she also wasn't going to be a pushover.

She didn't wait for anyone to respond to her words. Both she and the white portal behind us dissolved into mist and dispersed, leaving me and Kesstel in the middle of all the attention. Overhead, the second moon gleamed in the blue sky. As soon as she disappeared, the Association president, Anderson, stepped forward from the front of the crowd, his eyes locked on us. He looked cautious yet determined at the same time.

I completely disregarded him. There were more important things I needed to take care of.

Angling my body slightly behind Kesstel, I took out my cell phone from my Items Bag. It was exactly the same as it was when I last put it in. Even the battery charge was the same, since it was powered with an energy crystal and frozen all this time.

It was a long shot, but I dialed my family's phone number. It had been five years; anything could have happened by now, and this was the number to their old apartment. If they'd moved to the new condo, it might not be the same. Or maybe they weren't even in that condo at all anymore. There were so many things I didn't know.

But this was the only number I had right now to check on them. I had to try.

My body trembled with each ring that echoed in my ear. I could hear the president politely insisting on an explanation and Kesstel responding, but that was all background noise.

"Hello?" a woman answered on the other side.

My eyes widened. It wasn't Aliya's or Aunt Mina's voice. It was a voice from my past. The one who used to chase away all my fears. The one who made home feel like a home. One I'd been waiting ten years to hear again.

"M-Mom?" My voice broke.

Kesstel glanced at me out of the corner of his eye and shifted to block me from the view of the people talking urgently in front of him.

I bowed my head, hiding my red eyes from all the pictures flashing around us from all directions. "Mom, it's Jynn," I said, hugging the phone in one hand and clutching Kesstel's fingers for dear life in the other. "I'm back."

She gasped then let out a huge sob. "Jynn? Baby doll? I-Is that really you?"

On the other side of the phone, I could hear Aliya's voice. "Mom! What's going on?"

My mouth wobbled into a smile as my chest swelled in joy. I leaned forward until my forehead rested on Kesstel's warm back, feeling his soothing breathing. There were so many unknown things in the future, but for now, I felt happy. Whole.

I closed my eyes and listened to my mother's joyful sobbing on the other side of the phone, tears leaking through my own closed lashes. "I just wanted to say . . . good morning, sleepyhead."

A NOTE FROM THE AUTHOR: WHAT HAPPENED AFTER

Jynn Devhro and Kesstel Noblé

A year after coming back to Earth, Jynn and Kesstel set out to find the crystal vein in Colorado. It took a couple years to set up the company, during which they quietly got married. Even though they both owned the mine, Kesstel was the one who made all the decisions. While Jynn could do it (after surviving Kesstel's training), she preferred to be in the background, and Kesstel was content to spoil her that way.

Ten years later, Terre was born. It came as a surprise, because Jynn didn't think they could have kids at all, with Kesstel not being from Earth. They were good parents. Kesstel was the strict one—especially because Terre took after him—and Jynn was the more lenient, friend-type parent.

Jynn picked up the hobby of mount raising, aka hunting down monsters and seeing if she could tame them. She had a forty percent success rate . . .

Aliya Devhro

She became a nurse and worked in Eden's hospital, under Jonovan. She had a crush on him until she was twenty-five, when she met her husband, who won her over. It was odd for Aliya to become older than her older sister (when Jynn came back to Earth, she was still nineteen while Aliya had turned twenty-one already), but that didn't interfere with their relationship.

Aliya aged normally, while Jynn aged one year for every five. But Jynn was very active in Aliya's life and spoiled Aliya's two daughters and one son their whole lives.

Annette Devhro

She stayed in Eden with Aliya, watching her grandkids while Aliya and her husband worked. She never remarried, instead devoting her time to her family. After Terre was born, she lived in Mist Haven until he was ten, then moved back to Eden to become an art teacher.

Aunt Mina and Uncle Carl

The money they got from the cure made it so they didn't have to work— just like Aliya and Annette—but chose to anyway, mostly to give them a purpose. After Uncle Carl's depression and Aunt Mina's neck trouble and migraines were managed with medical assistance, Uncle Carl took a relatively stress-free position in the Noblé Company.

Jonovan

When all the Hunters' powers were reduced, he was knocked down to a high C rank, still maintaining his second-strongest-healer-in-Eden position. Healer Laurel also fell to a C, but she stayed a smidgen stronger than him.

After the Gates fell, he took over management of the Eden Hospital and was the first person to suggest that normal humans be allowed to join the Hunter nurses. (All the E healers had been reduced to normal humans at that point, anyway.)

He worked hand in hand with the scientists to make sure that the Dreamer cure was created and properly distributed, not just given to the rich. Since he spent so long paying attention to Aliya, he continued the habit after she was married and had kids. He kind of became an adopted uncle to Aliya's family. He got married later in life.

Maveric

He was injured during the last fight at Eden's Gate. Because all healing abilities were drastically reduced a couple days later, before he could get healed, he limped for the rest of his life. He followed Jynn to Colorado, since most of the monsters around Eden were killed off. He continued to stay a respected armorer his whole life.

Emma's Team

In the last battle, Billy and Morgan died. Kip was pretty beat-up about it, since Morgan died saving her. Nick also blamed himself for Billy's death because it happened when they got separated. The team stayed close friends for the rest of their lives, except Russel, who faded away.

Emma and Mason got married after a short courtship, joined the mount raising profession, and stayed close friends with Jynn until they died.

Mark and Penny

Wardyn Price died during the last fight, and the Stone Mace guild fell apart. Since Mark and Penny were already at odds with the guild, they didn't care to stick around to glue it back together. They joined another guild as monster exterminator team leaders.

Even though they were reduced in power like everyone else, they played a large role in clearing out the most dangerous monsters around Eden.

Their relationship was so close, it foiled all their other romantic relationships. After a while, they figured out they would never find another person who was more important than each other.

Rainbow Brigade

Blue and Orange died in the last Gate battle. Pink, Purple, Yellow, and Green joined the monster extermination teams. A couple months later, they bit off more than they could chew, and Green and Pink were seriously injured. Green's injuries never fully healed, and Pink carried a large scar across her back for the rest of her life. After that, the team found other jobs and started families.

Bethany Wilks

Bethany's dad died in the last Gate battle. Half of her bodyguards left or died then. Some loyal ones stayed and helped her figure out how to protect herself. When the battle ended, Paul Anderson took her under his wing and taught her how to do her father's job. Without daddy to protect her, Bethany had a large learning curve, but with the support of her bodyguards and real friends who stuck around, she stepped up and became a leading figure in the rebuilding of the world—not just a pretty face on a poster.

ABOUT THE AUTHOR

M. L. Reid is a walking contradiction. She loves art as much as science, so her collection of random knowledge is as eclectic as all the fungi in the world. She's a Kingdom Hearts and Final Fantasy fanatic and spends too much time reading Asian webnovels. Although a peacemaker, her favorite scenes to write are fight scenes. After her kids get older, she's totally going to start a sword collection.

DISCOVER
STORIES UNBOUND

PodiumAudio.com

Milton Keynes UK
Ingram Content Group UK Ltd.
UKHW021331290324
440175UK00006B/622